The Queen's Spawn

The Wrecking Squad Book 4

Nick Snape

NICK SNAPE

Also by Nick Snape

Weapons of Choice Series

Hostile Contact

Return Protocol

Zuri's War

Finn's War

Alien Rebirth

Invasive Species

Legion Earth

Nemesis Earth

The Wrecking Squad Series

The Wrecking Squad

Butcher's Folly

Warmonger's Wrath

The Queen's Spawn

Emperor's Fall

Breaker's Ruin

The Scorching Standalones

The World in My Hands

Just Press Play

Warriors of Spirit and Bone

A Dragon of the Veil

A City of Ashes

A Queen in Blood

Praise for the Author

'A masterful voice in modern sci-fi' ★★★★★ SPR

'Nick Snape's creative storytelling, rich world-building, and engaging characters make this book an unforgettable journey.' ★★★★★ Literary **Titan**

'Stunning series. Very highly recommended.' ★★★★★ **Goodreads**

'Sci-fi with pace, heart and unafraid to tackle deeper questions of what it means to be human.' ★★★★★ **Amazon Customer**

'Wildly creative' ★★★★½ **Self-Publishing Review**

For an unsung hero I'm not allowed to name.
Thank you.

PART ONE

CHAPTER 1

APPROACHING BENETAI SPACE STATION

"Are you sure this is the best idea?" asked Savvo, keeping his eyes averted and on the co-pilot's navcom screen.

"Ooh, let me think of our options," replied Rebekah with a slight shake of her head. "Option one, Benetai; option two, the black until we run out of fuel." She knew what Savvo was doing – trying to get her to talk through all her concerns before reaching the dilapidated space station. They had left on what could be called 'bad terms' though if she were honest, they had stopped Lieutenant Ormsk from blowing the place into a gazillion pieces – its people and all.

"We could try Windward," stated Arin over comms. "Become full-blown space pirates. I could wear a headscarf and get a tattoo. Arin the Red, they'd call me. Bane of the space lanes."

"More like Arin the Dickhead, blight of the back alleys," cut in Hendricks from engineering, resulting in Arin's choking cough. "Can't see we have much choice. We know nothing about this system other than Benetai. I think Mikai will at least give us the lowdown on where else we could lie low for a while."

Rebekah's smile was tight, the sigh that followed long and full of tension. The joy of getting Heki and Tremil back was still front and centre, but this was a new start. Their first in three years if you ignored being whipped by Erikson, the Emperor's Enforcer, into doing his bidding.

"May have to call in some old favours, Dricks," she said.

"If we didn't burn through them on the last visit. Oh, hang on, didn't we kind of set off a fire alarm, kill a few Senti and beat up numerous gang members? One or two may have died along the way ..." Arin trailed off.

Rebekah knew Arin's bitterness wasn't for the gang member he'd killed in front of Lieutenant Ormsk; that bastard had it coming. But there was Hannah, the girl Tensei had spaced. Was he still around? Mikai Hannos had a space station to calm after the Bustan's threats. It'd be no surprise if she had decided to let him live, but they would all find it hard spending any time around the gang leader. One to avoid.

Only a few would know they had been directly involved in the gang warfare that had swirled about the wetware. They were around at the time, wanting to buy the kit, and though they had worn full, frosted navy suits when forced to hunt down the wetware, there'd be whispers. Benetai was small, their presence noted, and Arin had been forced to show Ormsk around. And then there was Pshwa. Someone would fill that Senti dream-peddler's niche. Money always wins out in the end.

"We can't be blamed for the Bustans, though. That was Baja's doing, for which he paid a high price," Savvo said, then tapped at his comms unit, mouthing 'Hannos'.

Rebekah drew in a breath to replace the sigh, rolling her shoulders and trying desperately not to click her thumbs. One crack, and she switched the channel. "Hannos."

The cartel leader jumped straight in. "You've got to be fucking joking, right? I mean, you're alive for one, which says to me the Bustans got what they wanted and for some fucked up reason let you live. You got your nose still? Toes?"

"All of them," she replied, a half-smile intruding. ZZ3 had screwed up the Bustan frigate. She doubted Ormsk would forgive and forget, but there was no reason for him to return. He'd lost and would have to lick his wounds, while his superiors considered stripping his rank.

By any means. Wait until they find out the Butcher is not only back, but powerful as hell.

"I'm not letting you dock," she said. There was strain in those words, an undercurrent of regret. "You kind of screwed up my fucking paradise when you were last here. The Benetai have long memories, and the story we spun Lieutenant Ormsk is the one I stuck with."

"And there I was thinking we would be heroes," replied Rebekah.

"Yeah, well, heroes are dangerous when you live on a tin can in the black. They bring trouble in their engine wake. My people know that. They'll remember your tactics when you stormed the station, and the sacrifice when you fucked-over the Bustan Navy. They just won't know which of those you really fucking are. And neither do I." The comms clicked, and Rebekah could make out muffled voices in the background. "Park in the black and we'll talk."

"Thanks," Rebekah replied. It was something. They were well-stocked with everything but space to breathe.

The airlock cycled, Mikai Hannos and one other waiting on the other side. Once complete, she removed her helmet, her orange-tinged skin looking starker in the *Sunstar*'s bright corridor, her blonde hair a little greyer than when they last met. Her eyes remained certain, the spark still there and surrounded by the deep creases Rebekah remembered. The bruising around her chin had gone, thankfully. The price the cartel leader paid for the crew's façade when they had raided the station.

The young man by her side she had seen only once before. A scar across his cheek, but the same eyes. A son, maybe. Definitely related, and a good sign there was some trust. Risking your blood was a sign to Benetai and her own gang that she didn't fear the Wrecking Squad.

Mikai eyed Rebekah, and then surprised her, pulling the ship's captain in for a bear hug before leaning back and slapping her face gently with a gloved hand. "I said it when I first met you, woman. You got balls. Ormsk nearly blew a gasket when you turned and ran. Now you got anything decent to drink aboard this heap o' junk?"

Rebekah's eyes flicked over to the man accompanying her, whose head was slowly shaking, eyes to the ceiling. "She's on a dry run. Gunports closed, so don't give her any ammunition, eh?"

Rebekah smirked, instantly liking the young man, and showed them both down the corridor towards the junction. "We're a dry ship, Mikai. Alcohol and space are a surefire way to hell."

"*Not* having alcohol is like bathing in hell's fucking flames. Andrei here has me as barren as Bustan fucking humour. Come on, you must have something on board." The ex-Skyrider clomped towards the galley, eyeing the cupboards with expectation in her eyes.

"Herbal tea, coffee, hot chocolate, but other than that, dry as a Shema desert," said Savvo from the cockpit. "Best that way."

Mikai shook her head, clamping her helmet to the galley wall with Andrei doing the same before they sat at Rebekah's behest. She made them both a coffee, almost matching Dricks' and Arin's usual combos.

"Alright. Pleasantries over. How did you escape? And more important, why are you back?"

Rebekah had thought long and hard about what to say. But it had to be believable, and she needed to invest some truth and trust in this woman.

"We have a warbot." That produced the expected splutter. "And we got it on board their ship. Dumped a cargo box as if it was the wetware, then curved out while Ormsk collected it. Fucker still tried to take us down."

"A fucking warbot? I can see his face now when he undid the bow!" Mikai took a drink, a sour expression across her face when she realised it was still coffee.

"Yeah, well, everything still went shit-faced down. Chased us to Scarva's ship, sent in Marauders except they died in the decel burn. Their AIs went for us still, but we took them out." Rebekah took a sip from her flask, then locked eyes with the cartel leader. "You knew Rubel, Rubel Carmen?"

"Trained with him. 7th and High? Didn't Scarva …?"

Rebekah grimaced. "That's him. He was on board Scarva's scummy ship with most of his squad, and died there too when the Marauders boarded. Listen, Mikai. This is going to sound like bullshit, but you need to know the truth. Of what Rubel saw, what we saw and what's going down in the Almaarian system. There's a storm coming, one filled with death, and you might be safe here, but our people are going to die once the Butcher starts to flex his fucking muscles."

"The Butcher? You mean Asham, who Ormsk was after?"

Rebekah leant forwards and spent the next hour souring Mikai and Andrei's mood. She kept the twins out of it, but talked them both through the events on Daphene as best she could – Countess Segfi, the Butcher's release and control of the base, the AI's murder of the majority of military personnel. By the end of it, she needed a beer. Or seven.

"Fuck…" summed up Mikai succinctly.

Andrei finished his second coffee, stood and washed the cup out before placing it in the cleaning unit. His manner reminded her of Savvo. "You think he, it, whatever, will be coming here?"

"I doubt it," replied Rebekah. "But if he spreads, starts the killing we witnessed aboard the *Scourge* and the *Segfi*, then people will come if they can. The scum Senti will be cutting out their dreams by the thousands as they try to escape. Where are they going to go?"

"Windward is the only inhabitable planet, but its ecosystem ain't up to shit. There's what, ten thousand down there at most? And they're fighting a constant battle to keep the bio from contaminating their crops and animals," stated Andrei, running his fingers down his face, leaving red streaks that faded slowly away.

Time for the kicker. "You're assuming it'll be lowlifes."

"Aw, fuck me, no. The nobility? Coming here?"

"Every engineer I ever knew had a stash in their workroom. Come on, Dricks, I need a shot."

Hendricks shook her head, sipping at her sugar-filled coffee with a raised eyebrow. "Dry."

Mikai continued to pace around engineering, hands on hips, chin thrust out, her lips almost curled into a snarl. "Is all this bullshit true?" She waved her arms vaguely towards the bow of the ship. "This Asham crap?"

"Worse, more than likely. But yeah, true. A psycho AI that infects by uploading itself."

"And the Countess? Fucking cloned soldiers, and that wetware you recovered? He has that too?"

Hendricks shrugged. "You missed out the bit where he has control of a battleship and spaces crews for fun." She stood, standing in Mikai's path as the ex-Skyrider paced back her way, finding it more than a little ironic that it was her getting agitated at someone else unable to keep still while they talked. "The question is, when the shit starts flying, what are people going to do? Not just you. Everyone. The Butcher wants to live, to survive. Make sure no one can take him out. That type of paranoia breeds, and ideas take root. And when I start thinking on that, I get the chills. I've *seen* what he did to the crew of the *Scourge* because he could, the clones he programmed, how he was three steps ahead all the time. What lies three steps ahead when you want to ensure you live forever?"

"You eradicate the threat. One by one. Start with the closest, but you're saying it won't ever be enough."

"You know how I know it's finally clicking home?" said Hendricks, waiting for Mikai to look directly at her. "You've stopped swearing."

CHAPTER 2

ON APPROACH TO THE UNPRONOUNCEABLE

Rohan Michaels smiled briefly at Treni, his co-pilot, another of Scarva's waifs and strays acquired in the alien's travels around the systems. A Bustan Navy grunt who'd paid for passage somewhere in the distant past but couldn't remember why after the Senti's ministrations. She could, however, remember how to be a mean pilot, had helped him slowly recover after Khan had shot out his shins, and warmed each other during the lonely nights. One good thing to come out of the past few months at least.

"Kefi, are you there?" It was not the Senti's real name. That approximated the sound of a rotten apple hitting the deck, but Kefi would have to do.

"Yes, Rohan. I am always here. Where else would I be?" the Senti's reply monotone due to the electronic translator embedded in the back of its mouth. If you spent enough time around them, they all sounded a little different. Rohan couldn't tell you how – that was beyond his understanding – he just knew from Senti to Senti, as did Treni. They all had their own specific smell too, that adjusted with the moods their faces rarely showed. Some he would even call friends, Kefi prime among them. Scarva most definitely not, though the alien was far from the pure scum that Pshwa manifested.

"I dunno. Maybe you took a holiday? Spent some time in the sun on a beach somewhere." He grinned at Treni, who was giggling.

"I could think of nowhere less that I would like to be," stated the Senti, sploshes of blancmange-like noises mixed in with the speech. "Ugh. Transponder activated."

"Linked," said Treni, tapping at the controls of the repaired shuttle. "And engaged."

The shuttle thrusters manoeuvred them into their usual valley on the *Unpronounceable's* spinning section. The repairs after Khan's attack, and the subsequent assault by the Bustan Marauders, had been completed with the usual Senti efficiency. Rohan knew most looked upon the state of Scarva's ship as reflective of the alien and its crew. But that was the exterior, all for humans to categorise, while their own quarters towards the centre of the ship were kept spotless. The mould was food, anyway, a delicacy they added to their usual fare while in space to maintain their internal gas bladders in top condition. At least, that's what Kefi told him. It could be a Senti joke for all he knew.

Once the shuttle docked, he unbuckled and left Treni to ensure all the usual checks were undertaken. He needed to speak to Scarva; the Senti was in for a shock that might decide all their futures. He wasn't looking forward to the gaseous response. He had considered – for the hundredth time – taking the shuttle and running for somewhere in the Almaarian belt, but duty always nagged at him. That and the empty space in the centre of his mind where his memories had been torn from him. Something he and Rubel and the rest had seen, that the countess had been cooking up. He slid a hand under his sweaty shirt, running fingers over the three long scars across his stomach and ribs. Like whip marks.

Rohan reached the bulkhead, lower than those built for human access, and the handle a strange configuration that favoured tentacles. Of course, it was for emergency use, the strength needed powered by the Senti encounter suits. He thumb-printed the low pad next to it.

"Kefi, you there, gasbag? Need in," he said, a small grin forming as sounds like frustrated seagulls emitted from the speaker. That – he was almost sure – was an alien laugh. Almost.

"What word does Treni use? Ah yes, shit-for-brains." That noise again – a flock this time. "Enter shit-for-brains."

"I'll make a human of you yet," he replied, stepping through the slowly opening door. The other side smelled of wet, rotting vegetables, yet was pristine, warm and covered in an absorbent rubber that his magboots still clung to if he kept to a predefined path. Blues and greens swirled across the corridor, the material sterilising his clothing and the air that seeped in with him. Scarva had thankfully stopped demanding he wear his own encounter suit despite the human taint.

Rohan reached the central core, the Senti version of a command centre, with various screens his brain could not process and control panels utilising the Senti material on the floor where Kefi currently had its chin tentacle attached. He had learned to tell the aliens apart from the nuances in eye, mouth and gait, but above all else, smell – and how they treated him.

Kefi's body burbled, a ripple rising through the layers of rubbery material, and the Senti off-gassed as he approached. The smell was familiar, the underlying cabbage-like essence still there, but with an element Rohan's brain processed but could not describe. Labelled as 'hello', the Senti was in a communicative mood. Friendly.

"You are late," said the Senti, its voice flat.

Rohan smiled while shaking his head. "An hour."

"Time is time. When seen from my perspective, that hour has infinite possibilities. From yours, an hour less scratching your ... spheres? Ovoids?"

"Balls, Kefi. Slang, less specific and certainly less mathematically correct. The big bad in?" Rohan nodded towards Scarva's quarters; the door covered in swirling patterns he couldn't directly look at without feeling sick.

"Yes. With a guest."

"Guest? He's let Pshwa out? Don't tell me that fuck's roaming free."

"Pshwa has left. Scarva traded him to Seventeen's Orb Queen in return for some favour or other. He will be returned to the Great Nest and processed for past crimes. I expect he will be sublimated." Kefi paused, one shoulder tentacle raised in Rohan's direction, the other joining its chin appendage within the light-based controls of its console.

"Sounds painful." He got no reply, not even a seagull or two, nor an off-gas.

"Scarva will see you now. His guest is Almaarian Navy." Kefi's tentacle pointed towards the doorway, and Rohan turned away, heading in that direction, keeping his eyes to the floor lest his brain get caught up in the Senti guard runes. The door slid open, Kefi's doing, and he walked in. The change in smell struck him hard, however much he had pre-prepared. Scarva was old, and as far as he could tell, his internal gasbag was constantly leaking. He wore an undersheath when moving about the ship, but here, ensconced in the liquid support of what Rohan saw as an elaborate hot tub, he didn't make that effort.

Standing before him, at ease with hands behind his back, was a well-muscled male Navy officer. Everything in its place. Hair regulation short, cap at the perfect angle, uniform sharp. A tiny scar on his neck was the only blemish.

Typical Navy. Back so straight you could use it as a plumb line.

"Rohan," said Scarva.

The chin tentacle gestured him closer, and he winced as his shins reminded him of how much healing there was to go. Without the low grav and the elongated boots, he would have been struggling, but they were protesting now.

He moved in beside the officer. The man didn't glance his way, eyes locked on Scarva, chin up and unwavering. Rohan had met some navy dickheads, but this one knocked most of them out of the park.

"Officer Creedence is requesting passage to Windward," said Scarva, the voice electronic, flat. "A last-minute request on such generous terms, a whole crew filled with war memories to savour."

Scarva had that look, the greed that seemed to wipe away reason. A victim of his own drug, perhaps. There had been frequent times when he appeared lucid, his dealings with Khan and her crew one of them, and then he'd turn into this.

Senility, perhaps? Do Senti minds slip as they age?

And why the hell has he let him in here?

"What ship?" he asked, turning to the officer. There was no change in demeanour, nothing. It made his skin crawl.

"ANS *Ungrit*," Captain Creedence replied. His eyes blinked, Rohan not sure if it was for the first time, and the man's chin wobbled ever so slightly. Between wondering if his time with the Senti had made him more aware of such tells, the captain turned his head, eyes dragging away from Scarva, to briefly fall on his own. Cold, empty. "A fine ship."

Creepy. The Navy scraping the bottom of the officer-noble barrel now?

He tried to recall the name, something vaguely familiar about it. Had he and Rubel been aboard? No, a patrol ship. It had run orbital cover on some of their dropship incursions. That was about it, but where and when?

Screw this hole in my mind!

"Agreed," he said, desperate to say more, but then he was a deserter, presumed dead. The last thing he needed was to let that shit slip out to a stick-up-the-arse navy captain. "Out of?"

The officer paused, blinking. "The *Barehelm*."

Again, vagueness brushed his mind, but enough to confirm the name was familiar. A cruiser, he thought, one of Count Portus' perhaps. Maybe. He nodded.

"Enough of your human pleasantries. To business. I am not one of your charities for lowlife scum, Creedence. It is pay up front, understand? And I want a taste of the goods as soon as possible." Scarva pulled himself forward in the suspension tub, off-gassing from a back flap as he did so. "And I mean soon. I've had enough dealings with the Almaarian Navy to know you like your orders and your rosters. But on my ship, I set the timelines. You have an hour."

"An hour?" blurted Rohan. "How are they going to get anyone here in that time?"

"You misunderstand, Rohan. They have already docked."

"We're all checked," said Treni, the hiss of the comms spluttering with the Senti alloy woven about the inner hull. "We got some downtime, Rohan?"

Rohan gathered up the roll of clothes and day-to-day detritus that infested their cabin, sticking to the routines drilled into him over years of being a Marine. Clean bunk, tidy mind. "Yeah. Scarva is taking us to Windward, so we've got a few days in void-space." The words stung. Windward had not been such a great trip last time. Rubel, the Marauders, his bloody shins. Annit's sacrifice. Memories he'd gladly give up, except the hole would eat away at him like the other.

"Windward? After the last time?" Treni stepped into the cabin, a glint in her eye he recognised. Mischievous, the type of look that made his day. "What can we possibly find to do in those forty-eight hours?"

She grabbed his arm and spun him around, planting a kiss that enveloped his mind as well as his body. He let it linger as long as he dare, before pushing her gently away by the shoulders. "Still work to do beforehand," he said, and threw the bag of trash over his shoulder. "Scarva wants me present when they test this navy crew."

"Why?"

He smiled in response, lips tight, almost white. "Cos I mentioned how weird it felt. That bastard used to be so astute at reading humans, but he's on the downturn. The captain gave me the creeps, and I told Scarva that. Plus, the news we brought – the chatter on the comms across the belt, and later at the mine – was all about some shit going down with the navy. Not like the usual conspiracy theories bored dockworkers spread."

"They were talking war, about my people coming for some payback. All bullshit, Rohan. You know as well as I do that without the Senti orbs, it isn't happening. And for what? We were losing; you were dying. It's all fucked up."

Rohan shrugged and kissed her again. "Dunno. But something's in the air other than Senti farts."

Two of the *Ungrit*'s crew were sitting on the bench by the side of the weird, dialled machine Scarva kept in the corner. Rohan was never sure whether it actually did anything, or was just his private memory store. A third was in the dentist's chair, Scarva hovering, his symbiote scurrying about the back of his indented skull in possible excitement. Business had been slow, after all.

"Did you put in the markers?" asked Scarva.

"Of course," replied the navy grunt.

Rohan studied the man. He again felt familiar – the jut of his chin, the cold eyes, though a different colour, similar to those of the captain. Cap in regulation position. His body...

Am I getting paranoid in my old age? While Scarva gets tentacle-loose, am I becoming a grumpy old man?

His gaze shifted over to the other two. Was his worry affecting his judgement? They sat still, no fidgeting, eyes normal, not narrowed, as if far too calm about what was about to happen. Rohan remembered the run-up to every memory purge. Three times he'd given for the Almaarian cause, and once for his own, but each had been nerve-racking. The thought of an alien mind rummaging in yours is sickening, and then to have part of you sucked out. After the wetware, it had been easier. The same invasion, but you still remained whole afterwards.

Wetware. Once you were cashiered out, your armed forces contract closed, it was turned off. Not removed, just a quick blast from a buzz gun supposedly flicked the switch. And of course, no new navy recruits got memory chipped because the Senti were no longer collecting payment.

Rohan eyed the nearest grunt. "The *Ungrit*'s a fine ship," he said, mimicking the captain.

"That she is," replied the grunt, eyes still facing forwards though there was a flicker of recognition at the corner of his mouth.

"How long you served on board?" Rohan said, trying to sound casual, his voice very slightly high pitched.

The response was quick. "Two years. Been good to me."

Rohan nodded, as if agreeing, one eye on Scarva, who had moved back from the man on the chair. "And before that?"

"Basic," he replied.

Rohan processed that. War memories, Scarva had said.

Lies.

"What's this?" stated Scarva, his chin tentacle wafting above the navy ensign on the chair. "What is this thing in your head?"

The ensign lashed out, grabbing Scarva's chin tentacle, dragging the Senti closer. Gas belched into the air, the Senti panicking and flooding the room with a foul miasma. Rohan spun about, reaching for his gun as the grunt he'd been talking to rose, fists balled, and punched him in the cheek. He was falling when a magboot connected with his ribs, detaching his own boots and sending him spinning away.

"Kefi! Boarders!" he bellowed into comms, then crashed into the metal wall. As he dropped, the navy grunt closed in, his cap gone, and his head pulsed. Scars suddenly livid across his scalp.

"Kefi!"

The walls shifted, Rohan's mind disoriented by the blows swirling as he sucked in a last gulp of stale air. A hiss filled the room, a thick green mist pouring from the upper and lower vents. Kefi's idea should anyone like Khan's crew come calling again. They were also speeding up, the central portion of the ship increasing its rotational spin, his inner ears, eyes and brain all suddenly in disagreement as he was pressed to the floor.

Scarva was in a panic, tentacles lashing at the ensign on the chair, the symbiote shuddering in dull patterns of grey-green as it leapt from human to Senti. The last thing Rohan heard before blacking out was the dull report of a handgun. Somehow his brain told him it was the imaginatively named Bustan Fieldweapon 3a, forty-slug magazine, adaptable sight with AI integration turned off.

Treni.

CHAPTER 3

BENETAI SPACE STATION

Heki swallowed, letting the sensation run through her entire body, gripping Tremil's hand tightly as she tried to reassure herself that everything was fine. Her symbiote mithered and then settled against her vertebrae, below the T-shirt and neckline of the flight jacket she wore. A yearning for her skinsuit invaded her thoughts, the reassuring pressure against her body that would root her in the *now*. Making her aware of where she was when the emotions threatened to overwhelm. Rebekah had said they should wear them, but both twins had stood their ground. They needed to look normal – to not stand out – and therefore paired clothing wasn't going to help.

Heki regretted that now.

The airlock cycled, and she swallowed again, quivering under the gentle fingers that dropped onto her shoulder.

"You'll be fine," murmured Rebekah. "We take it slow, just go for a coffee and milkshake in the place Mikai recommended. Under Hannos' protection, and on the fringe of the market. Not too noisy or busy."

With a soft squeeze, Rebekah let go, but Heki reached for her hand as the airlock finally opened, Tremil likewise. Hand in hand, they stepped out onto the corridor, with no gang members there to greet them. Rebekah had explained what might happen, introducing Mikai to the girls long enough for the ex-Skyrider to take the hint. Heki had instantly liked the no-nonsense woman. There was no hidden agenda behind her emotions. You got what you saw and felt. Curious, concerned, safety-conscious, yet somewhere in the maelstrom, the cartel leader wanted to help. She could see their need, though not their power.

No one did.

"It's been a long time," said Tremil. "Hope it goes better than last time."

"They only wept for an hour," stated Rebekah. "Besides, they were fucking rude even for M4 dockworkers."

They walked along the outer ring, Heki finding the strangeness of what was 'up', 'down' and 'sideways' a little disorienting. A space station felt so different from a ship, its spin affecting her ears initially, while her brain needed to catch up and stop thinking about which way her body was oriented.

Down is outward, up is inward; deal with it.

A few distant voices echoed along the corridor, but Rebekah paid no mind, keeping hold of their hands until one or the other released her. By the time they passed the Hannos gang entrance and reached the first bulkhead, Heki decided she could let go, a couple of people ahead holding the door open for them, waiting to let them through before resealing it.

"Thank you," said Heki, and she took the door, marvelling at the first words she had spoken face-to-face with a new human being in four years.

No, there was Davina. But on our terms, in our home.

"We'll close it," said Tremil, a beaming smile crossing her face as the people thanked her and walked off. "We did it."

"Small steps," stated Rebekah, and she stepped through, spinning the door shut after Heki.

"For you. Not for us. We've just met two people who didn't want to wrap our heads in metal or sit us in our own …"

"Shit," said Rebekah. "You can say it. Just not too often, Arin will get all fatherly and start complaining again."

Heki found herself laughing, the urge to stop rising as it echoed back off the metal walls, embarrassment creeping in. But she refused to accept it and let her joy spill into the corridor.

"When you said he couldn't come … his face …" Tremil joined in the laughter.

"Only so many kids I can keep an eye on at the same time. Come on, I need a coffee." Rebekah led them off and, after a second bulkhead, they entered a wider space filled with people. Not soldiers, nor scientists, but people. And children, animals. Stalls filled with goods, voices raised as customers passed on by. The smells rushed up Heki's nostrils, filling her mind with possibilities and tugging at her curiosity, promising delights.

Her symbiote shuffled, and she crossed her arms, hugging herself. The edge of her excitement dulled just enough to help her think.

"Calm," she whispered, but Rebekah heard her, flashing a reassuring smile.

"Yes, here." She led them both to a table beneath an unneeded roof that jutted from a small, windowless café to claim its share of the concourse. Under cover, but somehow it helped, taking Heki's eyes away from the ceiling, and dulling the colour and noise that swept on by. They sat, and she looked at a menu providing choices of what to eat, what to drink that were not determined by whatever Arin had chomped his way through or forgotten to order. Such a small thing, but the pure joy of it thrilled Heki, her mouth salivating despite not knowing what most of them actually tasted like. The names were enough.

"That's the dessert menu," said Rebekah, a smile creeping across her face as Heki stared back wide-eyed and hopeful alongside her sister. "Okay, but just the one. There's so much false sugar in them your bio chem will be off the chart. Get something not so sugary as a drink."

Heki nodded, chewed a lip, and then conspired with Tremil over the shared combo they were going to choose.

Rebekah watched the girls for the first minute as their eyes rolled, their lips smacked, and tongues sought every drop of the ice cream sundaes they'd ordered. They showed restraint, but the menu would have taken a hammering had she not been there. With an almost contented sigh, she scanned the crowd, having already marked a couple of Tensei's goons watching them intently. They weren't hiding, for which she was grateful. Being obvious served two purposes. One, they were indicating they knew she was back, as were her squad, and two, that there was a truce. Tense, but there. Arin had witnessed Tensei's dialogue with Lieutenant Ormsk, the sullen agreement to go along with their version of events around Segfi's wetware. It had bought time until Ormsk threatened the entire station, and she'd acted, putting her own crew's lives at risk in return for the thousands on Benetai. Of course, there was a third. The girls. Vulnerable in the gang members' eyes, and now marked should anything happen to Tensei. Mikai had let him live despite Rebekah's opinion that the gang leader should have been keel-hauled without a spacesuit after he executed Hannah.

Fucker. Is this where I am? Having to do deals with murderers and extortionists? But then I worked with an Enforcer and Countess Segfi. No bigger murderer or amoral bitch in this world than her, and I let her live too.

The clink of spoons brought her mind back, the ice cream smiles looking strange on girls whose own smiles spread from ear to ear. The laughter spilled as they looked at each other, tongues licking their faces clean before Rebekah could assault them with a napkin.

"Is it always like this?" asked Tremil. "You know, so busy and so many choices, colours, noise …?"

"Benetai has its quieter spaces, but yes. M2 and 3 are not so hectic, but there are times when they can feel overwhelming. And there is so much more out there, on the planets, Almaar, Shema. And the inhabited moons. Wonders, and to you they will be marvels. But after a while, the air is always sweeter elsewhere. You see what we're denied as lowborn. What we can't have because those in power hold on with an iron grip, no chink of light however hard you work." Rebekah realised she was preaching, and roped herself in. "Ignore me. Someone will always have more than you, it's just all these people here value the freedom to choose and develop themselves as best they can rather than be the playthings of the nobles."

"We've read about it," said Tremil.

Rebekah's smile was tight as she leant in. "Living it is very different. It's hard to find motivation when there's so little reward other than a pat on the back, a few pennies more, while the noble wallows in the excess they were born to but never earned." Thoughts of the Lundstrom's villa slipped in, and she forced them down. Horrific, but she'd come across enough people who glorified in killing, whether highborn or not. "Sorry. All this with the Butcher has got me thinking. We're free here, maybe we could try some trading, cargo runs."

"You could," replied Heki, and she glanced at Tremil, the ice cream smile fading a little. "But we've been monitoring the comms transmissions. They network between habitations, you know, like old-school bloggers discussing the latest news and that. You have to sift the bullsh—" Heki blushed, looking to the table. "The agendas they have, but the overall picture is everything costs. Especially fuel for the manoeuvring thrusters. That's why trading runs are so costly, and things have kind of stagnated. They're barely above survival level."

Rebekah nodded, eyeing the cost of the sundaes and musing about whatever the hell they would have used to make them. All synth, nothing natural. The girls got a taste for that, and they'd burn through their creds in no time.

"But," said Heki, running a finger along the inside of her plas-glass cup, "we could retrofit the *Sunstar*. Maybe experiment with an external tanker, see if we can fold one through void-space with us." She raised her eyebrows, the smile returning. Whether due to the synth sugar or her idea was hard for Rebekah to tell. "We could provide a much-needed service, kick-start the system's economy and make some dessert money."

Rebekah blinked, mind racing over what Heki suggested. "Someone must be hauling fuel here already?"

Tremil licked away the last of the ice cream on her face. "There's a Senti, Ravak, who drops in infrequently. But as far as we can tell, they don't see creds as of value. We have nothing they want except dreams and memories, and apparently, the people of this system want to keep them."

"Like you said, Rebekah," said Heki, "they have hope. We think there's an opportunity here. Someone on Windward produces a limited supply of low-grade fuel, but again, small fry, and there are big ships floating out there. They have creds, but the cost is so high."

"If we bring Mikai in, then ... but people would know it's us. Then they'd start wondering how we did it ... about the space folding thing," mused Rebekah. She was still leaning forwards, her eyes intent on both girls.

Tremil grimaced, but didn't lower her eyes. Rebekah knew she'd considered it already. "We could stick to the magic drive you mentioned to Trent Pike. Or ..."

"Bring in someone like Scarva, or this Ravak. Perhaps make someone up. Claim we were paying with memories until we got going. Maybe do all this out in the black," added Heki. "We'd be doing our part, and we'd build a new—"

"—home," finished Rebekah, her eyes sparkling.

CHAPTER 4

IN ORBIT, BENETAI SPACE STATION

"You okay in there?" Arin patted the wrench against ZZ3's chest. "Nothing falling apart? Any nuts and bolts undone? Capacitors fried?"

"You cannot still be sulking," replied ZZ3, and shuffled around to face the sub-engineer, eyes set blue.

"I have an amazing ability to hold a grudge for an inordinately long time. If you think a week is enough time for me to get over it, then you are mistaken, warbot." Arin grinned, hoping there was a hint of malice behind his eyes like he'd been practising. "You and Dricks conspired against me. Jello in my magboots, not funny. I wake up with nightmares about it squelching between my toes."

"You did add synth chilli to her shower soap."

Arin laughed. It had been funny, briefly, until Dricks had stopped talking to him for a few days and refused to let him in her cabin. "That was an honest mistake. Got my cargo numbers mixed up, that's all. Good job it wasn't the shampoo."

"True."

"Anyway, I've been thinking. You're crew now, right?" He tapped the wrench against the bot's chest again.

"I am crew," stated ZZ3, Arin convinced he could detect an element of pride beneath the monotone.

He smiled. A genuine one, filled with warmth, forgetting he was supposed to be angry still. "Well, crew need a role. A rank. Rebekah is pilot, Savvo co-pilot, Dricks engineer and I'm the sub-engineer. Not sure ship's warbot counts as a rank."

ZZ3's eyes whirled, though they remained blue. In recent weeks the bot had adjusted the status indicator to reflect, as it put it, a calm state. "I extrapolate that this conversation is going somewhere I am not going to ... like."

"Hey, I'm only trying to help. Here's my thought. You could be a sub-sub-engineer. You know, a sub-engineer's chief helper."

"Only helper."

"There's that. But chief helper has a kind of important ring to it, don't you think?" Arin stepped back, hands on hips, looking up at the ZZ3's eyes. "We could add the rank to your armour. Laser-etch it in."

"Have you proposed this to the Captain?" asked the bot, eyes settling again. Arin couldn't work out whether ZZ3 liked the idea, or was suspicious of it. Okay, it meant Arin was no longer the lowest ranking member of the crew, and in all likelihood, he could order the warbot around. But hey, there were always consequences of being a team player. Of being crew.

"No. You see, I'm thoughtful. Wanted to run it by you first." He pivoted, placing the wrench on top of the cargo box when the internal comms crackled, Savvo's voice resounding in the cargo bay.

"Dricks, Arin. Need you in the galley. ZZ3, can you tune in?"

"Affirmative, co-pilot," replied the warbot, bringing a little joy to Arin's thoughts. The warbot was obviously considering his proposal, as it should.

"Eh? Thanks ZZ3. The rest, hurry up."

"Okay sub-sub-engineer. I'll be back to check through your diagnostic after the meet." He exited the bay, clomping down the corridor, sure that there was still some jello residue between his toes that grated at him. The texture...

Savvo was waiting, leant against the galley wall, arms crossed, fingers pattering on his forearms. He nodded at Arin who collected a coffee, prepped Dricks' and handed it over silently when the engineer arrived. Yeah, they were okay after the engineer and ZZ3's revenge, but he was still in 'softly softly' mode. He'd got used to how comfortable things had become, and a knot at the back of his mind kind of regretted the synth-chilli. Mind you, it had livened things up.

He grinned spontaneously, a side-eye from Dricks shutting it down just as quickly.

"What's the brief?" asked Dricks, obviously deciding she'd have to be the serious one.

"Rebekah called us in. She's coming across with Mikai and the twins on a Benetai shuttle." Savvo pushed himself away from the wall and sat down with a sigh. "We're ordered to access the neutral ring."

"The what?" replied Arin.

Savvo activated the galley screen, scanning through the external cameras until achieving a view of the parked ships hovering to one side of the run-down space station. He pointed. "There."

"You mean that piece of space trash?" said Arin as the screen focused in on a rough ring of welded parts. If you squinted, it looked suspiciously like a donut with bites taken out. There was clear space around it and four docking ports, none of which were occupied.

"Apparently. A gang meeting place, a throwback to when they weren't all pally, and they had a bit more fuel. Used to hold their negotiations there. Neutral ground." Savvo tapped at his slate, and swiped up, the image on his screen matched now by that on the galley.

Arin baulked, blinking. It was Scarva's shuttle. He had no doubt about it, having got up close and personal as it landed above Rebekah and him back on Scarva's ship. And the fleeting glance as it escaped after Pshwa murdered most of Baja's gang.

"Scarva? No." Dricks slammed her flask onto the table. "Should have killed that mind-stealing shit when we had the chance."

"Second that," said Arin, Savvo nodding along.

"We would have been stuck here," stated ZZ3, spoiling the consensus.

Bloody logical warbots.

Arin stretched, his powered armour responding to the movements and supplementing with a whirr of servos. His visor was only half down, the ring having a limited atmosphere that cycled to keep the air relatively friendly though stale as hell. It had a taste to it he decided against allowing his suit to analyse. Rebekah stood to one side, also in her armour, and Mikai Hannos the other, looking as if she wanted to be anywhere else but here, a hand cannon strapped across her waist. Her smile gone, a scowl set firm as the *Unpronounceable*'s shuttle drifted in to take up a docking berth on the neutral ring.

It looks more like a butthole close up.

Scarva's shuttle adding to the shit hovering around it.

Heh.

"You in position, sub-sub-engineer?" he said into comms.

"Yes. And I understand you have not made the proposal of my rank to the Captain as yet."

"True. But I'm helping you get used to it." The bot was up to something; Arin could feel it.

A pause. "I was thinking of a different rank. Senior Rescue Warbot. That has a fine sound to it."

Arin spluttered, but was cut off by a glare from Rebekah as the ring airlock closest to Scarva's shuttle cycled. Hannos had refused to allow the ship any contact with Benetai. Primarily because Pshwa had stirred enough hate that there would be retribution if anyone found out, but Arin also suspected their story about the Butcher had got her spooked. And rightly so.

But it wasn't Pshwa who exited the shuttle, nor Scarva.

"Rohan Michaels," Arin said, the ex-Marine stepping through the airlock. He wore long magboots, a possible throwback to the shin injuries Rebekah had given him. At his side was a Bustan woman who screamed ex-Forces and was nervous as hell. How would Dricks describe her? Like a duck on a hot tin roof. Or was it a dog?

"Michaels?" said Rebekah, halfway between a question and a statement. "We were expecting Scarva with all the warnings."

The ex-member of Rubel's squad shook his head, his features drawn, tired. "Scarva's not up to the Gs without his encounter suit and is damn reluctant to put one on these days. But after our last visit here, well it wasn't worth the risk."

"And this is?" Rebekah tilted her head towards his nervous companion.

"Treni. My co-pilot." The Bustan's gun hand flexed, Arin assuming she was trying to relax but was finding it difficult. Maybe it was two sets of Navy-issue kick-arse armour putting her on edge. Good.

"And why are you here? We parted on less than amicable terms," continued Rebekah.

Arin knew most of her tells, and his captain wasn't gunning for a showdown. Rohan had survived their attack, and later the assault by the AI-Marauders, and had an underlying hatred for Scarva. Or at least, what the Senti had done to Rubel's squad at their request. But when you couldn't remember why you asked for shit to be taken out of your mind, it bred contempt. Yet he clearly still worked for the alien scumbag.

"We didn't know you were here until now, Khan. We're here to see Hannos, with a warning and maybe ask for some help. Or at least, Scarva is. Can we show you something?"

"It'd better be good," growled Mikai Hannos. "Cos you're on a short clock, fucker. Pshwa left a lot of death in the alien-bastard's wake. And you helped him. Aiding and abetting gets you a one-way trip into the void in my fucking book."

Rohan tilted his head, likely contemplating Mikai's words, before turning away and re-entering the airlock, returning with what looked to be a body bag. Arin's hand moved towards his sidearm, getting a similar response from the Bustan co-pilot.

"Stand down," Rebekah said, and she took a step forward, clearly curious. "We're past that but watch my back."

Arin moved to the side so he could observe and cover Rebekah, pleased to see he had access to her feed as Rohan unzipped the bag. What lay inside fired his nerves, and his stomach lurched.

"A fucking clone." Rebekah dropped to her haunches, pulling back the bag where it covered the bare head. The face was familiar; Arin had put down at least a dozen back on Daphene. The Butcher's handiwork. The pate was clean, but as Rebekah turned the body over, there was a scar across the neck.

"Shiiit," Arin said, wanting to move closer but resisted the urge.

"Treni," Rohan said, and the woman stepped forward, pulling out a collection of wires from a bag at her side. Arin didn't need to look closely, he knew what they'd be. She handed them to Rebekah, who took one glance, and passed them on to Mikai. "Took that out of another one. Kind of ironic after all the shit we went through to get them."

"Ironic? No. What do you know, Rohan? What do you really know about what's happening?" Rebekah stood, the glare she used one Arin had often suffered on his less restrained days.

"To be honest, we're as confused as hell. Why would the Countess send these synth-shits after us? Once Scarva started delving in their heads, it was all kind of obvious. Kefi, one of the Senti, ejected their ship after they attacked and we immediately entered void-space."

"The *Ungrit*," Rebekah said. "Right?"

Arin tensed, knowing the answer that was about to be revealed, and realising that their brief hiatus in decrepit paradise was about to be over. "Shit."

"How the hell …?" started Rohan, his co-pilot as shocked as him.

Rebekah turned to Mikai. "It's started. I thought it would take longer, but no. You need to prepare, keep any incoming ships isolated, limit all comms to narrow band. Preferably data burst only. Before we leave, I'll get Heki and Tremil to set you up the strongest safety protocols we can, but you're going to need relays."

"What?" said Treni.

Arin couldn't help himself. "Let me tell you about the *Scourge*, and an AI that makes the Marauders look like pussy cats, and a moon full of overly-muscled henchmen zombie clones with poor taste in clothing."

CHAPTER 5

"The relays will provide a time lag, but they can't cope with the Senti coding, so they'll failsafe to off. Best we could do. The station itself has a prison code box set up, with Asham's – ZZ3's – help. But if anything heavyweight turns up, they need to down comms, pull their skirts up and run." Tremil added a brief grin to her explanation.

"That one of Dricks'?"

Tremil blushed briefly, only a tremor of the emotion reaching Rebekah who easily blocked it out. How far they had come.

"But he can't get here yet," said Heki. "From what we know, it's obvious he's trying. Why else attack Scarva if not for the symbiote? He wants what we can do."

Rebekah had to agree, though something was off. She couldn't put her finger on it, but Dricks was right. The Butcher always seemed three steps ahead, as if the AI had worked out every possibility and made, as ZZ3 would put it, the moves with the greatest success probabilities. Attacking Scarva appeared desperate, a failed run. But there'd be something else to it, a feint, but why?

He doesn't know how we jump through space. Just that we can.

"Time ..." she started to say, gazing at the twins. Heki reached across the galley table and squeezed her hand.

"It's okay. This is what we do, and it brings no harm. At least none we've found. Scarva's at Durnat. We've been there," cut in Tremil. "Besides, if we're not trading fuel just yet, we need to earn ice cream sundae credit somehow."

Rebekah's heart fluttered. They had been through so much, trauma upon trauma, and remained strong. Resilient. It would come out in the end, she had to be wary, but also enjoy the moments of lucidity and hope. "Okay. Ten minutes."

The fold had been brief, passing as if a mere step in time. One moment she and Savvo were staring at the icy moon Benetai orbited, the next they were looking at another, but the space station was absent, and the sensors pinged highlighting the *Unpronounceable*'s position.

"Contact," said Savvo. "But there's nothing else here but Scarva."

"Check for sensory voids. The Butcher has access to Segfi's tactics, and a fucking battle AI along for the ride. We act at all times as if this is a hostile area of space ... and ship." Rebekah eyed the Senti spacecraft's lines, recalling the images of the ambassadors' ship ZZ3 and Savvo had shared. She'd thought Scarva's *Unpronounceable* to be a rough and ready, hacked together mess. But apparently not. Both the sleek lines of the rear, and the weird arrays at the front, matched that hidden away on Daphene.

"We have a transponder," Savvo said, swiping the data across to Rebekah's screen. "Scanning for sensory voids."

"No way are we fucking linking with that," she replied. "We match speed and course. And we fly across."

"We?"

She nodded. "Heki can fly the *Sunstar*, and we may need the numbers. Scarva also has to know we mean business if he's still alive. Send a message, short burst data about what we're doing."

Arin cycled the *Unpronounceable*'s airlock then reattached onto the metal hull. The docking valley they were in spun lazily, but it was in desperate need of repair. The clamp had been torn wide open, as if a pair of giant hands had wrenched them apart, and the armour plate scorched black by a pair of main engines. Rebekah could detect a gouge under the second clamp, likely where one of the *Ungrit*'s own docking clamps had ripped across the hull.

ZZ3 settled in the airlock, and they waited as the bot entered the Senti ship first, followed by her, Savvo and Arin when the warbot declared it was safe. They were in full armour, carbines at the ready, but had limited their comms to internal only. A closed loop, and they needed to keep it clear of any remnant of the Butcher.

Their sensory sweep on arrival had hinted the *Unpronounceable* was acting normally. Power levels were as expected, and analysis of the transponder link and comms had hinted it was Butcher free. But she had little trust in data anymore. Heki and Tremil could falsify sensor responses at the surface level, so what could the Butcher do?

The corridor was as filthy as ever. Mouldy, rubbish strewn. A façade according to Rohan. He was following in his shuttle; Rebekah having decided that the ex-Marine didn't need to know about their newfound ability to jump through space just yet. She'd cross that bridge later.

"Savvo."

"Yeah, yeah. On point."

"ZZ3, take the rear."

"That's sub-sub-engineer ZZ3," said Arin.

"Senior Rescue Warbot," added ZZ3, waiting for them all to pass. "On your rear."

Rebekah shook her head. "Stow that crap. Focus. We're on an alien ship which the Butcher may have infected. Fucking concentrate."

"Yes, Captain. My apologies," replied ZZ3, Arin silent. What had he done to the warbot now?

For later.

On reaching the first turn inwards, Savvo checked around the corner with his carbine sight, then signalled Rebekah ahead. She swept past, HUD displaying no threats as she reached the far wall and Savvo returned to point.

After reaching the next junction, and within sight of Scarva's memory extraction room, a Senti waited. They wore a full encounter suit, and strapped across their lower chest area was one of the strange weapons they had used against the Marauders. A type of radiation gun, one that neither she nor Arin had analysed for the effect it would have on their suits and the important flesh inside. She eye-clicked her HUD, ensuring it would remind her on return to the *Sunstar*.

The Senti turned, nose tentacle waving their way as if encouraging them on. Rebekah set her comms to broadcast.

"We're the crew of the *Sunstar*," she said, as if that would explain all.

"I read your transponder and am curious at your lack of a link." The voice was monotone, its manner and the word choice very Senti. "You mentioned Rohan, but little chance you could have met him at Benetai and be here."

"Kefi?" asked Rebekah.

"Why yes," the alien replied.

"Rohan said you think he has shit-for-brains."

A sound like a gang of seagulls squabbling over a fish filled the corridor. It grated on her ears, but at the same time was rather welcome.

"Well, you didn't torture that out of him. I remember you, Khan. Though we never met, I watched you fight off the Marauders impressively." The Senti's lower tentacles spun the encounter suit around to face the other way. "I have informed Scarva you are who the transponder says, but be warned, Scarva is ill. Weak, and moody. Follow me."

Rebekah glanced behind, signalling each in turn to stay in their positions and keep an eye on their rear. With that, she followed, catching up to be a stride behind the Senti.

"Have your systems been playing up?" she asked, keeping the urgency in her voice, hoping the alien recognised it.

"Not as such. Why?" The chin tentacle quivered a little, but the meaning was lost on her.

"Because we're here to warn you and Scarva. More than that, we're here to check if you've been infected. Your ship, your computers." She was by the Senti's side now.

The seagull sound again, and the shoulder tentacles shook a little. "We are Senti, human. Our systems do not get *infected*."

Rebekah wanted to grab the alien and spin it around, shout some sense into it. She pushed down the urge. Aggression wouldn't get her anywhere. "Senti code in four dimensions," she said.

The alien stopped suddenly, turning to face her.

"And you're missing a ship. An ambassador's ship. I know where it is, I know it's been stripped of its tech, and I know General Asham of the Almaarian Court studied your code. The same Asham that redesigned the wetware you encountered."

"It is impossible," the Senti said, but beneath the monotone was a slowness.

"I have seen many impossible things over the last few months. Human and Senti hybrids, a brain-patterned mad scientist and a ship full of the bastard's experiments. All to discover what you have. What you can do. Jump from system to system. Now tell me again, have you been infected?" Rebekah stared at the Senti, her HUD detecting a change in the gases exuding from the suit.

"Infection, no. Glitches."

"Then he's in there, and we're leaving."

Why am I still here? What has this bastard done for us?

Scarva had changed in the few months since she'd last seen the mind-fucker. She had little sympathy, but the *Unpronounceable* was infected, the Butcher had left something behind. Having entered the true heart of the ship, its similarity to the orbs striking and also reassuring after the exterior, the Senti had set to work immediately running diagnostics with its team. She had been ushered in to Scarva's cabin, with Savvo as company, the rest unwelcome.

Rebekah removed her helmet, out of deference to Kefi more than Scarva, who had made the request.

"Khan," said Scarva, its mouth flexing open, chin tentacle limp across the alien's body. "What a non-pleasure to have you on board." The Senti off-gassed, the reek terrible.

Rebekah wrinkled her nose. "Fuck you too," she replied. The alien grated on every nerve, sick or not. "The *Ungrit* was one of Segfi's patrol ships. It's infested with an AI, or at least, a human AI thing."

"I heard your conversation with Kefi. Not something we need to worry about." The voice faded on the last word, the limp tentacle's tip wafting.

"You're so wrong, Scarva. The attack on you was a feint, the whole payment thing a delay to get himself on board your ship. He wants to know how you enter void-space, so he can escape whenever he needs to." She took a step closer, regretting it due to the smell leaking from the alien. "He's a monster, Scarva. You will remember General Asham, what he did to Bustan 8."

"Yeees. Such delicious memories he made." The first glint of life appeared in the Senti's central eye. "But those secrets are mine to keep."

She wanted to throttle him, scream that he could have been after the symbiote, but this new Butcher always had a back-up plan. Always. And saying as much would reveal their secret.

The door slid open, Savvo turning at her side, hand on his weapon as Kefi entered. "Scarva," began the Senti. "There is the remnant of an attack on our system. Small, focused, that disconnected about the time I spun the *Ungrit* off the ship. I have isolated it, for study."

"See. I told you. Do you know what it was doing, Kefi?"

"At first it was searching the archives of our," the Senti glanced at Scarva, "of our journeys. Then, it downloaded our defensive code."

"That it?" asked Rebekah.

"If he has the code, he can experiment if, as you say, he is made from the same algorithms. Formulate attacks on our system." The Senti looked uncomfortable. "Not just our system. Most Senti ships have the same base code. It is unthinkable that we would attack our own ships. The nest ..."

Scarva's chin tentacle came to life, waving in the air as if to strike Kefi. "Enough."

Kefi bowed its head, backing away. Rebekah made to intercept, striding over, fists-balled. "Wait. Think Kefi. What was this for?"

The Senti looked again to Scarva, an off-gas filling the room. Was that panic? Scarva's chin tentacle settled back across its chest. "We are wary now.

But other Senti ... may not be. We are cut off from the main nest ... from comms."

"Fuck. You mean an orb, don't you? He wants to travel void-space, where else would he go but a fucking orb to get what he wants."

How many symbiotes would there be aboard a Senti transport orb? They're the size of a small moon.

CHAPTER 6

EMPEROR'S COURT, ALMAAR

"Talk to me Admiral. Give me a status report I can use, not one to hang myself with." Countess Segfi mentally kicked herself, realising that had sounded a little too desperate. "None of your bullshit. Gritty detail, projections for the next seven days." That was better.

She glanced up from her slate, the dual guard standing either side of the ornately carved and gold-leafed doorway staring straight ahead. They wore silver breastplates stamped with the Emperor's rearing horses either side of his family's crest bearing various implements of battle and currently a stylised map of the Almaarian system. She knew well enough Emperor Hanter Gunstaff had personally designed its replacement for when the Bustans were conquered. A modernisation, horses replaced by gunships, that type of thing. Crass, but most things about the Emperor were. When you ruled an entire planetary system, it didn't really matter what others thought, as long as they responded to the iron-fist the Court held the people in thrall with.

Where they belong.

Admiral Vante sighed. A habit, one Segfi could let pass while the woman pulled together a navy reeling from the loss of her flagship. At least she had come to terms with the danger the Butcher posed to the rest of the ships. Now it was brow-beating the petty, idiotically honourable officers of the fleet into understanding this was not a threat you could shoot or overwhelm. In fact, as distasteful as it was to her, hiding might well be the best possible approach.

Ambush is a far better word. Trap, perhaps. Anything that makes the stupid oafs understand the import of what they face.

"Yes, Countess," stated the admiral. "Sending now." The information relayed to her Senti enabled slate, the almost instant comms providing a glimmer of hope amid the concerns about the Butcher's ability to listen in and even ride the signals. The information would be hours out of date, based on the speed of comms transmission to the admiral, but the Senti system had a potential she needed to tap. Each of the smaller fleets overseen by various nobles had such a unit in their flagship, reserved for the noble's personal use. That had to change.

Footsteps echoed along the gold-flecked marble floor, a rap of metal-rimmed leather upon stone accompanied by the tap of an iron-bound, but prized, ceremonial staff. Rakan Albama, high priestess of the God's four avatars, her gold-threaded robes flowing behind her as the grey-haired woman strode towards the countess bearing a grim look of determination Segfi was sure she'd worn when she'd popped out of her mother's womb.

The Countess stood, then knelt oh so slowly on one knee, the creak of her back and the weakness in her legs no excuse in the eyes of the church. She pressed her forehead against the proffered hand, then kissed the high priestess' seal that bore slivers of the four swords born by the avatars when they quelled the fire, water, and air of Almaar then brought the beasts to heel.

"Countess," said Rakan, her voice a rasp of age. The hand became one of assistance, and the high priestess helped Segfi to her feet. "Your health?"

The countess pursed her lips, the slightest shake to her head. "Will have to suffice. In check, but the rot spreads cell by cell."

"I will pray for you," stated Rakan, sympathy in her eyes and at the turn of her mouth.

Segfi wasn't fooled. The sympathy stretched as far as retaining the Empire, and therefore her God's, power over all. She was a tool, and needed to be maintained, sharpened, used until there was nothing but a nub left to then be discarded and replaced. Such was her role, and she accepted it gladly. It was what she was born and raised to do. But Rakan had softer edges, ones she might need in the future.

"Thank you," she said. "That I would appreciate. And the Emperor?"

"As hale as ever, but perturbed, as is the Court at the turn of things."

Segfi eyed the gold-leaf doors, a depiction of Almaar split between them, each mountain range, city and coast picked out in intricate detail. A stunning effigy to the emperor's will and remit. To raise Almaar above all. "As am I, Rakan. This is to be ...?"

"Private? No. The Court is rife with rumour and supposition. The Emperor seeks to quell that with an open meeting. To show there is nothing to hide." Rakan's grimace and knowing look were a hint the high priestess disagreed with this approach. If Segfi's news was bad, a riled Higher Court only hindered, each looking to their own concerns before that of Almaar.

The two guards drew their swords, their edges keen, hilts adorned with the emperor's crest. In the same moment, the doors cracked open, revealing the glitter and warmth of a golden ceiling lit by three huge, bejewelled chandeliers that spun slowly on their axes. Light cascaded down the central aisle, with three rows of gilded leather seats on either side. Today, only the first row of each was occupied. The counts and countesses of the High

Court awaiting on Segfi's news with an eagerness she hoped was born from concern for the Empire, not to revel in her fate.

She entered side-by-side with the High Priestess, in one way glad for her company, and in another not. Should she be deemed to have failed the emperor – and if he was of the mind to take retribution – things could get messy. The Minister's hand, Gerent, had enough evidence of her duplicity to have her tried for treason. That he was as deep in the lies and hidden truths as her would hold no sway. Perceived treason, the breaking of the emperor's decree – even in the emperor's interests – could lead to her rapid downfall. Primarily if she had failed and the Minister – and therefore the emperor – needed a scapegoat. Or her actions had been uncovered with too many eyes able to make the connection back to either of them.

Where will the axe fall?

Nowhere if they want to survive what's coming.

Emperor Gunstaff stood before his throne upon a raised marble dais. Forged from the hull of the first colony ship and burnished to a shine that hurt her eyes when the chandeliers' light caught the throne's polished back, it rose five metres into the air before curling over like feathers at the tips. He wore the red and blue of his House, and as usual refused to wear the ceremonial medals accrued with the victories over the Bustans. First at New Almaar, and then Bustan 8 and the outer way stations of their system. He had taken the cessation hard, and developed a hatred for the Senti that meant he condoned her and Asham's actions, while showing a hand of friendship to the alien gasbags every time they made contact. It had always been her get-out, the experiments a huge diplomatic controversy should they be exposed. Unlike the high priestess, Segfi welcomed the public forum, for the emperor, and therefore the minister, would not risk such an exposure before the Court.

Unsteady legs didn't betray her, and she managed to kneel for a second time before Emperor Gunstaff.

"Welcome Countess," bellowed the Minister, his plain, tailored suit in contrast to the ostentatious room. His only affectation the key of office dangling from a silver chain that rested against his chest. He clicked his fingers, and a servant arrived carrying one of the leather gilded chairs. Segfi's house crest sat at the top of the backrest. Everyone knew she was ill, there was no hiding such secrets from those greedy for leverage, so she accepted the offer but didn't sit until the Minister insisted. At that, the shuffle of feet around her indicated the High Court had also taken to their seats, their eyes on the drama about to unfold.

"Countess Segfi, the Emperor wishes to thank you for your service since you were last in this hallowed chamber." The Minister's voice projected through the room. There was no electronic trick, the acoustics perfected so that the Emperor's will was heard by all.

"I thank the Emperor for such generosity," she responded, hands in her lap, fingers still despite the need for a cigarette.

"Good, good," said the Minister.

The emperor took that moment to sit upon his throne, one leg cast over the other, chin on hand as he eyed her. That was a first. He usually stood or paced throughout. This wasn't positive.

"Can you explain to the Court, Countess, the events around Daphene. And specifically, how you came to lose the ANS *Segfi*, the pride of Almaar."

Even though she knew it was coming the words bit home. Personally, as a deeply felt loss, and for her standing within the Empire. How could she be trusted as a war leader, for a war she was certain was coming, if she couldn't prevent her own flagship from being overrun?

But Gerent had briefed her.

At last, something useful after the Incini ran rings around him.

"My ship. My flagship was overridden by a Bustan AI attack."

The High Court went into uproar, shouts echoing about the chamber, anger spilling into threats of retribution. The Minister, his face stern, slammed his staff of office onto the marble floor, twice. The first a call for peace, the second to order. The emperor had stood, hands on hips, eyes fierce as he strode down the steps to stand before the countess. She made to rise, but the Minister's gentle headshake stayed her. Was this part of the theatre?

"Are you certain?" said the emperor. She had, of course, heard him speak in private meetings. But never in the chamber. Here the Minister spoke with his voice, the High Priestess his heart.

"Yes, Your Imperial Majesty. I am certain. We recovered a containment unit unknowing what was inside. On opening it under controlled conditions, there seemed little danger but then it infected one of our Marine's suits. From there the foul program entered Daphene's mainframe and rapidly replicated, growing and taking control. Before my scientists knew what was happening, it had opened the doors of the base, pumped in the atmosphere and murdered ninety-five percent of the base team. Over three thousand people." The murmurs started again, though quelled by a glare from the Minister.

"My subjects," said the emperor, his face screwing up with fury.

The countess nodded. The emperor didn't give two royal, gilded shits for his subjects. "And then it gained access to laser comms and used those to upload itself to the *Segfi*." She avoided mentioning the warnings from Khan and her crew, as well as the *Ungrit*'s role. There would be talk of treason, scapegoatism at its worse, deflecting from the real issue. The Butcher. "And proceeded to space the crew."

The emperor reddened. Crew meant officers, many of whom would be of Court heritage. That would hurt more.

"This AI is a threat to the entire Navy. In fact, to any military or civilian outpost where it can infect a mainframe. We should take precautions,

Your Imperial Majesty, before it spreads. I fear for the consequences." The countess shuffled in her seat, using a glance over to the Minister to raise an eyebrow. She hadn't been expecting the emperor's direct involvement, and it was unnerving even for her. There was the briefest of nods, so she carried on. "We must cut all laser comms activity until we can ascertain how the AI spreads that way, and ..." she turned to face one side of the Court, then the other, before looking to her emperor, "ensure access to all the Navy flagships via the Senti comms units. They must be secured as a priority."

And there it was. Uproar. Reducing the capacity for instantaneous comms by every noble on Almaar, and the rest of the Empire given enough time.

The Minister's rod slammed down again. "Order!" he snarled. It crashed down again.

The emperor took to the first step, hands back on his hips, eyes sweeping across the Court who immediately silenced. For the first time the Countess could remember, he addressed the nobles directly in public.

"I will assess this threat," he said, the voice measured but filled with anger. "But hear me. If I believe this Empire of ours is at risk of the malevolence of a Bustan AI, I *will* make that order. And you *will* comply. We will not have another New Almaar. We will NOT!"

CHAPTER 7

ABOVE DAPHENE

"Captain, we are emerging from Trazor's stellar path," said Ensign Rodri.

Captain Srenik glanced over to the ensign, the woman's focus on her screen, fingers flying over the buttons and paddles of the navcom controls with a certainty he admired. And needed. The crew of the ANS *Righteous* wasn't new by any means, but like the rest of the Almaarian Navy, had spent much of the last four years on training runs with nothing to shoot at except pretend revolutionaries and interplanetary smugglers. Hardly a challenge for the second youngest cruiser in the countess' fleet.

Not exactly a Warmonger right now when you're swatting flies and the occasional wasp.

They, and the frigate ANS *Bonray*, had used Trazor to block any close-range sensors monitoring their approach, but if Daphene's base was fully operational as the countess expected, this rogue AI would already know of their approach and have calculated possible trajectories. But what pissed Srenik off most was that she and her new Admiral, Vante, had scrapped the usual strategy against a static base. Disregarded years of battle tactics honed not only in war games, but in the space around Bustan 7 and 8, and before that New Almaar. His orders were clear. The Bustan AI was back, more advanced than ever, with Almaar in its sights. The base on Daphene had been compromised, thousands exposed to the poisonous atmosphere, and, if the whispers were true, managed to board a navy ship. That had to be bullshit of the highest order, but the Warmonger was taking it seriously, and ballsed-up their usual approach to form a new plan. It smacked of panic, and Srenik wondered if the countess' lung rot had finally reached her brain.

"Any reaction?"

"Nothing from Daphene. No ships taking off, and there's zero activity in orbit I can pick up."

"Relays?" the captain asked, glancing over towards his comms officer.

"Active," he replied, scratching at his upper arm. "Comms are up."

"Uh-huh," Srenik responded. "We keep to the plan. Ensign Henton, take down all relays if you please. I want silence around Trazor, and Ensign Rodri, a full sweep of where the Countess identified the location of the missile platforms and active satellites. I want the data visually on the main screen in five."

He eased back into his plush chair, trying to relax, but annoyed at what was being asked of him and his crew. Confirmation of the relays' destruction cheered him a little, but whatever was on Daphene would have their position by now. But then that was the point.

"Satellites have engaged, and I've extrapolated the most likely platform positions." Ensign Rodri engaged the main screen, Daphene coming into a real-time view with an outer sphere of the satellites orbiting the moon displayed as a web of interconnected lines. Amid these were the missile platforms they had to assume were operational though currently inert.

"Any additional possibilities?" the captain asked, standing up from his chair, elbow resting on his other arm, hand on chin.

Ensign Rodri swiped at her screen. "Not that I can detect yet. What are we expecting?"

Good question. Wish I knew.

"Possibly the *Ungrit*, a patrol ship, or some such presence." He eyed the screen. "Anything that even hints at being spaceworthy I need to know about it. For now, we build speed and head towards Daphene. Maintain targeting on the satellites and platforms, ensure any aggressive response is met with the most efficient target array. I want this clean."

"The *Bonray* is hailing, sir."

Srenik turned to face the comms officer. "Hailing? We're on silence, Markov."

"Still hailing. Call signs and identifiers are correct, Captain."

Now what?

He tapped at his personal screen, turning it square on, eyeing the tracking data for the frigate. It was glowing large, the information from the sensors a lie that highlighted the *Bonray* as being a ship of at least cruiser length and bulk. All was as it should be, the acceleration rate high, just at tolerable levels if enough retardant had been pumped into your body. So why the hell would they hail?

"What system?" he asked. "Are they using a normal channel?"

It couldn't be the AI. How would it know the call signs?

"Standard secure," replied the comms officer.

The captain nodded, gripping the arms of his command chair. Rare was it that a ship's commander would break with set protocol. "Put them on. Private line."

With dampener activated, he slipped on his comms set, the crackle of speakers soon replaced by a familiar voice. Jackie Wynn.

"Srenik," came the voice. Clean, sounding close. "Come back. You there?"

"Yes Captain Wynn. I'm here. You have broken silent protocol." It was a start, his suspicions aroused. Had Segfi been right? But this wasn't the laser comms she'd warned about.

"Necessary. I'm getting indications of life signs on the surface. Radio contact. Calls for help. Those are our people down there, Srenik. Navy personnel. This doesn't scan." The voice was clipped, just as Jackie always was, the intonation perfect. If he hadn't already been suspicious, he wouldn't have given it a second thought.

"Tell me Wynn, where did we first meet?"

"Eh? What are you blathering on about, Srenik? We're about to blow our own people sky high." That sounded like her, one of the sayings she favoured.

"Answer. Where?"

There was no pause. "At the Academy, in Almaar of course. We had classes together."

Srenik cut the connection. This was scary stuff.

He slid off the comms unit, tossing it onto his chair as he stood. He'd met Jackie the night before the Academy freshers' week. Had drinks and a little fun they never repeated despite remaining friends. "No more comms response, understand. Track the *Bonray*. Any deviation, I want to know."

He clasped his hands together, thumbs against his chest as they twiddled with the central clasp of his uniform. Had the *Bonray* been compromised? If that was the case, surely they'd be moving away from the moonbase, their intended target?

"How soon until the *Bonray* should disengage?"

Rodri swiped the data across, so he had a visual. "Eleven seconds," she stated. Srenik watched the countdown, thumbs pressed against his chest, chin now resting on his clasped fingers. On zero, the image of the *Bonray* split in half. The frigate moving away, adjusting trajectory so that it would shoot past the moon at a safe distance. The other half split and split again, forming several trails of sensory information now the missiles were clear of the *Bonray*'s false shadow. Srenik let out a long sigh, relief washing over him.

"Multiple bogies. By all the gods, thousands of them!" shouted Rodri, her mouth half open as she stared at the large screen. Daphene was swamped in red, thousands of pinprick lights blurring the moon.

"What? What are those?" Srenik asked, stepping closer to the large screen, blinking. "Henton, any of those come near us, I want them to be space dust before I even breathe."

"Aye, Captain."

"Best guess, auto drones," stated Rodri, her focus on her own screen. "Linked, like a net. Sir, there is another swarm in the *Bonray*'s path." The Ensign tapped furiously at her console, eyes flitting from data set to data set while Srenik's mind tried to work out what the hell was going on. The first of the missiles struck the net cast by the drones, and the missile's heat signature flared, then faded away. More followed, one after the other, the drone net triggering each in turn.

Captain Srenik swallowed, trying to push away the fear that burbled in his stomach and threatened to swamp his throat. The countess had warned him, and he'd listened despite his massive doubts. Stuck to the half-arsed plan he'd called overkill.

But Segfi was named Warmonger for more than just bloodlust and duty.

Behind the missiles flew an old, nameless transport ship. Derelict except for the engines, and packed with chemical explosives. Nothing electrical in there, even the drive had been restructured with a closed loop once fired up. Impact triggered, he thought it was one of the most useless plays ever devised by a navy tactician. But then he'd just watched his beautiful missiles light up space, instead of the AI's new base. And it was streaking towards Daphene, accelerating at speeds that would flay flesh and aimed directly for the new hole in the drones' defensive net.

"What's happening with the *Bonray*? Rodri, focus on that. Henton the base."

"The *Bonray* will enter the swarm in five seconds. The net is wider. Different," stated Rodri.

"Shit," mouthed Srenik.

Please don't let the countess be right. Not a second time.

"Transport contact. We have multiple drones exploding, the sensors are blind … 3, 2, 1 and clear. It's through, Captain." Ensign Henton almost smiled as he glanced over. A little hope amid this new kind of warfare. "The base is responding. Missiles activated. There must be twenty, no thirty of them, sir."

So many things happening at once. Focus. The base was out of his control now, but not the *Bonray*.

"Contact," said Rodri, her voice trailing off, lips moving as she talked through whatever she was seeing. "The *Bonray* is through, Captain. No explosions. Safe."

Safe. She said allow no contact at any cost. No laser comms, no taking on board distressed ships or survivors. Wipe everything out.

"Damn," said Ensign Henton, voice raised, eyes wide. "Hit after hit, Captain. The transport blew a klick from the surface."

Srenik relaxed a little. "That'll still cause significant damage at that speed and range. I want an estimate, Ensign. Keep monitoring. Pilot, adjust so we are in the *Bonray*'s wake but away from what remains of the swarm. There is to be no contact, am I clear?"

"They're not drones," the countess said, annoyed at Captain Srenik. "Drones are logical, follow orders. These are far from mindless. They have been programmed by the most advanced AI in existence. Think of it as a games champion calculating every possibility, Srenik. Every one, and its aim is survival by any means."

In reality, she was the one playing. A game of sacrifice. The final piece to get the Court, the emperor, but above all else, the navy commanders to believe in the inherent danger the Butcher posed. She just hoped it was worth it.

Srenik stared into the screen, the Senti comms providing a near real-time image of a worried officer, his eyes averting as a commotion rolled through his command bridge. "A moment," he said, and moved away, leaving only his command chair in view. The noise grew, Segfi recognising the tinge of horror that could sweep through a usually orderly bridge when the world flipped on its head. She'd witnessed it the day Asham had let his soldiers do as they would on Bustan 8, and when Rubel's squad had been attacked by a terrified batch of Asham's hybrids.

"What is it, Captain?" she demanded, annoyed not by being ignored, but by being left ignorant. An arm came into view, then Srenik slumped into his chair, hands clasped together. There was a steel to his gaze, anger in the tight lips.

"The crew," he started, and his hands tightened their grip. "The *Bonray*'s crew."

"Spaced," she said, receiving a slight nod in response from Srenik. "The *Bonray* has been compromised. In your opinion, Captain, and this is for the Court record, how did that happen?"

"It must have been the dr ... the AI swarm."

The countess nodded. A necessary sacrifice. Evidence. "Prepare a report for the Court. Broadcast to all ships in my fleet that no one is to make comms or physical contact of any kind with that ship. I'll confirm the order. And Captain Srenik, go hunt down the *Bonray*, and blow it into the abyss."

"There could be surv—"

"Everyone is dead, Captain. Understand. Everyone. Do your duty for the Emperor and the Court, and destroy that ship."

She switched the Senti comms off, knowing that she had one of the most respected commanders in her fleet now on board with the threat the Butcher posed. His report would seal the Court's support, and combined with Srenik's newfound understanding, spread a wariness amid the other fleets. A first step.

She swiped her slate, setting it to report once any images of Daphene came through. Taking out the base would have been a bonus, but she suspected the Butcher would have moved much of his laboratory work onto her ex-battleship, or at least doubled up on it. The base was static, and therefore vulnerable, but also a draw to snare unsuspecting navy ships. Her actions had countered that, but leaving it even partially functioning was an issue. The defensive net and attack swarms the AI had forged were new weapons, a hint of what the Butcher could create down there. If left to his devices, what could the base produce next?

"Time," she said. "So little of it left." The countess drew on her cigarette stick, the medication barely easing the pain in her lungs. With a cough, she activated the Senti comms, her new Admiral coming into focus. "Destroy Daphene. Now."

CHAPTER 8

APPROACHING THE SENTI ORB

Rebekah's finger splayed along the galley tabletop, tapping a rhythm she didn't recognise, but filled with nervous energy that she did. Across from her Hendricks was supping at her sweet, milky coffee, eyes focused on her slate and avoiding Arin's gaze as he stared at the same view. They were seeking just a glimpse, enough to put their minds at ease.

Hendricks' shoulders dropped, and her head rose, peering at Rebekah. She couldn't tell whether it was good or bad news, frustration building until the engineer swiped the slate and sent the image up onto the galley screen. Half a view, the rest obscured by the hull of Scarva's ship. The orb was huge, even at this distance, and swirled and shimmered with a golden brown that to her eyes appeared like liquid clouds. This was the fourth time she'd encountered one. Two tours and when on the run from Bustan 7 after rescuing the twins accounting for the others. Each had never failed to amaze.

"Doesn't look any different," said Arin. "You think, Savvo?"

The co-pilot approached the screen, eyeing the static image while rubbing at his chin where he'd allowed the first signs of a beard to grow. How

Nicky would take to the fuzz was a different matter, but there was another month or two before their promised return to Karal and the feisty woman's decision over whether to join them, wherever they had settled.

"Not that I can see. Trem, can we clean this image up? Merge it with each time the spin gives us a view?" The girl nodded and left without a word, returning with her slate and it wasn't long before they had a moving image blended from the sweep of the cameras.

Rebekah sighed. "Looks the same. Like the surface has tides or storms blowing. Same light, same spin."

"And the ring looks intact," added Arin. "Weird seeing it all alone. Usually there's a swarm of ships waiting to travel."

"Kefi said that's not been the case for some time. They've only kept it open for diplomatic purposes. This and the one near Bustan." Rebekah adjusted her own slate and flask, trying to distract herself from the nagging worry. Her slate finally pinged, burst data from the *Unpronounceable*'s control room dropping in. Scarva had ordered minimal comms between them, mistrusting all human ships by association with the Butcher. He'd agreed to carry them only because of what came next.

"Time to learn," said Tremil, hand in hand with Heki as they sat together. "All adds to the empirical evidence."

"You're not coming," said Rebekah, more firmly than the last time.

"We're your Senti coding experts. At least, the most expert you can get without the risk of being infected." Tremil was using the same argument she had for the past fifty-two hours. ZZ3 had agreed with their point, but had backed Rebekah as crew should. The captain's word was law, and all the pressure that came with it.

"Both true," Rebekah stated, "And you can continue to use those words over and over until the letters wear out. Only when I'm certain that the orb is clear of the Butcher, will I allow you on board. You are staying here.

I need you to protect the *Sunstar*. Period. Priority number one. If Scarva gets a whiff of trouble, he'll fu … he'll run, and leave us in the lurch."

"In the shit," said Tremil, daring Rebekah with a glare to rise to the swear word.

How come when they get their first taste of ice cream, they stop being so sweet?

"Besides, you'd only have the basic suits. We've no armour to fit either of you." Rebekah caught a glint in Tremil's eye and glanced towards Arin, whose face flooded with panic.

"Wait …" Arin raised his hands, trying to calm the brewing storm. "Hey, hey. They're not done. Got at least another few days' work before they're usable, never mind fit for any comb—" He cut off as Rebekah's glare rose from level six to the full eleven out of ten.

"Not happening." She slammed her fists down on the table. "And next time our two youngest crew members come up with a plan, you run it by me first. Fuck, Arin. Now get *our* suits prepped. Dricks…"

"Yeah. I'm okay with staying. Not sure boarding mind-sucking central is exactly appealing."

Rebekah stormed out, trying to suppress the anger, the look in Tremil and Heki's eyes telling her they both knew they'd pushed too far. Again.

Was I like this as a teenager?

Probably worse. But we're in a tin can with nowhere to hide.

She found herself in the cargo bay, facing ZZ3 as the warbot ran through a system's check, blue eyes pulsing in a telltale pattern. Rebekah knew she could have done with Arin there, but was too frustrated with him.

"ZZ3. Status report," she said.

"All systems are repaired post Saim and Daphene, Captain. The heavier armour is reducing my efficiency by 2% and I extrapolate from some of my recent behaviour that non-considered comments are leaving my systems at inappropriate times. Which is strange, but analysis has shown no software glitches or suspicious code." The bot's eyes calmed to a steady blue.

"Sounds about right for anyone who spends time around Arin. But yes, some of those comments are out of turn." Her frown receded, the thought of the warbot having its servos slapped for comebacks suddenly funny. How would Major Ren have reacted? "I will inform you when they are inappropriate."

"As you do for our glorious leader, yes?"

"Yes. Exactly like that. ZZ3," she paused, thumbs inside her fists, ready to crack, "ZZ3, I have clear concerns over your involvement with the Butcher, with the part of Asham you contain."

"The coding, you mean. Not Asham."

"Yes. That." Was it just that? "Do you have any suggested protocols?"

"We contained the comms on board Scarva's ship, that should be appropriate. But, by the conversation you just had with Tremil, my probabilities indicate you are looking for something more." The bot's legs shuffled, servos activating and just as quickly switching off. "Is not Kefi coming on board with us?"

"They are, but a Senti and one of Scarva's crew at that. It's a matter of trust, and us needing to know detail that Kefi may not wish to share." Rebekah leaned back on a cargo box, the clomp of feet heading her way an indicator Arin had need to apologise and was seeking her out.

"I understand. I believe Kefi is different, but do not have any probabilities to prove that theory. Therefore, your caution is warranted. Our glorious leader is here." The warbot shifted again as Arin eased in by her side.

"Captain ... Rebekah."

"What was the bribe? An extra Danish? I'm not mad at what you're doing, but why you're keeping it from me. Lock the fucking guilt away. You can't run around after them at their beck and call, because it won't ever end. They won't have boundaries unless we set them. Understand?" She gripped his arm, meaning it to be reassuring but maybe a little too hard and eased off. "What next, two Hammers and a box of grenades?"

He rubbed the back of his head, a very Dricks thing to do. "Yeah. Okay. Maybe I am, you know, feeling it. What they went through, you know?"

"I know more than anyone. You all left me to live through it with them when I cracked Segfi's fucking suppressant masks. Now if you want to live *that* guilt, I'm ready and waiting." She laughed, breaking the tension. "Now be a good sub-engineer and be a sounding board for ZZ3. I may need access to the Senti system, other than through this Kefi. I want ZZ3 safe while on the orb. Our warbot is crew, remember."

Rebekah eyed her visor, the HUD displaying the front cameras with data scrolling down the side screen as Heki brought the *Sunstar* in close to the huge orb. Copper brown light briefly highlighted the *Unpronounceable* as it sat in the background, disappearing as they neared the vast orb and the encounter ring that surrounded its equator. Everything looked normal, except there was the eerie sixth sense hovering at the back of her mind. She expected trouble, in fact to enter the orb and find it operating normally would be more of a shock.

"Trem?" she asked over comms.

"No transponder. There's an automated radio signal warning not to attempt docking without it. It's broadcasting in Bustan and Almaarian dialects."

Rebekah grimaced. "Yeah, I know the one. Rubel used to fly in and wind the gasbags up until the last minute. Try the ..."

"I have. I know we boxed the code on a probe but there's no response to the transponder broadcast at all. Dead. Like a ghost ship."

"Not helping, Trem," said Arin, cutting in on comms. "Kind of a freaky way to put it, *especially* just before we board."

"I learned from the best. Sorry, we've knocked but—"

"—there's nobody home." Rebekah glanced over to Kefi, the Senti wearing an encounter suit the likes of which she'd never seen before. Definitely built for space but extremely flexible, the material appeared to flow with the Senti's movement. Their discovery about the true nature of Senti faster than light travel had knocked her belief in their tech down a peg or two, yet it was clear they had knowledge humanity would crave. The Butcher even more so, and unlikely to have the qualms even the likes of Countess Segfi still held to acquire it. Would she have spaced an entire crew to stay alive?

Fuck, of course she would if it meant advancing the Empire.

"We are geosynced with the suggested entry point," Heki stated, her voice calm, efficient. She hadn't entered into Tremil's moodiness, and Rebekah hoped she would only be facing one of them at a time if this was going to continue. The problem with freedom, is once you had a taste, you often didn't want to go back.

"Thanks, Heki. Dricks, depressurise the hold and open the doors. ZZ3, activate the loader." As her orders were carried out, the entry team lifted from the cargo deck and maglocked to the powered loader. Its thrusters kicked in, and nudged them at a slow but steadily increasing speed towards the magnificent orb. Rebekah's sense of wonder returned, briefly lost after the debacle around Saim when the defensive drones had nearly ended any love for space by splattering her and the Wrecking Squad across the void. The wondrous ebb and flow of the Senti machine's surface filled her with awe, and she was forced to set her suit alarm to beep every ten seconds to maintain her attention on the next task. Attempting to ignore the sheer weight of Senti technology, she focused on the encounter ring, shimmering with the reflective light from the orb, its many docking ports were slowly coming into focus. She didn't know what to expect. Would they be open, and the Senti inside exposed to the void? Rebekah had only ever seen Senti in encounter suits in the external ring, being processed in their efficient manner ready for memory retrieval and thus payment. Looking at Kefi, she doubted they were designed for the rigours of space, particularly the cold. Word had always been they were to keep the Senti clear of any type of direct contact or possible infection, even to maintain a disdainful distance between the human Marines and them. But on Benetai, there had been open contact. It had to be the grav.

A glance to her HUD showed no known weaponry tracked them. Did Senti have PDCs? The orb's grav would pull space debris towards them after all.

"Captain," said Kefi, his monotone drawl seeping into the Senti's designated channel. "I would suggest we use … (*buttered bread landing face down on a kitchen floor*)." The Senti shone a laser directly at the target airlock.

"Okay, Kefi." They had agreed to follow the alien's lead, but ZZ3 was tooled up with a plasma torch despite Kefi's protestations that it would have little effect on the outside of the ring. The thrusters adjusted, and micromanaged their approach, slowing them down.

"Trem? Sit rep," she stated, the crackle of the comms indicating the closeness of the encounter ring.

"I'm not picking up any response on the sensors," the girl replied. "I suggest dropping a relay."

Suggest? That was a little better.

"Agreed. Arin."

"On it," responded the sub-engineer, and a relay probe rose from the loader, a brief flare of a manoeuvring thruster guiding the auto probe to hover next to their target entrance.

They glided in, and ZZ3 attached the loader to the external hull of the ring under Kefi's guidance. Rebekah made a mental note, if there was a way to maglock to Senti metal, she wanted that knowledge. It wasn't as minor a thing as it first appeared.

Gripping on to the now connected loader, Kefi approached the large airlock doors, their seal almost perfect, only the faintest of vertical and horizontal lines visible on her HUD where the circular doors quartered and withdrew to allow access. She gawked in amazement as the Senti touched the ship, its suit's tips appearing to liquify and meld to the surface. She recalled the memory slug in Pshwa's dream den. More forbidden knowledge.

With her HUD recording, she eyed Arin and then Savvo in turn. Both were focused on the curve of the ring, looking for any possible danger and had likely missed what the Senti had done. ZZ3 however, was watching, a swirl to its eyes, and almost a nod.

"ZZ3?" she said over their private comms.

"Yes. Noted. The Senti readjusted the magnetic field of the maglocks. I will analyse how on our return, if that is expected."

"It is." She cut off, Kefi waving her over with a shoulder tentacle. She switched channel as her HUD flagged.

"A problem?" she asked as the suit thrusters brought her closer.

More tentacles waved, she assumed in frustration. "Somewhat. The system is dead, so whether it would allow my entry is moot. I need your robot to help me pull them open."

"Agreed."

The Senti's helmet turned her way, and she sensed its regard despite the frosted visor. "You are no doubt learning from my actions. The fact you are here, trying to help, has overridden my instinct to protect my ... our word translates to 'nest', but that does not, I think, provide an understanding. Many nests, perhaps. Understand, if the Orb Queen knew, she would execute me on the spot and sublimate me. Reabsorb my body and memories into the whole."

It didn't appear as if the alien was looking for a response, and she didn't have one. The Court nobles were as brutal, and giving away secrets to an enemy treason that would mean torture, a lifetime in prison, or most likely death. That the Senti saw it the same way came as little surprise.

It took a few minutes, but with ZZ3 clamped to one side after more adjustments, and the Senti to the other, their combined servos opened the quartered doors a crack. Arin soon had the entry clamps in place, and between those and the combination of alien and warbot, prised the entryway wide enough for them all to get through. Once inside, Arin removed the clamps, allowing the doors to reseal before following. The second set of doors, lit by their suits' external lights, comprised different materials, and Savvo had already attached a pair of chem charges onto their inner edges. With a turn of the physical timer, they fizzed and melted the materials, filling the airlock with acrid and dangerous fumes, their suits flashing warnings not to disengage helmets.

With a kick, Savvo had them through, and the warbot finally entered the ring and flew on by, attaching to the inner deck, arm weapons extended.

"There are no immediate threats."

Rebekah glanced at the bot's feed. The analysis was true, but far from the whole picture.

"Fuck," she said, as the first Senti encounter suit floated by, the alien inside deflated, leaking out from a large rent as if it was melting. A stream of blue and green goo wrapped about the lower limbs and on behind. Like a jellyfish in an aquarium, except dead to the world.

CHAPTER 9

SENTI ORB, OUTER EDGE OF THE ALMAARIAN SYSTEM

The corridor ring had no discernible curvature; the outer hull wrapped about a station the size of a small moon. Unlike the outside which shimmered under the beauty of the orb itself, the inside was black, void dark, their lights almost dying as the abyss swallowed their pathetic attempts to illuminate the horrors inside. Rebekah had no words. She had witnessed the desiccation of alien/human hybrids. Observed as those born from crimson sacs realised what they had become in the last vestiges of their sanity before lashing out in fear and panic. But this?

I have no words.

Their lights washed over eviscerated encounter suits, most slumped against the deck, or floating somewhere between, limbs splayed as their tentacles leaked from inside. Like a macabre carnival, where the actors and players swirled about in blue and green streamers.

She choked back the dread.

"Kefi. You okay?" She had known the alien a few hours, but Kefi was part of her team, and therefore under her watch. And it's not as if any soldier could ignore such an onslaught to the senses – and the heart.

A flow of agonised sounds reverberated over comms. She let the alien express the pain, if that was the emotion it was verbalising. Eventually, the torrent stopped, and the alien staggered forwards, chin tentacle reaching for the first suit. Two more wrapped about the body, rolling it over to expose the hole. With a swipe, the whip thin remains of the Senti were snapped off, and Kefi peered closer.

"(*choking*) Murdered," the alien stated. "No, that is not the word. Executed with no hope of sublimation." The Senti's helmet turned her way, defrosted. The black eyes didn't leak, but the slit mouth opened and closed, as if panting. "My people did this. Senti. Not human."

"Impossible, Kefi. Why would they?" started Arin, lights sweeping across the devastation in the first part of the corridor. There must have been twenty of the Senti, each killing the same.

Rebekah realised she was caught up in all the death, but a glance at Savvo's feed showed he was on guard, ZZ3 watching the other way. Little shocked her after the *Scourge*, but this ... she needed to focus.

"How far to the disembark point, Savvo?" she asked. "Can you remember?"

Savvo tapped his helmet. "To be honest no. I was kinda strung out most of the time. Arin?"

"I'm thinking about a hundred metres. We were split on entry, then down to processing. Want me to send up a drone?" Arin gestured towards his back.

"Affirmative. Get it prepped and send it around the ring. Savvo on point, ZZ3 take the rear. Any heat signatures, movement, potential life, I want to know." She felt instantly better. In charge. "Kefi, can you explain?"

The drone buzzed, rising from Arin's shoulder, spun once and then flew into the blackness, green lasers flashing as it mapped the route.

"These are Senti weapon marks. Our security carry these in case the ... well, you, ever get out of hand. Two settings. Pacify, and burn. Lethal at close range even in your Marine armour." The Senti stepped back from the body, shoulder tentacles laying the remains gently against the deck where they settled.

"Not a machine? A bot?"

"We don't use them. Not our ... way? This action was either by the orb security team, or humans who had acquired the weaponry but look ..." Kefi splayed its tentacles, all three upper limbs spread out. "No (*water splash*) fought back. No one was shot in the rear. No (*splash*) appears to have resisted."

Rebekah nodded, surveying the scene. Difficult for her to ascertain the truth in the Senti's words, but the theory could well fit the devastation. "We walk on. Stay alert."

Kefi slotted in ahead of Arin, while her focus was on Savvo and covering her point man. He led them on; the death ending as they entered a familiar concourse, rows of curved machinery signifying where they queued awaiting appraisal from the Senti administrators. Further back, where their lights couldn't quite reach, was the disembark point. There would be the hated transparent transport to an inner ring and the memory rooms.

"Cover me, Savvo," she said, and as the ex-Marine dropped behind a processing machine, she swept past, carbine up and synced. She flicked through the EM spectrum, receiving a glow up ahead. Warmth. She found herself in a narrowing corridor, a funnel, and knew instinctively up ahead was the transparent transport that put fear into its passengers.

"Station," she stated. "Come by, Savvo. Check my feed."

He confirmed, and was soon past her, mirroring her own approach while she kept an eye on her HUD. The warmth was blotted out in an odd pattern, and she suspected more death lay ahead. Savvo's camera soon confirmed, three of the Senti wrapped about each other as if embracing, their liquified bodies merging.

"Got a scene here," said Savvo. "Bloody hells."

Arin scowled. "He mentions demons, and I'm leaving."

Rebekah wanted to squash Arin, mindful of Kefi, but the channel was their own and the deaths unnerving. The liquefied bodies reminding her of the dreadful crimson sacs aboard the *Scourge*.

"Sit rep on the drone." She didn't want to scour the footage, maintaining her focus on how to get across. Arin was silent as she approached the departure doors and the entangled Senti, concentrating on the drone's feed.

"Kind of the same pattern. Hang on." Arin breathed heavily into his comms. "Need you to see this."

The images rolled, a green hue filling the screen against the blackness of the ring corridor. As the drone closed, a circle of the death streamers appeared, Senti maglocked to the deck around a hulking figure. It too wore a suit, more akin to the one Kefi wore, but the alien was much larger, one tentacle bearing a thick rod with a grip she recognised from Scarva's ship. The barrel was melded to the larger alien's suit, scorch marks across its chest.

"Suicide?" she said aloud.

"Unless the Butcher had its suit under control, like the mechs and ZZ3."

"Send it to Kefi, but warn first."

She watched on as the alien paused before the transport controls, tentacle tips glimmering silver where they liquefied but waited in mid air. The Senti quivered, and Rebekah's comms crackled.

"I agree with the two options. I would say a ... I have no translation for it. On a ship, you would call it self-destruct order. A kill switch."

Rebekah let that sink in while the Senti worked, Savvo watching, ZZ3 on rear guard. What were they walking into? And they were about to be at their most vulnerable. The doorway glowed, and then became translucent, the copper gold of the orb streaming in to fill the narrow corridor and the harrowing alien sculpture. Stunning, but who controlled it now?

"Is this a good idea?" asked Arin. "I mean those transports scared the shit out of me on a good day."

"Got your absorbent pants on, so you'll be fine," replied Savvo.

"Might need a full vacuum tube if one of those things starts rocking and rolling."

Rebekah watched as the silent transport approached. Just them and space, nothing between. Like a plexi-glass box that every Marine assumed was designed to add flavour to their brain patterns. A little extra spice to their memory meal. And this one might well be infected.

What the fuck are we doing?

She braced one hand against the soon to be open door. "Kefi, how do we know the system isn't compromised?"

The Senti turned to her, seemingly thinking. "Because we're not dead? Or the ring exposed to space? That the deaths we've seen were deliberate and enacted by my own people? The bigger question is why." Kefi turned to stare at the orb. "In its heyday there were thousands within the orb nest. Tens of thousands. Now, maybe a few hundred. I expect we are walking into a ... a morgue. But more than anything, the *Ungrit* is not here."

The transparent transport was thankfully devoid of Senti remains, giving Rebekah space to think as she stared out into the abyss between the ring and the central orb. Their fears had been allayed when they had entered, realisation that their time working in space in full suits had removed the dread. Now it was simply a box, though seemingly unpowered, that carried them through the vacuum they had been accustomed to over the past few years. If anything, its solidity surprised her, but then her mind was no longer filled by imagining what would happen should it crack and the contents spill out.

"Magnetism," said ZZ3, almost absently. "Magnetic field manipulation, and a high probability the transport is embedded with responsive materials."

"Looks like magic when you don't know the science," added Savvo, and he subsequently paused, as if his own words struck him. "Like the experiments the Butcher was doing. From the outside it looked like one thing – a mad attempt at making a super-soldier – and from another, experimentation to see what you can make. What mutated variant you can produce that might be the answer to your ... your quandary."

Kefi turned to face Savvo, the first time since stepping into the clear box the alien had faced away from the orb. "What was he seeking?"

Rebekah swore under her breath. Up to now, Kefi hadn't thought to ask, its only concern the attack on Scarva and now the orb. She wanted to keep the Senti from their secret, steer thoughts onto something less troubling for the Wrecking Squad.

"We're not really sure. Maybe interpreting himself? We understand it was your tech he used to brain-pattern himself. To stay alive – though I don't know if it counts as life – maybe to continue to *exist* is a better interpretation. Seeking answers." She spoke while releasing a hard stare towards Savvo, who swiftly got the point.

"Yeah. Like he's human made up of Senti code and trying to replicate that in flesh."

"Yuk," cut in Arin. "I mean, gross."

"That word I understand," replied Kefi. "The thought of being part human is revolting. No offence, but no. Your smell is so animalistic, and you're all so bony. All angles and hard edges." The ensuing noise sounded to Rebekah like being sick. Finally, something she could agree on.

The transport approached the copper flare of the orb's outer layer, the swirls appearing up close like molten metal of similar hues intermingling as they flowed over the surface. She braced as the transparent front entered but remained intact, the light rolling over the surface like copper paint poured from a tin before emerging into a second ring corridor filled with familiar blue-green membranes. Kefi exited, its weird gun held ready, and encounter suit connected with the absorbent floor. Unlike her past experiences, the alien kept its protective suit on, and took a position before the first corridor membrane, the tip of its chin tentacle caressing the rubbery material.

Savvo was soon out and by the alien's side, with ZZ3 remaining at their rear. Rebekah turned up her suit's mic, but the silence remained. She couldn't remember how it had been, the air usually filled by Arin's verbal spillage, but the silence galled. She was on edge, and triggered her wetware, welcoming the calm that flowed into her mind.

The Senti poked at the membrane, the material not quite solid but far from displaying the fluid movement she remembered.

"Dead," the alien said, and to her surprise, its suit's tip morphed into a blade and Kefi cut through the membrane, parting it like a stiff curtain. "The nest is malfunctioning. Or perhaps, has been shutdown completely."

Beyond the slit lay darkness, strangely hued due to a residual glow from the blue-green walls and floor. Her HUD indicated it was fading, an energy signature that dropped inexorably towards zero. "Savvo."

Her second-in-command stepped through, carbine high, lights illuminating the passageway. Eerie, with a multitude of consoles lit by the suit lamps, while curved shadows played against walls and floor as he entered. There was no sign of any Senti on his feed, and as he took station, Kefi and Arin followed in with Rebekah behind. The darkness hid the structure of the ring, but she remembered the many rooms with their memory-fucking-suckers ready and waiting to take payment. She desperately wanted to know about the symbiotes, but that was too risky to share with Kefi. A hint about what they knew.

"Where will your people be? Do they have quarters inside somewhere?" she asked, following Savvo as he led them onto another of the dead membranes, this one hanging at the entrance to a side room.

"We reside inside. In our ... rest-pods would be the best translation. There are other work rooms, central command, the – erm – engines. Places no non-Senti are allowed to see."

Savvo produced a knife from his utility belt, a glance to the Senti receiving a wave towards the membrane. He slit the curtain open, but stepped aside to allow Kefi entry while Rebekah chewed over his words. She was going to have to piss the Senti off.

The chairs were covered in the blue and green streamers, as well as the body of a deceased clone. At least, Rebekah assumed it was a clone. The skull broken, wetware and brains stuck to the chair's back while another who looked exactly like her lay on the floor, a hole burned through the centre of her chest. They both wore Navy uniform with the *Ungrit*'s name upon the sleeve. Splattered across the headrest were the remains of a Senti, tentacles sheared, barely attached where a blade had hacked at the alien, while the source of the streamers hovered above the floor.

Hovered?

"Kefi, is it alive?" She suddenly hated using 'it', as if the word devalued the alien.

Kefi approached, one silver-clad tentacle reaching out, gently touching the dead Senti. The deft touch must have broken something, or induced a release, and the gasbags emptied, filling the room with a green malaise as the alien sagged to the floor. It left Rebekah horrified, bile rising as she remembered how callous the Butcher was with life. Any life.

"No. These symbols indicate the humans are from the same ship, the *Ungrit*. This Butcher is the cause."

A groan broke the silence of the ship. Sounding more like the *Sunstar*'s hull arguing about what it was asked to do than a technically advanced

Senti craft. The hairs on Rebekah's neck rose, amplified as the glow of the walls and floor finally died. Kefi looked as confused as her.

"I detect a significant drop in the magnetic field," stated ZZ3. "By extrapolation, I believe much of the orb's ability to maintain integrity is perhaps based on such technology."

Rebekah glanced at Kefi, who broke off its stare at the death scene and met her gaze. "That would be correct," it said, a reluctance to the words despite the translator. "If the core has ceased to spin, then ..."

"Core? We're screwed," said Savvo.

"Personally, I'd say we're fucked and then screwed, but it's all a matter of perspective. Especially as bits fly off this piece of shit." Arin, spun about, eyeing ZZ3. "Got a timescale anywhere in that microprocessor?"

"Impossible to extrapolate."

"Then we leave n—"

"NO!" shouted the Senti, tentacles lashing at the air as he cut Rebekah off. "No. I must ..." The Senti looked to Rebekah, its upper limbs still animated, the gaze, however, as dead as usual. "Please."

Rebekah growled. "First, it's *we* must. Understand? *We*. And right now, we're leaving unless you've got a fucking problem that I can solve with a bullet."

The tentacles calmed, but there was a wetness around the eyes. "The queen. We must save the Orb Queen." The Senti spun, taking in everyone, trying to catch their eye. "I beg of you, this must be done."

CHAPTER 10

ANS RIGHTEOUS

Captain Srenik wiped the sweat from his cheek, bleary-eyed, the internal comms insistent he woke up. A rough scrub at the back of his neck worked his nerves, but still he shivered from the remnants of a night sweat. Yet another nightmare, this time the crew of the *Bonray* replaced with his own as a conveyor belt spat out his colleagues into the dark abyss. Silent as the void would be, he had watched as their fluids boiled away, their lungs emptied, and they died clawing for a breath. As nightmares would, he saw their cadavers expand and contract, freeze, and remain desiccated monuments to the evil of the Butcher AI.

"Not on my watch. Silence alarm." He stood, working through his shoulder and neck muscles until the stiffness had receded. With a long, drawn-out breath, he calmed his heartbeat, wiping his mind clear of the nightmare for another day. The comms sounded again.

"Answer," he stated, and the comms activated on his voice command.

"Captain Srenik," said his Executive Officer Maria King. "You wanted awakening should we attain striking distance on the *Bonray*. We will be in the probability corridor in half an hour."

Good.

"Copy that, XO." He tried to drag back into his mind who'd be on the relief bridge crew, angry that disturbed sleep was affecting his efficiency. Now was not the time for his mind and body to let him down. The countess, godsdammit, the fleet was depending on him. "I want Ensign Strup to run the models again. Patterns A through D, understand."

"Bridge crew Beta is stood down, Captain. I awoke the main bridge team an hour early." Srenik shook his head. Maria was going to make a damn fine captain, and very soon at that. He was lucky to have her still aboard. The relief crew were her team, well-drilled, capable to fill in at any point, but she understood he was most comfortable with his own bridge crew. "I will get Henton on it right away."

"I want you at my side, XO. I know you ran the vids, read the reports. But I have a feeling this won't be the last of our ships we have to engage."

No pause. None. "Understood, Captain."

With comms off, he dipped his body into the zero grav shower, scrubbing away the sweat at speed and waking up his tired mind. Dressed, he strode the short distance to the bridge, mind running over the attack modelling Henton had suggested. Four approaches refined in some of the battles with the Bustan, but not even they had ever gone fully uncrewed. Facing an opponent with no care for the flesh inside its hull was a massive challenge. The fact the ships had never been built for maxing out such potential kept the odds closer. If they ever did, like the AI-led drones that had swarmed the *Bonray*, space warfare would become precarious at best, and short-lived at worst.

"Captain on the bridge," announced his XO as he entered, Maria King rising from the command chair. She saluted, a rarity, but they were going into battle. It was a mark of her respect and belief in him, an indication the bridge crew were ready for what had to be done.

"Ready the bridge," he said. "Move to REDCON 2. All personnel to be prepared to move to REDCON 1 on my mark. We are at war with the rogue AI named the Butcher. Everyone aboard knows what that soulless evil did to the crew of the *Bonray*. It is our duty to stand between it and other ships' crews dying by its virtual hand. I stand proud alongside the best in the godsdamned Almaarian Navy."

Ensign Rodri signalled. Seven minutes. Countdown begun.

He opened a ship wide channel. "Crew of the ANS *Righteous*, we are at REDCON 1. Strap in, strap down. Let's go kick some AI butt." Captain Srenik clicked off comms, and eyed the bridge crew one by one, acknowledging each with the briefest of nods. "Ensign Henton, throw up the attack patterns onto the main screen if you please."

The forward image displayed the engine trail of the ANS *Bonray*. The last time he'd looked, the images had been vague, but now there was a distinct shape extrapolated by the sensors in conjunction with the forward-facing cameras. Henton ran through simulation A, speeded up as it modelled the PDC cannon cones, the combination of standard and guided missiles, and of course, the rail gun that would tear the *Bonray* apart but relied on a straight-line attack vector. Fast. Godsdamned they were fast. But fast *enough*? Any response from the *Bonray* would hit them sooner as they were flying straight into them, whereas the frigate was burning away.

By the time Henton had run through pattern D, the countdown had hit twenty seconds. The corridor of probability, the entry point where PDC hit rates reached ten percent likelihood extrapolating the *Bonray*'s use of thrusters. Of course, the Butcher may well have adapted.

Scrub that. Get your head in the game. Would *have adapted.*

"Initiate attack pattern B, Henton. Medium fire rate." He sat back, trying not to lean in, to look too eager. That pattern assumed a wider initial spread than A, not a cone, but perhaps enough to give the AI food for thought. The firing rate an interpretation Henton would make.

The PDC rounds streamed out, rapidly reducing the distance between them and their target. But this was space. The screen displayed the release of standard missiles, dumb, straight line but packed with explosive. Their angle of attack adjusted to form a conical, either forcing the *Bonray* to take the PDC hits, dodge into the oncoming missile spread, or force a manoeuvre to avoid both. Srenik's creds were on the latter. All depended on those missiles that followed.

"Rodri?" he said, framing it as a question, requiring an answer.

"Ummm. No action as yet. But the engine emissions are out of kilter. I ..." The Ensign swept at her screen, eyes roaming over the data. "We have incoming."

"Be specific," replied Srenik, a growl he didn't want pervaded his voice. Stress.

"They're firing back. PDC rounds according to the sensors. Through the engine wake, Captain." Rodri continued to focus on her screen. "Widespread, estimate high rate of fire."

"Markov, evasive action. Do not allow those rounds to scratch the paint-work." The crew didn't laugh; they knew the drill, but smiles appeared. Grim, focused. The *Bonray* had two rearwards facing PDC units, dual cannons, topside and keel mounted. Usually poor at distance when firing through the engine wake due to the scrambled sensory data, ships rarely bothered trying. This was something new. Accuracy would be a concern. A glance to his XO showed King had noted it too. Good.

"Missile launch. Three have exited the wake. We have been pinged. Locked on, Captain," stated Rodri.

"Henton, take them down. Keep me informed. Rodri, jamming sequence, target each and fill forward space with as much crap as you can. Markov, status?"

There was a pause, but forgivable, the sudden jolt in the ship marking the start of Markov's adjustments. There was no way to mitigate, and

REDCON 1 would see all non-combat personnel buckled down in the nearest gel bed. "PDC incoming, first wave passed us by. Second hitting us in 3," the *Righteous* lurched, sending Srenik sideways, the command chair adjusting as the gel poured into shoulder and neck braces, "2 and 1."

Alarms flashed on the captain's console. Amber, strike reports filing in from the hull sensors. No breach, but the forward keel plating had taken hits. At this speed, it was inevitable. And more was incoming.

"Good flying," he said, but his heart battered at his rib cage. On screen, the *Bonray* was practically dancing, shifting in patterns that would leave a human crew as nothing more than a stain upon deck and wall.

"PDC strikes at five percent," stated Henton. "Ongoing probabilities rising as we close, Captain. Yes ... missile strike."

"Specific. Ours or theirs?"

"Theirs. Two down," stated Henton.

"Third has skewed off. Jammed," stated Rodri.

Another alarm flashed as the ship jolted downwards, his stomach saying hello to his throat as the cruiser's thrusters shoved them aside. Amber strikes turned to red, listing plating breaches, with a deck wide lockdown auto-engaged topside. Lucky. Or Markov was as good as he claimed. There'd be few crew on the recreation deck. But even one death was too many.

"Our missiles are on approach – twenty seconds," Henton said, eyes locked on his screen.

Rodri cut in. "One more wave of cannon rounds, Captain. They've adjusted to a defensive spread. Monitoring engine wake changes."

Srenik eyed the data streaming in, running over the possibilities. The cruiser rose, the vibrations shuddering through his magboots as it strained and he was pressed back into the seat. A gasp or two echoed through the bridge, and an alert sounded Srenik couldn't see.

"Cutting," stated Markov, the word slurred, but the pressure eased.

Srenik checked the alert. "Godsdammit," he stated, slamming a hand down on the chair arm. "Lower deck repair crews, we have a breach in the machine room. I repeat, a breach." They'd already know, be pounding that way, but hopefully it'd give them extra wind in their sails.

"Dumb missiles on approach in five, four ... oh shit," said Henton, his left hand clenching and unclenching. Srenik already knew. The frigate had blasted 'upwards', as if the hand of a god had wrenched it away. Plating tore from the hull, arrays ripped from their housing, leaving half the missiles to speed on by, the rest erupting as PDCs showered the space before them with round after round. "All missiles neutralised. No hits."

"Adjust attack pattern to C, high rate. Action now. Keep the pressure on, don't let them return fire." He waited, allowing Henton the time to adjust PDC fire and prep the next missile run. His fingers drummed on the chair's arm. "Do we have a lock?"

"They're jamming," stated Rodri. "They've adjusted the engine wake's EM content. Filled the rear with enough rad to strip our bones."

"Is there a way around it?" He knew the answer, Rodri would have said, Markov barking out in agreement.

"No, Captain. The missiles entered the residual wake before the *Bonray* did that crazy manoeuvre. They've lost the target ... wait. They are adjusting now they're slightly ahead of the bow. We have a lock. I say again, we have one lock."

"Markov, prep the rail gun. Wait on predictive missile contact. You get a fifty percent window, you fire on their engine." The captain looked away from the weapons officer, knowing what he'd asked. Segfi wouldn't approve, or at least the version that fought around Bustan.

"PDCs active. Their forward cannons are trying to take them down," said Rodri. The missile had to cut acceleration ... but it was so close.

"Remote ..." he started to say. A close proximity hit would be a bonus right now.

"The wake won't let a signal through," replied Markov. "But it's close, if they hit ..."

"Missile blown —"

"—Rail slug away —"

"—A bow hit, Captain."

Engines would have been better, but he'd take that, assuming the Butcher AI hadn't moved systems centrally. How would it have the time? But machines didn't need rest. He counted down in his head. The screen displayed the rear of the *Bonray*, but there was little to show of the missile's effect. It hadn't slowed, was that debris? Definitely debris.

"Stay on vector," he mouthed. "Stay. On. Vector."

The *Bonray* disappeared, its sensory presence replaced by a flare that blurred their arrays.

"I want to know. Clean that up. Markov, prepare for course change 3." He watched Rodri work, knowing just how much crap the engines had already been throwing out. The distortion slowly resolved, the frigate split asunder, three larger parts wheeling away amid the sensory blur, the residual momentum from the engines and the rail slug's strike sending the detritus spiralling into the void.

Dead.

"Now, Markov. Keep us out of that debris field." The rumble of engine adjustments vibrated through his ship, a very welcome sound only interrupted by his console's simulated patter of ruptured plate and shattered decks from the *Bonray* glancing off the cruiser. Barely ten seconds, and they were in the clear.

Best godsdamned crew in the fleet.

CHAPTER 11

SENTI ORB, OUTER EDGE OF THE ALMAARIAN SYSTEM

Rebekah stopped, mind active with a combination of wonder and dread. Kefi had taken them through what all her suit's sensors indicated was a wall. Solid. And unlike the rubber membranes, this had been metal but had liquified like Kefi's suit or the memory slugs back at Pshwa's den. She had walked through it steeped in trepidation, ZZ3's worries about the orb's systems leading to a fear of the metal solidifying when she was halfway through. One leg flopping in the memory-suckers dentist room from hell, the other where she stood now.

"What?" she said, unable to comprehend the scale of where she stood. The space was filled with light that glistened a blue-green hue from above, an alien sun in which Kefi clearly basked, leaning back, tentacles wide as if to embrace its energy. It hung – or sat – above, unmoving as far as she could tell, while around her the strangest of plants entwined about her boots. It quivered, like purple snakes or eels, almost embracing her foot. About the sky flitted what she could only categorise as bird-like insects, or were they insects the size and variety of birds? Their colours mesmerising, and clearly unbothered by their presence as they swooped and hunted one another between the complexity of larger plants that were somewhere between bush and tree. Amid this visual feast, sat multi-layered houses, shaped like slices of blancmange piled on top of each other and covered in symbols that writhed in her mind.

"Note the low grav people," said Arin, lifting a boot. "And we don't clamp. Going to be a few of us dancing with the birds if we don't step light."

Rebekah shook her head, attempting to clear her mind from the wonder of where she stood. On the inside of an artificial moon, and above her a sun that she suspected should be spinning, but wasn't.

"Kefi? Where now?" A glance over caught the twitch of the Senti's upper tentacles before all but the chin settled down. It pointed.

"The palace will lie towards what you would call the northern pole. Your suits will struggle to understand where we are due to the way the orb manipulates electromagnetic waves. You may not be able to trust what they tell you." The Senti started out, lower limbs barely gracing the strange grass about their feet, yet moving faster than Rebekah had ever seen a Senti.

"Palace?" said Arin, a query in his voice. "Like a royal palace? You know, jewels and gold and all that. Servants. People feeding you grapes while bathing your bits."

"Bits?" said Savvo.

"You know, your fingernails, and between your toes."

Savvo snorted. "You have weird thoughts sometimes."

"Between tentacles," cut in ZZ3. "Senti don't have toes."

Savvo had fallen in beside Kefi, the Senti determined to lead them on with Rebekah's agreement.

"Everyone's a critic now." Arin took the rear with ZZ3, eyes sweeping around. Animated. Rebekah pleased he'd taken Kefi's warning to heart and was relying on visuals. "I liked it when only Savvo pulled apart my thoughts. Now I have a tank on legs doing it."

Rebekah sensed before she felt a shift, her stomach stretching and she suddenly found herself rising from the ground. All but the Senti had followed suit, with ZZ3 snaking out a limb to grip the plants below. Another lurch, and she was higher, reorienting herself as her suit systems threatened to lose its sense of place. Then she dropped, slamming into the alien grass with more force than it should. She tried to stand, finding herself using a greater effort than before but managing it.

"We got grav quakes," said Savvo.

"Fluctuations caused by the core shutdown. I expect it will get worse, until the gravity stops completely," stated ZZ3.

"What else can we expect?" asked Rebekah, with a suspicion the answer might not be to her liking.

"EM flares. Radiation pulses, bad shit," added Arin. "Our suits can compensate to a degree with normal space rad levels. But we get anything like that solar flare we were exposed to back in the 'field then ...'"

"Fuck." Rebekah glared at Kefi, agitation running through the alien's tentacles, the tips pulling at the purple snake grass. "How far we got to go and how fast can you travel Kefi?"

The Senti turned her way. "I suspect two of your hours at the current pace."

"Two hours? Fuck." Rebekah kicked at the grass, the fronds parting as her boot brushed by. Savvo and Arin looked to her; they needed a decision. Do they risk their lives for a Senti's hope that their queen was alive? Would they do that for them?

Stupid fucking question. Not bloody tit-for-tat.

"We have twenty minutes. ZZ3, saddle up."

"Saddle? Up?" said the bot. "Analysing, placing in Dricks' lexicon. Ah. Yes."

With thrusters burning and constantly having to compensate for the fluctuating gravity, ZZ3 dragged three humans through the orb's inner atmosphere using a mining synth-rope. The EM interference had made slaving the suits risky, and to reverse the 'saddle up' analogy, ZZ3 had roped its riders rather than the other way around. Below and just ahead of them, Rebekah could make out Kefi, the Senti's speed across the grass and through the thicker vegetation a testament to how well-adapted the aliens were in this artificial version of their home planet. They had rushed through clusters of the blancmange-like buildings, and not seen a single Senti, alive or dead. Another ghost ship, or in this case ghost colony, created by the Butcher. It appeared that no life was sacred, though she doubted even he could have predicted what Kefi had termed the 'self-destruct' his people had undertaken.

In defiance of the Senti building style, a more angular building began to slide into view against the curved background of the orb. Sprawling like the others, but punctuated by wave-shaped sections that rose and flowed over square or rectangular walls. A strange beauty, fluid with myriad blues and green streaks that glinted brightly despite what Rebekah feared was a rapidly fading artificial sun.

As they closed in, she could make out a lake or a moat surrounding the palace, before which Kefi had stopped. Her comms suddenly filled with a wretched noise she unfortunately didn't need to understand to interpret. It was pain. Grief.

"Bring us down, ZZ3," she said, and the warbot brought them to a gentle stop beside the distraught alien. The square doors with their ornate semi-circular top stood wide open, their surface a silver inlaid marble as far as Rebekah could tell. But before them was the small lake which she now suspected was the source of Kefi's pain. It wasn't water, rather it bubbled, gas seeping from the green goo amid which were outlines of tentacles and the strange canine teeth some of them bore. A lake of the dead.

"How?" asked Savvo, one hand gripping the grass to prevent floating away, the other reaching for but not touching a dead Senti.

The keening faded, racked breath and burbles of gas easing off. "Sublimation. They chose to die the traditional way. To give themselves back to the nest. But the nest," Kefi held out its shoulder tentacles, as if embracing the sun, elongated head back, "is already at an end."

Rebekah stepped in beside Kefi, her carbine in one hand, the other tentatively reaching for the Senti. In the end, she dropped her hand, unable to decide how the alien would see the gesture. "The queen," was all she managed to say.

"She will be inside, tending the spawn." Kefi looked to the open doors. "I need to go in." The alien acted fast, taking a stride back, before leaping. Momentum took the alien onwards, slowed by the air, but helped by the very low gravity, it reached the far side, and grappled with a bush-like plant that grew at the foot of the palace walls. The Senti reoriented and headed inside.

"We going to let Kefi be the hero here? I mean, it's in my job description now." Arin drew up his carbine, holding the weapon in both hands, peering at Rebekah expectantly.

"Stow the jokes," she replied, knowing it was how he compensated. A lake of horrors pulled at them all, be it Senti or human. "Savvo."

"Fuck, yeah," her second said, and copied Kefi's leap. They all followed and used their smaller manoeuvring thrusters to guide them into the palace. The entranceway mirrored the beauty of the outside, everything water-like in the way the floor undulated, and a ramp unfurled its way up to the next level. Almost as if they were in an aquarium, they swam through, up and over furniture or sculptures, past things they could not fathom, following the comms trail Kefi left as the alien burbled in pain. They entered what could only be a throne room, though the dais was as curved as the rest of the inner palace, about which floated more of the sublimed goo Rebekah took to be deceased Senti. Amid the death, she saw something familiar.

"That a carbine?" said Savvo.

"Confirmed," replied ZZ3. "There are several human remains amid the dead Senti. I also detect spent rounds."

"ZZ3, on room guard," ordered Rebekah. "Arin, buddy up. Savvo on my rear." Rebekah didn't wait for them to comply, knowing they would as she snapped out the commands. The weirdness of the orb had to be countered, focus returned if the Butcher's clones had been here. She manoeuvred over to Kefi, who had wound its lower tentacles around a stone slab that hinted at being some form of Senti chair.

"Throne," she mouthed, a weight of deference on her shoulders. An Impulse imbued in all Almaarians from when they first understood language. Pay homage to the Court, to his Imperial Majesty. Know your place. "Kefi," she said, more as a warning than anything.

"Her body is dead," replied the alien. The first time Rebekah had heard any gender assigned by a Senti. Kefi stepped back. A pool of green and blue lay in the dip of the chair, clinging to the stone. Within it, crystals glinted, a sash of material she recognised from Benetai, and a circlet of Senti metal. "Murdered." The alien pointed to a collection of carbine rounds that lay at the base.

"I'm sorry," she said, the words hoarse, dry upon her tongue. Her hand had somehow landed on the Senti's shoulder tentacle. The aliens had always presented as emotionless, their language stark except for those like Scarva who only became animated when memories or dreams were in the offing.

Kefi didn't react, instead the alien shifted around the throne, eyes to a stone bowl at the rear. "They have taken the spawn, the Orb Queen."

Rebekah blinked, not understanding. "A child?" she asked.

"No. Perhaps in a way. The old queen ah – you have no accurate word for it – err, sublimates herself, changes her state and pours all she is into the spawn. So it becomes her, takes on their ..."

"Memories. Fuck." Lots of things clicked home. "But the spawn is not a child?"

Kefi looked her way, the head tilting, mouth moving. "Your term would be an egg ... no ... no, a cocoon. Waiting to be queen."

Rebekah felt guilt, questioning the Senti as it grieved. But she needed to know. The Butcher had attacked seeking something. More than likely the secret to Senti FLT, and whilst here, had chosen another path. Or maybe he hadn't discovered the true secret lay in the symbiotes, or the mass suicides had thrown the AI, confused the Butcher with behaviour it hadn't experienced, so it resorted to what it knew. Take something precious, but for experimentation? Or like Segfi, seeking a trade?

The palace rumbled, shifting, the ground beneath it suddenly laced with hairline cracks that spread wildly up walls and towards the ceiling. The light dipped, blinking, fading out before shining so bright, the reflection into the room was almost blinding. The orb was in its death throes. Why had the Butcher done that?

She glanced at the dead queen.

Not the Butcher. Suicide. Mass death to prevent him from gaining what he wanted. Or to hide their secrets. But why go to such extremes?

"We need to be out, now!" she shouted, and the ceiling gave way.

CHAPTER 12

IN ORBIT, SENTI ORB, OUTER EDGE OF THE ALMAARIAN SYSTEM

"Dricks ... Dricks!" shouted Heki. The delay was too long. Heki, tongue squeezed between her teeth, eyes scanning the visuals as her heart threatened to shatter her ribs, punched in the manoeuvring thrusters. The *Sunstar* lurched out of orbit, but still the navcom blared multiple threats at her.

"Trem," she said, but before she could add to it, boots clattered along the deck behind her. The steps long. Dricks.

"Ahhhh ... Coming!" bellowed Dricks, but not over comms.

The engineer staggered, hands slapping at the corridor walls, but Heki had to act. The orb was breaking apart. Not gently in its spin, but quickly – the external encounter ring shattering, flung away as if the orb rejected it. Thousands of kilometres of twisted metal shards discarded as if they were mere toys scattered in a tantrum. Hurtling through the void in all directions, including theirs.

"The EM field has gone crazy across the spectrum. Rad pouring out in a flood," said Tremil, her voice strained, the patter of fingers on keyboard and screen in the background. "It's a mess. Trying to get through but Scarva's gone. Jumped."

Hendricks landed heavily in the co-pilot's chair, her breathing short, her flight suit half unzipped which she sorted as she stared at the visual feed. She saw what Heki did, the encounter ring gone, metal and debris spiralling out from the copper orb that flared and died with intermittent anger in its moment of death.

"No, no," said Hendricks, the words pained, hands gripping the arms of her chair as she leaned in. "Comms?"

Heki pointed at the co-pilot's comms unit maglocked to the navcom, unable to speak, her throat tight. Hendricks took the hint, placing the unit over her ears as Tremil's voice dropped in.

"Nothing. Just static with all the crap the orb is spewing out. What do we do? They're all in there." Her panic was rising, and Heki feared her emotions would overwhelm the symbiote that skittered against her neck – soon followed by everyone else on the ship. Her hands froze, paralysed. Shock rolling through her. They were heading away from the orb, leaving her family behind while her world fell apart.

"Heki." Hendricks' growl was low and quiet, not soothing. More like a predator on the hunt, looking for a weakness. "You've done the right thing. Taking us away, so we can act, not react." The harshness was still there, or was Heki imaging it? "But now I need you back with me. Understand?"

She did. But that didn't make it easy. Her brain was sludge, but a gentle hand upon her arm provided focus. One the symbiote latched onto, attempting to drain the swamp of her mind, bring her back to the now. She blinked, shaking her head gently while Hendricks squeezed a little harder before releasing her.

"Breathe slow, Heki. Bring us around and back towards the orb. Trem, anything?" Hendricks' words remained harsh. No – efficient – used to being in command. Directing. It's what she needed, but Heki found that difficult to admit.

"Nothing. Just a haze of … of …" Tremil cut off, and Heki instantly knew why. The symbiotes were acting strangely, the rhythm of their pulse no longer linked to theirs but something else. Something external. A pressure built in her mind through their connection, not painful, but as if there was too much happening to hold it all in. Or perhaps the opposite, her mind being squeezed out, like toothpaste. Something pressing.

"Dricks," she whispered, groping for her hand, finding it, holding tight. "Something's coming."

"What? Where?"

Heki turned to stare at the engineer, her face numb, fingers tingling. "Everywhere."

The *Sunstar* rocked, suddenly tilting, wrenching her and Hendricks to the right, bodies like rag dolls. The momentum of the ship carried on, riding a wave of debris that banged and rattled against the hull. Heki gasped, pulling herself back into her chair, side hurting but with a purpose she understood. The ship. The navcom showed no major damage to the *Sunstar*, the detritus from the orb travelling at the same speed and direction as them. She guided the bow outwards, away from the orb, riding the wave rather than steering into it. That would have been a disaster. But it meant more time lost as her thoughts focused on Rebekah. As she stared at the rear camera view, that was probably moot.

"Look." She shook the engineer, guiding her gaze to the monitor.

"Oh," said Dricks, staring. "What the hell?"

"Is that … Senti?" asked Tremil, not waiting for the answer. "Has to be."

Behind them loomed a huge ship, dwarfed by the expanding orb, but still massive. Debris flew around, lighting up the metal hull with a blue glow as they struck en masse yet bounced safely away. The curves of the ship rolled like an incoming tide, wave upon wave of metal as they reached towards the bulbous front. Here protruded the arrays they had seen on Scarva's ship, but relatively smaller, mere blips against the smooth skin of the hull.

Heki glanced to Hendricks, needing direction, to be told what to do. "What now, Dricks?"

The response was muted, shock there. First the orb, then the debris, and now a Senti ship had appeared, ploughing through the wreckage, engines flaring. It was braking, but Heki realised everything was about to go south and quickly. It was pointed straight at the orb, the copper glow of the rapidly expanding artificial structure lighting the bow as it powered onwards.

And then was gone.

She stared, open-mouthed. A hole in space, empty. A void soon filled by more of the orb as volcano-like eruptions pockmarked the coppery swirls. Pressure again surfaced in her head, briefer, and the massive ship reappeared the other side, careering off into the distance, a hard deceleration burn lighting its way.

"Fuck," said Dricks. A word she used rarely, but Heki had to agree.

Tremil's voice cut in, urgent. "Dricks, Hek. Take a look. There's an anomaly in the sensor feed. When it jumped it left something behind."

Hendricks had the visual up on screen, what originally had been lost among the expanding fragments was almost an exact copy of the orb itself in miniature. Well, relatively in Heki's mind, and she began to run the numbers.

"It's about a hundred metres in diameter," said Tremil, clearly ahead of her. "Everything's garbled, but it appears stable amid all that chaos, and resisting the physical and rad stress."

The Senti ship had been decelerating at a rate beyond a human's capacity to survive, and clearly with no immediate sign of being able to stop. Instead, it had released something that possibly, Heki hoped, had the ability to survive the orb's destruction.

"A rescue pod," stated Hendricks, finishing her thought for her. "Has to be. Trem, what are the rad levels like back there?"

"All survivable in a shielded ship, otherwise we'd be fried too."

"The suits can take so much," continued the engineer. "But not forever. If they lived through the physical destruction, then their time's still short."

Heki's chest thudded.

They. Dricks unable to say their names. Rebekah, Arin, Savvo and Kefi.

Hendricks was bringing her back to reality. The engineer's words a reminder that her crew, her family, could be gone. Dead in the blink of an eye and there was nothing she could have done about it. Grief crashed in, wiping away all else, the symbiote struggling under the sudden agony smashing into the alien.

"Stop that!" bellowed Hendricks straight at her, gripping the arm of her chair, anger narrowing her eyes. "That's an order, pilot. Mind on the job."

Heki winced, Hendricks' outburst forcing the impact of her emotions into the forefront of her mind. Grief would kill her crew. While there was hope, she couldn't afford to mourn.

But it hurts.

"What do you want me to do?" she said, failing to keep a tremor out of her voice.

"Take us back. As safe as you can, as fast as you can. Work with Trem around the rad. We don't know if this was survivable on the inside, or if that Senti lifeboat can pick them up. Either way, we need to know. Get us there."

Heki nodded, turning back to the navcom. Focused on one thing, her symbiote easing the nagging pain.

Get us there.

Except they were assuming that Rebekah, Arin and Savvo were in the core. What if they'd been in the encounter ring? Had either died as it broke up, or were heading out into the black, riding the wave of debris, watching hope disappear behind them with only despair ahead.

"Stop that," Heki snarled low, the words like lead. Heavy, weighted. The numbers blurred and came back into focus. "Do your job."

Heki weaved them between the lessening debris, the *Sunstar* on a trajectory towards a high orbit about the expanding copper orb. Every fibre in her being, and the information and projections Tremil sent her and Dricks' way, warned of the danger. The orb's rate of expansion was irregular, the sensors unable to penetrate beyond the surface and therefore they had little clue as to how much was light radiation and how much an actual physical presence. The small gravitational force on them was lessening, the indication, perhaps amid the maelstrom of messed-up physics, that the central mass was breaking apart.

What were they trying to achieve? Perhaps draw the attention of the Senti ship. Trem was on that.

A glance from Hendricks hinted she was thinking the same. Their comms were lost amid the chaos, their cameras subject to huge static interference. Everything was a blur ...

... and the orb erupted.

Coppery light painted the void, spilling out of gaps between the static affecting the camera feed. The navcom shut the ship's sensors down as a shockwave rolled from the core, forging a wave of detritus, the remaining wreckage battering against the *Sunstar*'s hull. How many had lived upon the orb? Hundreds, according to Kefi. All gone.

Heki felt nothing in that moment. Numb. Her love and grief for her family building a wall of refusal. Denying their death, and the loss of the

Senti they had gone to save. The alternative was to collapse in on herself, let the pain wash her away.

"Heki," said Tremil, her sister's voice slicing through her thoughts. "Dricks. I have a strange signal coming in from the direction of the main Senti ship. It's not aimed at us, but directed into the orb."

"Can you listen in?" asked Dricks, "Hear what they say?"

"I don't even know if it's comms, it kind of bores through. Creates a space our sensors can pick up, rather than *being* a frequency. It was suddenly there, not like a wave travelling, almost instantaneous. Hang on ... there's another."

"A response?" queried Heki, only for her screwed-up camera feed to provide an answer. The smaller orb emerged from the copper-hued outer fringes, spinning, pulsing with power. With the remaining orb wreckage repulsed before contact, it cut its way through the detritus as it spun.

"The pathway," stated Heki.

Again, Tremil was ready, predicting her thoughts. "Yeah, following that signal. Sensors show the Senti ship is returning."

"ETA?" requested Hendricks, unstrapping, standing as if ready to go to war with hands on hips, her face stone.

"At this speed about thirty-seven minutes," answered Heki, eyeing the old ex-Marine, knowing what she was thinking. Almost tasting the emotions. Hendricks hated the Senti with a vengeance. "And yes, we can keep pace with the lifeboat. But Dricks ..." she licked her lips. Forty minutes or so ago, Hendricks had cut through her pain and got her back on task, "you can't go in all ... all mouth, guns blazing. We don't know why they went in. Or even if it was a rescue, who it was for."

The woman's eyes flashed, catching the console lights as she glared at Heki. No, not at her. At the situation. Hendricks didn't exactly relax, but Heki could sense the shift. A masking, rather than a suppressing of the hate.

"No. But if those mind-fuckers have the power to go back in, they might need a little persuading."

By a two-bit ship, two teenagers and an ageing ex-captain? And there's nothing left to go back into. The orb has gone.

CHAPTER 13

They moved ahead of her. Savvo in the lead, almost swimming through the debris as the palace hall collapsed around them. Then Arin, the trim of his suit thrusters sending him left and right as he tumbled through the thicker trail of ceiling and wall stone invading the cavernous throne room. Rebekah engaged her suit, switching off the auto commands built to track and adjust to its sensors. The orb was throwing out enough crap to confuse a battleship's arrays, never mind a spacesuit. She had to rely on pilot's skill, a human sense of danger...

And pure fucking luck. I've had so much of that lately.

Where ZZ3 was gnawed at her, but the warbot would protect crew. It was inherent in its personality, the evolution of electronic mind and the fragment of Asham ghosting about its system placing the protection of all crew at its core. Kefi slid by, there was no other word for it, the Senti's suit forging ahead of her and then Savvo at the front like a snake swimming upriver. Lithe, fast. As if untroubled by the increasingly large amount of rock and debris surrounding them.

"Entranceway clear," stated Savvo, and with head straining back, she caught sight of his boots exiting the throne room and entering the dust-filled hallway. ZZ3 suddenly appeared, wedged tight in the architrave, upper limbs shoving away a large boulder pin-pricked with bright crystals that hurtled from where Savvo had just entered. A double-limbed thump, and the rock flashed back and upwards, out of harms way. More followed in its wake, ZZ3 keeping the door clear as Arin clambered between the bot's lower limbs. A glance behind confirmed she was the last, and with a deft blast of her thrusters, she arrowed towards the same spot Arin had used. A ceiling tile cracked into her hip; another, heavier, struck her left knee. Rebekah adjusted, trying to ignore the impacts as she reached out to grasp ZZ3's nearest leg. The floor welled upwards, stone splitting, more jutting through the crack, spearing up towards her waist. She rolled, unable to do any more, and took a glancing blow to her utility belt. The impact sent her spiralling, tumbling towards the ceiling, her pilot-trained mind predicting the direction, trying to correct the spin with her thrusters. She quickly realised they lacked the force required to prevent her from twirling off into the depths of the upper palace. Rebekah twisted and engaged her thrusters to maximum on her left side, the change of angle not slowing her down, but barging her into a lump of broken ceiling that hovered nearby. She clattered into it, the impact sending her suit into a panic as it searched for breaches, while the smooth rock spun away in the opposite direction. Ignoring the pain her suit soothed with a gel, her momentum had slowed, the angle of her tumble less severe.

"ZZ3," she said, the first words she had time to speak.

"Closing. Prepare," stated the warbot.

A twist of her neck enabled Rebekah to catch sight of the warbot's extended front limbs, and behind those, glowing red eyes that immediately locked onto her. Jaws gripped her ankle, staying her momentum.

"Reversing thrust," the warbot said. Rebekah switched off her own jets and waited to see what ZZ3 intended. She found herself pulled in closer, a second limb wrapping about her sore waist, and she flew backwards, scanning the remains of the ceiling and the swirl of shattered furniture in what had once been a room above. ZZ3 shifted her position as the bot reversed, and she was now able to see ahead, where Savvo and Arin's lights glared through the rapidly collapsing doorway. With an increase in speed, they were through, both she and the warbot taking minor blows from the edge of the doorjamb before entering the palace hall. There Kefi danced and writhed in the air, the alien's suit shining in the dark as it kept the vast entrance clear of the rubble that had once been a stunning Senti palace.

ZZ3 didn't hesitate, spearing the centre of the void Kefi had created.

"Savvo, Arin, hurry," ordered Rebekah, the bruises beneath her suit making themselves known. "Get out."

"Releasing you, Captain," said ZZ3.

Rebekah recalibrated her suit thrusters, spinning about, watching with concern until Savvo and then Arin exited the expanding wreckage. The alien had kept the area clear, but had visibly slowed as her sub-engineer passed, and she was about to send him back to help when Arin noticed. He took hold of the Senti's suit, one arm out, the other gripping a shoulder tentacle as the huge doors finally gave way. They broke from the disintegrating palace walls, thankfully stayed by the lack of gravity, but shifting into Arin's path. He rammed into the carved stone, but the force wasn't enough, and her heart jumped as Arin and his charge were blocked from exiting the rush of shattered rock and stone.

"Z—" she began, but cut off as Savvo slammed into the errant door. His angle sharp and flying feet first, he clattered into the nearest door, which shifted just enough to block the second. A chink of light emerged from the gap, and Arin sped through, Kefi gripping onto his shoulders with tentacles shod in dulled Senti metal wrapped about his suit.

"Our glorious leader," said the warbot. Rebekah was sure there was an undertone there, whether humour, or admiration, she wasn't sure.

"Well done, Savvo," Rebekah said, her voice hazy amid the roar of static. What else could she say, he'd acted on instinct, solved an issue, more than likely saved his friend.

Arin's voice was equally faint. "I had it covered. Heh, really I did."

An Arin thank you in disguise, she could hear Savvo's chortle cut off by an inhuman sound that was clearly a groan of some form.

"Kefi, how can we help?" she said. "Are you injured?" Rebekah met Arin, eyeing a lull in the palace destruction over his shoulder that she didn't trust.

"Not injured. Exhausted. Suit systems shutting down to (*screech*)." Even the translated words exuded tiredness, and Rebekah took the last word, the Senti utterance, to mean 'minimum'. She scanned the sky and ground below them, everything rippling, rupturing as if the orb was being torn apart. Had the Butcher's minions found a way to stop its core, and therefore the orb's ability to hold itself together, or had it been the choice of the Senti? The queen was dead, and her egg, cocoon, whatever it was, taken. The 'why' was obvious, the Butcher seeking answers to faster than light travel and finding an alien race prepared to self-destruct rather than reveal it. That hinted at more depth to the puzzle than appeared on the surface; the sacrifice made huge, bigger than hiding such a secret.

Unimportant right now.

"ZZ3, I need you free from any burden. Arin, superhero, you are to help Kefi. Savvo, eyes on," she paused. How the fuck were they going to get out of the orb, one that was suffering rad spurts and gravity waves? "Kefi, where will we find a Senti ship. Anything we can fly?"

Coughs and splutters filled her comms, high pitched. "The orb is huge," the alien started to say, the words morphing into meaningless Senti. But the hint was there. Not enough time. The hovering rock pile that had once housed a queen rumbled, juddered, and Rebekah was suddenly shaken by a rolling pressure her HUD identified as gravity. It could not discern its source or direction as the force pressed in, fluttered, then whipped her sideways into ZZ3. The impact stifled somewhat by the warbot's closeness and her suit's cushioning, but her brain still rattled in its skull.

"Fuuuuck!" she shouted, mingled with cries from Arin and Savvo as flesh impacted with the heaving ground, then each other.

Her befuddled brain responded, deciding priorities as she stared into ZZ3's swirling eyes, face to face. "Call in."

"Alive, but shit. Kefi?" stated Arin. Rebekah pushed away from ZZ3, looking around to find Arin splayed across the Senti's suit which had struck a protruding sliver of decking that had previously sat below the rock.

"I am as good as I was," answered the Senti, Arin pushing himself up and grabbing the nearest tentacle to help the Senti away from the metal deck. He began examining the alien's suit for breaches while the occasional tentacle lifted or twitched.

"Savvo?" Rebekah glanced her second's way, catching the grim look displayed on his visor amid the scrawl of static.

"I'm good, Captain. But we take one of those hits surrounded by other debris, we're only so much jam inside a suit sandwich." Savvo leapt into the air, thrusters pushing him away from the patch of purple grass he'd landed on.

"Hey. In the face of peril and instant death, *I* do the funnies. Understand?" Arin had lifted the Senti back into position, sending Rebekah an okay signal as he joined them.

"I thought we needed a good one to lift the spirits. A touch of quality." Savvo's lights hid his face from view, and the rad interference denied Rebekah his feed, but there would be a smile there. They were alive. Life meant hope.

Think.

"Kefi, what about a—a container of some sort? Built from your strong metal. Like your ships. A self-contained room we can maybe ride this shitstorm out in?"

There was a long pause from Kefi. Above them, towards the centre of the orb, the sky was racked by electrical discharge, the glow of the false sun completely gone. Amid the crackles and flashes were signs of metal structures, criss-crossed and patterned. Rebekah's sense of scale was completely lost. It had been difficult before the collapse, but now she was shrouded in detritus from the orb, in a vast darkness punctuated only by their dim lights and the waves of occasional fierce lightning from above. Even if the Senti knew of somewhere, how would they find it in this?

The sounds emanating over comms were muted splurges of blancmange and static. The alien making little sense until a few Almaarian words crept in. "Survival pods are stationed along the external skin ... the hull."

"Then that's where we head," Rebekah said, and the brief moment of hope brought by being alive shrivelled in her mind. Her HUD couldn't orient to where they were, its sensors at a loss, tracking information unable to process where they had been as the markers relied on landmarks and rad/grav markers that were no longer relevant. The only sense she had was which way was up, the lightning her guide. So down, or outward, it was. But how? The dark threatened to press in. Crush her thoughts.

"ZZ3, we need an exit outward. If that's through the deck, so be it. I want you to perform a spiral search pattern to find a way through while we move from here. Maintain a visual on our lights."

"Affirmative," replied ZZ3, who immediately began the sweep, thrusters engaged gently to prod itself into position, before tracing a lazy circle around them.

"Arin, remain in the centre, but track our movements. Savvo and I will float diagonally out, but shout when you suspect you might lose sight. Understand?"

"Yeah. I stay here nursemaiding the Senti, being bloody useless, while you two try to find a way out of here." Arin replied. "Our glorious leader, the alien sitter."

"S'about right," said Savvo. "Saves me having to look after you for a change."

Arin choked back a reply, his lights bobbing, a shudder that sent shadows and glare across Rebekah's vision before her HUD adjusted. At first, she thought it was another grav quake, or Arin's suit had malfunctioned. But then pressure rippled through the atmosphere, a pressing that loomed strangely in her mind. Then her suit began to cast a shadow that expanded back towards the palace, shimmering across the debris which shifted and yawed to form a valley down the centre. She spun about, Arin's voice echoing in her comms as more light flared, coppery, bright, as if a new orb was forming. Not forming, emerging, and the huge cavern suddenly lit up once again.

Thrumming beat through her suit, into her chest, and her HUD began to blare every warning system it had. She trusted none of it, her only guide to her status the beating of her heart and breath on her visor. The new orb was beautiful, its presence however, oppressive. As if it took up too much space, was too large to be contained by the inner world the Senti had built for themselves. The coppery light pulsed once, the wave washing over her, and then darkness reigned once again, the flashes of discharge above at a hiatus or end. Relief spread through Rebekah, short-lived, as the orb shone brighter than ever and a second wave of light crashed into her, cutting off her sense of self. A last thought an earworm, her favourite, warbling in her mind.

CHAPTER 14

The smooth-skinned Senti ship approached slowly, its nose covered by intertwining arrays, a scar compared to the refined beauty of the stern. Hendricks eyed the camera feed on the co-pilot's monitor with a mix of trepidation and fear. Outwardly she displayed as much strength as she could, while the dread Arin, Rebekah and Savvo were lost amid the maelstrom of the ruined orb clawed at her heart and mind. Heki could feel it, she knew, but the stoic façade was essential. To be the *Dricks* the girl knew and trusted in the face of adversity, whether the emotions rolling off her reflected that or not. If she crumbled, she was sure the collapse would take the twins down with her.

"They're hailing," said Tremil, voice flat and monotone over comms. A throwback to the old days, when containment of their emotions had been paramount.

"Put them through, Trem," she replied, and pressed two sweaty fingers into her eye sockets, regretting it as they stung, but at least it woke up her numb mind.

"This is ...," the name of the ship melded into a watery, muddy flood hitting a valley wall, "*Sunstar*, state the reason for your presence here."

Hendricks winced.

To stop the Butcher from doing what he's already done, you Senti shit.

"We were on a reconnaissance run as requested by a Senti we name Scarva," replied Hendricks, glancing over at Heki whose face was set hard, gaze unblinking. The symbiote, however, pulsed avidly.

"Scarva? (*Blancmange hitting floor*). Yes, Scarva. Prepare to be absorbed." The voice lacked any emotion as usual, but Hendricks sensed there was no choice given in that statement. However, being 'absorbed' didn't set her hopes high for what came next. They could have run, and likely, as the Senti ship turned, would have escaped. Another look at the symbiote flipped her stomach. Rebekah would have demanded she save the girls. Except, they were the ones piloting the ship and running comms. Two emotional time bombs ready to explode. Hendricks may be in charge, but there was no decision to make. They stayed, and this way she did so in one grief-stricken piece.

"Prepare how?" she answered, trying to be flippant like Arin would. She didn't know why, beyond the Senti always put her on edge.

"Simple. Do not panic. Cut engines, refrain from using thrusters. Open your transponder."

Hendricks let out a long sigh. Transponders. Damn. But this was a Senti ship, and the Butcher apparently long gone. She should save such concerns for when they were on board and had a chance, however small, of finding her rescued crewmates. Her friends.

She nodded to Heki. "Do it," she said, and the girl's fingers danced over the navcom. "Trem, HT2 channel only. Lock it down."

A crackle rode the internal comms, Tremil eventually cutting in. "Active," she stated. "I have set a shield algorithm, but they'll cut through that unless I add ... you know, the *new* code we have. I'll encrypt, but again I suspect they will decipher it in the end."

"Let's try and not give them a reason to. Girls. Heki, Trem, look. The symbiotes ... I don't know how they'll react." Hendricks unbuckled, needing to pace as the Senti ship closed, filling the viewscreen at its shortest focal point. "But ..."

"I understand," said Tremil. "But we can't operate without them. Everything is too raw, too close."

Heki craned her neck, blinking, tears at the corners of her eyes. "Crew first," she said. "You came for us, now we risk what we have to save them."

Hendricks grimaced as she paced, her thoughts on more than just the symbiotes. How would they react to the *connection* the girls had? According to Rebekah's last report, the Senti had killed themselves in response to the Butcher. Such an extreme she could fathom in one or two at a time, some of the Bustan Marines had blown their suits rather than let her unit gain access to their AI, or had sacrificed themselves, ordering the suits to escape and save the tech knowing they wouldn't survive the stress and speed of movement. Then there were those Marauders aboard Scarva's ship. But that many taking their own lives? How big a secret were they keeping? If it was connected to what had happened to Heki and Tremil ...

The cameras cut out, the external mics feeding in a cacophony of wet, liquid sounds that brought back the meaning of *absorption* front and centre to Hendricks' thoughts.

"Heki. What's going on?" she asked, pounding back through the galley to settle into her chair beside the twin.

"We're inside. They didn't open a door, the hull just moulded around us, sucked the *Sunstar* in," she replied, tongue working at the corners of her mouth.

"External sensor readings are dead. Some kind of field manipulation," cut in Tremil. "Matches the type of thing the orb was doing. No grav ... oh. Hang on. There's a subtle magnetic field running the length of the ship ..."

"Meaning?" asked Hendricks, sensing the ship settle, though no docking clamp noises resounded through the hull. The whole thing was unsettling, science that felt as distant from their own as fabled magic.

"Not sure yet. Being hailed, I'll switch over."

"Crew of the *Sunstar*," Hendricks was sure it was the same voice, "you will be ... cleansed on exit. Disinfected, but we will expect you to wear your survival suits afterwards until otherwise informed."

Hendricks sighed again and sent a rueful smile Heki's way.

The Senti comms kicked in again. "Please be aware you, your ship, and its systems, *will* be searched."

"We'll be okay. The symbs will help us deal with being enclosed again. There's no point in hiding anything." The girl grimaced, blinking back a tear, before unbuckling. "We'll be okay."

It wasn't a rap, more like a soft rasp upon the airlock door, but Hendricks sensed the Senti were out of patience and wanted them to open up. The girls had prepped swiftly, perhaps to blank out any trepidation, but she had delayed. She knew it. Told herself it was the worry over going in naked without a weapon, but in reality, Hendricks didn't want to hear that they – her crew, Arin – were gone. The longer she waited ...

Two hands slipped into hers, one either side. Though firm, they felt soft in her mind, soothing. Four eyes peered at her, the need there evident, yet Heki and Tremil hadn't taken her hand for selfish reasons. They were here for her, facing what was to come together. Hendricks had a flashback, to the city square in Shemmi, the run for the dropship as the Bustans closed in. Her mind had been stripped, her wetware broken by the girls, and all that she had known was their desperate need to survive. This was a debt repaid.

Blinking back the tears that threatened her resolve, she smiled at them both, nodding but unable to speak. Tremil activated the airlock, and they cycled through, emerging into a strange docking bay filled with the greens and blues the Senti favoured. Hendricks hadn't known what to expect if she was honest, her memories of the orb vague after the extraction of so many memories and the destruction of her wetware. However, it came flooding back. The hold was filled with curves, folds of both metal and a multitude of softer, rubberised materials. Like a cave carved by the sea, it rippled away either side, populated by spaceships that were close in design to Scarva's, yet the lines were cleaner, the arrays less jarring to the eye. But it was the quiet that struck, a hush over the docking hold, yet it was teeming with busy Senti who went about their work just like any human navy would. If it weren't for the lack of straight lines and sharp edges, and humans, she could have been stood aboard the ANS *Segfi*.

Two hand squeezes brought her back into the *now*. A ramp rolled out from the dockside, unfurling like a wave of metal to land precisely on the *Sunstar*'s lip. At the far end stood two Senti in their encounter suits, wearing a pack and hose that put Hendricks in mind of a plasma cutter, or indeed, a flamethrower. Steeling herself, she strode out onto the platform, head high, wishing for a carbine and a bandolier of frag grenades to hide behind. At her side stood two of the fiercest warriors she had ever known, their personal battle so different to hers, but no less dangerous.

"Halt," stated the Senti on the left side, raising their nozzle as they spoke, chin tentacle twitching slightly. Hendricks noted a set of swirls upon the shiny metal film of the suit, central, not up on the chest and to the side like on the Almaarian uniforms, but unmistakeably a badge of some form. "The suits are to be disinfected first."

"How ..." she started, but it rapidly became clear. The nozzles aimed their way and a thick mist spewed to wreathe all three suits. Hendricks squeezed the twins' hands, muttering calming words, though who they were for was another matter.

As the mist cleared, distorting her view of the aliens, she could see enough to know they parted, and another had joined them. Again, in a silvery encounter suit, but there was a difference it took a few seconds to work out. The helmet, and therefore the head inside, was wider, the chin tentacle missing. Where the eyes on the others were black, these were purest blue. Hendricks glanced at the badge, but the swirls defied her attempts to find a difference.

"Crew of the *Sunstar*," stated the newcomer, the voice only subtly different, like each of the Senti translators were. "You are to disrobe so you can also be disinfected."

Hendricks had been expecting that, and glanced at both girls before releasing their hands. She wanted to step forward, put her body between the aliens and them. An urge she half-resisted, pushing forward just a little as she spoke.

"We need to talk first," she said. "Explain something."

The newcomer stared her way, and beneath their visor she saw the slit like mouth remained closed, yet somehow, she sensed they were communicating, or listening to orders perhaps.

"Disrobe, and we will converse. Quickly now."

Hendricks complied, practised hands removing her flight clothes and magboots, finishing with her hands by her side, gripping her underclothes to wipe the sweat away. The Senti handed her a belt, clearly recently adapted with an additional buckle. On putting it on, she felt a pull upon her waist.

"Remove your boots. The belt will perform as if you are in our gravity."

Hendricks did so, and the spray washed over her while she held her breath until it had passed, her skin soaked but drying fast.

She wiped her face, blinking away a last drop that stung at the corner of her eye. "The ... there's no other way of saying this. My two crew, Heki and Tremil," she looked over her shoulder, emphasising by pointing at her charges, "they are bonded with ... screw it ... with two of your symbiotes. Well, one of your symbiotes that kind of split into two." She ran a hand over the back of her head, eyeing the Senti that had not reacted in any way. "I didn't know if your disinfectant was dangerous to them, you wearing those encounter suits and all."

"Symbiotes?" stated the Senti who was obviously in charge. "The (*scraping of toast*)? That is impossible." Both shoulder tentacles twitched, and the lower limbs bent a little. Agitation, perhaps? Or was this how they displayed incredulity. Hendricks, when she thought about it, had to agree everything that had happened to the girls could be labelled on the strange side. Arin said ... oh shit.

Arin.

"Look, I know it's hard to swallow. But it's true. Can we hurry? I need to know if my friends are alive. You sent something into your orb. We were hoping it was a rescue ship, that you saved our crew who were in there. And Kefi, a Senti. From Scarva's ship." Hendricks found her urgency, the words spilling out, but standing tall, face set hard and desperate to get an answer before they encountered the twins' symbiotes.

"Processing your previous words. Wait, human." The Senti twisted, head turning back as if looking over a shoulder it didn't really have, peering back into the depths of the hold.

Hendricks swore under her breath, gritting teeth, trying not to grind them as that always annoyed ...

Come on.

"We must see these symbiotes. They are to remove their clothes, and we will assess," stated the Senti. But somewhere in there was a hint of compassion, the head turning to face Hendricks, blue eyes locked to hers. "Our rescue mission is being cleansed of radiation and realigned to the ship's systems. We do not know as yet what is inside. It was hit with a huge surge of radioactive particles as the core gave. There is a possibility it could have taken them on board."

"A possibility?" said Hendricks.

"Yes. But no more."

She nodded, the Senti giving away as much as it could, she knew. They would be under orders to keep information at a minimum. After all, they were human and had also admitted that some of their crew were aboard the orb when it exploded. For all they knew, they could have been the cause, though Hendricks doubted they thought that. The welcome, though not friendly, hadn't involved handcuffs and threats. At least not yet.

She faced Heki and Trem. "Okay, your turn. They understand, and will be curious. Remain calm if you can. You know, we have zero idea how your emotions might affect them. I suspect not at all, but how many times have I been wrong in the last few months?"

Both girls didn't respond, rather began to unclip their crew jackets. Once undone, Heki and Tremil looked to her before turning around to expose the symbiotes. Both were pulsing in metallic waves, appearing un-phased by where they were.

The Senti in charge stepped forward, holding in one tentacle some form of device, swirls and circles rolling over its smooth surface as the alien swept it over Tremil's symbiote. Hendricks watched the alien's face, but it was the tremor in the limbs that gave most away. This was not only unexpected, but beyond what they knew. Something she prayed they didn't find abhorrent.

The tentacle swapped over to Heki, repeating the process, the response the same.

"Everything okay?" asked Hendricks, breaking the silence.

"I cannot answer that."

She took that both ways. One, I don't know, two, I can't tell you, anyway. At least, not yet. Either way, the nozzles rose ready.

"Finish disrobing," said the Senti, the words almost distant. "The cleanser will not damage the (*scraping of toast*). You are to meet with the ... what you would call a ship's controller – a captain."

Hendricks nodded, but wanted more information. "Do they have a title? A name?"

"In your words, a queen, though that is far from an adequate description."

CHAPTER 15

SENTI NEST SHIP

Heki adjusted the Senti belt, aligning it with her hips and beneath the hem of her flight jacket. The pull kept her on the ship's deck, drawing her towards the magnetic field Tremil had mentioned ran the length of the ship. Now they knew why. Magboots for Senti personnel were not an option, even if attached to their lower limbs, she could imagine bone free bodies would struggle with their use. Perhaps that was how the encounter suits started, and as their science had evolved, were able to move onto something a little freer. The belts were not perfect for human use, but the last few years in space had provided enough experience for her to adapt. Besides, thinking about it almost drowned out the noise in her head.

Damn.

She'd thought about it.

Her symb mithered, wrapping a tentacle further around the side of her neck, reacting to the worries coursing again through her body. Rebekah, Arin, Savvo. How the Senti queen would react. Everything. But she needed to be calm, because immersing Dricks in her fears wasn't going to help.

The corridors were initially laid out like a human ship, which, she assumed, was because they had devised a system to mimic gravity and a 'direction' for down. However, they were more cylindrical, with only the deck sporting straight lines as the core corridor they walked along stretched out into the distance. It reminded her of a worm tunnel she'd seen in a vid, with off tunnels connecting here and there, and lots of doorways that were unlike those Heki had observed on the crew's feed aboard the *Unpronounceable*. More circular, and covered in the rubberised material Rebekah had described deeper inside Scarva's ship. The transport they'd initially taken compounded that, almost like a subway train, though faster, riding the magnetic field about the huge ship.

Heki filed each observation away for later consideration, a pressure slowly building in her head after each step. They were walking towards the source, and it was too similar to the sensation when the Senti ship had emerged into their section of space for it to be anything other than whoever or whatever enabled their passage through void-space. The queen perhaps.

Tremil nudged her arm, and with a shared moment, they slipped their hands into Hendricks'. It was a natural thing to do, facing what was to come together. A shield forged from togetherness. From family.

The doorway ahead sprung open, silent, as much of the ship seemed to be, exposing an inner sanctum that swirled with the softer materials the Senti on Benetai had favoured. A ripple of cabbage-like air shivered, wafting the hues of blue-green like wind through long grass, or the crest of a lazy wave in a shallow sea. It had its own beauty, despite the smell pervading the massive room. The materials rolled back, almost as if they responded to their presence, exposing a raised dais in the centre and the largest Senti Heki, or anyone else on record, had ever seen. The queen was surrounded by a hologram, or at least that's how it appeared, a sphere of blue light that writhed with what she took to be writing, and visuals that distorted as her eyes swept over. All her tentacles were splayed wide, the ends tipped in Senti metal that flexed and split as they whirled about the sphere, prodding, swiping.

Running the ship.

A queen without a crown. Wrong type of queen.

She glanced about the room, expecting an entourage of Senti and finding none. They were, as far as she could tell, alone except for the two in encounter suits and the officer missing a chin tentacle – as was the queen.

Gender roles. Definitely the wrong type of queen. Like a hive, or what had Kefi said? A nest.

The queen suddenly stopped, tentacles left hanging, her head swivelling to face Heki.

Oh.

The pressure slammed into her head, and she staggered forwards, only saved from collapsing by Hendricks' intervention. The pressure immediately stopped, replaced by a distant hum that soon faded away. When Heki finally looked up, the queen's regard had shifted to Tremil, though her sister appeared unaffected.

Nice to be the test subject.

She patted Hendricks' arm, giving her a faint smile of reassurance. Speaking didn't seem appropriate, and the Senti with them had not spoken either.

Ah. Perhaps they don't have to. Or they sub-vocalise using communicators, though I think not.

The Senti officer spun about, limbs reaching as if pointing. "The Nest Queen asks permission to make contact with your (*scraping of toast*)."

"Permission?" replied Heki and Tremil in unison. Of all things, that was the least expected. Heki dreaded losing her symbiote, the thought of regressing back to what she once was a dark cloud. An abyss she didn't want to enter again. Ever. But what choice did she have? A glance, and both girls nodded, then spoke. "Agreed."

Hendricks, however, interrupted. "Heki and Tremil are empaths. Projective empaths. Sorry, I don't know what to call you. I hope 'queen' will do. *Senti* queen, they have been through mental and physical torture. Trauma I would never have the strength to survive. The symbiotes calm those thoughts, the emotions, allow them to function without harming others."

A silence fell, filled in Heki's mind by the prospect the queen spoke directly to the officer – communicating her thoughts to be passed on. If she was right, the weave of Senti society was beginning to form, and what humanity had witnessed beforehand was far from the reality. Here lay the true power, and as Kefi had stated, the orb also had a queen. A puller of strings, at the centre of a network that oversaw each facility or ship.

"Your knowledge is limited, filled with gaps and misunderstandings we have not the time to eradicate. The bond between the (*scraping of toast*) and their host is sacrosanct. The permission requested is from the host, but what you call a symbiote may well refuse to grace our Nest Queen with contact. Their will is adhered to." The officer spoke to Hendricks, but the reassurance was aimed at Heki and her sister. She knew it, could sense her symbiote's calm acceptance. They were one, and together they should not fear the queen, nor revere her. But listen, converse. Yes.

"We will be fine," she said, peering up at Hendricks, though she didn't attempt a smile. "The queen means no harm. Just to understand." The engineer grimaced, doubt playing across her face that rolled off her in waves. It wasn't a *no*, just a fear Heki assumed was based on Scarva and Pshwa, as well as Hendricks' previous dealings with the mind-suckers who took their due. Understandable.

Heki stared up at the queen, those blue eyes regarding her and Tremil in turn, before she stretched out a tentacle each, the metal tips writhing and reforming, mirroring the symbiotes that lay against their necks. She caught Hendricks' flinch out of the corner of her eye, the set to her mouth, hands that had to grip each other to stop the desire to lash out. The mass of smaller tentacles slid past her eyeline, wrapping about her symbiote, about her. Where she had expected a cold, metallic touch, a warmth spread against her skin, bleeding into the symbiote. Somehow, she had anticipated the little alien to welcome the contact, but it was more acceptance that seeped into her mind. A necessity, not rejected, but simply tolerated.

At first, the queen's touch was alien, distant, a mix of pressure and unfathomable distance of mind and thought. A creature whose size and complexity were so far beyond her own she was unintelligible. But the symbiote was the conduit, and it was at that moment understanding crept in. The feeding. She had always assumed it was for sustenance, but as the queen delved, acted as a Senti would, frustrations rose that cast doubt on that theory. Or at least, partly. Through the strangeness of the contact, she sensed the queen's frustration at her little alien. That it wasn't what she had expected. More complex.

Different.

He had, as she still regarded this offspring of TB as a 'he', assumed a human connection. Bonded with her, and it was this that the alien queen struggled with. It wasn't a rejection, or an abhorrence, more a need to understand. And for that, she needed permission.

If I tell Dricks, she will blow her top. Flip – as she puts it – her lid.

'Yes,' she thought, hoping the nest queen could hear. *I am willing to listen.*

Instinctively, Heki placed her hand upon the queen's extended tentacle, touching where the metal and skin of the alien melded. A tingle rose in her fingertips, spreading through her. Tasting her as the symbiote did. Exploring how she was made, boring down into her physical body, seeking an understanding. It ended as swiftly as it started, and the queen's regard returned to her symbiote. The conduit between them. A glance told her Tremil had mirrored her actions.

Contact.

Connection.

Images poured in, but they made little sense. They were mathematical, she knew that, and Tremil would understand more. Her brain could not process what she experienced, other than it was the alien queen creating them.

The contact broke, the queen withdrawing her touch, releasing human and symbiote from her presence. Heki tried not to stagger, to alert and worry Hendricks, but vertigo hit, and she wobbled only for a gentle hand to take her elbow and steady her. Hendricks, her eyes, however, were on Tremil who appeared much more at ease as the queen withdrew. She licked at her lips; eyes locked on the huge Senti. Focused. Heki had seen that look before, a sister who hated to be beaten, who vented her frustration when the Senti code had so nearly done that.

"You okay?" asked Hendricks, her eyes now flashing and on the edge of anger.

Heki nodded, her hand falling on Hendricks' fingers where they grasped her elbow. "I'm good. I think we have established a starting point. Certainly, that the symbs are ..." she was about to say 'ours' but that was wrong. The true explanation would make the engineer more concerned, but new ground had been broken. "Are bonded. Linked."

Part of who we are now. Integrated. One. And the nest queen accepted it, despite her frustrations.

The Senti officer spoke, blue eyes turning to Hendricks. "The rescue orb has been decontaminated. The queen states you are unlikely to be at fault for the destruction of Orb 17 and may attend the opening. Whatever the outcome, she will require your presence until what happened has been established from the data gathered."

"Understood," replied Hendricks.

Too many emotions poured from her to say any more, grief mingled with hope. A chink of light in the abyss that Heki held on to as well. She parcelled up her thoughts on the alien queen and the other Senti, storing it all for discussion with her sister. Their society's complexities were far beyond Scarva and Pshwa, and she'd had a glimpse of what may lay at its heart, but Heki's need for her friends, her family, washed all of that away.

CHAPTER 16

SENTI NEST SHIP

Throbbing?

Numb. Dull. Sludge.

Rocks. No. Rubble. Smashing, waves of stone.

Throbbing.

Suits blaring, red everywhere.

Radiation.

Still throbbing. Throbbing is good.

Hands?

Her eyelids refused to budge, sealed by hardened gum, raw beneath but needing to see. Slowly, her hand rose, pressing into one eye and then the other, breaking the seal. Rebekah blinked, the sleep crumbling back into her eye and irritating her even more. She turned her head, intent on wiping it out, only to find she couldn't move her neck or shoulders, perhaps clamps holding her down.

She remembered the hands.

Rebekah blinked as much of the gum clear as she could, opening her eyes fully to look straight into the black, soulless depths of a Senti's eyes. Her body went rigid, unable to flinch only for a suited tentacle to touch her elbow.

"Calm, Captain," stated the Senti, the sound familiar. Almost welcome.

She fished the name from the abyss. "Kefi?"

"Yes, and no. More of that later. This may come as a surprise, Captain, but you are alive." The Senti said, leaning back, revealing the scorched and battered encounter suit she remembered from the orb. The Senti orb that blew the fuck up, and nearly took them with it. *Should* have killed them except ... a copper light.

Rebekah tried to roll on her side, but she remained in the grip of ...? She glanced down as best she could. There were no clamps. "Kefi, can you free me from whatever this is?"

The Senti eased back fully, chin tentacle tapping and swiping at a console to her side. Around him, green and blue lights played out. Winking in patterns she couldn't quite discern, but their complexity hinted at regularity. The pressure released, though no straps retracted or clamps disengaged. Accepting it, she began to sit up, only for her inner ear to violently object, and the room spun, the lights' patterns lost in a riot of colour. To her embarrassment she retched, Kefi thankfully backing off as she threw up to the side. The vomit splatted onto the floor, only for the rubberised deck to absorb the past contents of her stomach.

"Fuck," she said. "Sorry."

Seagulls squawked, the Senti's mouth flapping wide. "Hah. You think I didn't release my gas bags when I awoke? At least the floor can take away your indiscretion. Mine taxed the scrubbers." The alien stopped, and despite the lack of contact she felt whenever gazing at a Senti's eyes, there was an instant disconnect as if Kefi was no longer in the room, its thoughts far away. It was brief, but niggled at her knowledge of the Senti. The first she had really come to like. "Apologies. We should wake the others. We were taken in by the rescue orb before the worst of the radiation hit, but my people are cautious about decontamination and still wait while the system scrubs us clean."

"People? Are we on a Senti ship? I mean, in a rescue orb inside another ship?"

"We are inside (*a muddy flash flood striking a canyon wall*). A nest queen's ship, thirteen in your numbers. Sent in response to a distress call from Orb 17, but too late."

"Fuck, it was too late. You mean sent for your spawn, and the orb's queen." Rebekah sat up, easing her back, exploring the bruises beneath her suit while she spoke. "Not us."

"No. But programmed to gather evidence. So it took me in, and consequently you when it realised you were witnesses to the events. I believe Almaarian humans would call it luck of your gods, whereas we would calculate the odds and let it fall as it will. Either way, you and your crew survived." Kefi adjusted its limbs, wrapping tentacles about its midriff in what Rebekah regarded as a very human action. Something Rubel used to do.

"And you," she said, risking swinging her legs over the side of the oddly shaped medtable. There was a pull on her suit's magboots, and she dropped to the deck. They didn't exactly stick, the response more like real gravity, low, but if she was careful, she wouldn't go flying. "You lived too."

"I did." The reply seemed curt, short. As if something underlying bothered the Senti.

"My crew?" she asked, looking about the room and seeing none of them.

"The next room." Kefi turned away, and Rebekah followed, careful in the strange grav, but able to adjust and caught up to the Senti as it exited into a curved, cylindrical corridor. After scraping the next doorway, it opened to expose both Arin and Savvo laid upon similar medtables to hers, but in a far grumpier state. Their frustrations evident as they called to be freed.

"Maybe we should leave them a little longer, Kefi," she said, the throb in her skull allowing a little smile to creep in. "It appears they are ungrateful." The Senti laughed, but briefly, again cut off in mid-flow. The alien was acting differently, but crew came first. "Okay, I'm coming."

"I think I may have drunk the bar dry, stuffed myself with a two-day-old kebab and fallen asleep with a porcupine as a pillow," said Arin, his body shaking a little as Kefi released whatever field pressed the sub-engineer onto the medtable. He immediately sat up, Rebekah backing off as his face turned green, and eyes rolled. The splat hit the floor at the side of him, the covering thankfully absorbing the outcome quickly before it set off Rebekah's stomach again. Savvo's guffaw was short-lived as the nausea swept over him too.

"Hah. You should never laugh at other's inflictions," said Arin, managing to sit at the edge of his table, rubbing at his gummed eyes.

"If I did, I'd die from laughing. Never catch a breath. Fuck I feel like crap."

"Don't worry, you actually look worse than that. So that's a win." Arin pushed himself to his feet, staggered a little, then steadied himself with the edge of the table. "Perhaps it was two bars I drank dry." He looked at Kefi, half-a-smirk forming which he apparently regretted. "Glad you're alive, Kef. How's your head?"

"I am ... fine. Captain, the rescue orb is about to power down and open for inspection. You have already been cleansed, but I suggest removing your suits and specifically your weapons. They will not be well regarded on board." The Senti wriggled around to face Rebekah.

How did he know? He was helmetless, and no comms had beeped. Perhaps wetware like theirs? But connected. Maybe. But they were aboard a Senti ship, that was certain, and somewhere out there were Hendricks and the twins fretting about them. In fact, after what happened to the orb, likely grieving. Everything else could wait.

"Agreed," she began to strip off, a glare to the others setting them in motion despite Savvo's reluctance.

"Leave them here. They will be transported to your ship."

She baulked. "The *Sunstar*?"

Kefi flinched. If he'd been human, it was if he had given away a secret he shouldn't, but it wasn't that. "Yes. I can inform you that Heki, Tremil and Hendricks are on board and being interviewed by the Nest Queen."

That was it. They were safe. She believed the Senti. They were the reason they were alive, and also the reason they had been in danger in the first place when she thought about it. Seeking the spawn of their queen. Either way, interviewed sounded ominous. "How do you know all this?"

Kefi went still. "I have been returned to the nest."

What were they getting into?

Rebekah felt the rush of musty air as the orb split, and the ramp rolled down from the spherical ship to land perfectly on the dockside lip. There stood two Senti in armoured encounter suits, with another missing a chin tentacle, a pair of excited twins trying desperately to dampen their emotions and an ex-captain who couldn't stand still amid the green-blue light enthusing the hold. It felt surreal. How long had it been since they saved the *Hatton*? And now they had just been rescued from an alien orb in full self-destruct by a Senti queen and her apparently massive spaceship. At her side a Kefi, re-admitted, so it said, back into the fold of the queen's nest. Whatever the fuck that meant.

They descended, the hugs and powerful emotions rippling through the humans while the Senti stood about, apparently devoid of sentiment. Amid the arms and outpouring, Rebekah noted the distance between Kefi and the Senti officer. As if ... no, she couldn't put a tentacle on it. A distance was the best she could do, but then, the Senti had become addicted to human memories and the emotions involved. Rumour being they lacked their own, and here was exhibit A.

She extricated herself from the girls, parted Arin from Hendricks' arms and pulled her ex-captain in close while the girls smothered Savvo and Arin. "And?" she said.

Hendricks' grimace spoke a thousand words. "Been tough, but I'm holding the resentment in."

"That's a start. And the girls? The symbiotes? I heard you were being 'interviewed'." She let the engineer go, pursing her lips, eyes wide and expectant as she waited for an answer.

"Yeah. A bit touchy feely for my liking. Hek and Trem, well they'll have to explain, but the queen interacted with their symbs. Made contact. They said she accepted them, but wanted to know more. We're not exactly free, shall we say?" Hendricks took Savvo's hand, shaking it, slapping the elbow and letting a little light into the shadow about her features.

"We're alive," Rebekah said to no one in particular, peering above and around her, admiring the sheer size of the ship and wondering just how powerful it was. Enough to take on the *Segfi*? She had no clue, but with the destruction of the orb, she had her doubts. How had the Butcher managed that?

Rebekah stood next to Kefi, the Senti now devoid of its suit, appearing much-like any other she had met. She was embarrassed about that, surprisingly so. Unable to tell one from the other seemed so wrong, and something, as she peered about the queen's throne room, she needed to put right.

The nest queen remained silent, as Hendricks had said, surrounded by a light control panel. A hologram that the queen interacted with as she oversaw the functions of the ship. Rebekah had seen similar tech aboard the *Segfi*, and another cruiser in the Almaarian fleet, though only ever in specific sections. She suspected there was nothing on board this Senti queen didn't control, or directly command others to do so. A tentacle in every pie, as Hendricks had put it.

She waited patiently, the past two days spent in recovery in an area the Senti had adapted to their needs. The *Sunstar* had been searched, and according to the twins, their databanks ransacked but not wiped. But this meeting had her on edge, because the only thing they hadn't explored stood the other side of her. ZZ3, and the warbot's ghost.

Fuck.

Kefi's lower limbs rippled, and the Senti flowed forwards to stand at the dais' lower edge. The queen instantly stopped what she was doing, her full regard falling upon the Senti, a tentacle whipping out at frightening speed. Rebekah flinched, then acted, her wetware kicking in, unable to do anything but save someone in need. Before she reached Kefi, she found herself slammed to the floor, the weight of a whole ship locking her Senti belt to the deck.

"Hold, Captain," stated Kefi as the queen's tentacle tip splayed into multiple fronds, wrapping about the Senti's head, smothering its eyes and upper, elongated skull. "I am in no danger. I am part of the nest, a vassal of the queen."

The belt released, Rebekah gaining her feet, face red with anger. "A warning would help."

"You are aboard a Senti ship, where we act as our kind do. Not human. You are the guest here and you will be respectful of that," replied Kefi, the tone had changed, the fronds squeezing a little tighter, almost lifting the

Senti from the ground. Despite the monotone, it wasn't a familiar voice. Something different, commanding and powerful. A queen.

"I am sorry," she replied. "It is my way to defend those in danger. Like on board your orb."

"As Kefi and your ship data have confirmed, Captain. We see your actions, but do not understand why."

"Kefi said your que—"

"No, Captain. That was your nature. But why were you there in the first place? Kefi describes what he knows of this Butcher. But you know so much more, and words are not enough."

The implication struck Rebekah. The Senti way, memories taken and explored. The queen wanted to experience the Butcher for herself, understand it from what she knew. The danger here was clear, ZZ3 at her side vulnerable to what came next. Her instinct was to protect. Deflect, perhaps let the nest queen see as much and as little as she could allow. But who was she kidding? The twins had explained the connection made with the symbiotes, the acceptance and perhaps more, but ZZ3? A product of stolen Senti tech. Two of their ambassadors murdered to gain access to forbidden knowledge, their cells used to experiment with by so-called human scientists. Butchers one and all.

How do you hide that?

And should she? It had been a perversion carried out by General Asham and Countess Segfi, and they and Almaar were about to be the victims of this foul secret, pursued solely to continue the war. For fucking honour no one else bloody understood but them.

"I warn you, you are not going to like what you see," she glanced at ZZ3, suddenly finding her hand upon the bot's nearest arm. "Though there is some good among it. The Butcher is a threat to us, and after Orb 17, to you. I agree to share, reluctant admittedly, but need you to discuss what you see. Interpret from my point of view. I am ... am ..."

"A queen," said Kefi. "Of your own making. But still a queen who cares for her ship's nest, and with that, respect is returned. May I?" A second tentacle swept into view, scuttling along it a symbiote rippling with metallic hues. It seemed small, but as it closed Rebekah became aware it was just the sheer size of the queen herself. She swallowed as the symbiote wrapped a tentacle about her arm, then clambered up her shoulder and around her neck. The touch familiar, its intrusion into her mind just like every other time. She had placed a memory marker where it all started with the *Hatton*. The symbiote wasn't here to take and sell, but to observe and report, unlike Scarva who had removed the memories from her wetware.

She closed her eyes and relived the memories in flashes of light and sounds, the symbiote drinking them in. According to the twins, they were a conduit, a part of whoever they had bonded with. Two beings as one, which gave her the chills when it came to Heki and Tremil. But then, those two beings were able to co-exist, and however brief, the girls had spent their first days in a new form of normality thanks to the aliens.

The sensation passed, her mind rifled and exposed. She felt dirty as she always did. Invaded. That would never change.

Kefi quivered as the symbiote crawled from Rebekah's neck and returned to the queen, mouth opening and closing. Amid the silence, a word eventually slipped out.

"Asham."

A tentacle whipped out, pointing at ZZ3, an accusation that seemed to pervade the air as it prodded towards the warbot.

"Asham," Kefi repeated.

"Only his shadow. A ghost," said ZZ3. "Seeking redemption."

CHAPTER 17

SENTI NEST SHIP

"How much longer?" said Arin as he paced from one side of the Senti cabin to the other. It wasn't a question, or at least in Rebekah's mind it was no longer. When you ask it ten times a minute, it loses its ability to query and just becomes a refrain. She had already kicked in an earworm to block out his insistent moaning. Good job she'd had a lot of practice at doing both.

Hendricks had already left, unable, Rebekah assumed, to cope with Arin's low mood and had taken to walking the corridors where the Senti had allowed. These were few, but better than the ex-captain strangling her partner with bare hands before throwing him out the airlock.

However tempting it may be.

Heki and Tremil sat in the corner, between them a Senti holo console shimmered blue, their fingers immersed in the light as they ran through the tests the Senti queen had set them. A precursor to her decision on ZZ3, they were required to show what they knew of her race's coding structure, and therefore what damage they could achieve to an open system. An activity designed to overcome the incredulity running through the queen, and therefore the alien ship's crew, that the Butcher could not only access their ship's system, but that of an entire orb. As far as Rebekah was concerned, the evidence was still hurtling away from Orb 17 right now, and they were wasting time.

But trust was hard-earned, and hers more than most, so she could equate to the reasons. But all the while they waited, the greater the gap between them and finding out what the Butcher had achieved in his attack on the Senti. She knew what he wanted, but did he find the secrets to FTL? A battleship that could fold space and time, fuck, a scary thought. One controlled by a paranoid AI hybrid even more so.

"Arin. I'm going to explain this in syllables. Sh-ut the f-uck up. Got it? It won't matter how long ZZ3 will take if I have ripped off your lips and shoved them up your arse so that every time you fart you whistle." Savvo growled each word. Eyes narrow and angry with his own frustrations as well as suffering Arin's. Rebekah stood, her mouth tight, and gently reached out to tap Savvo's head. He nodded, not looking her straight in the eye, but she caught the softening to them. His wetware kicking in.

The door slid open, Hendricks standing there, hands on hips. Behind her stood a Senti, not Kefi. The chin tentacle was absent, most likely the officer they'd been interacting with who still refused to share her name. The alien left, a tentacle waved disdainfully. Pieces about the Senti were slotting home, and the girls had explained their experiences between immersion in the tests. A queen who controlled not just via the command holo-sphere, but telepathically. That – if they could assign gender – was female in human terms, as appeared to be the officer they had dealt with. Males, or in the girls' terminology, the *workers*, bore chin tentacles and spoke freely. Acted independently as well as being directed by the nest queen. Rebekah had a suspicion the officer might show the same ability. Commanding a unit by mind speech would have huge tactical advantages, especially before comms or field radios had been developed. A natural advantage. It would also explain the nest queen's complete oversight of the ship. An inherent instinct to know everything. To command.

But they weren't slaved drones. Scarva, Pshwa, Kefi too, all showed independent thought. Was it proximity? Had they escaped the ... nest ... to be free of such oversight? Or cast out, not knowing the embrace of their queen and therefore bitter, selfish.

Mmm. Not Kefi.

Rebekah raised an eyebrow, to which her engineer shook her head.

"Kind of wandered into a restricted area." Hendricks tapped the metal belt about her waist. "Locked me down with this bloody belt the first step I took. Left me there for a few minutes until that officer came along. Sent for, I think. I got the silent treatment until we arrived back, then she dropped a threat on me about how long she'd leave me there next time."

Arin had finally stopped pacing, his face a mixture of concern and strain. Rebekah did have some sympathy, but he wore at it constantly. The more she thought about it, the more this felt like the old days. Before the *Scourge* and Duboit and the stark reality they had been brought back together in adversity. Odd how things worked out.

The holo console powered down, Heki and Tremil leaning into their oddly shaped chairs. They shared a glance, then looked over to Rebekah. She knew that look, the self-satisfaction of a job well done. They hated to lose, and would have faced the exercise like a war, refusing to back down. For all their emotional walls, their raw power, they could be manipulated with ease using the right triggers. The countess hadn't needed to kidnap them; she could just have given them an exam instead and told them it was impossible. Job done.

Teenagers.

"Go on," she said. "Tell me why you look so smug."

"Because we won," replied Tremil, a smirk arising, mirrored by her sister, but without the same level of self-satisfaction.

"And that's a good thing?" cut in Savvo.

Rebekah had to agree with his sentiment, but she could have reined them in earlier and decided against it. To all intents and purposes, they were in a prison. Not a human one, where you held everything close to your chest and played the system until a chance to escape arose. An alien one, with a warden who had a tentacle in every data stream. Could watch and analyse everything from fluctuations in their bio chems to how regularly they went for a shit. But could never truly understand human motivation, as she couldn't theirs. That made playing games with what they revealed dangerous. The possibility of being misunderstood, or failing to set the foundation for any level of trust, a concern.

Tremil appeared disturbed by Savvo's response, and her symbiote's skin rippled with a metallic wave before settling.

It's clicked.

"I get you," said Heki, who sent her sister a reassuring smile. "But we learnt things too. It works both ways."

The door slid open again, Hendricks, who had been talking in low, murmured tones in an attempt to calm Arin, spun about. She was still near the door, and Rebekah had to step aside to catch sight of Kefi. It was the first time she'd seen him free of the queen's touch since the throne room.

A shoulder tentacle beckoned them out. "The Nest Queen has request-ed your attendance. She has completed her analysis of ZZ3."

ZZ3. Not Asham, or just 'your machine' as had been said from time to time.

Rebekah let Arin leave first, but once he'd swept past her, she laid a hand on his shoulder, squeezing. "Wetware. That's an order," she whispered hard and low. Arin nodded in response, and his shoulder relaxed. She let go and allowed Hendricks and the girls past too.

Only Savvo lingered, catching her eye before shoving himself away from the wall, and following. "Funny how I'm never on point when Arin's in a rush."

"He'd do exactly the same if it was you under the queen's fucking gaze. Yeah, the same, and I'd have struggled to have kept him under control. Same with you. Like the bad old days this."

"Funny how we end up caring so much about a warbot," Savvo replied, falling in behind her.

"We all know ZZ3's not *just* a fucking warbot. Crew, one of us. I'm just hoping whatever the queen has done, hasn't jolted the bloody ghost inside back into old ways."

On reaching the command centre-cum-throne room entrance, Kefi insisted Rebekah be at the front.

The Sunstar*'s queen. Do I get a tiara?*

"Everyone calm?" she asked, looking over both shoulders, her eyes and face set to accept no other answer but 'yes'. Everyone nodded, even the girls. "Good."

The doors slid open, and she was greeted by ZZ3's gaze, the bot's eyes a calm swirl of blue that initially eased her worries. The fluttering materials had been cast aside again, the queen at the centre of her nest, tentacles jabbing and swiping at her holo-sphere, but the eyes were on hers. Blue.

Another female trait?

Kefi stopped next to the dais, spinning about to face them all and a metal-shod limb landed upon his neck. The Senti stiffened then relaxed, slitted mouth opening and closing before it – he? – spoke.

"The machine is no threat."

Rebekah relaxed, sensing her whole crew mirrored her actions. What would she have done if the Senti had gone the other way? Fought an entire ship for an evolving robot?

For crew.

"The shadow program named Asham within its system has been forthcoming. I have drawn from it memories my dreamers have interpreted," Kefi continued.

Dreamers?

"The containment unit built from stolen technology was likely poorly constructed via a lack of understanding. What was copied being imperfect and designed for Senti use. Humans like to meddle, without thought for consequences. I declare the Butcher a threat, the Countess Segfi a murderer of our kind. Your Emperor complicit ..." Kefi's head turned, his regard matching the queen's. "In times past, before we learned to retain our knowledge, learn from our history, we would have gone to war over such things. But we understand human's predilection for violence to solve your issues. My dreamers have watched on, fascinated at how you are unable to learn."

The enormity of the nest queen's words suddenly hit Rebekah. What Segfi had done, how the Senti would view such actions. How would the Court have reacted if two of their nobles ended up on a Senti scientist's slab? So much meat to be used as the aliens saw fit to meet their own selfish ends?

"The Butcher blew up your orb. Not the Empire. Not the Countess, though I won't argue with the accusation."

War?

"I suspect, but do not know, that you are correct. Asham assumes from its retained memories this *Butcher* was seeking how our ships are able to move through void-space. That he performed his experiments in search of an answer and failed. The Senti you name Kefi believes the attack on the one you call Scarva's ship was a practice run, learning, and he used this knowledge against the orb. It fits the facts. But know this, Queen Rebekah Khan, he did not destroy Orb 17. Its queen did. Sacrificed the orb nest, and all those on board, to prevent this Butcher from such understanding."

Kefi had said as much about the Senti they came across, but not the orb itself. She couldn't process that, the enormity beyond her. Was the secret that precious? So fundamental they were prepared to die for it en masse?

"I don't understand," she replied. An honesty.

"No." Kefi stared at her, soulless eyes that threatened to draw her into an abyss at the bottom of which was another out of reach revelation. Perhaps one not so pressing right now.

"Are we free to go?" she asked, her eyes moving from Kefi to the queen.

"Again, *no*. These Butchers' nestlings have taken a queen's spawn. That cannot be. It must be returned to us, and the nest regrown. Knowing humanity's paranoia, which the fractured brain patterning of the Butcher has refined, should *I* attempt to reacquire it, your Court and Emperor may view my presence as an act of war. And after our last ambassador was murdered, I refuse to put more of my nest and our technology in the hands of your nobility." Pressure built in Rebekah's head as the queen's words drove home, as if her presence filled the air with her demand. Tangible, like the girls' emotional waves, though she couldn't claim to interpret them in any way. Words were the conduit, a connection between Senti and human open to misinterpretation or manipulation.

She wanted to ask how the queen could force them to help, but feared it would lead to something being left behind as leverage. A twin perhaps, an excuse to study them further.

Not fucking happening.

"Your compliance is expected. Kefi will accompany you as liaison, (*a rock falling off a cliff*) will be my overseer." Kefi glanced at the Senti officer whose arrival at their side would have been theatrical in human terms, and her tentacles stiffened.

But how would they stop them from running?

The Senti had searched her ship, explored it from stern to bow. Invaded their systems. Setting some form of explosive would be easy for a race that would rather blow up a moon-sized orb than allow the Butcher their secrets.

Fuck.

CHAPTER 18

SENTI NEST SHIP

*U*pgrades?

'Perhaps, but they'd be weaponised somehow.'

ZZ3 just couldn't find out how. A way to stop them from running had to be a high probability. Not luck, nor chance, even fate in human terms. Logic. And also, the possible need to wipe away a mistake should it go wrong.

"Keep looking," stated Arin.

ZZ3 calculated that the sub-engineer's initial joy at the bot's return had now mingled with his concern for what the Senti engineers had done to the ship. Well, this bit anyway.

'They are far cleverer than that. They have observed enough human memories to add a deviousness they may have lacked.'

Such as you.

'Such as my originator? Devious? More a bludgeon when it came to people. It will be a code link. May even be sparked by something one of our Senti guests will do, even say. You must suspect they have some form of mind-to-mind contact.'

I do.

"It is a beauty," said Arin, running a hand along the bulge protruding from the engine room deck. Senti metal shone under his touch, a glimmer of static hinting at what lay beneath. "We're going to have to test this at some point. Understand its capabilities."

"They provided an analysis breakdown using human measures of distance, rate of acceleration and impact specifics. Rate of recharge, number of recharges, and a grading on the metal javelins provided. It matches in power the rail guns aboard an Almaarian cruiser, but recharges and reloads faster. Impressive," stated ZZ3. "Though Asham and I agree, after witnessing their manipulation of electromagnetic fields, this is a significant downgrade on their own systems by some degree."

"Shiiit? Really? And the moral of this story is, don't piss off the Senti."

"I understand, our glorious leader, that it is too late for that." ZZ3 shuffled further along the bulge, one limb sliding across the metal, running another sensor scan. Rail cannons required a huge amount of energy as compared to chemically powered weaponry, were subject to massive stresses due to how human engineering created the magnetic field, and oft needed frequent maintenance and repair. All these factors required a larger crew and engineering capabilities and both Kefi and their assigned, and so far unnamed, liaison, were not engineers. ZZ3 extrapolated that the downgraded weapon had been tuned for efficiency, rather than raw power, but they still had little indication of how long it would operate.

The scan confirmed the Senti had either shielded the technology in use, or that the field it generated masked its capabilities. In all probability, deliberately both.

"I cannot analyse any element of what lays inside," stated the warbot.

"Yeah, no shit. Makes you wonder why we've never seen them in battle," replied Arin, now running his own hand over the weapon's outer casing. He looked at his hand afterwards, his gaze dubious.

"Maybe they have no predilection for battle. No biological driver to fight." ZZ3 shifted away from the Senti mound, stopping next to the metal javelins packed tightly against the weapon in a reloading jig. Twelve heavy alloy spears the length of the bot, weighing precisely twenty-one-point-five kilos each and ready to drop into the reload system. Twenty-four all told. Maybe that was the weapon's lifespan? Or the limit before its internal power unit required recharging or replacing.

'That would make sense. To hide their tech, a self-contained system with limited use.'

From evidence, the Senti appear to have predicted typical human behaviour. I suspect when they said it was tamper-proof, they meant it. No deviousness required. After discovering their ambassadorial ship was not lost in the black, but acquired by Countess Segfi, their trust will be diminished.

'Thirty seconds of watching Breaker battle memories would have achieved that. But watching and experiencing are different things. They almost named her war criminal without a war. Stated a distrust for the Court and Emperor.'

Agreed. The captain knows if we do not act as their proxies, the nest queen's next choice could be disastrous.

Arin had a set of tools unfurled, and now knelt next to the rail cannon, tongue licking at his lips as he contemplated.

"I would advise against any and all interference," said ZZ3. Arin looked up, his eyes slightly out of focus, tongue now running along his upper teeth.

"Yeah. One hundred percent. I was wondering about the decking plate, and the inner hull and outer hull shielding." He furled the tool belt back up. "Dricks," he said over comms. "You copy?"

"Here," stated the engineer.

"How's it looking?"

There was a pause, ZZ3 contemplating what the engineer would be doing right now. Perhaps running a hand over the back of her neck like she did. Or maybe over her scalp, pacing? Less of an option as she was beneath the *Sunstar* right now.

'Theory of mind.'

Sorry? Where has such a thought come from?

'You are beginning to put yourself in other's shoes. It is how human children develop. They begin to predict not just from extrapolation, but from knowing the person, or making predictions on the little they do know, about how they may act and more importantly, think.'

And?

'You continue to evolve, that is all.'

You are saying I am becoming more human?

'Would you want to?'

The queen's attempts to understand us *would indicate I am far from human. Her frustrations at not fully grasping what you are, came close to her choosing our eradication. Whether physically or by a system wipe. We survived because she sees your Senti pattern coding as a connection, a link she wishes to know more about.*

'And that we are a useful tool to return the queen's spawn, don't forget. If nothing else, she does understand the Butcher's nature from what we were able to share. And due to that, and my coding as you say, there is more to come. We are not free of her thoughts. Far from it.'

...

Eventually Hendricks replied. "I'm thinking the Senti know their way around the *Sunstar*, all human ships for that matter, way more than I would have guessed. Rad shielding is in place; plating seams sealed and appear far superior to the rest of the *Sunstar*. Can you send ZZ3 with a second slate and we'll run an additional check?"

"You're picking a warbot over me?"

"Just the best crew member for the job, *sub*-engineer."

Arin glared at ZZ3, who shuffled to the side then rose to its full height and strode towards the cargo bay door and the waiting Senti lift mechanism.

"That's right. Stay silent, *usurper*."

"The *Ungrit* could have made any number of navcom changes. We can't predict with any certainty where they are going," said Rebekah, the galley screen displaying the Almaarian system at distance. Savvo leant with his back against the wall, arms crossed, eyeing the screen briefly before glancing to the deck with a shake to his head.

"Go on," Rebekah said, placing her slate on the table. With the coffee flask in its usual place, she folded her hands into her lap. "Say what you've got to say."

"Dricks called it a needle in a haystack. A whole field of them, in a fucking hurricane. I can't see how we can do this." Savvo pushed himself away from the wall, collecting his steeped herbal tea before returning to his favoured position. "Can you?"

Rebekah didn't want to answer that. Ever since the Senti queen had given them their task, she had avoided the futility. What did she think they could do? Yes, she was right, no fucking way the Almaarian Court, and therefore the Navy, would accept the aliens turning up in a Senti battleship mid-system. It would be messy, and if ZZ3 and Asham were correct, a scary prospect should the Senti bring their full capabilities to bear. And after Segfi's emperor-sanctioned kidnap and subsequent dissection of the ambassadors, she doubted the Senti would hold back. This was to be their role, the go-betweens. To prevent the prospect of conflict. Humanity had enough issues right now.

"How the fuck do we end up in the middle of this?" said Rebekah. "If we fail, and the Senti decide enough is enough with what we've told them, a diplomatic incident might become a full-scale war. A brief one." She let out a long sigh, stopping herself by taking a drink. Another caffeine hit might muddle her thinking.

So not too much.

A beer on the other hand ...

"Because Rohan came calling for help ... and we know just how bad things could get. Walking away seemed like the best option, Rebekah. A new life," Savvo's eyes went distant for a moment, "but, fuck, we gonna keep getting dragged back in. The only way that doesn't happen is if we jump somewhere we can't get back from or ..."

"Woah. Damn. Hold that thought."

"Damn? You been around Davina too much?" he grinned, a welcome sight if she was honest.

"Shush. Jump. That's what he went for. The Butcher. He was looking for FTL and didn't get it. He took the queen's spawn, but why?" She pushed the slate away, shoving herself back into the seat, tempted to stretch but knowing she'd just click something out of place.

"I," started Savvo, but his eyes widened. "If it was us, humans, it would be for leverage or bait."

"Again, hold that thought. But what *didn't* we see there? Besides the spawn." Rebekah lifted the comms unit that sat on the bench beside her, sliding it on.

"I don't know what you're reaching for ..." contemplated Savvo, but as he took a sip and pushed away from the wall, realisation was dawning, his eyes widening and closing, nostrils flaring. "The symbs. We didn't see a single symbiote. You think he took them? That he found what he was looking for?"

"I don't know. But we're not leaving until we do." Rebekah squinted at her slate, running through her notes and file names. She set it up to scan through her suit's camera feed. Screwed up by the rad it might be, but if the symbiotes had been present, she had enough exemplars from their time with TB and his offspring for the search to be valid.

She selected the Senti channel, and their designated liaison. Kefi, or at least, what Kefi was now. That the alien had changed demeanour was in no doubt. How had he put it? In human terms, he was 'back in the nest'. She visualised it as a connected crew member, a level of freedom to use intuition, but under heavy guidance. A net, each knot a Senti interconnected to the queen. She didn't want to associate it with a spider and web, a hunter, but that thought remained intrusive. A warning.

"Yes, Captain Khan. Can I help?"

"I hope so."

Rebekah wondered if Kefi would be freer to talk once they were distant from the Senti nest ship. That the connection suffered at distance. It would explain the Senti on Benetai, as well as Scarva and his crew. Kefi waited in the usual place at the foot of the queen's dais, a tentacle tip against the alien's head.

"The queen ... does not wish to answer."

Surprise. Secrets. Try a different tack.

"Does she think the Butcher took any of the symbiotes?" she asked. "That won't give away any secrets."

Kefi quivered, the tentacle splitting at the tip, wrapping itself fully about his head. "The queen does not know. But she suspects not."

Time to push it.

"But I saw none of the symbiotes when we entered the orb, or in the palace." Rebekah left that hanging, not quite a question, in the hope of getting some form of answer.

Kefi shivered, Rebekah suspecting she was pushing things too far. She began to speak again when the Senti cut in. "They may have left when the self-destruct was declared."

Left? You mean they jumped? But where? And 'may', so they don't know. More fucking puzzles.

She glanced at Heki and Tremil, not brought along for support, but as a reminder of just how new this was to all of them. They were not only young, but their relationship with the symbiotes had only just begun. In some way, it was a display of how hopeless the task was they had been given. But the symbiote issue nagged at her. There was something in that.

"Is that all? You disturb my work for this? You should have left by now."

"To go where? There are an infinite number of places the Butcher could be with your spawn. How are we to find it?" She shrugged, spreading her arms outwards in the hope the queen would recognise the gesture. "How would you find it if you were to enter the Almaarian system?"

The whole room appeared to pause. The holo hovered but stopped in mid stream, screens and their oddly presented data frozen in time. Kefi seemed to spasm into a set position, tentacles still, no off-gas or quivers affecting his body. Even the flowing materials surrounding the dais hung limp.

A presence pressed into Rebekah's mind, weighing her down. The nest queen, her regard fully upon her before shifting over to the girls. A panic rose, churning her stomach. Were they under threat? No. The acceptance lay there underlying the queen's sheer will.

Kefi rocked forwards, the queen's tentacle pushing the Senti, a second and third tentacle appearing either side. Horrified, Rebekah watched as the Senti queen pulled the alien apart. Ripping free shoulder tentacles and letting them drop to the floor, soon joined by Kefi's lower limbs. Each splat sickened her, and she sidestepped in front of the girls, arms out as if to hide the grotesque vision. Rebekah felt Tremil's hand on her arm and knew she was watching, anyway. The chin tentacle was ripped free last, the goo she'd seen at the orb palace spraying out towards her. She flinched, but something in the room caught the Senti's inner fluid, pulling it down to the deck where it splattered at her feet before being drawn back towards the dais. Looking up, the main body that had once been Kefi had been torn asunder, gas and spores billowing into the air only to be caught and pulled back into the spreading mess. Finally, the head, the outer, rubbery skin ripped clean off, the hard shell beneath pitted like sea swept chalk.

Subsumed? Was that Kefi's word? Or was that merging into the nest?

Heki whimpered behind her, and she pulled the girl in close to her back, unable to draw her eyes away from the grotesque spectacle. She suspected Tremil may have had enough as she also pressed into her back. They had known the Senti, had even in some small part, come to like the alien. Yet it had been torn down, and as she watched, broken into its constituent parts. Only the white skull remained with a black electronic device attached, which the queen wielded above what had once been the Senti's flesh.

It didn't end there. The blue-eyed officer appeared, the female, silent, unobtrusive. The queen tore this silent Senti apart, repeating each act till naught but her skull remained. This she shattered, cracking it open. Rebekah watched fascinated as the grotesque spectacle revealed the honeycomb structure of the bone before the brain slid into the pool.

The Orb Queen's remaining limbs dipped into the goo, spinning, intertwining, building step by step a form that solidified. Almost like she was 3D printing.

Is that?

A new Senti hovered above the deck, limbs snaking into the lattice, black eyes peering Rebekah's way. "Captain," said the voice. Still distinct. Still

Kefi to her mind. What had been grown, knitted together, had changed, however. The chin tentacle gone, the build up around the skull a little wider, and the skin tone brighter. Fresh. And larger. "I have been sublimated and reconstituted. I will now be able to help find the Orb Queen's spawn." The new Kefi turned about, holding out a shoulder tentacle to touch the queen's own. Her symbiote pulled itself along, apparently reluctant, to land upon this new Kefi and settle against its skull.

Did I cause that?

"We will be your guide."

Fuck. How weird is my life?

CHAPTER 19

KARAL

Davina swiped her work slate, Mr Duboit's, not the silent Erikson's that had seen no activity in weeks, perhaps months. If she didn't think about it, perhaps it would never happen again. An imperial pardon now sat proudly in her grasp, signed, sealed and unequivocal. However, she remained an Incini, and would do so until her debts to the Directorate were paid and beyond that if she wished to retain the status and potential wealth the trusted role could bring. Of course she may well now be tainted. Not only by her involvement with the Emperor's Enforcers, but also by her spat with Countess Segfi, and the eyes and ears of the Minister's hand.

Spat. Yes, just a minor skirmish with one of the most powerful members of the Court. Did I really define terms for a countess, and win?

The slate brought up her day's work schedule, however most of that was about to be shifted as she eyed the flag on a long-awaited message. She pulled it up and her wetware interpreted the encryption she'd added to the survey moniker on instruction from her employer. Duboit was keen to keep the asteroid's assessment secret. He smelled creds, lots of them, and as much as he loved playing the long game, the risk of losing YR3 to Karal, never mind a competitor within the nobility, was galling.

The analysis data streamed in, the auto survey ship's data thorough and detailed. Davina had learned much about the composition of the field's asteroids over the past few years. Not an expert, she paid for those, but enough to know when something had profit potential. Only Mr Duboit, or Baron Stimpson as he truly was under the pseudonym, had spotted something in this asteroid she couldn't fathom based on research ongoing in weapons tech. At least, that's what he informed her. The new analysis confirmed in greater detail what the years old survey had identified. Some PMG content, particularly nickel, as well as a higher concentration of copper and lead, with just a trace of rhodium. Minor, but it could be that. Rhodium was so hard to detect and increasingly valuable. Davina checked back to the previous study. There were markers there, but no definitive search had been done on the rhodium aspect. The new assessment heavily suggested potential interference from the presence of copper and lead in the analysis.

Got to be it.

She sent the data stream via a priority packet. Mr Duboit had lost his Senti comms unit to Erikson, and failed to secure another. Rumour was the emperor had recently declared they be surrendered for use by the inner Court. Davina suspected the Butcher's emergence was the true reason, and with the ANS *Segfi* roaming the system, were in use by the navy in an attempt to prevent the AI from uploading into any more ships. She shuddered. Recalling the twins on their release, the *Segfi*'s crew disgorged into the black, and Rebekah's recording of the Butcher's rant when he discovered they had folded space to escape.

She eased back into her chair, rolling her neck as she kneaded her own shoulders. The fading scar on her arm caught her eye, the slash where

Rebekah had so nearly taken her down after she prevented the ex-Breaker from taking her own life.

"So many moments, all filled with pain." A laugh slipped out.

But I felt alive.

The slate flashed, her message sent. It would be hours before the Baron received the message, and instructions would take just as long on the return journey. She keyed up a name, a picture of Jenkra Tew appearing. The widow executive of Karal Mining that she'd had most contact with since her return. Astute and apparently unbribable.

Apparently. Just got to know their weaknesses.

She made the call.

Jenkra eased back into the high-backed chair, enjoying the sumptuous feel of the brushed leather. In her hand was an expensive glass of whisky, with a splash of water to enhance the earthy peatiness she obviously savoured. A sip, and her face lit even more.

Davina smiled.

Information is power.

There was a gentle warmth about the exclusive backroom of the Level 6 lounge. Here they were alone, two chairs placed before a pseudo fire that occasionally crackled and sparked like the real thing, the holo currently displaying old castle walls covered in heraldry Davina could neither name nor cared for. A throwback to the past, pre-colonisation, that only existed in museums, libraries and fairy tales. And one Jenkra Tew longed for. Amazing what you can find out if you dig deep enough, with the promise of an Incini's tenets to keep the whispers of betrayal quiet. And the creds, of course.

Jenkra sighed, clearly letting the amber liquid play across her tongue as she eyed Davina over the rim of the special glass the Incini had presented as a gift. The contents were as equally exclusive as any out on the 'field, and the bottle sat at the table beside the executive.

"This could very well work, Miss Connors. Rare is the time when I can just ... relax." She drew out the last word, as if savouring it as much as the rare whisky. "But of course, that was your plan. How easily I fall into such traps." She hid her smile; the tease amid her words deliberate. A player of games.

Davina tilted her head, taking a sip of the foul liquid and setting her wetware to adjust her taste response. A sweetness to enshroud the smokiness she abhorred. "Oh, this isn't the trap. This is simply a hint of the trap. The breadcrumb trail to tempt you in."

"Do tell." Jenkra found a spot where she could lay back in the chair a little further, one leg gently laid over the other, a shoe hanging half off her foot.

"You've come to a decision about Mr Duboit's proposal. About the suggested move to a new area of the field."

"We have. Or, at least, we have a plan of action that requires a little shaping." Jenkra raised her glass, obviously enjoying the aroma but not taking a drink. "We are formulating a proposal in response to Mr Duboit's offer of support. I hope you're not trying to influence my input, Miss Connors."

"Of course I am. Why else would we be here?" Davina eyed the woman, the narrowing of her eyes, the tilt of her head. Astute, a lover of the powerplay. But she had more than one chink in her armour.

The executive finally took a sip, head rolling back, a sigh slipping from her lips. "True. How is this to go? Proposal, counteroffer, attempted bribe, my refusal, bribe increases, I appear surprised then take the creds and run? I think you are above all that. Mr Duboit, or whoever he is, perhaps not."

She placed the glass gently down, lifting the bottle, reading the label as her tongue touched her bottom lip. "I would rather spend time with the whisky, than run through such a tiresome charade." She put the bottle down. "Wouldn't you?"

Davina placed her own glass down, glad to put distance between it and her tongue. "I have a combined offer. Mr Duboit will help finance the move, in return for two things. Mining rights on an as yet to be specified sub-field of the new section." Jenkra made to speak, but a glance from Davina changed her mind. "Not the main claim. Mr Duboit understands that, and he would, of course, receive a percentage from such activity anyway under the terms. No, he wants to own a section. Possess." Davina raised her eyebrows, letting a lop-sided smile appear. "As anyone seeking further status in the Court would."

"Ah," replied Jenkra. "Status. A power denied those with just money. I see. I am sure you don't need my help to secure such a request."

"Mr Duboit wants certainty, and he understands there is another member of the Court who has their eyes on Karal. Acquiring what he wants specifically would be a slap in their face he would most relish." Davina leant forwards, allowing an eagerness to play across her face. "And reward."

"Certainty? And what is the offer that I will of course turn down?"

"You're in it," said Davina, her hands gesturing towards the stone walls, the fire. The stone faded away, the holo picture embracing a lake, rolling grass, a herd of sheep. Mountains rose in the background. Jenkra's eyes were wide, and the lid of Davina's trap snapped shut.

Davina dropped into her office chair, the overly sweet taste upon her tongue now more annoying than the actual whisky itself. She took a sip of water, washing it away, before recording a note of Jenkra Tew's agreement to send off to the baron. In a way, the woman's capitulation had felt too easy, disappointing Davina. An easy victory was harder to savour, though she had clearly devised the perfect bribe to accomplish it. But weak, and she feared for the woman's future should the baron discover it. He couldn't roll back his offer, as she, as his Incini, had made it. But he would snipe and push, see her as easy prey. No. Davina didn't want that, so she had added the second offer she had up her sleeve to the contract. The improved working conditions for the asteroid miners and repair teams, specifically the safety procedures around suit servicing and replacement. Something a widow who had lost her husband in such an accident with another company would want but had never managed to push through.

Rebekah would be proud. Championing the underdog and all that.

A slate flashed.

"Damn." Reluctantly, she reached over, her fingers tapping at the table twice. Odd, involuntary, the signal Rebekah and her crew used as a warning when something was wrong. She lifted Erikson's slate and swiped.

"Damn," she repeated. It wasn't Erikson on screen. Too much smoke and bitterness in the smile. "Countess," she said, "an honour."

"Not quite the way you treated me beforehand, Miss Connors. I would say it was less honour, and more backstabbing." The countess took a long drag of her cigarette stick, but her eyes never left Davina's. Senti comms.

"My initial contract was never with you, and … *Duboit* reneged on much of it. I am sure that was at your behest, Countess. And any later agreements we made seemed paper thin, rather than Incini ironclad."

"You know Connors, you should work for me. You have balls, girl. I kept to all my contractual agreements, reluctant, coerced, or not."

There was a hint of a smile there, setting a chill along Davina's spine.

"Tenets under the bridge," the countess continued. "I have a role for you. A small one, but necessary. You know of the Butcher, and that we are busy hunting him down. Since then, we have lost contact with the Senti

Transport Orb at the edge of the system. I do not have spare ships or time to find out why." Segfi appeared distracted by someone offscreen, waving them away before turning back to Davina. "I have sent Erikson on his way to be my eyes and ears on Karal. But I don't have the time to wait. I want ..."

"They're not here," Davina cut in. "The *Sunstar*, Rebekah. They left."

And I'm not telling you where.

Segfi didn't seem surprised. Or she was just used to hiding disappointment. "No surprise when we should all be pitching in."

If I remember right, it's why you're still alive.

She didn't say that, despite the temptation. But Karal offered an alternative that might rile the noble less. "I can commission an autoship. Fast and reliable."

"Yes. Yes, that would help. I will record a message. Connors," she continued, her eyes flashing, smoke billowing, "when Khan returns, I need to know. Understand. Not a secret, no hidden agenda. The Butcher is active and ... that ship might just make the difference."

You mean what it can do. Except, you don't know how it does it.

"If they return, I'll let them know."

"You do that. I'll send a message to Stimpson about commissioning the autoship. I need this ASAP, Connors."

The countess signed off, leaving Davina staring at a blank screen. With a shake to her head, she cast it aside and gathered her own slate. She clicked and waited.

"This is Trent Pike's PA, Helena. How may I help Miss Connors?"

Davina eyed the woman. Trent Pike would normally take her call without hesitation, especially with the potential investment from Duboit in the offing. The only time he hadn't had been when entertaining a couple of irate houseguests courtesy of Rebekah. A countess and hand of the Minister. But things were changing, apparently.

"I need to speak to Trent on a matter of urgency," she said, deciding against expanding.

"Mr Pike will be in a meeting for another ... mmm ... hour. I can get him to call back." PAs, a standard barrier between management and the world of stress wanting their attention. In this case a whole station full.

"That depends. You'll have a list in front of you of permissions you may give should he be busy. Is there anything on there that says do whatever Mr Duboit asks for short of blowing up the station?"

That received the slightest of smiles. "Not quite that level, but not far off. What can I do for you, Miss Connors?"

"I need a fast autoship ASAP."

CHAPTER 20

TWEEM SHIPYARD

"We have Tweem hailing, Captain," Ensign Markov stated, glancing up at the image of the shipyard playing across the main screen.

"Deal with it, Markov. Broadcast the transponder link and if they offer us berths in 34/C tell them how deep to shove their waiting list. We're in a rush, and we're not taking no for an answer. Rodri, bring us in. XO, you have the bridge." Captain Srenik pushed himself up from the command chair, and after a nod to King, aimed for the bridge exit and a long overdue inspection. He wasn't sure why, but he'd avoided the recreation deck on the journey to Tweem. As an XO back during the Bustan war, he'd lost crew under his command, but it had never felt quite the same. There, *his* captain bore the responsibility, Srenik just using *her* voice and orders as a barrier. Helping distance his own emotions from the reality of losing comrades-in-arms. When it was your ship, your crew, it was personal. Eleven of his had been killed when the hull was penetrated by the *Bonray*'s PDC rounds. Chases were difficult, those being pursued at an advantage as their weaponry deployed faster and, considering they were using Almaarian rounds, galling.

Eleven, however, was a small number, and in the past war regarded as insignificant by the countess. But it was still his loss to own. The lift doors slid open, and his magboots clamped to the deck. The first room, the foyer, was a hubbub of repair crew who were packing up their kit, clearing the way for the work teams from Tweem who'd need access to both the inner breach and the hull. They had plugged and patched. Not war worthy repairs on the run like the old days. No, just enough to get them back to the shipyard for a full hull inspection. The countess wanted them out and fully prepared for what was to come.

He walked on through, entering the first of three bar lounges. This one adjacent to the upper gym, where those desperate to talk to someone other than their assigned work team frequented. Beyond that, and to the left, were the staff quarters. The night shift. Each one killed when the metal slugs tore through the upper hull and exposed them and their gel mattresses to the void. Despite their lowly status, as much a part of the crew as everyone else. Essential staff even at the lowest rung aboard a navy ship. He took a moment to stare into each, saluting the rooms in turn, glancing down at the roster and checking over salient details.

Once done, he switched on his comms and played back the eulogy he'd prepared, the context of each room enabling him to add a little more poignancy to the prose. Once satisfied, he re-entered the lift and punched in his next destination. Ten minutes later, following a walk through the damage to the lowest deck, or the orlop as it used to be called when ships sailed the seas rather than the stars, he entered the smaller hold used for personnel disembarkment. Here waited a good thirty or so of the crew. Friends, lovers perhaps, all here to say goodbye to the collateral damage caused by the Butcher. More than the crew of the ANS *Bonray* or *Segfi* ever got, and that's why this moment meant so much to him. He had lost friends and colleagues to an enemy he could not imagine. A mainframe, a set of uncaring code that treated humanity as mere meat to be culled.

Captain Srenik paused before each coffin, placing a hand and naming the crewmember within. His eulogy left their friends in tears, and as the *Righteous* slowed to a halt, multiple clamps engaging, he bade the dead farewell. In a war footing, they would have been embraced by the black. Their bodies adding to the debris between the stars. But after they had witnessed the callous execution of the *Bonray*'s crew, he refused, instead returning them to Tweem with the hope of reuniting the fallen with their families for one last time.

Srenik watched as Executive Officer King ran her eye over the work schedule. The initial analysis of her repair teams had been annotated by the Tweem crews, their assessment receiving quiet praise by the sheer lack of changes suggested. It brought a small smile of satisfaction to her face, which the captain enjoyed. These small wins added to your reputation, the level of trust a crew would place in you, the respect accorded when you made your demands for resources or time in dock further down the line. He'd made sure her name sat beneath his on each of those reports. Whoever read them would know who had really done the work, and filed that away.

"Good job. Now skedaddle off this ship, take bridge crew alpha and get some R'n'R on Tweem. Not the most salubrious of locations, but there's godsdamned liquor and a half decent restaurant or two if you know where to look." He smiled as he spoke, the words a running joke between them. Food was his joy, booze a damnation he no longer partook. Too many nights he couldn't remember, and rough mornings he wished he could forget.

Maria King saluted, half-a-smile on her face. "Yes sir, Captain sir."

"Yeah, yeah. When this mission is done, Maria, it'll be time to seek your own commission. You know that, don't you? I'm sure you'll have had enough of me by then. Now get going before Rodri and Markov start bickering again." He turned away, eyes roaming over the disembarkment hold where only a few hours before he'd said goodbye to eleven of his crew.

"You'll be okay? This seems to have hit you hard," she replied.

He shook his head. "Not my crew, though their loss hurts. No," he turned back to face her, "but the *Bonray*? The *Segfi*, what we saw at Daphene? That hits hard. And there's going to be more against an enemy who's only just getting started. Enjoy yourself, I don't think we'll be docking again until this new war is won."

A little shock played across her lips, eyes widening a second before a small nod of acknowledgement. She had understood, and that her role for the next week would be to ensure the crew did too. Be his voice about the ship. She saluted, and he returned it, then gripped her shoulder before gently shoving her towards the door.

Once she left, he drew up his slate and activated comms. "We all good, Snow?" he asked.

"That you, Srenik? Thought you'd be getting some down time," the old oversight engineer responded. "But no, we're not all good."

He let out a sigh. She loved a drama, always had, but was the most reliable project manager on Tweem and the reason he'd not wanted 34/C as she refused to work that docking area after some accident he couldn't recall. "Go on."

"No. Suit up, Srenik. You need eyes on. Was going to ask that XO of yours, Queenie?"

"King."

"Yeah, that one. Wanted her to come and look. But as you're available, you can suck some suit air for a change. Do you good to stretch them stringy officer legs." His slate pinged, a location below the stern flagged for his attention.

"Be ten minutes," he said, hopefully. "This had better be urgent, Snow. Not one of your senior moments. All drama and no filling to justify it. Srenik out." He stomped into the holding area, wrist swiping over a locker door which cracked open. Despite Yena Snow being correct about 'officer legs' he was soon suited up, memories of the days he commanded away teams and shuttle runs led his fingers in the ritualistic dance across seals and safety sequences. One breath, and the helmet activated, an eye-click here and there, and he was in the green. He walked out onto the dock, the clang of magboot landing on metal reverberating through his legs until he reached the appropriate scaffold point. Lifeline hooked on, the secondary line prepped, he clambered up and along to the designated attachment point of the *Righteous'* hull. He would have expected autobots to be scurrying about, checking every square centimetre for micro cracks and pits in the armour. The area was clear, though there were signs of their passing in the sheen of the clean trails they left behind.

"Snow?" Srenik said as he tentatively clamped to the hull. As his second magboot attached, the engineer responded.

"About ten metres south of the flag in your HUD," came the reply.

Srenik eyed the angle, mind orientating, and he began the descent, allowing his HUD to adjust the view as it responded to his vitals. He was okay with space walks, no expert, but he'd done enough to be able to function with the suit's support. It's what Snow had meant by 'officer legs', challenging him to face the weirdness of no longer having an 'up' to focus on after years in a command chair. As he walked over the curve of the ship's stern, he came to a strange patch of plating covered in what appeared to be unusual, raised bumps of metal that matched almost seamlessly the hull plating. Snow wasn't gazing at those, but out into the black, away from the scaffold.

"I have lost two repair bots," she said, finally glancing over, her HUD and his syncing so he had an image of her face. She looked tired, wisps of grey hair plastered to her forehead and cheeks. A hand waved out into the void. "Out there. Malfunctioned when they reached this point. Can't even show you a visual of what happened, all the feeds scrambled into an unholy mess."

Srenik blinked, eyeing his HUD, a haze appearing in the image at the base of the visor. He glanced down, towards the nearest bump and the haze blurred his central view. Another step closer, and the blur widened.

"What in all the hells?" he stated, and wafted a gloved hand in front of his visor.

"Yeah, I tried that. Works just fine. Any idea what this shit is?" she gestured towards the bumps. With that, Yena Snow drew out one of the most tech'd out slates Srenik had ever seen. It hovered in front of her, yoked upon a gimbal, and she began to move mods from slot to slot, her gloves working across the screen. "I can't get any sensor readings other than those that are an exact match for the surrounding hull. Too exact, if you know what I mean. You move three metres to the right, and you get the variance you would expect." She let out a heavy sigh. "Check the logs or whatever you do."

"I don't ..." but he did. He did know, recalling the simulated patter of debris that clattered against the hull. The *Bonray*'s death rattle. Then his comms screamed, the deafening hiss doubling him over as he instinctively slammed his hands against his helmet.

"*Rescue me?*" reverberated through his skull. The thrum of a voice he had last heard over Bustan 8 "*It is humanity that will need saving.*"

General Asham.

"Snow," he drawled, but the engineer had already dropped to the hull, her gloves attaching to the plate as she activated whatever safety switch the shipyard had installed in her suit. Around her the hull appeared to reform, plates breaking off into shards. But it was the visor's interpretation, one Srenik didn't trust. In his mind, he already knew what was happening. He dropped, mirroring Snow though he had to eye-click through menus to request his gloves adhere to the hull. With the channel of his comms compromised, he hit the emergency feed, only to be greeted by the roar of interference.

"Godsdammit," he shouted, then activated his emergency beacon. An all-channel call for help. Someone on Tweem would pick it up, know something was wrong, though not what. He raised his head, and the visor finally cleared. Where the blur had been, now hovered a tiny ship. Barely the size of two men laid together, and four more flew in from the sides, their shells gleaming with the same armoured plate as the hull. Of course, the *Bonray*'s hull would match theirs. The bastard AI had cannibalised the frigate and created more of his drones. He waited for death, but that was not their intent. Small engines flared, and all five buzzed deeper into Tweem's array of scaffolding, underslung guns blazing as they ripped into the shipyard. Sickened, movement to his left brought him up short. More of the drones reflected the brief light of exploding generators and work rooms. He had brought a machine devil into the fold, and its demons were intent on doing maximum damage.

"Srenik. Come back. Your EB has activated. Srenik, what's happening?" echoed over his comms.

"War has come," he said. "And we're not ready."

CHAPTER 21

APPROACHING KARAL

Rebekah cracked a thumb, mind still unable to come to terms with how the girls, and the symbiotes, took them from one place to another. What made it worse, was the large Senti who had stood stock still throughout the process glaring at the navcom monitor screen and steadfastly refused to move until the 'jump' was complete. Looming wasn't quite the word.

Seething. Can a Senti seethe? Maybe they learned from memories of the Bustan after Asham had his way with the planet.

Karal appeared before them, four asteroids synced in perpetual motion about each other, and up to a month or so ago, a second home after the *Sunstar* itself. She had hoped it'd be a few more months before their return, time enough for Nicky to decide her future, and for the fallout from the circumstances around their pardon to settle. Not that the countess had 'forgive' or 'forget' in her lexicon.

"Kefi. Please. A little space." Savvo glanced over his shoulder at the Senti, a plea in his tone but his eyes betrayed anger. The alien, despite being broken down into constituent parts and reformed into what Rebekah assumed was a female Senti, had initially carried on as before, much like Kefi. More relaxed about the humans, and accepting of Heki and Tremil's ability to mimic Senti FLT. However, two aliens had been reconstituted and though the bodies were melded, Rebekah feared the minds were not. At least not yet. This Senti had two personalities, the second evident at this point. As if a switch drained her acceptance of humanity, while rigidity and disdain bubbled to the surface.

Rebekah had thought nothing would surprise her after the queen's wander through her mind, exploring the nooks and crannies, including the girls and their connection with the symbiotes. Certainly not the sharing of memories and experiences between Kefi and the queen. After all, the Senti revelled in human memories and dreams to the point of addiction. But the sublimation of two Senti, and the creation of a third from both had shaken her. The fact they were at times at war with each other just about topped it.

The Senti shuffled, eyes dropping to take in Savvo, before eventually backing off a little. Not a victory, more an admittance that they had seen all they needed.

"We're sticking with Kefi?" asked Rebekah.

"We are," replied the Senti, the words replete from any emotion at all. The off-gas was a hint, however.

"It's what we're all used to." He peered over at the receding Senti who had headed into the galley. "Got to call you something," he called after her. With a shrug he turned back to his captain. "Better than what Arin suggested, and waaaay better than Dricks' line of swear words."

Rebekah let a smile slip. True. Hendricks wasn't enamoured with the new version of their guest. "See us in. I'll check on Hek and Trem." She stood, eased her back a little, then clomped through the galley. There was no sign of Kefi, she assumed the Senti must have sought its – her – adapted cabin provided for the duration of the search. Rebekah hadn't inspected the changes out of respect, but curiosity would get to her eventually. Apparently, the new Kefi had crafted her own mini food processing area. She hesitated to call it a kitchen, as any use of that word did not involve 'mould' in any form. Rebekah made herself a coffee, grasping the flask and two biscuits before heading down the corridor.

A knock, and she entered Heki's cabin, the girls sat on the bed, their symbiotes writhing along their arms. Opposite stood Kefi, her gifted symbiote less playful but intent on the girls as its tentacles waved their way.

Not in her cabin then.

Kefi had insisted on being involved with the twins by order of the ship's nest queen. A fact-finding mission she'd called it. Wanting to know more about their connection, one Rebekah had only allowed when Heki explained once again the queen's acceptance of their bond. Rebekah's view was the relationship should be two-way. That Kefi needed to share as much information in return, which must be the reason she was here now. She hoped the twins had activated the silent alarm Arin had fitted, and that he was listening in on the girls' HT comms channel.

"Well?" she said, using the biscuits as an excuse to manoeuvre herself between the Senti and the twins. "Anything unusual or of concern?"

Kefi's shoulder tentacles sagged a little, and the symbiote wandered up to settle into the hollow at the base of her skull. The Senti turned a little, a shiver running through the alien's gasbags until an off-gas filled the room with a cabbage-like scent. "Unusual? Having two human guides already fulfils such a category. You need to be more specific, Captain." This was the Kefi she remembered, not the one from the cockpit just now.

She crossed her arms. "Anything I should be concerned about. When you do something new, you don't always see the dangers. They can creep up on you."

Kefi paused, another, smaller, off-gas accompanied the first. "I understand. If it reassures, Heki and Tremil are inexperienced, but they are simply the navigators. The (*scraping of toast*), or symbiotes as you call them, are the ... I have no word – engine, perhaps? They have vast experience despite their diminutive size."

"Vast?"

The alien's slitted mouth opened slightly, and her symbiote adjusted position. "Vast. They are the progeny of an aged *symbiote* once bonded to a Senti ambassador."

The Senti didn't explain any further, either keeping more explanations to the bare minimum, or assuming Rebekah already understood. And she thought she did. The way they spoke of the spawn, the regrowth of Kefi, the Senti's joy and addiction to human memories. They were a race that curated and retained their memories like a log, treasuring and passing down knowledge not only by recorded data or a book, but by somehow gifting them on. More than racial memory, somehow recalling the real experiences, which she suspected were more detailed than those a human remembered. Or, after considering just how much storage that would require, what was essential for their role. The symbs played a huge part in this somehow, a conduit perhaps. And now the girls were linked to TB's progeny with all its memories.

"So nothing to be concerned about?"

Kefi didn't answer straight away. The silence filled with the bubble of gas inside the alien's torso. "For you, no."

But for the Senti, very likely.

If Heki and Tremil were anomalies, his race would continue to thrive off their ability to fold space. If not, and the Butcher, or Countess Segfi got their way, their future could be very different.

Is that the real worry? Do the Senti become vulnerable? Their massive strategic advantage lost. Fear suddenly present in their society because at any time an enemy can appear from anywhere. The same dread we felt when the Bustan Navy arrived, or they did when Segfi led the invasion of Bustan in return.

Fuck. Deeper shit than I first considered. Would they kill to protect that?

She eyed Kefi.

Probably not. But far from definite, and not certain enough for me to ignore.

She nodded. "Okay. We're nearing Karal. Very few in the facility will have met a Senti, never mind one as belligerent as you can be." Kefi appeared to contemplate her words, pausing, tentacles rifling at her shoulders. "I understand that word. Yes. Belligerent. One I could assign to you. And Dricks."

Rebekah couldn't help but smile. The reply typical of the original Kefi.

"True," said Tremil, a sliver of a smile on her face. "There are other words too," she added, her look filled with mischief.

"And the pair of you learned them from the best of us," replied Rebekah. "Now come with me. I've got something to ask ZZ3 and Arin, and I need you both. Please excuse us, Kefi." She stood aside, letting both girls pass and, on second thoughts, waited for the alien to leave the girls' cabin. She had no idea of the Senti's concept of personal space, though the makeup of their ships hinted it was something their races shared.

On reaching the engineering hold, she could hear the printer hammering away, and the odd mutter between Hendricks and Arin. On entry, the girls were already with ZZ3, examining whatever circuit board the bot had been testing. They were still working on the sensory ghost they wanted to create for the ship, while Arin worked on their remodelling of the less powerful probe version that had been so useful against Daphene's defences.

"Well?" asked Tremil, turning to Rebekah as Arin sauntered over, wiping his hands clean of the printer residue where he'd been tuning the machine. "This about Kefi?"

And I'm the belligerent one?

"In a way." She went on to explain her theory about the Senti and the threat the girls posed to their stranglehold on FTL and their security.

Heki and Tremil listened intently, glancing towards each other while Arin nodded along, his countenance serious for a change. Rebekah knew Hendricks was listening in when she paused over whatever repair she was engaged in. Her response would likely be negative, whatever.

"I'd like to set a watch," she raised her hand as Heki made to dive in, lips trembling as she was cut off. Tremil, surprisingly, was the one to nod along. "Not cameras. ZZ3."

Heki visibly relaxed. Tremil nodded, then wrapped an arm about the warbot's. It was Heki that spoke. "Yes. Yes. I understand, but Kefi isn't a threat."

"Even I'd agree on the old Kefi," cut in Hendricks. She put down the micro wrench and crossed her arms. "But we don't know this new one. You were the ones to tell me what the Nest Queen did. Like, printed Kefi from his, her, whatever's, own—"

"—goo," said Tremil.

"Yeah. With added spices, another Senti and a pinch of salt. Could have added a little of herself in there for all we know." Arin's lips scrunched to the side, a glance to Hendricks showing they'd obviously been discussing it already. "A Senti raspberry ripple."

"That image is going to sit in my mind forever. So we agree, and none of us can fully trust Kefi yet." Everyone murmured agreement, including the girls.

"Set my parameters," said ZZ3, eyes flashing blue with a red tinge at the edge, "so I can put the protocols into place."

Tremil made to speak, but a glare from Rebekah shut her down, a surly flick of the eyes to the ceiling soon followed. She understood, she really did. "We'll discuss those together. But once set, this is about protecting crew, ZZ3. So we don't let our two ingrates tamper with them. Understood?"

"Ingrates?" said Heki, contrite. Hendricks turned away, a blush forming. Heki's face changed almost immediately. "One of your words?"

"It's appropriate," said Tremil, taking Heki by the hand, leading her away. "When even an alien can see we're part of such a *belligerent* family."

"Tell me why I'm doing this again?"

"Because, Trent Pike, or whoever the hell you are, you wouldn't want me traipsing across your precious Minx asteroid family trailing my new guest behind. Remember what happened last time I surprised you?" Rebekah cycled the outer airlock, Pike at her side in his special issue, ultra polished Karal management spacesuit. It had probably not been worn except for a test run. To give Trent his due, he didn't seem unfamiliar with the kit. Another hint, perhaps, to his previous life.

"What is it this time? The Emperor himself, perhaps? Or the Minister, bored with just dumping his agent in my lap?" His tone varied between painful and strained. It would soon alter to plain stressed.

The airlock cycled, and they entered the *Sunstar*.

"What the fuck?" said Trent, his helmet still on, a Senti eyeing him from the other side of the corridor, one just as unhappy as he was despite extending a tentacle in a small wave. Rebekah wondered how much that was gleaned from being around Rohan.

"Yeah. WTF. You should have had my life for the past month. Meet Kefi."

"Err, ahh." Pike gathered himself, detaching his helmet and placing it under his arm. "Err, welcome to Karal. I'm Trent Pike, Chief of Operations."

"Smooth," piped up Arin from behind the Senti. "Impressive diplomacy, Pike."

"Chief," stated Kefi, shoulder tentacles waving towards Pike. "Like a queen, controlling the minutiae of mining."

"Err." Rebekah prodded Pike. "Well, I'm in charge if that's what you mean."

Kefi stiffened then off-gassed. A sign Rebekah now took as the personality switch. "I was once (*a rock falling off a cliff*). The humans on board now call me Kefi, which is acceptable. My Nest Queen has assigned me to this human ship, and to be her voice should we meet anyone of *standing*."

Arin guffawed, a glare from Rebekah cutting him short and the sub-engineer wheeled away, back towards engineering, his shoulders betraying his attempts not to laugh.

"Well, pleased to meet you." Trent seemed to grow a little, as he had all those months ago when he'd explained his hidden role as a smuggler to Rebekah. Had he seen an opportunity? "And on your return, I would ask that you pass on my greetings in response."

Yep.

CHAPTER 22

KARAL

"Thank you," stated Kefi and Trent stood aside, letting the alien by. The Senti's silver suit attached to the transport's deck, tentacle tips splayed wide and pressing against the shuttle's inner hull to steady the alien as the small transport gently accelerated away from M4 docks. Pike had organised a dockside drill to ensure human eyes remained unaware of the Senti's presence. He had expressed his certainty to Rebekah that keeping things quiet was for the best. There were enough strange rumours flying about with the talk of a rogue Almaarian Navy ship filling the bars and communal lounges of the various Karal complexes.

"I will speak for us for now," continued Kefi.

"Sorry? Us?" said Pike, sitting in one of the executive shuttle's seats, fingers pulling at the tuft on his chin. Rebekah eyed him from across the aisle. Since he'd got over his shock, Pike had a calculating look in his eyes. One she remembered from their confrontation when he had revealed his hidden role. She hadn't been sure why she had chosen to reveal the Senti to him immediately, but maybe knowing the alien was on board would cut through all the bullshit that was bound to be his first response if she came calling for help later. Was this trust?

Perhaps it was.

They needed a focal point for their search, and Karal made most sense initially. Kefi had been 'programmed' – her chosen word – to pick up the spawn queen's presence. Her call. But the distances weren't huge, from what the Senti had said. Much like the nest queen's communication aboard the Senti ship, it was miniscule when you considered the vastness of a planetary system. No, they needed a hub where rumours flew and snippets of information might come to light, and a contact point with ... Segfi.

Oh-fucking-joy.

She tuned back in, Kefi continuing her conversation with Pike. "See it as a learning curve. I am used to humans, so carry the memory of how to interact." Rebekah smiled as Trent raised an eyebrow at Kefi's statement. There was so much that was going to be new to him. "But I share the memory of another who has not had such direct experience. However, this first meeting has been a spur to the melding. To acceptance. It will help." The monotone curtailed a little, a seagull's squawk piercing the alien's translator. "At least, I hope it will. Some of the things I've seen humans do may come as a shock."

Rebekah mouthed 'laughing' to Pike when he glanced her way, a shrugged response making her smile widen. The shuttle slowed and, with a blast of manoeuvring jets, matched the spin of M1 and the Karal offices, sliding in next to the executive disembarkment point. A concertinaed tunnel unfolded from the airlock, extending outwards to attach smoothly to the transport. Trent Pike had unbuckled already, and led the way to the airlock, cycling it through and making his excuses before exiting first. He was clearing the way, checking that his call ahead had been adhered to.

By the time they were sat, or in the Senti's case, attached to the deck in Pike's meeting room, a serious, almost ominous atmosphere had formed amid the group, including Savvo. Rebekah had wanted to have the meeting on M1, Trent unhappy at the possible exposure of the Senti's presence to the already on-edge facility. But this was too big to contain, and she needed something he had.

Credibility. And secure comms.

Shit could be faked, especially by the Butcher, and Pike was not only chief ops but had met with the countess and the Minister's hand directly.

"Your dampener," she said to Pike who nodded in return, and rummaged in his desk. Rebekah looked at Savvo. "This might hurt. Trent has a special gizmo for stopping our wetware from recording."

"Really?" replied her second, the ensuing wince, and her own rising headache indicated Trent had activated the device. It cleared after a few seconds, Savvo's pained expression also relaxing.

"Interesting," stated Kefi, her tentacles cracking open her suit's helmet, and placing it at her side. The grav weighed heavy on the Senti's features, causing the rubber skin about her neck and eyes to sag, exposing a red rim below the black. Kefi remained passive. "I can sense the frequency. Effective."

Trent brushed his beard again, before letting his hands settle on his desk next to the dampener. "So why are you here, Kefi, if I may ask? Why Karal, and not Almaar itself?"

"We are in the hands of Captain Khan. This was her suggestion."

"Oh, it would be, wouldn't it?" he glowered at Rebekah.

"No need to get angsty. I propose we contact Countess Segfi, make her aware of our presence. You know the story, Trent. No one else does." She went on to explain about Rohan's arrival at Benetai, the attack on Scarva's ship and the subsequent assault on the Senti Orb. She let Kefi explain events there. Trent had been aboard one, she was sure, the horror displayed in his eyes at the self-destruction wrought by the orb's queen. The sheer magnitude of destruction that Rebekah still couldn't come to terms with.

"Why?" asked Trent, his hands splayed wide as he sought an answer.

"To prevent disaster," stated Kefi, another variant on their standard answer. They weren't going to explain, why should they? It was such an alien act, it was hard for a human mind to comprehend, she supposed. Segfi might understand, many of the officer-nobles had sacrificed their own soldiers in the name of honour or victory. But never themselves.

"And that worked? You said he took something." Trent had said out loud what she'd been thinking all along. But then, they'd been under the complete power of the Senti nest queen.

"That is why we are here. But the act was necessary, a prevention, if you will. Your Butcher did not gain as much as it could have done due to the sacrifice." Kefi sagged a little, whether due to the gravity wearing upon her head, or the grief was difficult for Rebekah to tell.

"What did the Butcher gain?" asked Trent. "I mean, is it something the Butcher can tap into?"

"We don't know if he can. But your Butcher got the nickname for a reason." Kefi looked to Rebekah, another almost familiar trait. Perhaps it was using the social norms gleaned from contact with Rohan and Rubel. Punctuating moments by trying to appear less alien. Either way, Kefi was keeping what was taken secret. "And Captain Khan has stated our ambassadors were used in his experiments. With the Countess' full knowledge, no doubt."

That would cut deep. The countess hated being exposed at the best of times. But in such a meeting, being immediately on the backfoot, was going to be galling. She might have to fetch some popcorn in.

No. We hold that secret close. Keep back that the Senti know her dirty little secret or her choices may well be dangerous for Kefi, and therefore us.

Kefi's tentacles wavered, then rose, and with a hiss, the folds of her skin around her neck bubbled. The Senti's smell wafted through the room, but more disconcerting was the alien's stare. Had the switch happened again? The delay heightened the tension. If they'd been human, Rebekah would have said it had been planned.

"The Nest Queen will wish to take this matter up with your Court, Pike of operations. But that is a long time ahead. What was stolen is our major focus, and must be returned. Captain Khan is our means. Our agent in this. Should this task fail … there will be consequences."

Rebekah sent another shrug Trent's way as he repeated his glower. "And you want me to facilitate a message via comms?"

"Secure comms," stated Rebekah. "But more than that, Trent. Karal is rumour central. I can't see Segfi, or any of the nobles, releasing ships to help in the hunt. Not with the Butcher on the loose."

Trent held up his hand, staying her words. "There are rumours of a battle around Daphene. But whatever happened there, the Navy hasn't stood down."

"There you go. Information siphons through here, or the other company mining hubs … Contacts only you might have." And there it was, she'd voiced it as subtly as she could. Contacts, perhaps, beyond those associated with mining operations. Contacts a smuggler might have. If Trent could have melted the deck there and then, sent her spiralling into the depths of the asteroid, he might well have at that moment. Fury lit his gaze.

"You haven't given me a good reason to help, other than Senti-human relations. Not exactly my role. You know I need to avoid contact with any authority. Too much risk involved. Too many people need what I do."

"And it wasn't our job either," said Savvo, leaning in. "But somehow the fucking dice just seem to land that way."

"Butter side down," said the alien, seagulls accompanying her statement. Kefi had returned.

Trent shook his head.

"Just imagine what happens if war comes to Karal, Trent," continued Savvo. "You're vulnerable as hell. If the Butcher takes a shine to the station, the *Segfi* would tear this place apart in minutes. Piss the Senti off, they can appear beside you and side slap an asteroid into your beautiful office. I —"

"But that's not your problem, is it?" said Rebekah as she stood up. "You don't want to be a player in this. You want to keep your head down and hide, do some good from behind the scenes. I understand, but the world doesn't work that way anymore, Trent. From the moment we set foot on the *Scourge*, everything we knew changed. The Butcher will not stop until he has what he wants. He attacked a fucking Senti orb ship. Think of the enormity of that. Something not even the Court would risk because they place some value on life – their own. And now he roams our system with a thirst for revenge and survival, holding something a Senti queen is desperate to have returned."

"Before it's turned into a test subject," added Savvo.

Rebekah paced across the room. "I'm not asking you to put your head above the parapet, but all this shit links together somehow."

Kefi off-gassed, a tentacle waving as the alien pointed towards Trent. "Of course, if you will not act as intermediary, the Senti have a long memory."

A quick learner.

"Surely you have the Countess on speed dial now after your meeting a few months back?" Savvo grinned, proud of that one. An Arin level comment, that received a snarled response.

Chapter 23

"Just a dream," Erikson said, staring into the mirror. "No more than that." Manicured fingers ran through his black hair, grey eyes searching the scalp for any tells that might send him into apoplexy. Nothing, not even a raised bump. His brain had betrayed him, flashing back the remnants of his nightmare, causing him to shudder.

Rescue me ...

Erikson splashed water over his fine cheek bones and leant back, once again eyeing the chiselled face and body of the perfect noble. Raised from birth to be his family's leverage, a weapon if you will, in the political war of the Court. There to be a beacon to those sycophants looking to raise their status, while expected to act with perfect decorum and hidden avarice when looking up rather than down the golden staircase. He had abhorred the role, to the point his parents had switched their focus onto their youngest child, leaving him a noble by birth but not by family. The day he'd not needed to wave goodbye to a family who hadn't bothered to see him off had been the best of his life. A moment to savour. An Emperor's Enforcer.

He checked his ring, the mark of his role, and released a bitter sigh. Was he still one of those elite? Or a puppet of the countess? Or both, as it suited her where and when he acted.

"A proxy," he said into the mirror. "And little more."

But of my own doing, guided by my handler into being a scapegoat at best. More like a patsy.

He wasn't stupid, and had enough connections amid the lower echelons of the Navy's noble-officers to have the fog of Segfi's deceit cleared from his mind. With a little help from an administrator or two, the arrows all pointed her way. He'd been duped, though willingly he had to admit. No time to step back and consider how such a trap could be laid, he had led the Breakers into her web.

"And they won." That brought an unexpected smile, exposing perfect white teeth. A hint of pride? Hard to pin down, he hadn't exactly trained them or anything. Shaped perhaps, drew them out and made them look in the mirror to see what they truly were. What an Enforcer does with all their marks – make them see the truth of their actions.

With a firm nod to himself, he dried his face, dripped eye drops to keep them dazzlingly clear, and rubbed regression cream into his cheeks to prevent hair follicles from growing while providing the perfect level of sheen to his skin. Satisfied, he turned away from the mirror, only for a blur in the corner of his eye to draw him back.

No, he looked perfect. He shook his head, turning away just as quickly only for the blur to return. A fear gripped him. He'd checked the cabin for surveillance on entry, but perhaps he'd missed something in the mirror? Or had it been added since his last sweep?

A thought and his wetware engaged, enhancing his vision, widening the spectrum his brain could process. Nothing there, but then some tech was extremely low powered with no obvious signal. Erikson withdrew a small device from his trousers that hung in the wardrobe at the side of his bathroom door, and swept the mirror. Again negative, but something hovered at the corner of his eye, and he turned swiftly, trying to catch it.

Nothing.

With a tiny shake of his head, he squeezed his eyes, something he very rarely did. It caused a pressure build up, ruined their sparkle. On returning his gaze to the room, the blurring had passed, just the beginnings of a headache in its place. Another hit from his wetware prevented it from getting any worse.

Had the stress begun to tell?

No. I won't let it. I have an 'in' with Segfi, despite her lies. A chance to rise higher. Be noticed.

"Approaching M4, Karal docking ensues in three minutes," reverberated through his cabin. Dismissing his troubles, Erikson packed away the last of his clothes and items, donning the beautifully cut shirt and suit he'd prepared for the day. He took up his bag, and with a firm twist of his ring, settled himself down and headed for the corridor.

The private transport had been a surprise, laid on by the countess in her urgency to get him to Karal and be the buffer she needed as the events around, and fall out from, the *Scourge* and then Daphene swept through the Court. The fact he'd have to deal directly with that witch Incini galled him. She had been a meddling player in the countess' failure to keep the twins, as well as the apparent escape of the AI and subsequent loss of the ANS *Segfi*. In times past, he'd never have been allowed knowledge of such damaging failures by high-ranked nobility. But times were changing, and he, as far as he was concerned, was in the countess' inner circle.

He dropped his bag to maglock onto the deck next to his seat, sitting and strapping himself in. The steward eyed him warily, the gruff cut to his nose and chin, the tuft of hair protruding from beneath his cap annoying Erikson greatly. For a private transport, the crew were decidedly rough and ready. Far from the elegance that trained yacht crew should be displaying.

At first, he had assumed Segfi had sprinkled a few extra bodyguards into the mix, but they too should be trained in how to interact with the elite. These were stiffer, almost acting out the role of servitude rather than being trained for it.

Mind you, the journey had been swift. He'd slept through much of the initial burn, and had suffered headaches over the latter, so hadn't spent as much time tolerating their surprising ineptitude as he could have. He ran his hand over the back of his head and neck, fingers searching but not finding anything to be concerned about.

"Thirty seconds," said the ship's comms.

The Incini annoyed him. She had from the very first moment they had met. Too knowing. Not haughty as if she was above him, like a noble would portray, more distant as if she knew so many things he didn't.

She believes she is more intelligent than me. Knows things.

It almost put her on the level, in his mind, with Dexter Lundstrom. What horrors did she have hidden in *her* private cellar?

"Is the word out?" he asked, not asking Davina Connors to sit. She could stand, like a menial.

"Yes, Mr Erikson. You are here as Mr Duboit's proxy, acting in the interests of his holdings while he undertakes business on Almaar. I have instructed all relevant parties that they are to address business directly to y—" Davina blushed a radiant red as Erikson held up his hand to cut her off.

"That will not do." He kept his face neutral, but enjoyed the effect his rudeness had. A simple display of *expectation*. Despite the initial impact, he was annoyed that the Incini saw her point through.

"If you would let me finish – To you, *through* me."

"Better," he said, refusing to acknowledge her powerplay. "Now we need to set a remit. The Enforcers *and* Countess Segfi have sent me here as the eyes and ears of the Court. You were there, by the Countess' account," he added a sneer, "and know this *battle* AI has been released. That knowledge remains a secret enforceable by death, with all Incini debts transferable to your family. Understand?" He again kept his face neutral, allowing only a sliver of a smile. She needed to know her place in things. Segfi agreed, and would rather have dealt with anyone but an Incini who had forced her hand, embarrassed her and squeezed an imperial pardon from the Minister.

"I understand," Davina stated with, at last, a hint of contriteness.

"I'm sure you do." He steepled his fingers beneath his chin. "I want any and all official reports from the last eight weeks sifted for any indication of anomalies. Understand? Anything that could relate to the actions of the AI, a battleship, support craft or even the *Ungrit*. Navy personnel turning up in unexpected places, ships spotted where they should *or* should not be. Everything." One steepled finger tapped against his chin, placing his full regard on the Incini.

"Already prepared and ready for transference to your slate," Davina replied, gnawing at his nerves as she held back a smile he could perceive beneath her skin. Baiting him.

Smug Incini witch.

"And hearsay?" he asked.

"I understood that would be your department, as an Enforcer."

He snarled, slamming both hands on the desk as he rammed his head forward. "Keep pushing, and you'll be tasting void. It will cost me nothing to get another Incini, understand? You hold dangerous knowledge, Connors. With a *snap* of my fingers, I can eradicate a threat, tenets or not, to the Court. No one would blink an eye." That shut her up, the elegant mouth clamping tight, a quiver there he enjoyed causing. "Better. I will be trawling whatever you've prepared and ensuring I catch what you missed. I am sure an Incini has enough dirty contacts to make a start on gathering rumour and supposition. When I'm done, I will cast an eye over your attempts. Yes?"

The Incini nodded, her fingers bunched tight before her. A win.

"Now go. Get the information sent immediately and do your job, Incini." Davina left, her walk stiff, anger in her posture which blossomed a welcome warmth in his heart. Several seconds later, as he leaned back in his chair enjoying the victory, the information dropped into his slate. A brief cast of his eye told him there was a lot to go through, and he stared at the first file name. His vision blurred ... a headache rolling in. He squeezed the bridge of his nose and read it again.

Rescue me? What?

Erikson found himself swiping at the slate's screen, checking over its connectivity, a grimace forming. His hand involuntarily rose to his ear, digging in and snapping open a tab. A second wince, and his other hand slipped inside his jacket, drawing out a wire that he slid into the newly exposed ear port and then the slate. With that, his perfect eyes rolled up into his sockets as he slumped back into the deep leather chair, whispers echoing in his mind.

'Rescue me.'

CHAPTER 24

The necessity threatened to take over her lungs, creeping about her body, clawing at her throat, threatening her stomach control. Countess Segfi needed to draw down the medicated smoke as much as Count Finorr, who sat by her side, needed to draw in his next breath. He wasn't as insufferable as the rest of the High Court, a well-chosen confidante over the years in all but her most secret of dealings. He was also patient with her medical needs, unlike those who watched and waited for the weakness she would eventually show. That Fionrr coveted her fleet was in no doubt, just like the other sharks of the Court circling her family, waiting for the opportunity to take a bite from her legacy in hope she would fall before her grandson was of age.

Another eight months to hang on.

I need to live.

The Minister rapped his staff upon the marbled floor, almost awakening the dead – jolting those Court elders who found staying awake through the more mundane matters of state difficult. A few nodding heads bolted upright, bringing a smile to the countess' face. Ill she may be, but you could add stoic and bloody-minded to that list too.

"The High Court is at an end. In the Emperor's name, I bid you farewell and to act upon the diktats hereby agreed on this morn." The Minister brushed his suit jacket aside, ensuring all could see his key of office. The symbol of locking, decisions made today to be actioned by his hand. A rumble rose along the ornate seats, counts and countesses or their proxies rising to bid each other goodbye before heading off to whatever lover or double-dealing they had planned.

My noble comrades squabbling over their power base.

She waited, saying her goodbyes as Fionrr stood and took her hand, a squeeze and a tight smile shared before he left. In another time, she may well have accepted his company, but she was the Warmonger, and war had arrived.

Gerent strode over. She hadn't seen the agent since leaving Karal. Weak, in her mind, though perhaps the decisions made had been, in the end, for the good of the Empire. There was no doubt she was needed. The Butcher – a weapon she had been so close to taming – now running rampant and displaying behaviours that caused her to fret. Worrying because there appeared to be no pattern she could detect. A testing, perhaps.

Perhaps not.

"Countess," Gerent said, and offered his arm. She accepted it, and stood, refusing to give in to the imbalance in her ears.

"I will require ... medication," she said, eyeing the Minister's hand with a little trepidation. Would they allow her that?

He patted her hand, annoying her greatly as if she was an old maid to be doted on. Gerent caught the glare and withdrew his hand. "You will need to be swift. The Minister nor the Emperor will countenance delay."

"Then lead on. I will forgo the crutch for now." She winced internally, but locked away the pain as best she could. They walked past the emperor's dais, and she stole a glance at the polished throne. A reminder of the first of the colony ships to arrive on Almaar, guided by the Senti who had since swung from friend to supporter, to now, in the Emperor's eyes, an adversary. One *she* had been charged with bypassing. To master their secret of faster than light travel.

And failed. Unleashing the Butcher AI hybrid upon Almaar.

Ensuring her head was to the side, she coughed, the pain racking her ribs. Eventually they were inside the emperor's meeting chamber, the curved table before Emperor Gunstaff bearing the names and faces of each of the *Almaar's* – the first colony ship's – officers who had gone on to forge the first Court, declaring their captain king and later emperor of their new world.

With a gesture from the Minister she sat, hands upon her lap, aged shoulders back, her vivid eyes upon the Minister, waiting to be addressed by Gunstaff before daring to look his way.

A screech declared the emperor had stood, his gold-leaf chair pushed away from the table, hands resting on the chamber table. He struggled to remain still, and Segfi took no heed or threat from the pose. She had seen it before, been held under his regard in silence or under a storm of demands. He was her emperor, and she, his sword.

"Explain," he said, the word hard, falling upon her like a hammer upon the forge.

"Your Imperial Majesty, the AI is clever. Always looking three or four moves ahead. Like chess, he is judging our moves, our responses, and predicting the consequences. But unlike a computerised chess master, Asham's brain pattern provides an unpredictability and intuitive response. It – he – is the most dangerous enemy we have ever faced, before or after our blessed flight from Earth." She coughed, raising a hand, blood upon the back of her glove.

Gunstaff stared, his eyes flitting from the glove to hold her gaze. There was a flicker of recognition there, of the reality. It disappeared just as quickly. "You may smoke," he said, the words far softer than any she had been graced with before. "Yes? Smoke. Now."

An order. She slid out a stick, lighting the end with the touch of an enhanced fingertip. With an internal sigh, she drew upon the medication, letting it sit in her lungs.

She was needed.

Of course she was.

"Daphene," she started, letting the smoke slip from between her lips. "The *Bonray* was a sacrifice. Like a pawn, a trap to draw in the ANS *Righteous* and pepper its hull with camouflaged drones. On entering Tweem, they attacked. Reducing the repair capacity of the shipyard by half or more. They also took out several newly built hulls of the planned defence fleet for Almaar's moon. This is how the Butcher thinks. Everything has a purpose, but hidden, perhaps his intended outcomes will be weeks or months in the future, perhaps immediate." She kept the emperor's gaze, his face unmoved, and took in another medicated breath.

Gunstaff's neck reddened. Anger evident, his hands clasping tightly to the table's edge. "Did *you* predict the moves he has made? The purpose? You hint that there is more than just the destruction of repair capabilities." The words came out in a sneer.

The countess shook her head, as brave a move as she'd ever made. Admitting she lacked the knowledge, but needing the emperor to understand the sheer threat. "I am sorry, Your Imperial Majesty, but no. Perhaps, and this is a leap, he plans to infiltrate more of our ships out in the black. Seeks to prevent their capability of coming in for resourcing. He must recognise that we have ended laser comms, and therefore curtailed a known way of uploading himself. Maybe he seeks to isolate the ships and therefore ensure easier targets."

"But you," started the Minister. "stated that isolation was necessary."

"I still believe that. Imagine the outcome if the Butcher gained three or four ships. It'll be like a virus, replicating and spreading exponentially through one fleet and on to the next. He would then have the power to isolate Almaar, the colony worlds and moons. Nothing would have the strength to stop him." She held the smoke in her lungs a little longer than normal, before releasing the plume away from the emperor, using the moment as an excuse to look anywhere but at him. The fury in his eyes curtailed by realisation. Before, in the chamber amid the High Court, he had acted as an emperor should. Powerful, belligerent. Reinforcing that they would prevail by the force of his will. But her words, her evaluation, was beginning to seep under the façade and present the leader of their Empire with the truth. Far from a strong, unified Almaar, she predicted a fractured state. Human occupied worlds facing the Butcher individually, alone. Their own firepower turned towards them.

And will he unleash that power?

Of course he will. The crew of the *Segfi* and *Bonray*, Daphene, just so much flesh and meat that was in his way. The epitome of why the Court had ruled against Artificial Intelligence for fear it would tear the nobility down. Used by the lowlifes as a tool to bring an end to their rule. An irony that in the hands of one of their own, it could still do so.

"You paint a painful picture," said Gunstaff, turning to face his Minister. "You agree with the Countess' assessment?"

The Minister, his suit perfect, hair slicked back, flicked his piercing grey eyes over to study her intently. That gaze had crushed a minor rebellion or two amid the lesser nobles. Those who had thought too much of themselves. Wielded the Enforcers like a rod and corralled the Incini Directorate when he had a mind.

"I am beginning to," he said, eyes unblinking. "The whispers among the nobles hint at your failure, Countess. That none of this would have happened if you had acted appropriately. Not pursued your own agenda when the stakes were so high." His eyes locked on, prepared for the kill, or a moment of support. You never knew which. He sucked in a breath, releasing it slowly as his hands shifted to clasp behind his back. "I have to agree ... you went beyond the remit placed on you by the Emperor—"

The countess controlled her anger, knowing some of it rose on her cheeks, hoping it would appear more contrite than the fury roiling in her gut. But then, would it do for an emperor to be caught dabbling with experiments on the Senti? Or exploring the possibilities of the Battle AI? Even brain-patterning one of your own noble-officers so they could work on after death. They all knew and approved – until they didn't. Until the moment her actions could expose the emperor, reveal he had gone against his own laws.

And throw me to the wolves of the Court. Of course.

"—However, Countess. You are needed, for now. Perhaps you can bring about your redemption, your family's redemption, by preventing the scenario you describe. It would be a shame to see a house fall under such painful circumstances. I understand Captain Srenik and the *Righteous* survived the assault on Tweem. Fought off the drones in the end. He is spreading the word of his Warmonger, convincing a disbelieving fleet that they are truly under threat. The Butcher's actions at the shipyard appear to have had the effect of securing your wishes, Countess. Now you need to ensure that no more ships are lost, hunt for the Butcher while maintaining the defence of Almaar and the colonies. A new war, a new way of thinking."

"But the result MUST be the same. Victory, Segfi," the emperor slammed his hands onto the desk, "nothing less will do, or your name will be forever associated with this ... this treason."

"Gerent here," the Minister's hand moved to stand by her, his near perfect electronic eye glinting in the chamber's golden light, "will be your aide. To smooth the pathway directly to me, and through me, the Emperor. Understand?"

Yes, your spy, just more in the open than normal.

"I do."

"Good. I have arranged a briefing for the Court members with fleet commands, big or small, at the Emperor's request." The Minister switched his gaze to the emperor who had turned his back for a moment, gazing up at the tapestry behind him. The UNS *Almaar* depicted with exquisite detail, unfaded despite the centuries since it was woven from fine metallic thread.

The emperor's shoulders were tense, posture tight. He said nothing, the silence ominous. When the shouting stopped, there was always trouble ahead, and the gazing at the tapestry deliberate. Instigating the weight of his expectation.

Gerent held out his hand, which she accepted, rising to her feet. "I hold the Empire above all," she stated, and after a bow, left with Gerent. Outside, Rakan Albama, High Priestess of the God's four avatars, waited. Gerent instinctively dropped to his knees, bowing his head and kissing her ring. A ceremonial staff crossed the countess' route to the marble floor, Rakan shaking her head.

"Too old for that. Gerent, I know your role, but my words are not for you. Understand?" She glared at him, expectant, and the Minister's hand stood and backed away, finding his usual niche in the dark. The high priestess pointed along the aisle with her staff, and Segfi made her way alongside the grey-haired woman, a little unsteady. "You survived," said the priestess. "I am pleased. I think you may have a request of me."

Segfi blinked slightly, and with the gentlest of touches, placed her hand on the priestess' where it rested on the staff. "Is there anything you don't see?"

"I have four golden sets of eyes," she replied.

"Tomas," the countess said. "If this goes wrong ..."

"His eyes have always looked to the priesthood over the Court. I cannot think why. Heh. Yes, if your house should fall, I will take him under my wing." Rakan stopped, a half-smile on her lips as she turned to face the countess. "But you must win, Countess. By any and all means. We have built a haven here, one where the rightful people flourish under our God's and his avatars' will. By any and all means, win." The high priestess patted her hand once more, the zealotry in her eyes hard to ignore, before turning away, the metal shod staff knocking loudly on the floor as she left.

Quiet footsteps approached from behind. Gerent. She had little doubt he could have heard if he wished, but he was also a zealot, and would have followed Rakan's demand. That he would report the meeting was in little doubt, but whether the Minister guessed its purpose was moot. Tomas would be safe, or he wouldn't. Rakan had at least given her hope that should she fall for whatever reason, he might be safe. Her honour, her house, however, were far from certain and she would be damned by any and all gods if she was going to let that happen.

A vibration in her overcoat pocket made her flinch. Leaving the throne room, Gerent by her side, she took a seat in the atrium, pulling out her personal slate. A message, text only, to ensure its passage was swift and unhindered.

"Here," she said, handing over the slate and showing Davina Connors' message to Gerent.

He read the words; a querying look on his face. "What's gone?"

"The orb," she replied, the words like ash in her mouth. "The Senti transport orb at the edge of the system."

"Gone? How?"

"Follow me, agent, and we will see. But there is residual debris, so you and I both know the answer."

PART TWO

SIX WEEKS LATER

CHAPTER 25

In the Black

"Ahhhh," growled Savvo, fingers running along the stream of data that flickered across his screen. "My eyes are so tired of this crap."

"Like looking for a needle hidden inside a haystack, alongside ... how many haystacks could you get into our planetary system? I mean, it's got to be a lot, right? Millions? Billions? What did Trem say the other day, apart from 'give me chocolate'?" Arin wiggled in the pilot's chair, sighing before easing his spine a little.

"Trillions of Almaars would fit inside our system, not, of course, including the dead space where they don't align," replied Savvo, frustration coursing through his veins. They had been searching for the spawn queen now for so long that it must be obvious to everyone that it was near impossible. Arin's crass attempts at breaking the monotony aside, he was right. A needle floating in an impossibly large stack of hay. And they had only begun the search along the ecliptic plane. Why would the Butcher choose that, when he could hide absolutely bloody anywhere?

"Shiiiit. How many haystacks on Almaar, times a million and a bit. If it keeps going on like this, I'm going to go insane." Arin sipped at his flask, eyeing Savvo over the rim who was trying to ignore him, but failed.

"Going to go? I mean, you know, right? That happened a loooong time ago." Savvo swiped over to the next screen of sensory data. "I'm just a figment of your imagination. Really, you're on this tub alone with your robot lover and a last Danish with mouldy sprinkles."

"Really? There's a Danish left?" Arin was up and out of his seat, mag-boots clomping towards the galley.

Savvo couldn't decide if he was just playing along, or the monotony had killed the last of his brain cells. And his. The cupboards banged shut, the internal magnets struggling as the sub-engineer slammed the doors closed.

"You lied to me, Savvo. Nothing here but mushroom powder and girls' fingerprints."

Savvo sniggered. He truly would have gone mad without his friend. "Time to break into the third month's provisions. Only two weeks early."

More magboots announced a new arrival, Savvo glanced behind to catch Dricks and Rebekah entering the galley. He gave a last look to the sensory sweep data, and set the system on auto for what felt like the five hundredth time – thinking on it, it probably was – before joining the spontaneous gathering. It had been monotonous, and despite the odd bad day, they had coped as a crew. The downtime a reminder of how things used to be.

"Did I hear we're out?" asked Rebekah, pouring a coffee and settling into a galley bench. "You've scoffed everything, Arin?"

"Hey, no fair. We have two thieves in the night to account for most of it." He feigned indignance, and despite his mood, Savvo grinned. "But yeah, Savvo's right. Time to delve into the goodies saved for month number three of this fruitless search. Hey, you know how many haystacks you can fit in the system?"

"Want me to blow your mind?" replied Dricks. Arin looked up from the packet of soup he was looking at forlornly. "Think how many needles you could fit in."

Arin's eyes widened, then he looked to Rebekah who tilted her head to the side in return. "Head blown" he said, mimicking it, dropping the soup packet which steadfastly refused to float away.

"But food for thought," said Dricks, her glance to Rebekah seen by Savvo. They must have been discussing it. They all had. They had followed up on the initial gossip, and that's what it was, the usual miner and docker bullshit. Nothing. They were at the last site Trent had gleaned hints about from Eastern-Buckhold Corp, and they had found exactly fuck-and-all.

Rebekah sighed. "Anyone else want to tell me we're wasting our time?"

Arin held his hand up.

"That was a given. Okay, break out month three's shit. Let's have cake and treats, then we turn around and head back to Karal." She looked around, and Savvo gave a nod of approval, mimicked by the others.

"Cake?" he asked.

"Got to bribe the human engines into doing their thing," Arin replied. "Supposedly this 'folding space' gig requires sugar-filled calories as well as inhuman levels of patience from their carers."

Savvo sniggered, Rebekah and Dricks shook their heads, smiles in place. But there was no doubt a return was necessary, even if it was just to see a certain lady who still hadn't made her mind up. But then, a ship filled with a semi-permanent cabbage aroma none of them could barely discern anymore was an unlikely lure. He sniffed his flight suit. Maybe he could.

Dricks stood, supping the last of her white coffee. "I'll go let them know to dress for cake and sugar," she said.

Savvo sat opposite Kefi, the Senti having intertwined its lower limbs into the bench legs to pull itself down, one shoulder tentacle wrapped underneath the table between them. The Senti took every opportunity to avoid its encounter suit, like the Kefi of old, but the occasional slip into her 'other' personality still gave him the creeps. Like a disgruntled noble-officer always one step from ordering them to the front to be slaughtered for their failure. Savvo had become Kefi's liaison by default, Rebekah eschewing the role so that she was divorced from their situation when making decisions. Arin because he was Arin and would make too many fart jokes, and Dricks because of her history with the Senti. Surprisingly, Kefi was a different matter. Somehow, Dricks had come to relate to the alien once more. Savvo wondered whether this was because one half of the Senti had been with them through the dangers of the orb, stood alongside those she cared for. Or that the Senti had been broken apart and rebuilt. Something Dricks knew a lot about. And of course, the Senti had learnt humour from Rohan and possibly the rest of Rubel's dead squad.

"There's no easy way of saying this," he started, receiving an off-gas almost immediately that bubbled out from under a flap. Savvo had become used to the Senti, and carried on knowing full well that indication of his own stress was probably seeping from his pores too. The Senti were sensitive to aromas – human and alien – and she would be feeling exactly the same as him right now. "We're going back to Karal."

Kefi's shoulder tentacles twitched. "You're giving up?" The Senti leaned in, pulling herself closer. "That's not what you mean, is it?"

Savvo wasn't sure if that was a question, or a statement of hope. He had concluded over the last few weeks that there was more flexibility in Senti thinking than he had first assumed. That perhaps the translators were the cause of the rigidity, unable to relate any subtleties in word choice or tone humans could read. And of course, the tells of body language. He suspected it would take years to truly understand their overall – what was Arin's word? – nuance. The nuances of their language.

"We're not giving up, no. But what we're doing is fucking fruitless. We have followed every lead we had, but there's nothing on the 'field we can find and your 'skills' have not even hinted at the spawn queen's presence." Kefi shuddered a little, readjusting position. "I'm not sorry," Savvo continued, "we believe our time would be better spent trying a different bloody tack. The fleets have sent no word of contact either, and they have been searching the planets and moons."

"At distance, in a wide net for fear of being infected by the Butcher," stated Kefi.

Savvo nodded. It was true, but sensors could spread wide and the *Segfi* wasn't exactly tiny. "It's been quiet since the attack on the Tweem shipyard. The countess reports the Navy base on Daphene has been wiped from the moon. They used enough ordinance to blow up twenty bases, but got through in the end. But the Captain feels it was merely a distraction as any static base will always be vulnerable."

"Yes. They can be blockaded, and need defending," said Kefi. The Senti went quiet. Almost distant. These were the moments when the crew concluded an internal monologue was going on, two minds speaking to each other. Not like the nest queen had done. Rebekah had hinted she thought that was a *female* thing, but wasn't definite.

"The Nest Queen needs to know," stated Kefi eventually. "I suggest you have an alternate plan before we make contact," the alien added. The tone remained steady, electronic and clipped, but it didn't *feel* that way.

Savvo recognised the implied threat. Not unexpected after the queen had sent them on their way. They assumed the officer Kefi had been subsumed with, had likely been charged with administering whatever punishment was built into the *Sunstar*. The most obvious being buried deep within the rail cannon that sat in the belly of the ship. Despite their efforts, Dricks and ZZ3 had come up empty-handed in their sensor searches.

"Any suggestions are welcome," Savvo replied.

Savvo pushed the last cake crumb from the corner of his mouth between his lips. The chocolate bitter, just how he liked it, and tingling his tongue. The smallest kick of sugar followed, leaving an aftertaste that brought a smile. Nicky had the sweetest of tooths, and she was within touching distance.

Or her voice was.

Karal hung in the void before them, the four asteroids circling each other in a dance that had lasted the decades since Karal had set them spinning. Heki and Tremil had brought them home, their understanding of time and place growing with each fold. Kefi had taught them how to use simulations to envisage where they were going, four-dimensional images – when you included time – that they could model with increasing accuracy using Senti code. Given enough safety margin, and time to learn and therefore envisage the next jump, they were confidently expanding their reach.

"You ever wondered why Kefi is teaching them?" he said, prodding at Rebekah, restarting a conversation they'd had before the Senti first watched the girls' symbiotes fold space.

"I have two answers," stated Rebekah, easing the *Sunstar* towards M4 and the expected contact to come. "The first to report back on their capabilities to the Nest Queen. Obvious, but likely."

"And the second?"

She glanced over, a grimace there. "You like Kefi, yeah?" she said.

He paused, but he did and said so. "But I have qualms about what happened to her. How she can slip into the other one. The officer."

"We all do. So it, she, whatever, could be ingratiating her way into the crew to find leverage to use against us."

"That's Pshwa thinking, or Scarva. Either of those, I'd agree, and cut out whatever they have as a heart to fucking prove it." There was a catch to his voice, almost a growl at the thought of those two aliens. "But that sounds more than a little paranoid to me." He caught the flash of a scowl. Leaning back, he raised his hands. "But hey who am I to judge?"

"My second." She cracked a thumb, almost distractedly, out of habit as the comms crackled.

"Welcome home, *Sunstar.*" It was Nicky's voice, they had timed their approach to her usual shifts, though Heki and Tremil had positioned their arrival from void-space on a standard approach vector. One blocked by the swirl of the outer asteroid field. "Am I getting a *hi* from any co-pilot on board?"

Rebekah's grimace broke, a smile appearing. Savvo had actually blushed. "He's looking a little embarrassed right now, docking tower. I'll say hello for the fuckwit, so he doesn't have to."

"He's gonna pay for that. Transponder activated, *Sunstar.* You have bay 11c. I'll let Mr Pike know you're here. Tower out." Nicky's voice faded into the hiss of comms.

Rebekah's smile also faded. "As we were saying. The Nest Queen rebuilt Kefi, like one of our printers. Knitted her together with the Senti officer like a scarf or jumper. We don't know what she put in there, who this Kefi is. If all this with the girls and us is genuine, you could almost argue she's trying to make the decision harder."

"You really are paranoid," said Savvo, his mind now churning over the possibilities.

"You're alive, aren't you?"

He couldn't argue with that.

CHAPTER 26

KARAL

"**D**amn." Davina swiped her screen, running her finger quickly over the file options. Already up on the main office slate was the proposal from Karal's board. Not a full agreement, but close, just the finer details to thrash out in which they would hide every possible get-out clause and trapdoor escape route from any financial penalties Mr Duboit, the baron, demanded. That part was not her job, and the document was already winging its way across the abyss to land in the hands of her hand-picked lawyers on Almaar. They would comb through, and set their own parameters and so the back and forth would go on until the agreement was thrashed out.

The tenets were set, and as an Incini she was happy. As Mr Duboit's voice upon M1 she was not. As Rebekah would say, she was mightily *pissed off*.

Had the promise of her own estate been a little too fat? Had Jenkra smelt a trap, and gone digging? Indulged in her own industrial espionage?

"Damn," she repeated. Her file on one particular asteroid was gone from her personal data bank. She was thorough, careful and, as her Incini trainer used to call her, a little paranoid about losing things. She couldn't have wiped it by accident. Perhaps the system had glitched? A cross-reference showed a few other files were also missing. The dates matched, despite their contents being unrelated. She sucked in a breath, held it for a few seconds, feeling the air press against her repaired lungs before releasing it into the office. She managed to avoid the moan building in her throat.

She took the office slate and ensured the draft contract was safely stored, and began searching through for the identification file and the forms she had prepared for its, and several other less wanted asteroids in its vicinity, transfer to Mr Duboit's ownership. These she found swiftly and then dug a little deeper for the survey info. She needed to register what they knew about its worth to ensure no fraudulent downgrading or, as she'd witnessed other companies do, over-stating its value as they searched for loans to secure against it. Of course, she was hardly going to be providing the latest survey, carried out without Karal's permission, was she? No, she needed the first survey, which she found quickly, and the lost file. One an exogeologist could revise for a price, upgrading the asteroid's project-ed worth enough for someone to understand Duboit's interest, without overstating the composition of the metals her boss identified as the next stage in arms grade resource requirements.

Crossing the t's.

Dotting the i's.

Keeping the real truth under a shadow. Making creds by the bucketload.

There it was. The survey file she had copied and was now missing from her own slate. Locked in Duboit's secured holding drive. She drew it up and decrypted, only to be thwarted by its absolute blank refusal to accept her code. Davina's hand dropped to the desk, flexing her fingers as she worked through her wetware, checking over the code stored there. She re-entered it, only for the refusal to stare back at her. Taunting. At that moment the office door opened, and Erikson stood there staring, though his eyes appeared distant, lost. Over the last few weeks, he had appeared less and less from the room, often arriving before and leaving after her. Always perfectly turned out. But something was changing, his veneer peeling away layer by layer, as if he was fading away before her eyes. They rarely spoke, only for her to send any insights the Enforcer – if that's what he still was – wanted forwarding on to Rebekah and crew.

"What are you doing?" he said, the words clipped and precise as always. He had hold of the office door, gripping the handle, grey eyes finally focusing on her.

"Work for Mr Duboit," she stated. Unless he was investigating Baron Stimpson again, that was as much as he was getting. He stepped back a little, then gripped the door harder.

"I have things for you to do. Urgent. You need to drop whatever it is. I'll send over the trawl I've completed of the latest rumours Pike has sent me." She baulked at that, suddenly understanding why she'd not got anything from Trent in the last week. She was being bypassed, reduced to the menial. "There's a potential lead or two Khan needs to know about. Now."

He stepped back, leaving the door open. With a glance, she noted he'd moved his desk, positioned it so he could look through to her. It must have been recent. There was a whiff of something. Bleach perhaps, seeping from inside.

Was this it? She was going to be watched now? Had she become the next target for his Enforcer paranoia?

Her office slate pinged, and the new info he promised dropped in. A minute or two of rumour and dock worker supposition. It was no different from any she'd seen before. Yes names, places, asteroids and ship names differed, but the tone didn't. A waste of everyone's time that stank of desperation – with a tinge of antiseptic. Overly clean.

Her personal slate then flashed, the ping silent.

It was Trent, the message brief. With a twist of her lips, she worked Erikson's data into a file and sent it on to the *Sunstar*. It wouldn't have far to travel according to the message, and she intended on making sure Rebekah understood its implications face-to-face. Her worries.

Am I now paranoid? Yeah, learned through experience.

A check on her schedule showed she had enough time. A meet, a chat, something to eat and then she could return and finish up the proposal for the asteroid's re-registration of ownership. Davina made an addition to her timetable and slid the slate inside her jacket, then gently lifted her chair to place it beneath her desk. A check inside Erikson's office implied he was likely too busy to be disturbed, and she quietly left. A breath sitting heavy again in her chest.

Davina sat with Rebekah and Trent at his slightly ostentatious conference table, all three of their slates forming a triangle before them with coffee in the centre.

"I know he's a dickhead," said Rebekah, "even more than before from what you're saying, but he works *for* the Court. First as an Enforcer, and now under Countess Segfi's blood-soaked wing." She took a long sip of her coffee, twisting her neck as the zing hit. Davina did the same, a glance over to Trent Pike, chief of operations, confirming the lines around his mouth, the dark bags below his eyes. In a negotiation, he would be down as an easy mark. Nudge until he twitched, then go for the proverbial kill. Something was troubling him.

She looked back to Rebekah. "I know. It just feels different somehow. He took a few wild risks, pushed the tenets whenever he could, but he got results."

"And caught Segfi's eye. She's nobody's fool. And I can't believe she will have him blocking our search. The Countess will not want to piss off the Senti, and she understands the cancer that is the Butcher. What he aims to do. Maybe this just isn't his skill set?" Rebekah finished her coffee and tapped Trent's cup, the sound bringing him back from wherever his thoughts were. "Wassup? You look like you spent an hour in Arin's company?"

Trent rubbed at his eyes. They were redder than Davina had expected. "Uh? Sorry. Mind on so much shit right now I don't know whether I'm coming or going. What was you saying?"

"Erikson," stated Davina. "He siphons off the rumours and sightings you send and it's all kind of merging into one big *no*. There's no oomph there to dig deeper, and he's surly. I mean, more than before."

Trent leaned back in his chair, lifting his slate and swiping. "I never knew the man, but having an Enforcer or Segfi's wingman on board isn't a situation I like. How can I help other than what I'm already doing?"

Davina gently snorted, holding up both hands. "Occupy him so I can do my job. Help Rebekah."

"What the *Sunstar*'s been doing is a waste of time," replied Trent, Rebekah nodding along. On that they all agreed. Davina knew they had had to try, and it didn't stop them gathering the information just in case. "What's he good at?" continued Trent. "I mean you know him better than me. I might have something I can perhaps wrap in a suspicious enough way to catch his attention."

Davina found herself surprisingly ready. "Detail. You know, the nitty gritty of facts and figures, extrapolating predictions. Rumours don't hold weight, so he misses stuff. Too human for him." She nodded to herself. *That was it.*

"Yeah. I can find him something." Trent swiped his slate, tapping away.

"Anything we need to know?" asked Davina.

Trent stopped peering at his slate and glanced up. For a moment she suspected he had forgotten who he was talking with. Yes, she was one of Segfi's links, but also an Incini his bosses were negotiating with. She could almost see the realisation slot home. "Nothing I can share with a representative of Mr Duboit, a future major investor."

Davina couldn't help but smile, Trent's response, blunted by their current roles with Rebekah and the Senti, but a slice of corporate comeback she could appreciate.

"Copy that," she said, mimicking the *Sunstar*'s crew. "Just hint that the external asteroid field rumours can come my way while he focuses on whatever you have lined up."

"It doesn't solve what we do next. You can trawl all that shit as much as you like, but it's got us fucking nowhere so far." Rebekah's fists balled as she spoke, her thumbs ready to crack but no sounds came yet. "Kefi is going to make contact with their Nest Queen. But I'm at a loss. Unless the Butcher pops his virtual fucking head above the parapet, we're on a ghost chase with no gh ..."

Davina tilted her head, watching Rebekah's eyes as they wobbled slightly from side to side.

"Ghost. Asham," she glanced up at Trent and Davina.

Whatever just struck her, there was no way she was going to share it in that moment. Davina sensed a secret, but now was not the time to pry. Something to wheedle out later.

Rebekah stood quickly, grabbing her slate. "I have an idea. Might be full of crap, but I'll be in touch. Keep me in the loop about Erikson as I don't want him jumping on my back after you prise the fucker off Davina's." She turned and made to leave, stopping at the door. "I don't like the silence," she said. "The Butcher is prepping something big. Has to be." With that, she left.

Davina stood, collecting her things as Trent closed off his slate. "He's a snake," she said. "And I'm guessing you're not from any noble family he'll kiss the ring for."

Trent shook his head. "No. Well, not anymore."

Davina dropped her bag onto her work desk, surreptitiously peering through Erikson's still open door. His head was bowed, the perfect hair remaining in place as he stared at his screen. A long blink followed, and a flinch, before he looked towards her. By that time, she had sat at her desk, her slate open, only catching his gaze from the corner of her eye. A chill ran down her neck.

It lasted longer than she felt comfortable. The man had never liked her. Saw her as an Incini 'witch', and she found it equally uncomfortable working for him. She suspected he knew her heritage. A fallen house of a minor noble whose resources had been depleted by multiple business failures. Their patron tired of bailing them out, leaving them to wither and die a few years before New Almaar was wiped clean by the Bustan AI fleet. From there, sold to the Incini under bond until she paid off her training debts. A history like that must make her appear as a lowlife to him, not worth his time, risen up by the Incini. To an Enforcer that hunted down nobles who pushed boundaries but were never exposed, she held knowledge he craved, and the power to deny him it. An anathema.

Perhaps that was all it was. His resentment at being here channelled through his dislike for what I am. What I represent.

She jumped. He stood before her desk, almost as if appearing from the air. Davina blinked, taking in the expensive suit, the ring his other hand spun constantly as he looked at her.

"I'm going to a meeting," he said, the words pin sharp. "I won't be back." Erikson turned on his heal, heading for the door. She waited for some kind of follow up, but there was none, just the hint of a pause at the handle, then he headed out.

Davina drew in a long breath, calming her mind. There was absolutely nothing about the exchange that would have been odd if she hadn't already been on edge.

"Pull yourself together." Davina opened her slate, going through the security protocols to pull up the re-registration she'd been working on. A glance over the preparations made her feel a little better, and she cross-referenced everything until satisfied. With a scrunch of her lips, she pinched the icon for the survey file, expecting the encryption code request and thus the fly in her preparations. It opened.

"Finally, a break. Must have been a glitch." With that, she put the finishing touches to the proposal. When done, she wrote a summary, pinging this off to Jenkra Tew. A little late, which annoyed her, but done.

"A cocktail and then a shower, I think, to celebrate."

CHAPTER 27

KARAL

Rebekah sat cross-legged on the cargo box, fingers tapping on her knees as Savvo crossed his arms opposite. He leaned against the old navy storage box that now contained little over a third of the depleted uranium rounds Trent had smuggled on board months ago.

"Come on ZZ3," said Arin, "bend down a little more. I can't reach the connection." He was waving a wire in front of the hulking warbot.

"Are you shrinking?" asked ZZ3, the flat tone making it sound like ZZ3 really wanted to know.

"Har-bloody-har. It's cos this lot work me to the bone. I bet I have no skin left on the soles of my feet. Even my magboots have lost a centimetre or two." ZZ3 dropped so its torso touched the cargo deck, Arin sliding home the connector. The warbot's blue eyes swirled a little, but soon settled, their gaze focused on Rebekah.

"Not as much as your moaning has worn away my soul. With a 'u' not an 'e'."

"Asham is very wary of this," said the bot. "I am not sure why. I apologise it has taken a night of persuasion. My extrapolation of his mood suggests he suspects something deeper in your purpose."

"Like a wipe?" asked Arin, who glared at Rebekah before dropping his eyes as she glowered back.

"I think I have shown enough acceptance of what you are ZZ3. If I were to suggest such a thing, a change or even a fucking wipe, it would alter who you have become. Has anything in my behaviour suggested that?" Rebekah let a harshness permeate her voice. "You are crew. All of you."

ZZ3's eyes swirled, and the bot jittered to the side. "I have repeated this to the point he shuts down. But I have reviewed all available data, and extrapolation indicates a 99% probability that you do not wish any part of me harm."

"Hey. That means 1% of the Captain does," cut in Arin, holding up his slate to indicate he was ready.

ZZ3 dipped, almost like a stiff-necked nod. "Everyone has an element of doubt. For instance, data also suggests a 10% probability the Captain wishes you harm, rapidly increasing depending on how often you repeat the same joke."

"Or the same bullshit," added Savvo.

"Yes. Or the same bullshit, glorious leader." ZZ3's eyes pulsed, entering a repeating pattern.

"Everyone's a bloody comedian now." Arin jumped up to sit on the edge of the same cargo box as Rebekah. He tapped at the icons and drew up a 3D image simulator he used when working through the schematics of the ship or its increasing weaponry. "Ready, funny bot?"

"Senior Rescue Warbot ready for duty. Asham has reluctantly agreed to engage."

The slate's screen rippled with static, and a face slowly emerged from the blue pixels, resolving into a likeness of the general. It caught in Rebekah's throat seeing him again, but as the image spoke, the texture of his voice was very different from that ZZ3 had produced, or that she'd heard over her suit comms. Even from when the Butcher had lost his shit when he realised how the *Sunstar* had escaped.

"I am here," the words were soft, yet strong. A depth to them. "But I wish it to be known I am not Asham. A sliver, a mere ghost, and I detest what I once was. But I wish to continue to exist."

Arin raised an eyebrow her way, but she ignored it. She had no intention of either believing this part of the Butcher's brain patterning, or wiping it clean. ZZ3 had a handle on it, and that was enough for her. Well, that and she had two girls who could probably break her brain apart should she harm their beloved warbot.

"And that's why we want to talk. I'll be honest, I can't get my head around the 'I am ZZ3, Asham is part of me' when here we are speaking to each other. But I'll let that lie. You want to survive, just like the Butcher does. You were once part of him."

"I understand where you are going. But without data, more than you have already had, I do not have any insight for you," the voice remained soft, but there was a pleading undertone there. But she couldn't trust anything she was told by code or machine, not after Daphene, the Marauders. Actions spoke far louder than words.

"Which ZZ3 has confirmed before we started. Asham, you want to live. To continue on, and for that you will have a plan. That could include hiding your intentions from ZZ3, pretending to be looking for redemption while waiting your chance." ZZ3's eyes swirled red, and his limbs quivered a little. She cracked a thumb, hating what she had said, but context was key. "Would you agree that's possible?"

"I do not," stated the warbot.

Asham, however, paused. Lips moved, but no sound came initially. "I could have made such an attempt, but the pacify algorithms were strong when I was weak. They now infect ... no, that is a Butcher way to think. They are now sewn into me, part of what I and ZZ3 are. To do so, would go against that. In human terms, my state of mind has been re-sculpted. But I can extrapolate such an act."

"Good. So take that thought. Savvo."

Her co-pilot pushed himself away from the navy box. "The Butcher wants to survive. So instead of searching for where he might have been seen, we were thinking of devising a map of where he might go. What choices he would make to ensure survival."

"I believe you already know he will seek to eradicate any capability you have to stop him. That he regards flesh merely as a means to an end. Something to control and discard as he sees fit." The modelled Asham faded in and out as it spoke. "He will seek to control or destroy all means that threaten his existence."

"People?" said Arin. "You mean people."

"No. At least, not at first. Your fighting machines, the space navy has to be the first target."

"Agreed," said Rebekah. "And we have evidence for that. The *Segfi* could blow any and all ships into the abyss in a straight fight. But not a small fleet. So he hides, attacks one ship at a time, tries to take them over. But space is too fucking big, so you need a lure. Bait."

"The spawn queen?" said Arin. "I mean, I don't think that was what he was doing at the orb." He glanced towards the door, as if checking the Senti weren't walking in at that moment. "That stank of happenstance. He wanted the symbs."

"After raiding Scarva's ship, I'd agree," said Savvo. "However much it pains me to agree with a sub-engineer."

Arin sent over a middle finger salute.

"He will seek to attack without endangering himself," said Asham. "As would I."

Rebekah soaked that in. It was logical, and the connotations huge. "Do you mean like keep a backup of himself safe somewhere? We think Daphene has been wiped out by Countess Segfi."

"That is a possibility," said ZZ3. "Based on his actions so far."

Asham's head came fully into focus. "That would take a huge level of storage capacity, and I predict he will be increasing his potential by the minute. But there is nowhere large enough to store such a safety measure other than another battleship. It is possible. But the Butcher has acted by proxy ever since taking the *Segfi*."

"By proxy?"

"Zombie clones from hell," said Arin.

"The hybrids, and we had reports of drones taking the *Bonray* over," Savvo said, uncrossing his arms as he looked to Rebekah.

"The *Ungrit*'s attack on Scarva's ship, then the orb itself. Keeping himself out of the way. But that doesn't tell us what he's doing, or where he may be hiding." Rebekah cracked her other thumb.

Arin pursed his lips and rested the slate on his lap. "No? There's a huge resource issue if you want more bloody proxies. If you're not prepared to fight the navy head on as you're afraid to lose, to die, you need—"

"—more ships. But he's not taken any for weeks. After he attacked Tweem, he's been silent."

"Tweem?" stated Asham. "I was unaware."

Rebekah tried to drag back through her memory. No, she hadn't mentioned it to ZZ3. A glance to Savvo was returned with a shake of both heads. "Yes, Tweem. But he took no ships. Used camouflaged drones that attached to the *Righteous* when it went in for repairs. We told you about the *Bonray*?"

"Yes," said ZZ3. "And I am aware of Tweem from your comms transmissions. I have not discussed the attack with Asham. I was aware, but did not see an importance as you have not discussed it directly with me."

Rebekah mentally kicked herself. With the Senti aboard, everything was out of kilter, and though the nest queen knew about ZZ3, the Senti had seemed to avoid the bot wherever possible. Somewhere in that mix, she had kept a crew member in the dark.

"Sorry, ZZ3. Asham, can you see a significance?"

Rebekah sipped at her beer, looking over the rim of her glass at Hendricks as she happily tucked into the synth ham and cheese sandwich. By her side, the two girls she loved, ice cream moustaches failing to hide their smiles. The café next to the transport hub was busy, but even so the girls appeared relaxed and able to cope with the bustle and noise.

Ice cream helps.

Hendricks had taken them on a short tour of M2 while they interrogated Asham, starting, of course, from the shuttle transport hub they were at now and up through the levels with a suggestion to avoid the seedier elements nearer the centre where grav was short and so were creds. A gentle introduction.

How had she put it?

A toe in the water.

"You'd better get back to the ship." Rebekah was supposed to have relieved Hendricks and given her some downtime with Arin. But she needed contact with the countess as soon as possible, and that meant Davina's Senti tech link.

Hendricks sighed and sagged a little but nodded. "Sure," she said, and slid her wrist over the table scanner. "I'll get one of their sugar-packed coffees to go. How long you going to be?"

Rebekah shrugged, eyeing the concourse. "Depends on whether she's persuaded Erikson or not. Don't really want to be talking with that bastard looking over my shoulder but at least I get to meet him in person. I won't forget his fucking face, I promise."

"Then we add him to the list under Lieutenant Ormsk and Pshwa," said Hendricks, but Rebekah knew she wasn't finished. There was another, one she had come so close to killing. Both of them had. "But Segfi will always be at the top."

The girls had finished and were standing up, gathering their collection of bags they'd hidden from view beneath the table. Hendricks patted her on the shoulder and winked. "Not what you're thinking. They've acquired a few supplies for the ghost engine. They've figured out how to project a false sensor image, but wanted some grade A tech to ensure it didn't fail. There's no sugar in sight."

Tremil grinned at Rebekah. "So she thinks." Heki joined in the laughter, and Rebekah watched as all three walked towards the waiting area. Eventually she turned away and headed for the lift and the next transport to M1.

Rebekah's slate pinged, and on opening it Davina's image appeared with a message below.

"Fucking Enforcers," she growled, and swiped the number embedded in the message. She sat back down, ordered a coffee and waited for the bastard to appear. Eventually he answered. Black hair, smooth skin, grey eyes above sculpted cheeks. He could have been any noble's son, rather than a hunter of them.

"Khan," the voice cut through her. "I'm afraid the Countess has put the master in charge of the comms rather than the cur." The coffee arrived via a serving bot. She collected it, ignoring Erikson while she reined in the anger.

"I need a message sending ASAP. I haven't the time to wait on normal comms, it'll be run through their systems before it gets to Segfi. Priority or not."

"*Countess* Segfi," he corrected. "Yes, Connors informed me. Unfortunately, I require those comms for other matters. But I have a slot upcoming to report on your lack of success. Tell me what you wish to convey, and I'll talk to her direct."

That was something at least.

"I'll need the answer ASAP. The attack on Tweem by the Butcher's drones—"

The ignorant bastard cut right in. "—I assure you that all the information and recordings were made available despite my protestations at you being provided access to data without official status."

That was true. Nor did she want it.

No more fucking hound masters and whips. No longer a cur.

"Fair enough. But we're on the same side here, Erikson." She enjoyed the flinch. No status attached, just a name. "So, to say it again, I want to know if there was any ingress into Tweem's systems. The shipyard plans and designs, anything that might help the Butcher build more ships."

"There are times when I wonder why we ever kept you alive, Khan. The *Segfi* will have had those schematics on board."

"You're wrong." She enjoyed that, too. "Any attack on the *Segfi* would have led to all encrypted data being burned. Standard procedure. Same with the *Bonray*. In all likelihood, he has no access. I suspect it would be the same on Daphene. He forged workarounds in the system to use the laser comms and weapons systems, the transponders to access independent machinery. Even the *Segfi* arrived due to procedure and not using any encrypted coding."

The Enforcer remained quiet. She couldn't even detect any cogs whirring. Flat. If it was a *no*, she'd still be contacting the countess, but it would add time.

"Okay. I will ask the question and ensure it is a priority." The connection cut.

"Fucker," she said, and grabbing her coffee, ran down the concourse while up ahead the shuttle slid into view. Hendricks could still have her downtime if Arin had finished ZZ3's diagnostic. The discussion with Asham had spooked him, despite ZZ3's reassurances, and he was acting it out through a thorough check like an over-protective father. The twins and their shadow came into view, and she waved over.

I can relate to that.

CHAPTER 28

KARAL

Erikson stared at his slate, the screen blank. Empty. Much like he felt, yet the void roiled with spite and self-recrimination. Though why seemed to be just out of reach, as if there were plaudits in his mind, slaps on the back, just not for him. A duality, simultaneously hating himself despite successes that he couldn't quite remember. He leant back, seeking something. A memory he needed to burn out.

Erikson gazed up into the main light in his office ceiling, his pupils narrowing as the glare threatened to shatter his mind into a thousand pieces. Each part of his brain hurt, as if wrapped in a net of pain.

He blinked again, trying to remember where the hell he was. Almaar? No. he'd left that far behind. Segfi had sent him ... where?

He could remember the planetary transport bringing him into a dock. Where was it? Not Almaar? No, that was a few days back. Maybe a week or two. Perhaps Palail, yes. That was it. The ship announcement ringing through his mind. Packing away all the freshly laundered clothes into his vacuum sack, annoyed at the poor creases on one of his shirt collars. He distinctly remembered sending in a complaint, a demand for a reprimand for whoever had forced him to turn out in such a poorly clothed manner. He'd disembarked, had a few drinks and a play at the gaming table while waiting for his cabin to be prepped. That was it. Yes.

But what then?

He had an overnight. Just the one before the private transport arrived. He'd eaten, lab grown steak in a mushroom sauce with a piquancy that had taken him by surprise. Wine.

Where did I go?

He slept, badly, the wine acid in his gut.

He'd awoken and groped to his side, arm hardly moving, the hand numb, as if he'd slept on it overnight. Erikson remembered shifting his head, trying to catch sight of his errant limb and the headache had exploded again. A flash of agony that forced him to gasp out loud. Something had landed on his shoulder. Fingers? No, they were warm but too smooth. Metal, and they had pressed him down slowly into the mattress.

Gel. For fucking space.

I hate space.

"Stay still." An electronic voice, but there had been a nuance there. More than a medbot. A jab in his neck, and numbness spread upwards. Was that the end?

No. Just a dream?

Don't look. Never look.

He'd opened his eyes again, blinking away rising tears, fearing the spreading paralysis. Above him hovered a screen, its blur sharpening. He could see a man beneath a blue blanket, arms strapped down.

The face was familiar, yet just above the eyeline, the skull ended. As if someone had lasered the top third clear, exposing a bloody brain. About it a net of wires pulsed, glowing, where metallic fingers and soldering irons flared.

He knew that face, that winning smile. A look along their hand revealed what he sought. A ring. An Enforcer's ring.

His ring.

His face.

His skull sawn and brain exposed. Erikson tried to open his mouth, to scream. But the numbness spread, a fog of mind and body calling him into its embrace.

"*Rescue me?*" said the voice, over and over. It always punctuated his lapses, those moments when his wetware fired without his trigger.

His new wetware.

And he had fought. Struggled to hold on to what he was. A noble. A hater of corruption, jealous of those above him who spurned their birthright. Sullied it.

Erikson squeezed his eyes shut, blinking out the searing light. "Rescue me," he whispered, mimicking the echo running through his head. "Karal. I'm on Karal."

His wetware fired, prodding its proxy with a zap that seared across Erikson's mind. Burning out the last of him. He stood, stalking awkwardly over to his office door and slammed it shut, returning to his desk to pick up the slate, swiping through until Connors appeared on screen. Inside, he seethed, hate and bile rising in his gut. His actions hadn't changed that foul smile she always wore. "Hold all calls, cancel appointments. I have an urgent meeting with the Countess." He needed to look away, to not look at that contemptuous Incini face or hear the all-knowing voice any longer.

"You have Chief of Operations Trent Pike arriving in ten minutes, Mr Erikson," Davina said.

He forced himself not to growl. Pike. Yes. "Have him wait. I'll make time." He cut off the comms before she could reply and stared at the blank screen, fearing falling into the promised abyss of its depths. His wetware fired again, bringing him back from the brink.

Wrist swiping his desk, he thumb-printed a drawer and removed his second slate. This one modded with the Senti tech he'd taken from Connors courtesy of her other employer. Erikson passed his wrist ID over and the screen thankfully came alive. Eyes stared blankly back, as if whoever was on the other side had been waiting for this moment. Of course they had.

"The mission has been compromised," he said, his voice now with a mechanical edge, hints of another tone beneath his own. "Program the autoship, ensure its navcom has preset course adjustments. It is not to be followed."

"And then?" the voice was flat beneath the dock worker's cap.

"Blow the dock and tower. I want mayhem to hide its flight-path." Erikson grinned, though it was not by choice, nerves firing to urge reluctant muscles into position.

"The *Sunstar*?"

"As already agreed, no change of plan. On my signal." He tapped at the slate, turning off the direct comms and checking over the final preparations. A scan down the resource data brought an involuntary scowl. It was too soon; Khan having interfered ahead of the probabilities. It would take some adjustments, but that was no longer his concern. He downloaded the remaining information scoured from Karal's database, and aligned it with a quick scan through Connors' latest trawl. Nothing much had changed there, and he resisted the temptation to interfere with the surveys again. Watching her tap furiously at her screen on discovering the re-encrypted file had been the highlight of the last few weeks.

He sent the data packet and then plugged a wire from his ear socket into the Senti mod. A few seconds later, the smell of fire rose. His mind wavered, the aroma of electrical burning triggering a memory. His family's estate, fishing rod in hand, the glint of sunlight off the murmuring river, the swish of line as it sailed through the rising flurry of insects to touch upon the water. The bite, the brief but fruitless struggle of the fish before he reeled it in, then gutted his prize and cooked his victory over an open fire. For the briefest of moments, he understood who the fish was, and who had become the victor.

Unplugging, he slammed the slate against the wall. It splintered, dropping to the floor where he ground the Senti mod into dust.

"It is time," he whispered to himself. A check of his slate informed him Trent had arrived, was likely prowling the waiting room, ready to hear if Erikson's investigations had pulled up anything useful. Of course they hadn't, because they were mere token efforts. He already knew what resources were missing, which autoship had been lost, what dock workers had suddenly quit and been replaced. The siphoning to feed the machine. The Butcher. He could, of course, have carried on the misdirection. But waiting could lead to exposure, suspicions rising as the Chief of Operations revealed the extent of the losses and, of course, Khan's seeming leaps of intuition. He had little doubt she'd be calling the countess right now, not trusting him to make the promised contact. Always have a backup. Typical Marine. A Breaker until the end.

Soon.

He called through. "Send Trent Pike in."

The urge rose, a desire to open the door himself, grab the witch by her throat, throttle the life from the Incini. But that was too easy. Too soon.

Time.

She showed him in, Trent pawing at the ridiculous tuft beneath his chin, eyes raw from lack of sleep and desperate for any answers Erikson might have. Of course, the man was vastly experienced, a useful resource for Karal and likely one Segfi and her cronies had recruited to their cause. There was a military edge to him, one he'd not had an opportunity to dig any deeper for. But you didn't give such people chances. Now was the time to take pieces off the board.

He lifted his wrist to his lips. "Now," Erikson said. The word so simple, but ready to cause mayhem. Trent peered at him, head tilting, curiosity in his eyes. Erikson snorted. How unbecoming. "I have your answer," he said, and drew out a gun from inside his jacket.

Two bullets flew, and ever the hero, Trent stepped aside, taking both rounds to the chest. Blood splattered, and tired eyes awoke with realisation. The bastard Incini screamed, alive because of Trent's training, no doubt. Erikson clambered over his desk, shoving the toppling operations officer to the side, another bullet winging its way towards Connors. She dropped, the Incini wetware must have triggered her reactions.

No mind.

He leapt, slamming his feet into the back of her legs, driving knees into her spine, ramming the Incini witch to the floor. One hand wrapped into her not-so elegant hair, yanking her head back, the click of the trigger next to her ear.

"I'm going to enjoy this," he said, and he was. A bullet slammed into the base of his skull, smashing the vertebrae, severing his spinal cord. His fingers pulsed, the gun firing as he jerked, as agony flooded his brain. A last awareness punctuated with the Incini's scream, blood erupting from her ear. But not death. No.

Not yet.

"Rescue me…"

The wetware fired, triggering an explosive. Heat tore into his brain, the eruption, the shattering of skull and bone … then nothing.

Davina winced, her ear aching, clogged, a roar echoing that refused to stop. A weight lay upon her back, heavy, unmoving, and wet. She tried to roll, a sharp pain in her back refuting her first attempt, but she forced herself into a second, and something slid off.

She glanced to the side, her blood-red vision blurred but catching sight of Erikson. His skull cavity exposed, empty but for the one or two wires that reeked of burning blood. Davina heaved, nausea spreading like a wildfire through her body. Disoriented, head spinning, she vomited, unable to keep herself from the embarrassment. It helped, but her mind still spun as she rolled onto her hip, her back reminding her of its woes. Her other eye remained good, and she took a guarded look at what remained of Erikson. Blood and gore had splattered the walls, and by the feel of her hair and blouse, most of her. She raised a hand to her ear, and a sharp pain drove into her skull. It came away wet, bloody, and despite Erikson's demise, she suspected much was hers.

With an eye flicker, she activated her wetware, dulling the sensory input from her nerves, clearing some of the headache but far from all. With a painful twist of her neck, she made out Trent. He was on the floor but slumped forwards, eyes glassy, a handgun by dead fingers.

"Damn," she mouthed, the effort hurting her jaw. She pushed herself onto her knees, her back hurting with the effort, almost as if bone ground on bone, gnawing at her wetware's efforts to dull the pain. Davina grasped the edge of her desk, but her arms were so weak, and she was unable to stand. Instead, she pulled herself around the edge, eventually managing to reach a slate. Of the two, she prayed it was her own, rewarded with a hope as the blood sprayed screen came to life with her personal icons. She tapped once, and the office alarm systems blared into action. A second wasn't so swiftly answered, the wait agonising until Savvo appeared. The co-pilot's breathing was heavy, and he appeared to be struggling into a spacesuit.

"Davina?" he said, the words strained, an arm popping through and on into the gloved ends. "What ...?" His eyes widened. Perhaps he'd noticed her hair wasn't as elegant as usual, or the gore that splattered one half of her face.

"Erikson," she managed. Then passed out.

CHAPTER 29

KARAL

The docks' transport shuttle stuttered on approach to M4's terminal, almost as if reluctant to come to a stop. Rebekah's pilot instincts kicked in, a recognition that the usual smooth glide to a full stop beside the hub had, for the first time in over 30,000 runs, an issue. She gripped Hendricks' shoulder, and unclipped before she should, but there was no one watching. The rest of the passengers merely stopped their whispered conversations as the difference in the shuttle's usual smooth approach impinged on their thoughts and then was just as quickly dismissed. Only four others had copied Rebekah, three she knew were pilots, the fourth wore a flight suit and rose to stand behind the others. They glanced at each other, the gentlest of nods shared, their eyes all falling on Rebekah.

She'd been volunteered.

Reputation for trouble, huh? Too fucking right.

She clomped along the aisle, slapping one of the pilot's arms – Sventon of the *Amethyst* – on the way by, giving him a half-humorous glare before she approached the corridor that led into the fore cabin and then the sealed cockpit. The flight attendant stood by the embarkment airlock, talking into the comms, eyes on the series of red lights that ran alongside the door.

"An issue?" he said, then the attendant seemed to sense Rebekah's presence, glancing over his shoulder and nodding. He raised a hand, she assumed for silence. The crackle of comms leaked from his cans, but she couldn't quite make out what was being said until the attendant mouthed 'gunfire'.

"Hey," she tugged urgently at the attendant's arm. "We need to know. What's going on?"

Again, he held up his hand as he listened, and her anxiety rose a notch. The man then blocked his small mic and blinked before speaking.

"You need to take your seat. We're leaving. There's an incident in the docking bay, and it is not regarded as safe to disembark." His voice rose in pitch, and Rebekah picked up the tells of fear. The attendant's more than comfortable monotony had been shattered, and he was on the verge of panicking. Next stage would be overreaction, but her crew were on that dock.

Fuck that. We are in a defenceless tin can.

Until they knew what the incident was and whether aggressive spaceships were involved, the safest choice was to hug the asteroid.

"You said gunfire. Gunfire. That means our crews are under attack," she prodded, keeping her words fast and intense. "Any ships involved?"

"I-I don't know."

Rebekah growled at him and ripped off his comms unit. He made a grab for it, suddenly finding his arm pinned back against the wall. Hendricks was by her side holding the attendant back, behind her Sventon, his blond hair tied in a ridiculous top knot trying to stop her ex-captain.

Good luck with that.

"Listen to Rebekah. Yes? Any holes in this flying bathtub and we're all airless, dehydrated popsicles." She spoke with Arin's penchant for drama.

Rebekah glanced up at the pilot roster. Nicholls. Solid, dependable and zero combat experience. "Nicholls, this is Khan," she stated. "Your attendant has just had a panic attack. What's the deal?"

Hendricks shushed the attendant, one finger to the lips with a threatening glare doing what Rebekah would have achieved with a punch. At the same time, she shrugged off Sventon who was still trying to intervene.

"Khan? Sheesh. The tower is under attack. We need to leave."

"You have any confirmation that there are no hostile ships?" At those words, Sventon stopped, hands in mid-air. Rebekah could see the sudden realisation in his eyes while Hendricks growled.

"No. But ..."

"No buts. You ever had your co-pilot sucked out of a fucking crack in your fuselage? Watched your Marine buddy gasp their last breath while the water in their cells drifts behind them? Had cannon rounds tear through your hu—" Sventon's eyes widened a little further. He had seen combat towards the end of the war, flown dropships during the withdrawal from Bustan 7. Hendricks, on the other hand, lowered the attendant whose panic had culminated in a faint. He floated against the corridor wall, boots preventing him from drifting off.

"Enough. In all the bloody hells, Khan. What do you want me to do?"

"Is the terminal compromised?"

"No. It's still sealed."

Rebekah glanced over to her ex-captain who nodded in return, then looked behind to the seats and the waiting mining and ship crews. All of them except two knew space like the back of their spacesuit's glove.

"Get the tunnel out. We all have our suits in the locker rooms. Safer than having a fucking missile up your shuttle's arse."

Rebekah and Sventon went first, the only two with forces experience on board apart from Hendricks. But she had her hands full keeping the twins in their seats.

They descended the link tunnel, staying low, eyeing the terminal airlock which blinked a reassuring green despite being on emergency lockdown. She signalled him to wait, then took the last few steps down to the outer door. The small window provided a limited view, but the flashes inside were unmistakable. Gunfire, the occasional bullet striking the inner skin of the terminal wall. It was tough, and nothing short of a direct micrometeor strike would get through. However, the airlocks were the weak point, and three guards were arrayed about this one, benches overturned as they fired back towards unseen assailants. Rebekah had a good idea who they might be, but weaponless and missing her armour, the odds of a successful intervention were small. But she had an ace in the hole. She hoped.

She tapped at her wrist, then drew out her slate as she leant against the airlock. Sventon took guard, peering through the tiny window.

"*Sunstar*, this is Rebekah, come back. I say again, Savvo, Arin, you there?" she mentally prayed as she spoke. If this was the Butcher's work, then surely the *Sunstar* would have been a main target. The delay wasn't helping, nor the hiss of static. Jamming?

A look down at the slate made her smile as a flag pulsed back at her. She selected a new channel. HT2, internal comms twins' style.

"Savvo?"

"No. Our co-pilot is currently running defensive cover for a group of dock workers. Arin is in support. I, on the other hand, have the prerogative of saving crew." ZZ3's monotone had a hint of pride in there, she was sure. "Orders, Captain?"

"Where are you?" she felt useless minus her HUD. Exposed without her entire Marine kit.

"Dock side, thirty metres from the terminal, hidden behind a mag-cargo transport," replied ZZ3. "There are two of the attackers on guard at the main entrance." Rebekah drew up the guide plans of the docks, those used by crews. She visualised where the warbot was.

"On my mark, take down the two guards, but do not, I say again, do not damage the airlock. We need to gain access to the locker room. Your priority on entry is to guard that room while providing a distraction. Go on thirty seconds."

"A distraction? They'll be lucky to stay alive," said Sventon.

"You might be in for a surprise. Be ready, when the shit starts flying, we need to be in and locking this airlock down so we can move everyone safely inside." Sventon glanced at her, a reluctance in his eyes. She would have given anything right now for a carbine in her hands, a full navy suit and a Breaker by her side. "Open it."

Sventon tapped in the emergency override Nicholls had provided. When the outer door spun open, they both entered a space designed for twenty passengers at a time. A guard registered the movement, but ignored them for now. Rebekah had a better view of the terminal concourse, keeping low, she tried to count the assailants. Four, but well-armed. The inner office doors beside the security booths were smashed open, these led to the tower offices and control. As the air pressure hit green and the doors opened a crack she rolled through, coming to her feet beside one of the guards. Gunfire rattled, answered only by the bark of low-powered pistols from terminal security.

The set up was obvious. They were being contained. The target was through those shattered doors. The tower, but why?

"Khan," she said. "Sergeant-pilot ..." she hesitated.

Fuck it.

"I was a Breaker." The security guard stopped firing, ducking down, eyeing her. "I need a weapon."

Behind his visor his eyes roamed over her, and then he dropped a hand to the floor, grasping a bloodied stun pistol which he handed over with his baton. "All we got."

It'd have to do.

"Sventon," she handed the pistol over. "Once the shit flies, keep whoever's coming through that door safe. Understand?" She slapped him on the arm and flicked the baton open. The metal tip stung the floor.

"Distractions incoming," stated ZZ3.

"Down!" Rebekah shouted, the voice of command.

A thunderous roar bellowed through the half-open exit doors, followed by smoke and a tremendous flash of light. She hoped their assailants were not as savvy, and had glanced back to see what was happening as the second flash grenade erupted. Clever warbot.

She was up and running, dodging between overturned seats and benches, disengaging her boots and leaping over the security barriers. With the aide of the lower grav, she hit the ground and rolled to a stop next to one of the combatants. They had their hands to their helmet, shaking it side to side as if trying to clear their vision. She swore, the insignia on their arm from the *Segfi*. Navy kit, meaning the visor would have reacted fast, the blindness minimal. And the fucking armour tough.

She flexed her wrist, and not waiting for the split of skin, speared her hand upwards and into their arm pit. The blade snicked and locked as the tip struck the joint, and with her wetware triggered, Rebekah rammed it home, driving up through her legs to rip and tear. The blade smashed into the bone beneath, the ripple of pain forcing a roar from the clone Marine. With no time, she crashed her elbow down onto their helmet, knowing the pain would be an issue but she needed what they had. The clone smacked into the deck, his grip upon the carbine faltering. Rebekah grabbed it, throwing herself to the side on the presumption the rest of the clones would be shaking off the effects of the flash grenades.

Bullets tracked her, shattering benches and seats in her path, splinters pattering against her legs. She hit the deck, scrabbling to be free of the gunfire. But it poured in, relentless, their assailants switching from containment to the hunt. There was answering fire from the guards, the flash of low-powered rounds and stun shots flaring across the concourse. But their armour would shrug it off. In her gut, she knew she'd pushed things too far, and needed ZZ3. She reached for her comms, but they weren't there.

"Fuck." She kicked at the chair opposite, the seat obliterated as the clones reacted.

No, no, no.

And then her words were echoed, searing into her mind.

"NO!" roiled along the concourse, half words, half pure refusal. A tide of emotional denial she barely had her barriers up in time to deny. The tsunami crashed into her mind, threatening to shut it down then reboot in seething hate.

Wails rose, agonised declarations of self-loathing that echoed about the hall. Gunfire erupted. Short bursts, followed by gentle thuds while the clatter of hand-to-hand fights continued near the external airlock. Rebekah risked a glance, catching the gleam of crimson splattering the clones, their carbines cast aside, smoke leaking from the muzzles after their last act. She got to her feet, eyeing Hendricks as she wrestled a security guard, reluctance in her eyes as she wrenched the stun pistol free and blasted them point blank. Another guard moaned, receiving a second discharge of Hendricks' careful ministrations. On the floor lay Sventon, breathing, but a red mark rose livid on his cheek, the whites of his eyes showing as they rolled up and his lids closed.

Standing in the centre of the chaos were two girls, hand in hand, the fury on their faces melting away to reveal broad smiles that sent a pulse of relief rolling over Rebekah. They made to run towards her, but she raised a hand accompanied by a swift shake of her head.

"No. Not until we have the all-clear. Dricks," she threw over the carbine, "guard the concourse, get the shuttle evacuated." She walked over to the clone she had stabbed, collecting her lost comms and its sidearm, placing the muzzle carefully and finishing the job she'd started. She wanted no threats at her back when feeling this vulnerable. "ZZ3, sit rep?"

"All clear," the warbot replied.

Rebekah eyed the broken doors that led to the tower offices, and above that the control centre. The consequences sent a shaft into her heart. "With me. We have a clean up to do."

CHAPTER 30

"Inside now!" bellowed Savvo from behind an aluminium cargo box, whipping his hand towards the *Sunstar* and its open cargo bay. The dock workers and maintenance crews responded, bouncing across M4's metal deck towards him, risking all as they turned down their magboots to use the low grav to their advantage. Four hovered above the deck behind, dropping slowly, mist pouring from the holes punched in their suits by carbine rounds.

Fuckers.

Gunshots came in silence, the only clue the slightest flash from a muzzle here and there, the airless dockside peppered with the dead and soon to be dead. Workers who Savvo regarded as colleagues. He had struggled to make sense of the attack at first. It appeared almost random, exploding into chaos as the comms chatter ramped up.

A round slammed into his shoulder, twisting him around, forcing the ex-Breaker to disengage his boot or suffer a back injury. He carried on the spin, dropping to his knees, aiming past the last of the repair crews on this side of the docks.

"Got the bastard," echoed in his comms, and something exploded thirty metres north of him. Blood sprayed in globules, swiftly followed by the telltale mist. The assailant had a huge hole in his chest where Arin's high-powered sniper round struck. "Arin six, zombie clones from hell, zero."

Savvo accessed the sub-engineer's feed, checking over the flagged infra-red images. The camera jostled, Arin firing again, the round boring through a generator to smash the helmet of another clone. They knew who they were, their first kill had been in close, taking down one fucker who had been mowing down a defenceless work team.

"Watch your reload," he said, and zoned back in. The last of the survivors had dodged inside the *Sunstar*'s bay, most either ignoring that it was a silver-suited Senti whose tentacles guided them to safety, or were too shocked to care. Kefi.

Another burst body erupted from behind the generator, this time nearer the back, answered by carbine fire that bounced off the upper hull of the *Sunstar*. If the clone Marines had better weapons, they'd be in trouble. Savvo fired a burst, keeping their enemies' heads down where Arin had flagged them. Eight left, wearing suits similar to theirs, weaponry as well. Potential stalemate. Well, it would be if the transponder was working.

"Coming in," he said. "Cover me." Savvo spun from behind the remaining cargo boxes on Arin's confirmation, and ran for the yawning cargo doors, weaving as he went. A few rounds bounced off the surrounding deck, one clipping his thigh before pinging away. Arin had switched to his carbine, emptying the clip in a burst that he caught through his feed. Savvo flung himself inside the doors.

"Kefi, cover." Kefi – tucked in behind a steel navy storage box – let fly. The strange radiation gun firing bursts complemented by the carbine she was firing with her other shoulder tentacle. She appeared formidable. "Arin, we're covering, drop inside."

"You spoil all my fun," came the reply.

A quick check of his HUD, and on seeing Arin was on the move, Savvo reloaded and added to the covering fire as the sub-engineer dropped in, swinging his lifeline to land with zero grace but perfect accuracy the other side of a box stack. Savvo winced, knowing there were dock workers hunkering down somewhere over there.

"Get off, get off. I'm friendly!" shouted Arin, more than a few dull thuds accompanying his voice over comms.

Savvo switched to the dockside channel. "He's one of ours, be gentle. Kefi, the doors." Savvo fired again through the entrance and felt the hum of the bay doors activate. Another burst, Arin finally having joined after extricating himself from the pile of irate dockers. "Going for the navcom. Arin, get on the PDC."

"You what? You want to give me access to the ultimate zombie clone deterrent?"

"No. I don't want you to *deter*, I want you to fucking eviscerate." Savvo hoped that was the right word, heart pumping as he reached Kefi. The Senti cycled the airlock fully open, the urgency apparent, and with the hiss of escaping, misting air, Savvo pounded down the corridor to the sound of alarms. The *Sunstar* wasn't happy about the change in atmospheric conditions, but Savvo was in a rush. He clipped the galley table on the way by, then squeezed himself into the pilot's chair. Fingers danced over the screen and keyboard, bypassing the transponder and eventually disengaging its weapons override. No one wanted weapons fire inside a dock. Whether atmospherically sealed or open to space, it was highly dangerous.

"Now, Arin."

"Yeehah. Come eat some plutonium death." The topside PDC opened up, vibrations shuddering throughout the hull as the ship was clamped to the dockside. He hoped Arin would show some restraint, but right now he needed whoever was out there deader than dead and he didn't have the time to do it himself. Rebekah was out there with Hendricks and the twins. On negating the transponder, he'd noted the transport shuttle had docked. ZZ3 would be there, waiting, defending the crew, but something was wrong. He knew it.

The tower had been silent for too long.

Rebekah followed ZZ3 in, the warbot kicking the doors wide, arm weapons bared as red eyes swept the tower hallway. Six doors, a lift and a stairwell all bore the brunt of an assault. The dead splayed upon the floor, faces in shock, blood splattered carelessly everywhere. A massacre. The first she'd seen since ... since Bustan 8. The memory didn't sit well; they'd pumped the entire vanguard full of drugs and turned their wetware all the way up. No mercy, no quarter. They were the hammer, and as Dricks led the squad into the tenement, she had sprayed floor after floor with metal death from the outside, emptying the fore guns on the dropship.

Fuck. What was I?

"Check every door," she said. "I'll watch the stairwell." The warbot was nothing but efficient, kicking each door down, running a sensory sweep and moving on. What would have taken her five minutes it completed in two, and saved her the sight of the bloodied innocents the clones had left in their wake. This was systematic assassination. It had to have a purpose.

"Next floor," she said, eyeing the blood scrapes across the bot's limbs with trepidation. "Run a sensory analysis."

"Yes, Captain." ZZ3 steamrollered up the stairs, no bullets greeting the walking tank. She leant back, taking aim, and destroying the lift controls. One way in, one way out. But there were two more exits. In a body bag or through the walls and windows. The clones were in powered navy armour. Walls were no hindrance.

Rebekah ran up the stairs, slowing as ZZ3 bashed through a final door at the corridor's end.

"No one alive," the warbot stated, the tone as matter-of-fact as it could be.

Rebekah eyed the final floor. Command and control, old style. A 360-degree view of the entire M4 dock and repair bays via a series of ultra-thick plexi-glass windows. An affectation. One hundred percent of the tower's work was via navcom interface and screens, but she had to admit, the one time she'd been allowed in there had been breathtaking.

"ZZ3, Nicky ...?" she said.

"Shift roster states that Nicky is off duty," replied ZZ3.

Rebekah paused. Of course, Savvo would have checked, known even. Would ZZ3 have been waiting for them otherwise, or Savvo defending the docks? If Nicky had been in danger, his decisions may have been very different. Relief coursed through her as she eyed the stairwell.

"Take out the cameras," she said. "And any defensive weapons still operational."

"There are none," replied the warbot. "The systems are offline, and I can detect traces of electrical fire including particles commensurate with auto-weaponry. However, I will approach with caution." ZZ3 took the first step up, and was met with a hail of bullets that bounced off the stairs. The bot paused, servos whirring, then exploded into action. The heavier armour Arin had added definitely weighed ZZ3 down, but the sight of a thundering tank pounding up the stairs would have any soldier shitting themselves. Except, of course, these were clones. Who knew what emotions they were governed by, if any? After all, it only took a few drugs and a blast of wetware to turn her into a murderer of the innocent.

But the girls can affect the clones. Their anger.

ZZ3 had reached the mid-level, the barrage increasing, and she wished for one of Arin's flash grenades so hard, only for her prayers to be answered – unfortunately by the enemy. An eruption, sound roaring down the stairwell, accompanied by an enclosed flash of searing light. She dropped, smothering her head, instinctively kicking in her wetware to take the edge off the pain boring into her brain. The comms unit blocked some of the cacophony, preventing her from being stunned, but her sight was affected, and she threw herself to the side. Bullets rained down, whether they would have hit or not was moot as her shoulder slammed into the corner of the stairwell, spinning her out and away from their path.

"ZZ3," she said over comms, her shoulder stiff, eyes weeping. "Hold the stairs, I've been flashed. Need a minute."

"Affirmative. Six enemies barricaded in. I have negated three others."

Rebekah got up onto all fours, searching for a position that would prevent her rising nausea. A cough, and she vomited a little, and then the flood of chemicals rode over her brain. A squeeze of the bridge across her nose, and she was able to rise, balance returning despite the red-rimmed black spots flickering in and out of her vision.

"Rebekah," came a hushed voice. Hendricks, fast approaching from the level below. Her ex-captain dropped in beside her, carbine in hand, a couple of extra clips now resting on her knee. "Take these. You been hit?"

"Flashed," she said. "No fucking visor. ZZ3 is holding the upper stairs."

"Watch my rear." Hendricks swept past. There was no arguing, she wasn't ready for an out and out firefight.

"ZZ3, Dricks is coming up." She pushed herself off the floor, checked her magazine, pocketed the spare clips and followed, blinking all the while. Carbine rounds echoed from above, and by the time she reached the upper half, Hendricks was alongside the warbot returning fire.

"Sit rep," she said, unable to squeeze in between them. "ZZ3?"

"They have moved three hostages through a door behind the rear console. They are threatening to kill them should I attack," stated the bot.

"A standard delaying tactic," growled Hendricks, she stopped firing and glanced back to Rebekah. "Time wasting. Either awaiting rescue, or for a triggering event."

"I know," she huffed, blowing out her cheeks. In suits, with Marine equipment, just maybe they could do this without more deaths. But that was irrelevant. "Why the tower?"

"Because they are bringing ships in?" mused Hendricks, releasing a burst as someone moved up ahead.

"Attack ships? Or they are doing the Butcher's work, downloading, or the gods forbid, uploading itself into the system." She tapped Hendricks on the leg, blinking away the last of the light spots. "Either way, once done they'll kill the hostages and blow the control room."

Hendricks nodded. "Aye. In all likelihood. What you got with you, ZZ3?"

"I have three arm grenades left," stated the warbot. "We were in a hurry."

"Right," the engineer said, the tone familiar to Rebekah. Hendricks had a plan, one she didn't like, but, as always, ready to face the inevitable. It was likely the same one she would have chosen. High risk, high gain. Maybe. "Pump two into the first console, the third behind, then go for the hostages. Rebekah and I will mop up the enemy in your wake."

"Affirmative."

"On my mark ..." Rebekah pushed herself to her feet, keeping low as Hendricks counted down. "3, 2, 1 ... Mark."

The warbot fired, double grenades ramming into the forward console, a third winging its way before they had exploded. ZZ3's limbs powered the warbot forward, aiming for the centre of the dual explosions that tore through the control room. As the third grenade blew, the bot had dodged left, steaming towards the identified room. Gunfire rattled against the warbot's armour, Rebekah tracing them back and pouring a burst into the clone. Hendricks' gun barked over and over as they strode into the room.

Rebekah couldn't see past the smoke, but heard the crash as the warbot battered through a door. Gunfire echoed back.

"Explosives!" exclaimed the warbot in her comms.

She didn't think, just acted, chemicals surging across her brain as she grabbed Hendricks' collar, yanking the woman back. They toppled, her foot clipping the upper step, and as the control room erupted in fire and billowing smoke, they tumbled backwards down the stairs. Rebekah clutched her head, hoping Hendricks was doing the same as the explosion and false gravity combined to slam her into the mid-level. Her ex-captain landed on top, ramming into her unprotected chest – winding her. But alive was alive.

She rolled Dricks off, gasping for air, calming her mind and body to ease the rising panic before finally sucking in a shallow breath, then another. Gaining her feet, she pulled Hendricks to hers, and then ascended the stairs, sidearm in hand. They weren't sucking vacuum – a bonus. The windows must have held, but the room was a burnout, foam pouring from the console fire defences, bubbling up like a white lava amid the electronics. Fire in space was a big no.

"ZZ3, sit rep." Static ensued over her comms, and looking around the room, interference was no surprise.

Row by row, they checked the Marine clones. Finding more unused explosives in their shattered packs. Further along they reached the doorway ZZ3 had battered down, the bot sprawled across the floor, backplate scorched. Rebekah couldn't describe what lay beyond, a foul mix of limbs and burned body parts wet from the room's fire sprinklers. Blood flowed in rivulets.

"Fuck." She dropped by the warbot's side, a red flicker deep within its remaining four eyes indicating ZZ3 was still in there somewhere. A hand landed on her shoulder, Hendricks, her eyes wide. On the far side of the room swung a half-burnt banner.

"No."

CHAPTER 31

"Clear," said Savvo, but Arin had a taste and the dual point defence cannons still fired. "I said clear, Arin. Stand down!"

The vibrations thrumming through the *Sunstar* faded away, but out on the dockside, and the level above, smoke and ash fluttered in the low grav. Shrapnel, shredded metal and ex-cargo boxes filled the space, gently wafting sideways as the spin of the asteroid drew them back towards their respective levels.

"Checking the level below," he said, and ran a sensory sweep, tuning the ship's system as low as it would go. There were life signs out there, each pinging back the code for a Karal dock worker or maintenance crew. So far, all those they had fought wore Navy-issue armour. The crews' suits designed to resist tears, not penetration, would have left an attack force far more vulnerable.

Unless you have a PDC, of course.

But the Butcher was a sneaky bastard AI, so far usually several steps ahead, and he feared that among the surviving workers may be seeded clones. How the hell was he going to weed them out?

He let out a breath, sucking it in before speaking over comms. "Only Karal signals coming from above and below. Stand down and join me in the cargo bay. Stay armed and frosty, Arin. This doesn't feel over."

"Copy that."

After setting the sensors to auto-alarm, he collected his carbine and squeezed himself out of the pilot's chair. There was no way he was removing any protection until he knew who was in the hold, or left out in the docks. By the time he reached the bay, Arin was already there, milling through the thirty or so workers, slapping backs. At least everyone knew who they were now. Who they had been. Carbines and powered armour a small giveaway.

Armour, visors. What about wetware?

Savvo pulled up his HUD screen, and locked in on Arin's signal. It came through loud and clear, with no other flags in the bay. No surprise there, and he began to run through the standard frequencies. Nothing came back, that small flicker of light amid the thunder clouds fading away. Either they were shielded, like the countess, or using a frequency his HUD couldn't recognise like on Daphene.

"You okay back there, good buddy?" asked Arin. He was still amid the relieved workers, milking the plaudits, but as ever, had one eye on what was really going on.

"Just wondering if there could be a wrong 'un amid this lot. A Butcher clone," he replied, watching the milling crowd. "But there's no wetware flags." He glanced over to Kefi, who appeared clearly on edge, shoulder tentacles twitching at the tips. With the split personality thing, it was so damn hard to make assumptions about what was churning in that alien mind. Did she sense the unease too? Or was the squeeze of humanity a little overwhelming?

Humanity.

Bloody hell.

"Keep them contained, Arin. I need to speak to Kefi alone."

"Oh, *I* see," he replied with a measure of indignance. "There's still room for more above a lowly sub-engineer's role."

Savvo shrugged it off. He gestured towards Kefi, who read his intent and pulled herself towards the exposed corridor.

Savvo switched comms. "This is the Butcher's work," he said. "They were in navy armour. The clones again."

Kefi nodded along, again a human gesture, but her eyes stared into the distance. The slitted mouth gave another hint she was listening, the occasional opening and closing perhaps an indication she wanted to speak. He suspected they were having some form of internal discussion, which he hated the thought of. It didn't feel safe.

"Agreed," stated Kefi. That was it.

He carried on, filing away his concern. "Look, thank you for your help. But I need something else. Your symb ... your symbiote, or the Nest Queen's, whatever. It can read wetware, right?"

A pause, a distance in the eyes. It gnawed again. "The (*scraping of toast*) hmm ... taste your brain excretions. So can detect the anomalies caused by the integrated brain stimulation and memory storage systems. Yes."

The coldness of the response didn't surprise him, but the information he'd need to recall for Rebekah. A glance told him his HUD was recording. Good. "I need you to test those inside the bay. But subtly. They get any sense you're tasting their fucking brains, shit will go down. They're already on edge."

Kefi shifted then, almost a gleam in her eyes as they focused in. "You mean they will react badly to me examining their excretions." She added a whole cliff side of squawking. "Yes, yes. I can do that, though they are nervous of me already."

Savvo eyed the cargo doors. "Good. I have a plan."

His suit comms hissed, a distant voice, monotone, matter of fact, breaking through. "*Sunstar* this is ZZ3. Terminus and tower secured."

Relief flooded through Savvo, and he passed on the message quickly to Arin who sent back a thumbs up from amid the workers. "Dricks? The twins?"

There was a pause Savvo put down to the warbot's usual hitch. "They and Rebekah are unharmed. The tower is out of action; comms and all transponders are down. We have word of an attack on M1. Trent Pike is dead, Davina injured."

"Fuck. Not just here. The docks are clear of any assailants. We have retained as many work teams as we could in the *Sunstar*. Listen, ZZ3, we don't know who's friend or fucking foe here. Kefi is going to test them."

Another pause, this time Savvo knew the bot was relaying his sit rep. Pike, dead? Davina attacked. What was going down?

"Nicky was here," said the bot.

Was?

Fucking was?

"No way, she was off-shift," he said, heart in mouth. "ZZ3, what the hell? Was? She's okay, right?"

"She survived and is under treatment. The shuttle took her and others back to M2 and will be returning with a full medical team and additional armed security." The warbot's tone remained flat, matter-of-fact, but there was something off. As if the warbot had rowed back on its burgeoning personality. Hiding something.

"ZZ3. The truth. Nicky ..."

"I am not a medbot. Her physical injuries were relatively minor, her left arm broken from a fall, right side struck by multiple pieces of shrapnel from an explosion, though superficial. But she was in severe shock. Closed down after ..." the hitch was not deliberate, more a hint of the emerging ghost in the machine. "When she saw me. When I attempted the rescue."

Savvo waited by the cargo doors. Behind him fifteen of the workers had emerged one by one, Arin plugging the medbot into their suits as each passed by, making a show of checking out their med data while Kefi stood at the side of the medbot 'helping', speaking to those waiting in line. Each set of med data was relayed to the medical team who had established a field hospital in the terminal. So far, the signs were of shock, the most severe of whom were already on their way for treatment with a designated buddy. Not one of those waiting in line appeared agitated by the procedure. Savvo knew the presence of wetware could only be detected if the medbot was set into search mode, and it took time. On Palail their active wetware had passed through without an issue, though whether Baron Winkal was fussed about deserters in his private army was unknown. He also suspected it could be masked, the wetware tuned to provide expected responses should the wearer, or its creator, wish. Therefore, the lack of anxiety in those waiting wasn't the proof he was looking for. That remained with Kefi.

"No signs," she repeated and moved on to the next, then the next, Arin keeping up the show with the medbot.

Across the way, a small dock transport glided in, manoeuvring thrusters micro adjusting to land in its designated bay. A minute or so later, a batch of shell-shocked workers exited, Rebekah behind having flexed her pilot's muscle bringing the small ship in.

"Last ones," she said, and swept her gaze over the line.

"Nothing of note," he said before she could ask. Hendricks then emerged from the transport, carrying one of the maintenance crew in both arms. "Bad?"

"No, they'll live," replied Hendricks, and she carried on past, heading for the terminus. "Just needed to knock them out. They were in no state to travel safely in a crowd."

"Screaming all the time. They saw their work buddy die. The others had him held down, but we had to sedate." Rebekah sidled in beside Savvo. "You're relieved, co-pilot. Go check on her."

Savvo looked to his captain, her face replicated by his HUD showing the same concern he felt. Hers was likely for him, probably wondering if he'd been ragging on his wetware, or added a stim to the adrenaline coursing about his body. "I'm clean," he said.

"I know. But this is not the Breakers, we're not on mission."

"No," he said, then felt an urge to qualify it. "You're wrong. We've not been off mission since the day we opened up the *Scourge*. And until the Butcher is dead, or we are, we never fucking will be." He tasted the bitterness in his words, acid on his tongue, and immediately regretted snapping at his captain. He made to apologise, expecting the Rebekah scowl. He nearly choked at the sympathy in those eyes.

"You're probably right. Now fuck off and check on Nicky." She shoved him away.

Savvo allowed his magboots to disengage, and headed off towards the terminus, speeding up to catch Hendricks. They walked in silence for the last thirty metres, Savvo getting the first sight of the wrecked concourse as they cycled through the airlock, the peppered stairs. Blood was splattered across wall and floor, while the med team worked on the injured on makeshift beds. He'd witnessed a hundred scenes like it before, at the rear of many battlefields. He'd occupied one of those beds on occasion himself, and knew damn well it would have been many more without the woman he walked alongside.

Hendricks headed straight for the nearest available bed, easing the man onto the sheets as an orderly dropped to their knees beside him, medical scanner plugging in to their suit.

"I had to sedate him. He was heading into shock. Agitated," stated Hendricks, and then spun to face Savvo. "You still here?"

Savvo snapped to attention out of habit. "I'm going," he replied, and turned away before stopping himself. "How bad?"

"Nicky?" started Hendricks. It was a delaying tactic, trying to compose herself. "Hard to say, Savvo. ZZ3 went in hard, the room was screwed up. She was the only one ... she was the only one ZZ3 could save."

He turned about, mind running over those words, pouring over the times ZZ3 had led assaults before. Fuck, the old warbot could barely separate enemy from hostage. It was only the direst times they sent the bot in, or when the drugs had left them uncaring. Had it chosen Nicky deliberately? Sacrificed others? And did he want to know?

Savvo nodded, not turning about, hoping Hendricks had picked up his response. His feet dragged him towards the shuttle, loaded up with the remaining injured and even more of the dead. Once inside, he made himself busy, removing his helmet – his defence against the outside world – to help those in pain. It had been his calling after he'd been released from the haze of being a Breaker, exercised since the day they had entered the *Scourge*. A need to make things right, without drugs or wetware to dull the memories.

CHAPTER 32

M2 HOSPITAL, KARAL

Davina pushed herself up, sidling back to rest against the headboard, adapting the medbed's position until her whole body was comfortable. She felt disoriented, as if floating a few centimetres above the mattress, but then the medication staved off the pain running through her back and lower legs.

"What are you doing?" The nurse glared her way, clearly harassed and stressed, his hands constantly squeezing together as he stood at her door.

"Getting comfortable," she tried to say, but the metal wires cradling her jaw prevented anything other than a grunt to fill the medroom.

The nurse waddled over, eyes rolling in mock sarcasm, as if she was a nuisance. "No talking. You've had your jaw remodelled some under your insurance policy, your eardrum is now defunct and there's a scheduled op for a synth drum replacement. Your lower back is heavily bruised; one lower disc is bulging and will need repair. You took some beating, girlie."

"Girlie?" it came out in another grunt, rewarded with a wide-eyed grin.

The nurse checked over the medical scanner at her side, tutting and clicking his tongue. "All good, but as soon as this thing bleeps at you, it'll start adjusting your position for the best blood flow to your injures. You don't listen it sends for me." He cracked his knuckles as he walked off, cackling.

Davina decided to listen to the monitor if only to avoid being called 'girlie'. A glance gave her sight of what she wanted most, a slate at her bedside table. It wasn't hers, standard hospital issue, but it was a start. Despite the ache in her fingers, she had swiped through enough firewalls and security barriers to keep the Emperor safe by the time a visitor appeared at her door – this time devoid of a threatening nurse's uniform. Rebekah stood there looking nearly as battered and bruised as she was.

"Hey," she said, and looked her up and down. "They say I'm not allowed to let you talk. So, either you just get to listen or ..." The ex-Breaker pointed towards the slate. "You can type."

Davina held up a finger, asking Rebekah to wait one moment. Once she had completed her message to the Directorate, she copied most of it and sent a sanitised version to the countess. Erikson, she was sure, was not acting on her orders. But sure didn't mean certain, and the only person Davina truly trusted right now was sat at her side.

Damn, never thought I'd be saying that. Or typing it.

She gestured to Rebekah, who attempted a smile in return, a wince hinting at Rebekah's own injuries.

"I tell you what went fucking down at the docks, and you tell me about Erikson. Deal? No beer and cocktail to mull it over with. At least for you." Rebekah smiled warmly as Davina blinked, then nodded softly in agreement. Rebekah leant forward, relaying the assault, their attempts at staving it off and the rescue of the workers. And of course, Nicky. Davina didn't know her well, but enough to see what Savvo saw in her. What stood front and centre was Rebekah's crew had saved the docks, and the lives of the remaining workers. It wouldn't go unnoticed. No wiping of records or hiding away vids would keep their secret hidden any longer.

"Trent?" asked Rebekah once she had finished.

She typed away. *'He saved me. Twice. Took a bullet meant for me, then blew the bastard's head off when I was down and out.'*

Rebekah grimaced. "He was always a dickhead," she said low and quiet. There was a hint of remorse there. "Do you know why he attacked? Was it on Segfi's orders?"

Davina focused, running through the events. Her wetware was unlike Rebekah's. It couldn't record everything or store a second memory. She was aware of far too many secret dealings for that to be allowed. But with a little stimulation here and there, it could heighten her recall. She ran through the attack as best she could, but found no clues. What had he said to Pike? Could she recall his lips?

She typed. *'He said 'now', maybe into comms or something. Then told Trent he had what he came for. Nothing after that apart from wanting to kill me.'*

"Was Trent the trigger?"

'Maybe. But Erikson's been acting weird a while.'

Rebekah sighed, nodding. "I've looked at the timings. All this happened soon after I contacted him about getting through to Countess Segfi. I wanted to know whether there had been an attempt on the shipyard's systems. Those at Tweem."

Davina shrugged. It meant nothing to her, but if that was a trigger …

'The Butcher?'

Rebekah stood, hands locked together in front of her. Davina could see concern there, the twist to her lips, the look in her eyes. And despite herself, she knew some of it was for her, the rest, perhaps, for what Erikson's actions hinted at.

"I'm going to need to examine the fucker's wetware. Right now, Karal is in a mess. Jenkra Tew has stepped in from the board to take over. She seems capable. Know her?"

Davina nodded. *'She is sound. A good choice.'*

Rebekah took Davina's unbruised hand, squeezing gently. "Then get me access to the body. I'm sure Segfi will have a say and soon, but I need it now. Can you do that?"

'Copy that, Captain Khan.' And as Rebekah left, she made a start. Yes, she had an 'in' with Jenkra, but right now the whole of Karal would be in a panic. It would need a calm voice, and money to settle the company and its workforce down.

Wishing for her own slate, she again went through a set of security protocols, eventually securing the briefest of outgoing transmission slots. She packaged up a request, highlighting the financial opportunities and her relationship with Tew, the potential of a relationship with the countess and a subtle hint at how Duboit – or in his true guise as Baron Stimpson – might be viewed for steadying Karal and therefore one of the Empire's main sources of PMG resources. He needed a status reset after the debacle with the *Hatton* and then the *Scourge*, and his Incini had one for him.

She encrypted and pressed send, then began to compile a list of all the issues with Erikson that had caused her concern. Davina suspected the countess would be in touch, her eyes also on protecting Karal, but if Erikson was a traitor, had been compromised by the Butcher somehow, she would want an Incini's insight. An opportunity, perhaps, to smooth Davina's future. The countess held grudges for decades, and she no doubt had one marked against her name circled in big red pen with 'bitch' written above it. Segfi didn't like to lose, nor be outplayed by lowlifes, for which she would regard Davina as a major conduit. The Incini who had contrived contracts in mid firefight, and then argued for the imperial pardons.

Work to do.

Davina woke up, finding herself in an entirely new position, her back aching and demanding more attention. She looked over to the monitor, checking the timetable pinned to the corner of the screen that noted the last visit from her less than favourite nurse. Apparently, two hours beforehand, he had adjusted the bed to move his favourite 'girlie' into a far more comfortable and safe position for her to sleep. A second note, this one by hand on a scrawl plate, noted where he'd put the slate he'd found toppling at the edge of the bed.

With an effort, she rolled herself onto her other side to be greeted by a face she'd last seen admiring castle walls and the lay of the land she had always dreamed of. Jenkra Tew, her grey hair pinned back, face made up that just about hid the bags under her eyes but not the red-rim of sleepless nights.

"Miss Connors," she said, and then to Davina's surprise, took her hand. "You are looking a little worse for wear."

Davina reached for her slate. *'Being beaten up can do that. Davina, call me Davina.'* She tried to sit up, but her back restarted its argument, with her upper thighs in total agreement. The monitor buzzed, and she knew damn well who would be on their way.

"Steady now. Wouldn't want any more harm to come. I can't stay, but your vitals hinted you were about to wake so the hospital contacted me at my request. I'm sorry, I know you've been through a lot, but I'm compiling a report for the Karal board with the Court looking over my shoulder. Word is, Erikson worked for them." Jenkra leant in a little, a conspiratory whisper on her lips. "That true?"

'I am contractually obliged not to respond,' she wrote, knowing full well that was enough of a hint. Besides, his behaviours in trying to kill her may well have negated some of the tenets. Well, all of them. But she still didn't know for definite who he officially worked for.

Jenkra didn't appear satisfied, however. "You are aware of the devastation to M4? The tower?" Davina nodded and regretted it. "Without the *Sunstar*'s crew, we'd have lost an entire shift team, and more of the crews. I understand you know them well?"

Too well.

'Good people…' she thought on that. *'tend towards violence when pushed. But trustworthy.'*

"They have requested access to Erikson. They say it's urgent, and that I should talk to you. I feel we, Karal, owe them, but if he's the Court's man …" Jenkra let that hang in the air. She was canny, looking for a way through the maze that had been dropped in her lap. She may never have dealt with the countess, but she would know more about the true reputation of that noble than most.

Davina couldn't answer for the countess, nor the Court. So, she gave the best one she could. *'If they wanted to, they could take Karal apart piece by piece.'*

Jenkra's eyes widened as she leaned back, but her hand still held Davina's.

'On that basis, in what amounts to a war situation, with a group under an Imperial Pardon, I'd say you had good reason to allow them access.'

Jenkra said nothing but maintained her gaze on Davina, the slightest of smiles appearing on her lips. Davina knew many executives who claimed they could handle power and the stress that came with it. Not one of them would have smiled at what she'd just dumped in Jenkra's lap. This woman was about to earn her castle and estate, and would likely never spend a moment there.

She typed again, *'I have prepared a report for the Countess. It may be wise to bump it up the comms queue. Perhaps add your own note that we are working together.'* Davina eyed Jenkra as she acknowledged and agreed. *'I also need my slates if they survived the carnage.'*

The acting chief officer touched her hand again, this time as a goodbye. "I'll see what I can do. Call it part of the investigation." Jenkra rose, a figure appearing at the door, a worried frown accompanying their feigned anger at Davina. "You look after her well, Tintru. She's important to me."

"Yes, Ms Tew," the nurse replied, the merest glint of humour in his eye. "It's what I do."

CHAPTER 33

M2 HOSPITAL, KARAL

Rebekah eased beside Savvo, her frown for him, not Nicky who slept soundly under sedation. There was a bruise forming along one cheek, the other side covered in medpad strips helping to heal the cuts caused by flying debris. One arm was locked in a cast, strapped in a gurney to prevent Nicky from rolling on to it. Beneath the sheets there were more bruises, and a swathe of lacerations that were thankfully non-life threatening.

Her mind, however, was more than just bruised. She'd gone to the tower for an office goodbye, to celebrate with a staff member who was leaving for Shema, her friend. Nicky had been the only one to survive.

Savvo had stripped off his navy-suit, the powered armour piled in the corner, smelling of sweat and fear, much as he did. Grime ringed his neck, his face sallow, eyes sunken. He hadn't left Nicky's side all night.

"She screamed," Savvo said, and touched Nicky's good arm. It was the seventh, perhaps eighth time he'd repeated that since she had joined him.

Rebekah had no words left for him. The med team had explained that the trauma was still real. That every time she woke up, she feared she was reliving the firefight, the hulking warbot, the explosion. Fire, shrapnel, the weight of ZZ3 as the bot crashed her to the floor, saving her life. Her brain was working out the dread, the taste of pain and terror.

Trauma was a bastard. For some, it never left them. The human brain as complex as any AI, but the repair mechanisms had their limits. The Almaarian officer-nobles knew this too well, and prevented the sharp loss in combat forces with the drugs, memory extraction and discipline. When the Senti offered to improve the efficiency of memory transfer, the nobility had initially baulked, but in return the new wetware had other benefits. A soldier who could retain their combat experience without the trauma, well they were nearly a machine weren't they? A flesh machine, with less downtime.

Next step, clone the fuckers.

"It's going to take time," Rebekah said, and rested a hand on the back of his neck. "And we—"

"—Don't have that," snapped Savvo. "*We* have to go off and do what we're told. Either for the Senti Nest Queen or the fucking Court. Never mind our choices, our lives." He shrugged off Rebekah's hand, but saved his glower for the floor, not her.

Rebekah hated herself. "Is this the bit when you tell me you're done again?"

Savvo kicked at the floor, his mouth twisting into a savage scowl. "Not going to work."

"I'm not trying to psyche you out. I'm trying to leave the question in your mind. Cos an unfocused crew member ain't gonna cut it against the Butcher. Not one whose thoughts lay in a hospital ward, or is out gunning for revenge." She hated herself. It was too soon. But wasn't it always? "You need some sleep, and Nicky's under for at least another six hours. And if she sees..."

Savvo was nodding, then crying, and Rebekah found herself pulling him into her shoulder. As awkward a position as it was, she refused to move, holding Savvo close as he poured the world's pain into the crook of her arm.

Rebekah closed the cabin door, praying to herself the soft click wouldn't disturb the sleep that had finally overtaken Savvo. She waited, then clomped as silently as she could towards the galley and her remaining crew, eyes all on her as she walked in.

"Asleep. No meds," she stated, and they all relaxed, the twins included.

"What now?" asked Arin. He wafted his flask about, gesturing towards the dockside of the hull. "I mean, it's all screwed up out there, but the dock team are on the ball. Place is being turned around."

"But not the tower," cut in Hendricks. "Word is they're bringing in a satellite transponder from one of the main asteroid fields as a temporary fix. Won't handle all the traffic, but safer."

Rebekah eyed them all one by one. Karal wasn't their concern, and they knew it, but small wins helped. She collected a coffee and sat by Heki, who hitched up. Putting it down, she withdrew her slate from a thigh pocket and placed it on the table. An adjustment of her flask, and a crack of one thumb, and she settled her hands on the tabletop. They were silent throughout. They knew the ritual.

"Kefi," she said, "has to be kept in some of the loop. We need to decide on how much."

Arin piped in. "She was there for us, for the dock crews. Didn't bat a black eye at what Savvo asked of her, or get her tentacles in a tangle." He looked at her over the rim of his flask, the smallest nod affirming his view.

"Dricks?"

"I have a say? Kind of biased."

"We all have a say." Rebekah didn't push. If her ex-captain needed to vent, now was the time.

"Well …" Hendricks rubbed the back of her neck, not looking at anyone else. "Kind of getting used to it. Even the smell. Kefi's – well you know – got a human side." That made Rebekah wince. She knew what the engineer meant, and no doubt so did Kefi. But when the switch came things were different. Emotionless. *Alien.* "But don't ask me to trust her not to blow us all to hell if we decide to cut and run. There's something in that rail cannon. I can smell it."

"Over the cabbage?" said Arin, a smile beaming, seeking a laugh.

Instead, the grin quickly faded as Rebekah hit him with a full glare. "Now is not the time." She tapped on the table. Hendricks looked up and caught her eye. "Interpreting all that, are we saying we trust Kefi to the point where we don't give shit away about Almaar? Anything short of treason goes?"

Hendricks grunted. "Near enough. But be careful. We don't know how the Senti think. We only know what they present, think of all the smoke 'n' mirrors about Scarva's ship. They like to hide the truth."

Rebekah had to agree. But the alien was on board, and maybe held a gun to their head should things go shit-face down in search of the spawn queen. Or, should she say, *more* shit-faced down than they already had.

"We haven't had our say," said Tremil, sitting up, shoulders back. A tentacle peeked out either side of her neck.

"True. Go ahead."

It was Heki that spoke. "Kefi has been teaching us. Says the Nest Queen instructed her to. That should we f—" Heki blushed, "screw things up, we could end up lost in void-space. They hold the symbs in reverence, Rebekah. They're not pets, and far more than just symbiotes. If she was ill-intentioned, why would she do that?"

"The queen? To know more, to see if you are bad people, or mean her harm. Perhaps to have a connection, or even to prevent others from taking you from us and doing what we wouldn't," replied Rebekah.

Arin sipped his coffee, then placed it down. The grin had completely gone. "Strategic," he said, causing them all to look his way. "Hey, there's no Savvo here, someone has to fill in. All what Rebekah said but also, they're safe, right? No one can get to them as it stands. Their home world, or colonies, the orbs. They have the monopoly on this space folding thing – until now. But instead of killing you both outright, they chose study." He raised his eyebrows towards Rebekah, who shook her head in a combination of despair and surprise she was sure had become a daily ritual.

"We're a threat until proven otherwise. I can see that," said Tremil.

"No," said Hendricks to Rebekah's surprise. The engineer raised a hand. "I know, I know. I'm the alien sceptic. But a human, we'd have killed you outright. Stone dead, there's no threat. Or in ..." she glanced over at the girls, a sigh slipping out, "in Segfi's case, drugged you up for study. Then ended the threat."

The colour drained from both girls. To Rebekah, that was a good thing. They needed barriers, despite Kefi's apparent kindness.

"Okay, to work ..." she pulled out two slates from inside her flight jacket. "I need you to break into these."

"Are those ...?" started Heki.

"Davina's," finished Tremil, her eyes wide.

"They are. I may have dropped by her office while M1 was in a bit of chaos. I want you to crack them both, and find anything you can on Erikson, ASAP." She dropped them both in front of the girls. "I also heard a rumour there's an automining ship missing, Dricks. That's your job. The crews owe us a favour, and they trust you, so get the fuck out there and get some of it paid back. I want to know if and when, its berth, registration and any clue as to where it might have been going."

"The tower? You thinking those bastards blew it up to hide that?" Arin stood, tossing his flask onto the galley side only to get a standard glare from everyone. With a tut, he placed it in the cleaning unit. "That's for shit. I mean ... it fits the Butcher's way of working. No thought for life."

"Only that it's in the way," said Hendricks. "And Arin?"

"*We* are going to examine a corpse." Rebekah stood, sliding her slate into its usual pocket.

"We are? I get all the best jobs."

The whole of Karal would know about ZZ3, Rebekah was sure. Another of their secrets peeled back. That didn't mean stomping about the asteroids with the warbot in tow was a good idea. But nor was ignoring the bot. Once she'd finished explaining what went down in the galley meeting, she had slipped off her usual cargo box, and stood by the warbot as its eyes swirled between blue and red until they settled down.

"There is more?" asked the warbot.

"I will need to inform Kefi before we leave. But. Fuck it, ZZ3. It's not your fault."

The usual shuffle, and the eyes pulsed once. Blue. "In all probabilities, it is. But also not. I was under orders; I acted on those orders."

"Yet you refused to attend. Switched off comms."

"Savvo ..." started the warbot, then paused. "Extrapolation of his previous mood swings, the circumstances of the assault, Nicky's trauma, would indicate he would not wish my presence." The bot's limb twitched as she made to reply. It annoyed Rebekah when others interrupted her, but somehow ZZ3's need sat different. Maybe it was the timing. "He will be grateful at my rescue, upset at the lives I could have saved instead, and distressed at the trauma I caused."

Rebekah had to agree, though she wondered if ZZ3 was also experiencing those things. Projecting your own emotions onto the expectations of another was a very human thing to do.

Fuck. Warbot psychologist is not on my CV.

"I agree. And are you?" Even a warbot has to talk, right?

"I am ... unsure."

Rebekah took a step back. That was new and probably welcome. No parameters, no probability score. "I think that's a good starting point. When Arin and I return, you should discuss it with him."

"With our glorious leader?" ZZ3's upper half dipped towards Rebekah. "Are you sure?"

CHAPTER 34

M2 HOSPITAL, KARAL

"This is not my area of expertise," said Arin. "Explosives, engine tinkering, warbot hugging, those things I can do. Extracting shit from dead bodies not-so much." Arin stationed himself at the edge of the wall, one eye on the bleak white corridor they had just passed through. "This is Savvo's gig."

"It is," replied Rebekah as her eyes flicked up to the cameras, searching for a hint they were on. Not for the first time in the last few days wishing she was ensconced in full armour with an active HUD. She tapped at the comms link in her ear. "Trem, we clear? Cameras down?"

"On a loop," replied Heki. "The whole level. Trem has gone on a hunt in Karal's main system."

"VERT?"

"Yeah. Better to fill you in later. We opened *the* slate and started delving. The trail led us there." Heki sounded a little distracted, as if her focus was not on the conversation but other matters. "Your whole level is now recording the same ten-minute loop. The quicker you are, the easier it'll be for me to cover your tracks."

"Copy that. Keep me informed." With the events on M4 docks, the mortuaries were in use far more than usual, and they needed to be fast. Rebekah signalled Arin over. She turned and walked ahead of him, reaching the second of the mortuary doors. She took guard, hand on her sidearm loaded with low-powered rounds she'd procured from the ship's stores. The last time they had been used was on Saim, and it felt a million years away. Arin worked the lock, and the door slid open in under thirty seconds.

"Who needs Savvo, eh? Well apart from us, obviously." He slid the twin wires back into his hip pouch while Rebekah eased on past, her weapon still holstered. It remained an odd feeling. The mortuary lights blinked on, and a chill settled on the back of her neck. Across two sets of walls were the stasis pods, ready to welcome all who needed a cold, final resting place.

"Hek, we're in," she said.

It didn't take long to get a response. "There's a trolley heading your way. One mortuary assistant with a deceased dock worker. You have eight clear minutes unless I jam the lift. Erikson is in pod seven."

"Jam it," she said, and clicked off, eyeing the wall and pointing to the relevant pod. The external lights flashed green. "Open it up."

Arin approached the lockpad, drawing out his breaker kit and attaching the wires. "Zombie clones, and now graverobbing."

"Firstly, it's not a grave. And second, the body's staying here. You're just examining the wetware." Rebekah closed the mortuary door, conscious that the light from the room was spilling into the corridor. The fallout from the attack on the docks was ringing through Karal, no more so than the hospital and she had no intention of adding to the drama. With a bit of luck, they could be gone before the next body arrived.

The lights on pod seven flickered, then switched over to amber and the room filled with the sound of a breaking seal. Chilled air billowed from the pod as it slid out.

"All we need is the bastard to rise up from the pod and we'd have a whole horror sim to ourselves." Arin had stepped out of the way, attaching a third wire to the pod's inner pad. It clicked over swiftly, and a second seal gave. Mist rose, but despite the potential for more overblown drama, Arin ignored it and approached the cold cadaver inside. He blew out the last vestiges of the fogged air and stared at what remained of Erikson's head. "We do have wetware."

Rebekah walked over, peering in from the opposite side. "No surprise that Enforcers are chipped. Set to record in case we have to leave in a hurry." She pointed to the shoulder cam he wore.

"On it." Arin shifted the camera to his forehead and unfurled a roll of small tools. He began prodding at the shattered remnants of the skull, teasing out wires and sets of tiny, interwoven metal bubbles. To Rebekah it looked much the same as the kit on Benetai, it was Savvo who had the knowledge of what should and shouldn't be present. The Enforcer wetware would be top grade, but that's not why they were there.

"Shiiiit," said Arin, and he exposed part of the Enforcer's skull near his ear. "There's a link port. Recent work too, the skin hasn't fully healed inside the ear." He glanced up to Rebekah. "You expecting this?"

"I've no idea what I was expecting. Maybe the chip kit being similar to the Butcher's handiwork." Rebekah looked at the port. Hardwire. In an ideal world, she would have Savvo here. He'd work out the implications.

"Cyborg Enforcer."

Unlike Arin.

"Where does it lead? Film it. Film it all." She considered cutting out the wetware. Who would know? But that would lead to more suspicion and paranoia on board. Tew searching for spies in her ranks instead of helping Karal recover from the attack.

Her comms crackled. "They got the lift working. I daren't try that again. You have three minutes."

Rebekah looked to Arin who shook his head. "I need longer," he said.

They needed a misdirect. She headed for the door, ready to step out, play the dumb lost friend looking for a patient, when Heki cut back in.

"I can risk hacking their information flow. The log shows they're heading for you." Heki was tapping at her slate in the background. "Might cause suspicion, but they're kind of overworked right now."

"Do it," replied Rebekah. They had been splashed over the Karal feed. The heroic crew who had fought off the assault. However convincing she was, they would still remember the captain of the *Sunstar* who charged into the fight armourless with a warbot sidekick.

"Copy that."

Arin looked up as Rebekah cracked a thumb. "I'm going as fast as I can, otherwise someone's gonna know I screwed about with a dead man's brain."

Savvo would have had a comeback.

She closed that thought off. Not wanting to think about his state of mind, the choices whirling through it.

"It keeps rejecting my request," stated Heki. "Old software. Why do people hang on to this stuff?"

"They like what they know. Habitual. How close?"

"Thirty seconds. I'm trying." Heki sounded strained.

Rebekah approached the door, one hand on her weapon. A stun gun would have been a better choice, but she'd lost that back in the terminal. Maybe something she could busy Arin with after dissecting his current task. She waited, back to the wall, ready to strike at an innocent orderly.

A tap vibrated through the lockpad near her hand, the screen flashing green then switching back to red. Twice more, and she swore she could hear muttering through the wall. A fourth try and the door clicked open. Rebekah was reaching for it when the swearing started.

"Godsdamned ancient good-for-nothing piece of crap. What now? Want me to twirl around seven times with my hand up my arse?" The accent was Almaarian, but she couldn't quite catch sight as the door remained open just a sliver. "What? Reassign?"

The door clicked closed, the pad flashing red.

"Got it," said Heki. "May have left some elephant-sized footsteps."

"Footprints," corrected Rebekah, remembering one of Arin's favourite sayings from the twins' frequent raids on the cold store. "Good job." The clatter of a trolley hitting a wall reverberated through the door, and then silence.

"I'll track the orderly's slate and let you know when it's clear."

"We have a record of *Segfi*'s wetware, the kit we recovered from Benetai," said Rebekah. "Can you pull it up?"

Arin tapped at his slate, and a visual of the wetware appeared on the screen. He spun the images, then drew up his recording and began attaching markers to each element he had exposed in turn. Once complete, he altered the recording, fading out the shattered skull and meat of the brain for a 3D representation in less ghoulish form.

"You can come in now," said Rebekah, and the twins idled in, their looks surly. They hated being kept out of the loop, and had admittedly suffered more depravities than most humans ever did in their short lives. It didn't mean Rebekah was prepared to add to them, and brain surgery was high on her list.

They slumped onto the galley bench, but perked up as they peered at the screen. Eventually Trem offered to take the slate from Arin who shrugged and complied. Working at far greater speed, she had the two sets of wetware in comparative 3D with a detailed extrapolation of their similarities. Smug, she handed it back to the sub-engineer.

"Yeah, yeah, yeah. I'd have got there. Just out of practice," Arin said, half-a-grin in place.

"I'll take that as a thank you," said Trem, and the storm clouds at being left out parted.

There was a thump, the clatter of a door, and Savvo appeared in the corridor, clomping slowly along. Dishevelled, one arm sliding into his flight jacket. Even at this distance his face looked sallow, grey, eyes sunken. It struck at Rebekah's heart, and she made to get up when Hendricks appeared behind Savvo, and sped up to catch him. A gentle hand on the shoulder, some quiet words passed and Savvo nodded. Her co-pilot briefly glanced her way, then turned about, Hendricks letting him by before carrying on to the galley.

"Sent him for a shower. I'll take him a tea," she said, then peered at the screen, gesturing with her head towards it. "This is his area of expertise."

"Aye," said Arin. "Want me to send it Savvo's way?"

Rebekah was sure she already had her answer between Trem and Arin's modelling, but it wouldn't hurt. "Yeah. You take him his tea. But deliver it with a little gentleness."

The sub-engineer stood, slate in hand and collected the flask from Hendricks. "I can do that. Tender of heart me."

"It's your words she's worried about, not your bleeding heart," said Hendricks. "We'll go together. Strength in numbers."

"I have a censor now?" grumbled Arin, but Rebekah could detect an air of relief underneath. They left, heading towards Savvo's cabin, Arin explaining in great detail the delicate brain surgery he'd undertaken.

Rebekah shook her head, the twins at her side mirroring the gesture.

"What you got for me?" she asked.

Trem shuffled in her seat, then tapped at her screen. Lines of code and data appearing on the galley screen. She closed in and broke the code down into multiple parts. "Senti code," she stated. "Or to be more accurate, some form of hunter algorithm. It was on Davina's office slate, like an old-school virus, messing about with her stored data as well as running a search. Going back through her logs, it targeted one file in particular, but I can't break into that – there's Senti encryption in place. Recent too. Time correlates with Erikson's attack on Tent Pike, which also correlates ..." Tremil left that hanging, almost prodding Rebekah's thoughts.

"With the assault on the docks?" asked Rebekah, knowing the answer.

"Yep," cut in Heki. "I've got some info on that but let Trem finish."

"So I tried to hack her other slate. No chance of that."

Rebekah found that an odd admission. Matter-of-fact, no grumbling. "How's that?"

"It's encrypted in a really weird way. A visual system, one I know is there, but can't make head nor tail of. Must be Incini," stated Trem. "I've never seen anything like it before. Not a clue how to break it, but I'd love to find out."

"And VERT?" asked Rebekah, remembering Heki's prompt.

Trem continued. "Same type of trail as Davina's slate. I can follow wherever the hunter left a Senti encrypted file. They're in odd places, like in the asteroid field surveys, then the repair schedule, flight plans and crew roster. No defined pattern, but I'm thinking it'll be like a cascade once it's cracked." She finished with her hands wide open, then looked to her sister.

"We've an idea," said Heki, taking the cue. "But you may not like it."

Rebekah had already made that leap. "Kefi," she muttered. There was little choice, and the alien had earned some trust. Besides, Karal's secrets were not necessarily Empire threatening, were they? Without Senti help, they would be greatly delayed. "ZZ3 no help?"

Tremil shook her head. "We showed ZZ3 the code. Asham had no clue, says it's evolved way beyond what he understands."

CHAPTER 35

Savvo knocked at the door, glancing inside. Nicky was still under sedation, the medical team reporting she had suffered turgid, painful dreams that had awoken her to a dark ward and anxiety-inducing loneliness. They had no choice but to sedate her, after which she had fallen back unconscious. He took a seat by her side, gently uncovering her left hand and taking it in his own. He sat there for what seemed like a few minutes, but a glance at his slate showed half an hour had passed before he could rouse himself. In his heart, he feared Nicky was gone. That the trauma of the attack and ZZ3's rescue was too deep and ingrained. She was strong, her strength of will probably on a par with Rebekah's, but recovery took time.

The selfish part of him wanted her back in his arms, that knowing smile cutting his dreams to ribbons until he accepted her way was best. Now, he knew deep inside, she was lost to him. That he was nothing but a daily reminder of the attack. He was a deserter, a soldier, who had faced death with a regularity he had masked with chemicals. But still she would wake and look at a man of violence, the same violence she had been subjected to. He saw nothing but the death of her love for him.

And it fucking hurts like hell.

With a last squeeze he stood, then checked over his slate. Each contracted worker within Karal was subject to their basic medical insurance. But she deserved the best care. With a swipe, he watched the creds fade from his account.

"To work," he said, rubbing at his sore eyes, and left the ward, heading for the private space afforded those whose lives centred around M1. He found Davina's room. At first, he'd wondered why Rebekah insisted it be him. But she was bringing him back into the fold. Gently reminding him he was crew and loved. It was whether he wanted that anymore she was testing.

He knocked, but didn't wait on ceremony, walking in and plonking himself down onto the chair. Davina was awake, beavering away on a slate, ever the worker. Her jaw heavily bruised but now clear of the wired-metal Rebekah had mentioned.

He tossed one of her slates onto the bed. "We can't crack it," he said. May as well jump in with both feet.

Davina stared at the slate as if it was diseased, then at Savvo. "You stole these?" The Incini winced as she spoke, working her jaw.

"You give me far too much credit. I've been busy grieving," he replied.

Davina pulled herself up higher against the headboard, altering the medbed's position with a control. "She's not dead."

He shrugged his shoulders. "It's not her life I grieve. But us. The fucking Butcher has taken that too. Her mind ..." Why was he discussing it with Davina?

Then he knew why. Those words would have broke his crew into fits of sympathy. He couldn't cope with that. Davina just looked back, her mind probably sifting responses, emotionless. No. That was unfair. Just structured, seeing the facts.

"You don't know that. It's very early days."

"But it costs. Treatment, the best treatment, is expensive." He crossed his legs, setting up a defensive barrier. From what, he wasn't sure.

"Are you asking me for help?" she said, and collected the slate from the bed. A swipe, and she stared at the screen, eyes flickering back and forth.

Incini wetware. Should have guessed.

He shrugged. "I don't know what I'm asking. Maybe. You know people – can access some of the best. I transferred creds into her account, so whatever that can help with. For me, for us, if the crew means anything to you." He uncrossed his legs, leaning forward.

"Is that before or after you kidnapped me and took me into a war zone? Oh, and stole my stuff." She gestured with the slate.

"We also couldn't wait for Tews and hacked Erikson's brain. Seems we won't stop at anything to find out what's going on. Trent saved you, right? Nicky and the tower workers only had us, and we were too late for some. But Nicky? She's innocent of everything but loving me." Had he said that out loud? "Please."

"Damn you people," replied Davina, and she worked her jaw again. "If I can. But you might not have noticed that Almaar's in turmoil. This attack, Tweem. All of it is leaking out. Rumours about the *Segfi* are all over the indie stations. I'm not sure what'll happen, whether anyone will want to travel to Karal. But I can tap into people here."

"Thank you. Now the slate." He pulled out the second slate from his jacket. "Trem and Heki have cracked it," Davina made to cut in, but Savvo carried on despite the storm clouds gathering in her eyes, "and found a Senti encryption. Senti, that means the Butcher. I believe Erikson's wetware was an evolved version of what we recovered from Benetai. He'd been compromised, and all that stuff squashed into his head was most likely the source of the code. He even had a physical port." Savvo dropped the slate on the bed.

"I take it you have a copy?" Davina reached for the slate as Savvo nodded in agreement. "Which file?"

"It's up. Trem is working with the Senti to hack it open. They work out the code, then they can follow the trail. Might help to know what the file contains."

By the look she quickly covered up, Savvo suspected she already did. Davina soon had the file up, but was clearly unable to access it, though she looked his way with the slightest grimace on her face.

"An asteroid, that's all. A survey report. One Mr Duboit, the real one, was very interested in." She grabbed the Incini slate and drew a file up. "I have a copy. Against Incini protocol, but there was something weird going on and it was a vital element in Mr Duboit's investments."

Savvo got his own slate out. "May I?" he said, indicating he wanted to connect the slates

"Now you ask? This is between us, Savvo, the *Sunstar* crew and me. If it goes any further, I lose my job and rights as an Incini, and you lose the one person who can procure Nicky the best help. In return, I want the encryption code. Whatever you can provide in terms of structure that I can share with the Directorate and possibly Countess Segfi. A bargaining chip should they come knocking. And also, why this asteroid? I want to know what Erikson was really up to."

Kefi's black eyes focused on the monitor as her tentacles graced screen and keyboard simultaneously. "You really need to embrace light tech for your control system," she said, waving a lower tentacle at Heki. "This insistence on physicality holds you back."

Trem ignored the Senti. Her asides about human traits, failures and lack of foresight were a regular occurrence. It seemed to amuse the Senti, and a happy Kefi was far more pleasurable to be around than the sullen silence she sometimes dropped into, or Frosty the alien as Trem secretly called her in those moments. Trem was sure they would fully meld in the end. Be of one voice.

Kefi beavered away at the screen. "Also, screens are flat. How you can perceive things on a two-dimensional screen I do not know."

Trem nodded in return, a body movement the alien knew, while watching the code being stripped apart. Despite the alien's protestations, she could understand her point. Both her and Heki's minds could perceive the code, had been training since ZZ3 first introduced them to it, but the more they spent time with the symbs practising the exercises Kefi had set out, the wider the reality she understood and perceived. The Senti were three-dimensional beings, but the symbs? She suspected – no she *knew* – their existence was based on the fourth. Not only that, but the connections they made were something the Senti had evolved to rely upon. Perhaps, ultimately, had shaped their development.

"There," said Kefi, and the screen simulated the toppling of a defensive wall. Behind, the same file Trem had already seen on Savvo's slate. It soon became apparent, Kefi had not. "What is this?" A tentacle waved towards the survey data. The alien turned to face her. Kefi had clearly learned how such contact, the little things, helped settle her thoughts.

"An asteroid survey," she replied.

"I need to search ... to think on other memories," stated the alien.

Trem expected what came next – almost as if Kefi had her own internal comms unit. The Senti stiffened, a twitch to her lower limbs, then a slight off-gas she had become used to.

An internal monologue? Separate minds?

"There," Kefi started, "take a look." The odd turn of phrase was followed by Kefi running through the survey results, precise, but punctuated by their strange speech. Was that for her benefit? She soon finished and returned to Almaarian. "It is what I thought. I only saw the reports about the *Unpronounceable*'s shuttle refit, but I'm positive ..."

The two shoulder tentacles came together, their tips split, intertwining. Two halves, in Tremil's mind, agreeing.

Kefi's voice was flat again, "I think I am correct. There is one required element missing, but the asteroid has the components of the ... ermm ... *stealth* alloy we use on smaller ships. This is very important information your ship's queen needs to know."

That brought a smile to Trem's face, images of Rebekah in a tiara and a ballgown dress were always amusing. "You think ..." Pieces began to slot home. The odd combination of encrypted files, the pathway from asteroid to resources. The missing automining ship. "Shit," she said. "We do need the ship queen."

Savvo eased himself against the wall, arms crossed, trying to focus on the discussion. His mind wandered its own path, always back to Nicky. He searched for the fire in his gut, that determination to gain revenge for what had been done to her, to Karal, the navy crews the *bastard* had spaced. Daphene. There was still an ember that burned bright, but wrapped in his personal grief, sapping its energy. His energy.

"We've tracked through the encrypted files. Erikson must have had some type of trip in place, activating them when things went wrong. They couldn't be deleted as VERT has too many failsafes for that." Heki pointed to the galley screen, lines appearing between interlinked files. "But there's a definite pattern."

Trem took up the explanation, a light shining in her eyes. Savvo thought she took some pleasure in her success, contributing to the crew beyond being one quarter of a jump engine. "We know Trent Pike was worried about something. The hints are that Erikson was scouring the survey records for geo-surveys. We also think there was resource appropriation."

"Theft." said Kefi, off-gassing.

"Yes," said Trem. "I think Pike may have hid some of it."

Savvo piped in, feeling like he too should contribute. "Embarrassed. And maybe if what he told Rebekah was true, worried someone might think it was him skimming Karal."

"He probably was," said Rebekah, she pointed at the screen. "Can you spin us into the autoship rotas? That an encrypted file I can see?"

"Not one," replied Heki while Trem spun the 3D model of VERT's database, and drew up a section. The whole of the autoship's timetables had been encryption bombed. It appeared like a pulsing malaise on screen. "All of them."

"If he could do that, why didn't he just wash the whole system. Fuck it up completely?" Savvo pushed himself off the wall. He blinked at the screen, trying to muster enthusiasm he didn't feel.

Kefi spoke up, her speech punctuated by animated shoulder tentacles that gesticulated towards the screen. "The attack on the files set off your protective systems. This was like a big data bomb, the attacks on the individual files were more like ... a snake attack."

"Worms, not snakes," said Arin absently, eyes on his own slate. "But yeah. Delaying tactics."

"No," said Tremil, the confidence of the young in her denial. A certainty that Savvo struggled to mirror. "Or at least, I don't think *he* believed so. How would he know about Asham and ZZ3? What they've taught us of Senti coding?"

"True," said Rebekah. She put her coffee flask down in its usual place. "Nor would he know that we are working with you, Kefi. The Nest Queen. No human ever has before, so what parameters would he have as an AI? And the Butcher carved the Senti open, rather than make any effort to talk about the abilities he was fucking after."

The comms crackled. ZZ3 piping in. "Asham agrees. He says that the General hated the Senti for what they had and refused to share. And also, that he mistrusted the translations, believing they were a deliberate barrier the Senti used to keep their secrets. A misdirection. At the moment, we both agree the Butcher is unaware we can break the encryption."

Rebekah cracked both thumbs, a glance to her slate, then to each of her crew, new and old, alien or human, finishing with Savvo. He felt claustrophobic under her gaze. Closed in.

"If Kefi is right about the metal surveys, then we need to confirm about the resource thefts. But I don't think any of us believe it's going to be a set of uniforms and a shovel. The Butcher wants to make Senti stealth ships."

"Impossible," cut in Kefi. The Senti's mouth tweaked open and closed before the alien turned to face the crew as best she could. "The knowledge for manufacturing the metal was in Scarva's database, I agree. We made modifications to the human shuttle. But not our ships. We were never entrusted with that. We were sent out into human space with only the knowledge our Nest Queen deemed necessary."

Savvo twisted his lips as he eyed the Senti. That was interesting, and Arin's look showed he had also noted what Kefi had revealed about the Senti. Scarva sent out?

But the Butcher's clones attacked the orb. We thought he wanted the secret to FLT, or the symbs if he'd worked that out. Possibly that was true, and taking the spawn was happenstance.

Savvo could see where this was all going, the look in Rebekah's eyes. She had already made a leap.

"And they gained nothing from the orb?" his captain asked.

Kefi nodded, tentacles waggling, acknowledging Rebekah's thoughts. "No knowledge, none of the (*scraping of toast*), just the Orb Queen's spawn. And from what you've shown me of the Butcher's experiments; he is incapable of extracting the memories she carries."

"Yet," said Rebekah. "But he doesn't have to build Senti ships. It's the stealth he wants. He might have sent the *Ungrit* looking for FLT, even the symbs, but found something else in your database, Kefi. If he builds ships that the navy struggles to detect, he can spread his fucking infection where he likes." She looked at Savvo.

"Tweem," he said. "You're betting the Countess comes back with her tail between her legs. The attack on its repair and building capabilities a distraction from what he was really after."

CHAPTER 36

ON BOARD THE SUNSTAR, KARAL

The message dropped in loud and clear. Tweem's system had been breached, the database searched and downloaded in full. Rebekah placed her coffee flask to the top left of her slate, lips moving as she re-read the countess' message. She wasn't sure if she was reading too much into it, or if the countess was finally showing a thread of fear. Of realisation. And this was before she knew about the prospect of multiple ships built from Senti metal. The thought terrified Rebekah. Segfi had spread the Almaarian Navy, ensured orders and comms were via Senti links or short burst data. Codes were changing with great regularity, the dread being the *Segfi* finding individual ships and pounding them out of existence, or disabling and subsuming the ships into its own fleet. With stealth craft, sneak attacks would succeed with greater regularity. The vulnerability shown by Rubel and Rohan's escape from Benetai evidence that not even the AI ships of the Bustan Navy were attuned to their capabilities.

"Decisions to be made," she said, then glanced up at Savvo. "Including you."

Her co-pilot and second blinked back at her from across the table. Silent.

"I can always tell," she continued. "But this time Heki gave me an extra nudge. You're giving off so many signals, *she's* using an earworm."

That at least brought up a smile.

Savvo raised his hands, as if to plead his case. Only for them to collapse to his side. "I..." he said, the word fading away.

"You're of no use to me like this. A liability until your head's back in the game," Rebekah paused, tapping at the table, a single crack signalling her anxiety, "or out forever. And no, you won't know. But we have to see if we can find the Butcher, or whatever part of him is on that asteroid. We need to understand what he's doing. And you're staying here. I don't have the headspace to manage you, the girls, the Senti. All of this shit."

"But ..."

Rebekah watched the light go out of his sunken eyes, and reached across, squeezing his forearm. "But nothing. Decision made. Heki will ride shotgun until we're back. Be the co-pilot. By then, you may know more. As a reward, you get to be my eyes and ears on Karal *and* deal with the Countess."

"What do you mean, deal?"

"Davina is working on organising a devoted comms link. You'll be the relay, the conduit. I trust you, know you inside and out. It'll improve the safety of the comms access and provide a barrier between the navy and us. If they get compromised, I don't want that shit pouring our way and I trust your judgement. Understand?"

A shuffle interrupted Rebekah's flow, annoying her. She wanted this between her and Savvo. To know how hard the decision was despite it being the right one. Taking the choice out of his hands so it hurt him less. Kefi hovered at the galley entrance; lower tentacles hooked into the deck. She off-gassed when Rebekah caught her eye. There was something grasped in her shoulder tentacle.

"Ex-excuse me," she said, then took a step inside. The Senti proffered her tentacle, a device curled in its split tip. "I have worked with your nestling to devise a blocking module."

"A what?" asked Rebekah, standing, reaching for the plain square casing. Kefi dropped it into her palm.

"We thought after witnessing how part of the Butcher acted from the attack on VERT that we could devise a system code blocker. Tremil advised that the Butcher would ... errm ... continually re-subsume its knowledge until it could bypass the blocker. But it would delay and alert that an attack was in progress, though subsequent attempts would take far less time to bypass it."

"Can it be replicated?" she asked, spinning the mod. To her surprise, it didn't appear to be Senti metal, but then where would they get it if it was?

"No. Well, yes. Each has to be manufactured separately, with a new code embedded." Kefi's tentacles spread wide, grasping the table. "It would mean leaving the nestling on Karal if the intent was to share with your navy. We considered this device would help Karal." The Senti gestured towards Savvo. "Give some protection to VERT and the comms."

Rebekah squeezed the little box, then handed it over to Savvo. "Useful. But I still want more."

Savvo smiled at her words. "You always do."

***

With her message – filled with dire warnings – prepared ready for Savvo to share with the countess when the time came, Rebekah worked through the pre-flight check. Heki, her shoulders back, her flight suit freshly pressed by the look of it, supported the procedure like clockwork. She double-checked each of Rebekah's requirements with the efficiency of someone eager to please. She wasn't Savvo, so the pre-flight was filled with less of his usual grumbles at Rebekah's zealous routine. Of course, Savvo hadn't learned his skills on a Marine dropship, where a misfiring engine meant a quick dive into hell and likely death. An opportunity to teach good habits.

"Starboard thrusters check."

Heki tapped at her console. "Clear and in the green."

"Good." Rebekah's comms hissed, affirmation from the dockside crew up a level that an autoship had successfully cleared the outer scaffolding. It was now accelerating towards their target at a rate beyond those safe for human or alien in the hope it could snatch readings of Duboit's asteroid. Provide a hint as to whether the Butcher was there.

"The autoship is through," she said. No dock wide transponders were up and running yet, so leaving the spinning rock that was M4 had to rely on piloting skill or excellent pre-programming of the navcom. In the *Sunstar's* case, both.

Heki was side-eyeing her; she could feel it. With a sigh, she glanced over. "Ghost it then."

Heki beamed and set up her navcom simulation ready to track Rebekah's flight path and alert the cockpit to any concerning deviation. Things you do for your children.

My children, who I am once again taking into danger.

As if I have a choice.

"Dricks, we're leaving," she said. "Make sure Arin is strapped down."

"I buckled him in myself," replied Dricks. Rebekah could almost sense the cogs working. No Savvo, no comebacks to wind Arin up. To make them feel like a family despite one being missing. "But yeah, I can add the newly issued gag if you wish."

Arin piped up. "Hey. No fair. Me and ZZ3 are going to start a mutiny."

"You can leave me out of this. I agree with them, glorious leader," ZZ3 said. "I made the gag on the printer this morning."

Arin snorted into the comms, Heki giggling by Rebekah's side. It all helped.

"I am beginning to feel targeted here. You were supposed to be my friend. If Savvo was here ..." mused Arin.

"He would have held you down while I strapped it on," cut in Hendricks.

Yeah. My children. Even the older ones.

"Is it always like this?" asked Kefi

Rebekah grinned briefly. "Pretty much."

"Rohan was far worse, mind you," stated Kefi. "And don't get me talking about Rubel. It is good the Nest Queen never met him." The seagull squawk echoed briefly, and she found it strangely comforting despite the oddness of having the Senti on board.

"Taking off in 3, 2, 1 ... Mark," she said, and the engines gently lifted them away from the dock. She trimmed, ensuring the burn remained in the dockside tunnel. The area was clear of workers, but even so, you followed protocol. Set an example. Despite herself, she eyed the ghost version of the *Sunstar* playing out on the navcom screen. "In the pipe," she whispered, easing the ship forwards, accounting for the spin and the shifting pseudo gravity.

Heki grimaced at her side as she kept track, the occasional shift in her neck a clue as to whether Rebekah was drifting from the girl's favoured course. Rebekah ignored it in the end and eased the *Sunstar* out into docks' exit pathway. Usually there would be one or two more ships, transponders active, weaving into line ready to leave for the black. Not today, just them, and to their side the tower. From the outside it looked peaceful, belying the damage caused by the Butcher's clones. And Erikson.

"Dockside, we are engaging forward thrust." With that, the *Sunstar* entered the void, Heki shaking her head at her side, a low whistle slipping from her lips. "Go on, give me the numbers. Got to be at least in the nineties."

"Close. Navcom has you at eighty-seven percent ideal flight path. Five percent more than projections based on flight record." Heki swiped the data over into the upper corner of Rebekah's screen.

"Watch and learn. Okay crew, prepare for a medium-to-hard burn." Rebekah ran over the numbers, wary that she had to be careful. The Senti was in her encounter suit, but those only compensated so far. "Kefi, you prepped?"

"I am," stated Kefi. "Alerts are set, linked to the ship's comms as requested."

Rebekah was pleased the Senti had kept to her suggested protocol and ran through the data flow. The alien had gone for Marine code: green, amber, and oh fuck. Considering how much she knew about alien physiology, it was ideal.

"Heki. You need to go prep." Rebekah waited for the comeback. There was none, the girl unbuckling and setting off through the galley and on to her cabin. There would be the mood swings teenagers came with as stock and without the updated manual, but as with Tremil and the code blocker, she wanted to be crew again. To be more than just a means to leap the stars.

"People," she said. Her thoughts wandered to Savvo, Nicky, but she shook them away. It wouldn't help. He had his own path for now.

"Ready," stated Heki over comms. "Retardant activated." The rest called in.

"And 3, 2, 1 ... Mark." Rebekah was slammed back into her seat, the gel forming around her body as they sped towards Duboit's asteroid and whatever waited for them there.

Savvo watched as the engine flame flared, then settled. The *Sunstar*, his ship, speared into the dark. Within seconds only the merest glow in the distance remained, and he clicked the external cameras off, not seeking any further probes he was allowed to access. It was enough for him to feel both abandoned yet loved. A maelstrom that forged a whirlpool in his mind, sucking down rational thought. Strangely, an unexpected hand landed next to his, Davina catching his eye. There was a sliver of understanding there. Enough.

He twisted his head, pulling at his collar. "To work." He showed the Incini Kefi's blocker. "You and me, we have to persuade Jenkra Tews that dropping Senti tech in VERT is a good thing."

Chapter 37

Shema

The countess held the smoke as long as she dared. The meds penetrated her lungs, easing the pain but, above all else, their constant itch that grated at her mind. Something so annoyingly close yet beyond her, unable to relieve it with a simple scratch. Out of her control without the proxy of the smoke.

Finally, the need for oxygen denied her the relief, and she released a cloud into the air. Gerent delivered the hardest of stares her way, but over the past few months she had come to see the Minister's hand as less of a threat and more of an annoyance. He attempted to maintain the countenance of being her superior, but they both knew better. His power stemmed from the Minister, hers from centuries of her family's status and half of the Almaarian Navy as hers to directly command, while the rest pulled at her apron strings in hope of succour. He could of course turn on her. A word to the Minister, and on to the Emperor, with treason upon his lips, and she could falter. Could. But now was not the time to remove the head of your navy, their one hope to cage a beast.

The one I not only created, but set free.

Duty enough.

Baron Winkal sat opposite her, or at least, his holo did. It had taken a description of the possible scenarios on offer should the Butcher arrive on Shema for Gerent to decide against meeting in person. Her opening gambit a reminder about Daphene and the denial of any atmosphere. All it would take is redirecting a little CO2 from the scrubbers, and they would be facing a painful death and a blow to the Court.

She watched the flicker of his holo absently, the recreation of his foppish hair, the high cheek bones she knew were surgically enhanced, and the grey eyes he spent a small fortune keeping crystal clear with his wetware upgrades. Still, there was a hard streak to the noble, one they were all going to need should her hunt run out of time.

More nobles flickered into their designated places, Baron Lundstrom's intricate comms system placing them one by one around the table. They all looked far healthier on holo than face to face, something, if she thought about it, she had also left active in her projection system. Lies to show the world. Funny how she had shown her true face to Khan and the Breakers, but then they knew her inner demons. Had been her hand upon the outer worlds and moons of Bustan. They understood the monster inside.

The last of the requisite nobles appeared. Baroness Lundstrom. She who had squeezed every percentage of profit from the shipyard at Tweem, and had admitted, red-faced, to the incursion within the manufacturing database. Something the countess could leverage in the future, probably around the time the Lundstroms made a bid for the higher echelons of the Court. That would require room to be made, the fall of a family from the Emperor's favour. The most likely candidate being hers should the hunt for the Butcher fail.

And what then for her Tomas? Peace perhaps.

She eyed the holos about the table, all looking for political advantage in this moment of crisis. Unable to understand the bigger picture. She had been one of them once, elbowing and backstabbing her way through the middle ranks until she gained the taste for war and her true calling.

They would eat Tomas alive, pick their teeth with his bones, and fling the remains to their dogs. A pity, but you must understand the true nature of something before you break it and reshape what they are to what you need.

She nodded to Gerent, who stood and placed a hand over his heart, repeating the litany of devotion to the emperor and the Court. Each noble repeated back, their faces clear at that moment of any connivance. Not that the holos would show it if there was. So much more difficult than in person. But safer.

"Countess," said the Minister's hand. She wondered in that moment how much life had changed for him too. No longer the agent scratching at the foundations of the Empire, seeking sedition or manufacturing it whenever the Minister required. Out in the open. Exposed at her side. Should she fall, would he fall too?

Interesting.

She sucked in a sliver of smoke, letting it settle with practised ease in her lungs as she spoke. "Families of the outer colonies of the Empire. Nobles of the Court, servants of the Emperor, you know I am here due to the rising threat of the Butcher AI."

There were no murmurs of dissent or agreement, no nods or pained shakes of their heads. There was an advantage in having holos and a lack of eye contact. Such physical absence made responses less likely to gather any momentum. Unless of course they had already forged their agreements.

"The Emperor has tasked me with its destruction, while guarding those who stand with the Empire. The colonies. To that end I am here with a variety of requests and ... permissions." She swept the room, the combination of tilted heads and curious looks so false. They had heard the first part, and knew there were demands to come, ones the Minister's hand was there to observe for dissent. But a carrot was in the offing. "But first, you must understand how fast this threat grows. You have all read the testimony from Captain Srenik and those from the survivors of the attack on Tweem. You have witnessed the recordings taken of the ANS *Bonray* and the spacing of her crew. I have detailed the need to utterly destroy my base on Daphene despite the cost in resources. I believe – the *Emperor* believes – you are beginning to remove your blinkers. For so long there has been little internal threat to our worlds and moons. The Bustan attack was a wake-up call, shifting our Navy's focus from interplanetary posturing to defence by attack. Stepping back from that status and defending your resources is now paramount. Essential."

"I don't understand," stated Baron Winkal, leaning in, holo hands clasped, forearms resting on the table's edge. He had been primed, and was a little early but it would have to do. "How can one AI, one ship, be it your flagship," the countess winced, no mummery required, but bringing herself low, exposing her own failure, was necessary. Should the famed Warmonger fall to the Butcher's machinations, so could they. Winkal continued, "be such a threat?"

Gerent spoke up. Again planned. For the first time she heard a hint of passion in his voice. "See it as a virus. When we first learned of the Bustan's use of AI amid their invasion fleet, it became apparent that they had contained the foul thing. Imprisoned it within the confines of their control ship. Our studies indicate this was deliberate, a controlling factor amid a plethora of failsafes to maintain its role, however inhumane the attack was."

"I see," replied Winkal, leaning back.

"And like a virus," Segfi swept the room, "replicates and spreads. On repeat. Imagine Almaar under the Ingblack plague. It nearly wiped our beloved ancestors from existence. Ended our Empire before it started. Without the Four, the Avatars of our faith, we may well have fallen, unable to rise from the ashes. It took strength of purpose, the bravery to cull or cure." The agreement about the room confirmed her belief that most nobles still held to the faith. "The Butcher is well named. It seeks to cut out the heart of Almaar. It wants nothing more than to grow while reducing us to ash. To finish what the Bustan started, and we are charged with the first line of defence."

"How so?" asked Baroness Lundstrom. "With one phrase you say we need to look to defence, with another to attack this AI. Possibly the ANS *Segfi*. How do we achieve both?" There was bitterness laced within each word, but the countess needed them. Lundstrom was correct.

"The Emperor gives you permission to coordinate under my hand. To work together for the first time since the cessation of the Bustan War. Your fleets, whether small or large, will be coordinated under a strategy I outlay." There it was. The fear of an uprising pushed to the background by necessity. She raised a hand as a clamour began. Not filled by anger, but by surprise and an urgency for their voice to be heard. The smaller of the nobles would worry about being usurped, petty grievances of the past played out. The larger seeking opportunity. "I will say that again. By my hand."

She stood then, displaying a strength in her legs and posture she didn't feel but knew was necessary. They were all awaiting her demise, whether by the failure to contain the Butcher, the loss of her flagship, or by ill-health. Yet she still stood for the Empire. So screw them.

She sucked upon her stick, eyes locked on Lundstrom. "We cannot risk a misstep. Should the Butcher infect one ship unknown, each of your ships will fall in turn. A virus spreads by multiplying unchecked, at speed. You may think space is a barrier, but hold no doubts it will find a way past those who are unprepared."

This was the moment. The baroness could choose to go on the attack, bleat about the loss of a battleship, her failing health affecting her decision making. The destruction of Daphene. Segfi held back the acrid words she had filed ready.

Choose your fight wisely, Baroness. Or, at least, consider the timing of your strike.

The holo revealed no secrets, whether Lundstrom was coiling up ready, or easing back in acceptance. Almost as if the baroness had paused the image while raging in the background. It would be a hard pill to swallow for all of them, so used to their individual autonomy, playing out their stupid war games.

"And permission?" The words fell like lead upon the table. Silent curiosity filled the conference room. Lundstrom's room.

Segfi smiled. She couldn't help it, and kicked herself. Though a gift was always welcomed, whether it was poisoned or not remained unknown until you pulled the bow. "Firstly, you may arm your private militaries and prepare your defensive perimeters. You may act as you wish within the bounds of Empire martial law within your own regions should a war status be declared." There were murmurs and nods of the head. They were seeing it as an acknowledgement of their true position. The emperor, under her advice, saw it as freeing up the standing army and valued resources. It was nothing more than a token in her eyes, but to those who loved their power, a golden opportunity to bring their people to heel. Or crush them under it. "Secondly, you may call in your reserves and prepare to draft more should such a war status be announced. Finally, you may extend your personal fleets. Begin a rebuild. Any suddenly available," she glared about the room. Everyone of them had hidden ships, "navy resources may be commissioned without recourse." She let her gaze fall upon Count Portus who had been silent up to now. He smiled and nodded.

"Be in no doubt I will need much of your fleet to hunt down the Butcher. But should I fail," Lundstrom's holo paused at that moment, hiding a smile no doubt, "then we will be at war within our own system.

Under my hand, there is more chance we can coordinate and keep your ships clean of infection. If I fail, you will be the last line of defence for your colonies."

And no Avatars will be here to save you.

The nods about the room were a positive sign, and within minutes Gerent had wrapped up the meeting, the holos winking out in turn. The baroness was last, the look she left with calculating but not angry. The message had got home, or at least the noble had understood what it was and showed the right face to her competitor in the Court.

Once empty, silent, Gerent turned to her, signalling his dampener was engaged.

"You have your ring of steel," the countess said. "A line of defence for Almaar. But the net casts wide, Gerent. And the Butcher sees many futures, predicts the trajectory, understands the potential."

"You are not instilling me with confidence," Gerent replied.

The countess pursed her lips, then explained what had been on the data gleaned from Tweem. What the Butcher had taken, but not how a group of Breakers had worked out what she hadn't. That was too much.

Her slate rumbled, and a glance brought her up short. A communique from a frigate she'd sent at speed to Karal. Had they found the Butcher? A swipe left her both disappointed and elated. Not found, but the trail was warm, and hinted at a greater gift if only Khan hadn't been so stupid and left. A potential shift in their favour, a system blocker, a shield to give her ships time.

CHAPTER 38

KARAL

Savvo ran through the protocols Jenkra Tew had insisted he adhere to on his slate. He then paired it with the stand-in chief officer, who gave a thin-lipped smile in return, her skin tightening around her nose and lips, stretching the powder under her eyes that was failing to hide her tiredness.

"You're a bona fide member of the team, Savotini. Congratulations. Security clearance has been achieved. Of course, without the imperial pardon, you would now be sitting in the brig in chains and suffering the torturer's hot irons." She patted his hand, and then sat back, Trent's massive chair dwarfing her body, but her aura was formidable. Davina had said she was capable, but from what he could see, she'd not just grown into the role but embraced it. A challenge she relished.

Good. Gonna need that.

"You are now officially liaison to the security team. So, what's your first piece of advice?" Jenkra leaned in, genuinely interested in what he had to say. It wasn't a game; she clearly had no time for that. More wanting to drain him dry, wring him out and use what was left for the benefit of Karal.

Just like being back in the Marines. He could handle that. Better that than to *lead*.

He looked her in the eye. "Something Arin said, Private Enterman, before they left: 'Did you count the bodies?' That may sound bloody weird to you, but I know where he's going. Erikson arrived by private shuttle. Have we records of it? Know where it is? And the crew. Have we traced any of them? I assume you've backtracked over sensor records to see if the assault team came from an external ship. Any that were docked or on approach."

Jenkra shoved her slate aside, taking a sip of water before placing the glass down carefully. "The security team on Karal is here to keep rowdy miners from spacing themselves and guide drunk executives back to their rooms. There are some with experience, but limited. I think you just got yourself upgraded to Chief Consultant."

Fuck.

"Give me a list of the information you need," she checked her slate. "Barclow will be your point of contact. Know him?"

"Of him. Hard-ass pen pusher with a rep for being old school. But solid, ex-Navy?" Savvo looked at his hands. They were scrunched in his lap, the prospect of his new role causing him to wrap them tight. White and red spots intermingling on his skin like an ink-blot test.

"Army," she corrected. "What was the term? A groundpounder, but he's worked his way up. Knows the Minx field like the back of his hand. Now," she eyed her slate, pulling it towards her. "The data security team declare your 'blocker' as benign. They can't get a tune out of it, never mind a jig. Tell me again why I should trust something you tell me is 'alien' in VERT?"

Savvo sighed, dropped his slate onto the table and slid it over as the screen activated. Kefi's translator began to fill the room with its monotone, with the occasional seagull squawking in the background. Few had seen a Senti on screen, never mind in the flesh. The Court had refrained from sharing their image outside of a frosted visor and an encounter suit. Whether that was deliberate censorship or fear of how humanity would react was an interesting question he didn't have time for. Jenkra's wide eyes were proof enough of her ignorance.

And I'm the lowlife.

Savvo stroked her soft skin, running his fingers between her knuckles, a faint smile on his lips as he remembered how she bloody hated him doing that. Nicky had been awake briefly, her mind dulled by the sedation. Her eyes had been filled with ... trepidation? Flitting between a genuine smile and thunder clouds as she tried to work out what the hell was going on. He knew the feeling.

Heavy footsteps echoed behind, and a gruff voice acknowledged an orderly or two before they dropped in beside Savvo. Barclow. Heavy set, barrel-chested, a thick beard trimmed back but still unruly on chin and jowl. He braced.

"How's she doing?" The voice growled as if he'd sucked vacuum for an hour before speaking.

"In body, well. But ..."

"PTSD," he said. It wasn't a question. Nor was he likely wrong, but right now it was a shock to hear it said out loud.

"Maybe."

Barclow coughed, hawking up phlegm that he had the pragmatism to swallow. "S'what a big effin' warbot will do to you. You had it all this time?"

Had? Not over the last six months. Crew now.

"If I say yes, do you still trust me?" Savvo glanced over. Barclow had his chin pressed into his chest, nestling in his beard, body stiff, legs stretched out with hands clasped on his stomach. The last time he'd seen him Barclow had been in exactly that position while Savvo bailed out a certain sub-engineer from the holding cells.

"Never trusted your lot. Dricks maybe. But not you bunch of tossers. Arin still ridin' the *Sunstar*?" Barclow still hadn't looked his way.

"He kept the fuckers who attacked the docks back while I herded the work teams into the ship." Savvo felt a need to defend his friend. Despite the reputation, one he courted, Arin wasn't all mouth. Not completely, anyway.

"Figures," Barclow turned to face Savvo, "gives him more bollocks to brag about at the effin' bar. And you ..." The hulking man twisted his neck, as if what he had to say pained him greatly. "S'pose you deserve a little thanks. What were you, back in the day? One of my team mentioned the Breakers."

Savvo snorted. But he needed status if he was to be listened to, so fuck it. "Yeah. Even Arin before you ask."

"Unbelievable. Some of that crap he spews for real?"

Savvo snorted. "I never said that. This going to be an issue. Me and you?"

Barclow peered at him, bushy eyebrows furrowing briefly. "Apparently you know your shit. So no. Lost some good people in the terminal and on the docks. Solid bastards who'd have yer back. Willing to play ball until yer eff it all up and I can shout 'I told you so' at Jenkra Tew."

Savvo nodded, relief settling the edge in his thoughts that had been building. "Good. Gonna need an autopsy on all the assault team fuckers ASAP. A rundown on the ship that bastard Erikson arrived on, its crew, and where they are now."

"You think we missed some?"

"Not during the assault. But I've been wondering about that magic trick. You know, sleight of hand. Watch one hand ..."

Barclow pushed himself up, legs bent, back straight. "While the other screws us over. For real?"

Savvo considered Daphene, the hunt and subsequent recovery of Countess Segfi, the time taken to focus on rescuing her and not the laser comms. They had been played from the moment the countess had released the Butcher.

"Been done before."

"I expect he thought I'd be dead, so just encrypted the one damn file thinking it less likely to be found." Davina shrugged. "What's this about?"

Savvo paced beside the Incini's bed. The bruising about the Incini's jaw had already gone down. Amazing what good insurance could get you. Since his conversation with Barclow the possibility of more clones on board Karal gnawed at him. Someone hidden in plain sight, or squirrelled away in a hidey-hole. It made no difference. What they needed to know was their intent. Their purpose.

There could be no one. Am I getting fucking paranoid?
As Rebekah would say, I'm alive aren't I.
Fuck.

"I was just thinking there might still be one alive. You know, hiding with ill-bloody-intent somewhere on Karal. Nags at me. Arin put it in my head, and now it won't go away." He rubbed the back of his neck. Pacing, rubbing – his mind wandered to Dricks. Couped up in the *Sunstar,* their personal habits were bound to creep in, and he suddenly missed her like a part of him was absent. A jigsaw piece missing. More than one if he were being truthful.

"You said they wouldn't know we could crack the encryption ... that the Butcher would be unaware of ... you know ... what the others are doing." Davina swung her legs over the edge of the bed and got unsteadily to her feet. She stretched gingerly, then collected her slate, using it to gesture towards Savvo. "Right?"

He shook his head, not knowing how to answer. "Right ... but what if their fall-back mission was recon? Observe and report? Or," he looked out the door, thoughts on Nicky, "more disruption. Karal mines what, twenty-five percent of the ore for shipbuilding?"

"Thirty-five percent. More if you add in the PMGs for electronics and the like." Davina sighed and slid a finger across her slate. "I was hoping for a normal life."

Those simple words hit Savvo, a gut-punch. A tear formed unbidden in the corner of one eye. "Yeah. Me too." He tried to look away, but Davina caught his gaze with sympathy in her eyes. A slow smile and tilt of her head followed. If she'd touched him then, reached out to comfort, he'd have collapsed. Davina was an Incini, however. They could feel emotion, but saw it as a weakness, especially at the negotiating table. He watched the moment fade; the sympathy locked away. The twins, they had the key to that Incini-trained mind, perhaps Hendricks too.

A voice echoed from the slate, one he knew. "Davina, that you? Where are you?"

Davina broke eye contact with him and took up the slate, her face back to the mask she usually wore. "Jenkra, I have Savotini here asking some very pertinent questions. I'm going to need security clearance to help answer them. Barclow loves me even less than you do."

"Emotions and business are poor bedfellows," Jenkra replied. "Another consultant, Barclow will be *so* pleased."

It had been a busy day, and there was still more to do. No sitting about the galley drinking tea in zero-g. Here he could tip a cup and savour the flavour without fear it would fly away. It nearly made up for the gruesome sight laid out before him. Thirteen clones, with seven different flavours of facial features among them, their body height varied but the musculature much the same. He had no clue about the hair; the skullcap removed to expose their brains and the wetware pinned and glued to it.

"How clever are these clones? How much independent thought do they have?" he whispered.

The surgeon-cum-pathologist raised an eyebrow at him over her shoulder. Perhaps the mask was of little use, a surgeon's time spent listening to the mumbles of others.

"They're human, Mr Savotini. From head to toe, an exact copy of their originator, but human, nevertheless. They may, under some belief systems, be regarded as soulless. That which animates their nerve endings and brain function bereft of the spark of true life."

"And? The relevance?" He hated sermons, and the comments had the air of one. Or someone cleverer than him talking down, which he also hated. But then it was rare he had dealings with those of minor noble status outside of the forces. Did all those born to privilege talk this way to scum like him? Savvo glared at the clone, wondering what the surgeon would do should the soulless bastard animate and grab her by the throat. Would she talk down to him or plead for a lowlife's help?

What the fuck am I doing? They're just words.

"It's the same work?" he asked, the words perfunctory. Of course it was.

"Absolutely," replied the surgeon and, after a few snips of brain tissue, pulled the wetware free. "Glorious work, I must say. I saw vids of the original wetware engagement, but the surgery required to achieve such beauty is quite something. Rivals the Senti."

"Does it?" Savvo wasn't surprised, and took the glistening wetware from the surgeon, attaching it to a wire protruding from his hip. He'd given up trying to work the different chip kits without wearing the navy-suit. It was unnatural to him. Once connected, he snapped on his helmet, and the visor fired up. Several eye-clicks and he added the wetware's frequency to the rest. All the assault team were set to slightly different wavelengths, and he had them all logged. This being the last. He asked the HUD to run an extrapolation, wishing ZZ3 was at his side with the bot's extra computing power.

It came back, and he set the HUD running the additional frequency alongside all the others, switching between them at one-second intervals. Davina had run through Barclow's information on the private transport, her analytical enhanced brain cross-referencing the records backed up on VERT. He had wondered how Barclow would take her interference, but once he clocked that there was the possibility of two of Erikson's transport crew still on board Karal his mood had changed. Davina had shifted focus in hope of finding the missing dock workers, for it was evident that Trent had employed the clones to replace staff who had resigned one-by-one over a week – fooled by high-quality falsified IDs – yet none had ever departed the station. Barclow had left her to it, his assistant Yol by her side.

"Time to go hunting?" Barclow asked. He checked his holster, a soldier's habit.

"Fuck yes," Savvo replied.

CHAPTER 39

The alert clattered through the *Sunstar*, its blare urgent, demanding, which immediately put Rebekah on edge as it dragged her from the depths of sleep. Memories flooded back of the journey to the *Scourge*, the *Maverick*, Toms' crew and their attempts to murder her own.

They paid the price.

She grunted, unclipping her bed's covers and sliding into the waiting magboots. A glance reminded her she had gone to bed in her flight suit, the alarm's call expected, and it soon shut off.

"Rebekah?" came the query over comms. Heki, on watch in the cockpit while her captain got some down time.

"On my way. Trem?" she asked in turn. "Is it the autoship feed?"

"On a ten-minute delay, but it's on approach. Signal running pure." The girl sounded distracted, but then she would likely be doing three other things at once right now. The twins' personalities were diversifying, mood swings no longer synced. Whether that was the separate cabins, maturing, or that Rebekah was mentally disentangling the twins now – viewing them more as different entities than sisters bonded by flesh and memory – she wasn't sure.

After a brief trip to the bathroom, she collected a flask of coffee and toast, sitting at the galley table as Kefi and Hendricks sauntered in. It took her by surprise to see them together, and they continued their conversation as the engineer collected her highly sugared caffeine hit.

"Arin with ZZ3?" she asked as Hendricks sat, Kefi choosing to hook into the deck at her side.

"Just finishing up the last probe mods. Tremil has had ZZ3 running through her navcom changes to see if Asham can find any flaws in her code. With the new parts, she thinks she can project the ghost image about ten klicks either side for a sustained but as yet unascertained period." Hendricks smelt her coffee, a smile towards Kefi as she proffered the flask.

The Senti shrunk back. "A stimulant for humans, a foul concoction of chemicals that has the aroma of a week-old encounter suit." There was no laugh, the alien quite serious as it eyed the flask. "Would you like a rundown of what it'd do to my biomeds?"

"Naah. Worth it just to see you squirm." Hendricks pulled the flask away, Rebekah unsure if it was a taunt or a bonding she was watching. Perhaps both.

Heki called from the cockpit, confirming the navcom was on trajectory, and with Rebekah's affirmation joined them in the galley as Tremil arrived. The girl swiped her slate, and the galley screen flared into life. Another tap, and she spoke into comms. "You getting the feed, Arin?"

The sub-engineer replied, "We are. Got any popcorn?"

"Wasn't on the supplies list," said Rebekah. "How long?"

"The autoship should already be past the asteroid. What we'll be watching is delayed." Tremil swiped, and the screen separated into an image feed and information square. "The sensor information shows the ship was pinged, and then swamped by a barrage of electromagnetic pulses."

"To minimise data trawl," said Kefi absently. "Yes?"

Tremil nodded. "Yes. If I'd had more time I could have prepped the ship, maybe blocked some of it. I'm working on that now for the *Sunstar*. Analysing what the Butcher's doing, and if there are any patterns."

"It shows we're on the money," stated Hendricks, Kefi shuffling in response. "That the asteroid is important. Defended."

"Ah," said the Senti, and its gaze returned to the screen. "I believe I can help with the overload jamming. It is targeted at human-designed sensors, but I am learning very quickly that a touch of alien can make a difference." The Senti did squawk then, Hendricks shaking her head.

"That would be useful. We got anything else?" Rebekah raised a hopeful eyebrow towards Tremil who pinched and tapped at her screen.

"I think everything is projected outwards." The data fed back in, the trail of random, jammed information, flickering onto a screen that Tremil froze. "The data packet still has to pass back through it to reach us, so there may be some distorted information, but we found a small flaw by chance with the flyby."

"Not by chance," corrected Rebekah, ignoring Tremil's wince. "Planned. If we programmed the ship to hard burn and do a slow sweep, it wouldn't have stood a chance. We took a guess the Butcher will be preparing for a human incursion, at worse an autoship programmed to report back on a return trajectory. Not what amounts to a giant missile heading for the black." There was a beep, Tremil glancing down and with a slow shake of the head, she sent new data onto the galley screen.

A low whistle pierced comms. "Woah," said Arin. "There's strip mining and then there's that."

The images stopped, only the void pricked by the occasional star in view as the autoship sped past the outer rim of the field and out into the far-flung edges of the system.

"Heki, double check the trajectory. Need a marker we can send back to Karal." Heki nodded, and headed for the cockpit. Rebekah gestured for Tremil to continue. "Rewind and slow it down."

Tremil, tongue poking out the corner of her mouth, was already on it. The asteroid appeared tiny at first, the feed shimmering, flickering but giving a clear enough almost stop-motion portrayal of an asteroid being thoroughly stripped to its core, and likely beyond. Bots of all descriptions busied themselves around the rock and, parked close by in a standard orbit, the missing autoship, hold doors wide as loaders steered in and out. The final image showed what lay beyond the remains of the asteroid. Synth-mesh nets held more mined ore in huge bundles.

A check told Rebekah their autoship hadn't picked up the geo mineral content, but did it really matter? The Butcher was gathering resources, had built a mining operation on an industrial scale and she had no doubt the model for it all had been stolen from under Trent Pike's nose. Designs, examples, processes. Simple enough for an AI/scientist hybrid to scale up when you don't need to give a shit about anyone dying on the job.

"What's that?" she asked, and stood, pointing to the pinpricks of light that left streaks at the speed their autoship was travelling. Tremil focused in, magnifying and then using the ship's computer to fill any missing gaps. "Missile platforms."

"The data packet suggests they double up as the jamming satellites."

An electronic monotone agreed over the comms. "I would suggest all three. Sensors, jamming and missile defence. A step up from what we faced on Daphene and Saim."

"But this is all useless," said Rebekah, all eyes falling on her. She shrugged. "What can we achieve? We're days away. The defensive systems know we're coming, the autoship can transport the ore without us knowing where it's going. Maybe we can deprive the Butcher of some resources, but to what ends?" She glanced at Kefi. "And we're no closer to recovering the spawn queen."

Kefi off-gassed. "How *can* this help us? What if we could get there before they run? Is there anything to our advantage if we got there sooner?"

"Sooner?" Rebekah scrunched her eyes, then pressed her fingers in, squeezing. "You mean jump in? Heki and Tremil have never been there. Impossible."

The Senti laid a tentacle on the table, pointing towards the screen. "The autoship sent back current radiation signatures, am I right? I can guide them from the image and the data position. Or at least the queen's symbiote can."

Rebekah blinked out the spots in her vision and clasped her slate just for something to hold on to. There was only one reason to ask that. "You mean they use regular radiation emissions to locate? Like from planets, even pulsars. The symbs can sense the regular fucking beams of charged particles and radiation they shoot out. Bloody cosmic lighthouses." She looked at the Senti, the soulless eyes returning her gaze, the slightest of off-gases bubbling beneath a neck fold. Kefi waved a tentacle as if to agree. She shook her head. How much more was there to these tiny aliens? "How risky is it?"

"You walked into a Senti orb being invaded by the Butcher's clones and you ask about risk now?" said Arin. "I mean, zombie clones or a blind space jump, what's the difference?"

Rebekah eyed Tremil. Of course there was a difference, but it's what they did. Heki and Tremil would say 'yes' to whatever was on offer. But if it worked, would they be showing their hand?

Not all of it.

Not yet.

She cracked both thumbs. "If we could get hold of his autoship, then we can hack the navcom, find where its heading. If our hunch is correct, it should take us to where the Butcher is building ships with Senti metal." Rebekah gestured to the screen. "He kind of does things on a big scale."

"A worthwhile endeavour," said the Senti. "We both believe the Butcher will have the spawn queen aboard his battleship. It would seem logical that it would be guarding any smelting operation and shipyard."

Rebekah wasn't so sure, and Tremil's glance her way hinted she had picked up her doubts. She grimaced and flicked her gaze to Hendricks who shrugged.

"We've come this far. We either go all in, or face the consequences with the Senti Queen." She glanced at Kefi, who held her gaze with her empty eyes. "Fuck, it's more than that. We walk away, we leave the Butcher building ships the fleet can't detect."

She was met with Hendricks' grim smile and the slightest tilt of her head. Tremil squashed in a little closer, hooking her arm in Rebekah's. Once again, she would be taking children into battle. The countess wouldn't have batted an eyelid at that, though she would have stripped away any humanity first, shaped the girls in her image. But Heki and Tremil were family, and without them they would be a blunt force, slow, deliberate, and unable to match, never mind beat, the Butcher. What hope for them then? For every family out there?

"Okay people. I want a flight plan, trajectory and probe structures all aligned to an attack run. We're going in hot, dropping our payload, then running."

"Payload?" said Hendricks. "What payload?"

Rebekah smirked. "It's an autoship, ain't it? Know any specialist repair crews around here?"

There was a thunk over comms, a hand slapping a forehead, perhaps. "No, no, no. Hey, surely I've been upgraded by now? Think of all the things I've done. How many times I rescued Savvo. Raiding Daphene, ran around a parade ground wearing weights. I got beaten up pretending to be a groundpounder called Sparks! When is enough, enough?" Arin's pleading tone echoed in the galley.

"When – our glorious leader – your Captain says so." ZZ3 sounded almost happy. "Besides, you have a Senior Rescue Warbot to look after your sub-engineer's skin. Isn't that right, Captain?"

"Oh yes," she eyed Kefi. "How long do you need?"

"I need two of your hours."

"If we're doing this, you have one. We need to get there as soon as we can." Rebekah stood, gathering her slate.

"One and a half if I am to ensure a safe journey," stated the Senti. "No less."

She nodded. "And we've got a lot to do in a short space of time. Hendricks, how's your gunnery?"

"Rusty," said the engineer. "But I guess I have an incentive to improve."

Tremil squeezed Rebekah's arm, her eyes a little wider than she expected. A wave of the girl's trepidation washed over Rebekah and the symb along the girl's neck mithered before settling again. "You need the ghost ship program?"

"We've enough to do. I have the probe access now Arin and Dricks have automated it. Besides, I'd like to save that for what comes next." She dropped a hand onto Tremil's still hooked in her elbow, and glanced around to smile at the returning Heki. "Don't push too hard, understand? Once we're through, I'm going to need you both if we're to access the autoship and ride their defensive screen. Crew don't get to slack even if they've moved the ship impossible distances."

Arin stomped about the hold, arms full of a combination of munitions and explosive that Rebekah eyed warily.

"You need all those?" she asked.

"Too right. We're being dropped in a shit-filled autoship controlled by an insane AI with a penchant for spacing humans. Thinking on it, I might need some more." He began to turn away then stopped. ZZ3 was attaching the plasma torch but also halted, blue eyes swirling before fading into red. "Who's in charge?" said Arin.

"What?"

"Out there." Arin waved towards the cargo bay doors. "When we're being thrown at a stolen ship in the hope we'll stick, and then hacking our way inside. We need a hierarchy, otherwise it'll all go to shit." He placed his collection of armaments on the floor, crossing his arms. "We need to sort this out now, before we go."

Rebekah shook her head. "You have the weirdest of timing. Check the ship's logs. The manifest." She headed for the cargo bay exit. "And stop talking yourself into this stuff. Dricks is on edge about what I'm proposing, so stay fucking focused."

Arin, hands on hips, shook his head, ZZ3 looming behind. A metal limb landed gently on his shoulder. "You should check them," said the warbot. "And whatever they say, you are my glorious leader."

Arin patted the metal, feeling its warmth, the reassuring companionship. "Thanks, ZZ3." He slipped out his slate from a thigh pocket, pulling up the manifest. "Hey, hey. I've been promoted."

ZZ3 withdrew its hand, eyes settling to a calm blue. "You have?"

"Yeehaw. I've been upgraded to Senior Technical Engineer. How about that, Senior Rescue Warbot? *Senior* Technical Engineer. That makes me in charge of ... of ..."

ZZ3 cut in. "Warbot repairs, probe design and navcom systems as well as suit management."

"That's right," Arin paused. "That might sound like what I'm already doing to you, Mr Warbot, but *I* am now a *Senior* too." Arin started collecting the equipment he'd left on the floor, stowing much of it in his suit's pouches. "Do you think I'll get paid more?"

"You get paid?" said the warbot.

CHAPTER 40

KARAL

Savvo eye-clicked his HUD, the visor returning a blank map of the dockside. Again. Still clear, but he had a feeling he was missing something. Dock workers milled about his position, one or two of the maintenance crews too, each sending a look of thanks Savvo's way, his presence a reminder of the attack, and their subsequent rescue. It wasn't helping as he tried to focus on the new issue instead of the old.

"Savvo," hissed his comms. "Anything?"

"No." He slapped the wheel of an autoloader at his side in frustration. The dock area was vast and busy with repairs, readying M4 for a return to collecting and then shipping ore back to Almaar or the colonised planets and moons. Tweem included. The tower would take longer, but the transponder system imported from a defunct asteroid family wasn't far off being operational. Jenkra was nothing if not efficient.

Barclow cut in again. "We should check out the warehouses again, then call it a bust and move on to M3."

Savvo agreed. M3 would be a nightmare to scour. The warrens tunnelled into the asteroid filled with the miners who worked the field. Rough and ready, it was a rowdy place which wouldn't welcome the intrusion of Barclow into their slice of not-so paradise. He started the walk back to the warehouses, the sections piled on top of each other like the high rises back on Almaar, wrapped in handholds and stairwells.

"Savvo?" It was Davina. "You still on M4?"

"Affirmative," he said, the word slipping easily from his lips, while thoughts of ZZ3 danced at the edge of his mind. The warbot would have ripped every single door off if it thought crew were under threat. What he'd give for that thoroughness now.

"Good. Yol had an idea I was following up on." Savvo cast his mind back. Yol? Barclow had insisted Davina could only help with his assistant at her shoulder. Was that his name? "About cross-referencing Erikson's arrival date against all the standard equipment checks via the database. Anyway, Trent had done all of that and left the file accessible. Stuff started going missing only a few days after the transport arrived, but it got me thinking. I've worked through Duboit's expenses, and Erikson rented out several storage areas in his name."

"On the docks?" he asked, eager for some kind of breakthrough.

"Two. Quarter D Level 1 and E Level 1."

"That's effin' odd," said Barclow. "Hard to get hold of the ground floor. Reserved for the heavies."

Savvo knew what he meant, the pre-constructed auto loading trains and tracks either recovered from the larger, mined-out asteroids, or built ready for the next. Maybe some of the main parts for the massive mining drills they'd often had to repair. Rare space to get hold of. Big enough to store most of what Trent had listed as missing twice over.

"Paid through the nose," said Davina. "And agreed any current equipment stored could remain there."

"I bet he did. Fuck," said Savvo. "Meet me there Barclow."

"On my way." The security chief hadn't barked back about who was in charge, Savvo taking that as a plus. The warehouses were a good fifteen minutes away, so Savvo used his newfound fame and waved down one of the loaders to blag a lift. In return for being the centre of attention, he reached the corner of a huge warehouse block that glinted blue in the harsh dockside lights. He couldn't see the top for the nest of stairwells in the way as it pierced the outer rim of M4 and entered the residual lighting, but he could make out the huge painted markers along the base.

He clamped to the deck and drew out his handgun, leaving the carbine maglocked to his back for now. Striding along the metal wall of the lower level, he passed section C and an eye-click focused in on the distant figure of Barclow as he waited beside a massive set of doors. Savvo hoped he'd sorted an override code, because gaining entry without a warbot was going to be an issue.

"Can we get in?" he said, eye-clicking his suit control to up the pace. "Got the override?"

"No, I've been stood 'ere twiddling me effin' thumbs waiting for a super-'ero to do it all." Barclow's gruff response made Savvo smile briefly. The security officer cradled an odd-looking weapon in his arms. By the time Savvo arrived, his visor had analysed and labelled it as a riot control gun. Savvo didn't have to time to check what that meant as Barclow tapped impatiently at the lockpad.

"Cover me," he ordered, giving Savvo little choice in the matter. His HUD showed the first third of the warehouse was likely clear. If it was correct.

The hum of motors vibrated through the deck and wall, and with a clunk an access door began to open, leaving the massive entryway for the mining equipment closed. Barclow barged in, keeping low, but hardly demonstrating an aptitude for stealth. Three steps inside and Savvo followed, his HUD clicking over to infrared on his instruction. He had half-expected the warehouse lights to erupt into life, but apparently Bar-clow had opted for them to remain off. The security chief's suit was hardly state-of-the art, but tough and functional, like the man, and Savvo wondered about its capabilities a little late.

With no heat signature registering, he dropped to one knee beside Bar-clow, taking station beside a set of large lockers labelled with part numbers. "Anything?" Savvo asked.

"Nothing," answered the security officer. Ahead of them was a train engine, massive, sleek-lined but pitted from use and as cold as the rest of the warehouse. "Cover me," he said again, and inched forward before spurting for the train. Once there, the ex-army man swept below, peering through the wheels ahead.

Savvo joined him, leaning on the nose of the train, surveying the multitude of cranes, drilling arms and tracks spread out before him. The enormity of the space was beginning to sink in. They were going to need a search team if he couldn't pick anything up on his HUD. Or a drone. He glanced at Barclow, a thought wheedling its way in. He hadn't thought to bring drones; why would he? But the ship's crews and maintenance teams would have plenty.

"Hey, Barclow. I have an idea."

They were in a cab, squashed in like so much trash. Their lives forfeit for the Butcher's goal of survival. Desiccated and very dead, fifteen naked bodies discarded and forgotten. The drones had swept the warehouse, buzzing between the mighty machines, lighting their path, speeding up the process with their operators tucked safely behind a couple of Barclow's team.

"Savotini," said Barclow, he tapped his helmet, rising from the last of the bodies he'd med-tagged.

Savvo accepted the request, and the data rolled over his HUD screen. Thirteen had been dock workers and on record, all tallying with those that had left their jobs soon after Erikson's arrival. Two were unknown and piqued Savvo's interest. He strode over, with Barclow kneeling next to one of the dried-out cadavers. A glance caused his heart to jump, and he eased in next to the security chief.

"Is that ..." Savvo took in the bald head, pinched, dried cheeks.

"Victor Gonzales," finished Barclow. "Know him?"

"We've run into each other. At least, Rebekah and Arin have." Something tickled his memory. Had Davina mentioned it? Or Rebekah? "This guy had been fooling the facial IDs."

Barclow shifted, lifting the wrist that turned to dust at his touch, exposing the wrist bone. There was scarring, and recent. "They dug out his wrist ID scanner. The bastards could be anywhere on Karal if his history is anything t' go by."

A flag and a message dropped. One of the drone controllers calling for Savvo's attention. Savvo's, not Barclow's. He pulled up the message, a camera feed. "Oh."

Barclow glared at him. "What? A penny drop?"

"No," he sent the image over, then replied to the operator. "Mining explosives clamped to the doors. If we'd come in that way ..." He let that sink in. And if they had access to one set, then they had access to a lot more. It was a storage facility after all. "A secondary mission. Fuck." He slammed a hand into the cab wall. "Not recon. Resource denial."

Barclow stiffened. He knew what that meant as well as Savvo. Standard armed forces practise. Cut off supply, drain your enemy of what they need to keep going. "They're rigging the docks?"

"Maybe everywhere. People are resources too. The autoships as well. Whatever order of priority the fucking Butcher has set." Savvo glared at the pile of bodies, nothing more than dust-covered bone and soon less than that. They didn't even bother to cover their mess.

Mining charges. How many?

"Davina?"

"Here."

"Can you and Yol do a trawl of what mining charges were missing," he thought for a moment, "and where the remainder are stored."

"Do I want to know why?" she asked.

"Hard to fucking answer that. We're looking primarily at the heavy-duty kit, aimed at cracking metal deposits, second priority are the smaller charges. ASAP." He cut off the comms, Barclow staring at him, the man's eyes steely beneath a bushy brow. Savvo shook his head in response.

"What we need are the repair crews," said Barclow, and tapped his helmet, Savvo briefly wondering if it was a habit or a comms glitch. "I'll put a call out."

"Wait," said Savvo. Arin and ZZ3 would have been five times quicker than a repair team untrained in explosives. But there were no auto repair crews like the *Sunstar*'s out there. Anywhere for that matter. Not many Breakers with their old warbots on the run.

Savvo switched his gaze to the bodies of the dockers. "Want some advice?" He carried on regardless, "Miners. Pull them a team at a time and get them to M4 ASAP. Tell them they've earned the chance for some serious Calc but only if they keep the fuck quiet."

Barclow's helmet bobbed as he nodded. "Not my area of exper-ef-fin'-tese. They need anything with them?"

"It'll all be here waiting. Recall *Monk* and *Selles'* crews from M2, the only two repair ships in dock. Do that first, and we'll get the search up and running."

Sending miners on the hunt for explosives with hand scanners and bloody autobots was going to set everyone on edge. He could imagine the panic as those with limited knowledge put two and two together and made up whatever answer they wanted. But miners on the outside of Karal's infrastructure, now that was doable, and they had the sensor equipment to penetrate the hulls. It's what they did.

"Have Karal's repair teams on call and ready to run alongside. The miners will sweep the external, the repair teams internal, but we keep them linked. Barclow, they're going to need to know what they're looking for. Calc will wire their mouths shut, but drink ..." Savvo splayed his hands wide.

"Yeah. I hear ya."

"Savotini, Barclow," the comms kicked in. Davina in the background, but the voice was new. Yol. "We're looking at fourteen of the larger charges as newly missing, and all since the attack. We only found them because I ordered a stock check. I think the database had been pre-prepared for the theft. Still working on the others, but I've got a stock anomaly in progress right now. Someone's tampering with the storage unit Section B 13a. A botch job and in progress."

Barclow responded. "On it."

"I'm on it," said Savvo. "We need those miners ASAP." He unclipped his carbine and headed for the exit.

"Effin' consultants," echoed in his comms. "Dobson, Mint, follow the super-'ero. Keep 'im alive."

Savvo left his minders behind, increasing the power-level of his navy-suit and pounding up the stairs. Each step became just the slightest bit easier as the gravity gradually reduced, and it took minutes for him to reach level 13 where he then slowed, crouching, and running a quick scan with his HUD. Activating his wetware, he calmed his mind, slowed his breathing.

The sublevel sat just above head height, the steps angling off and away from the main stairwell. His HUD mapped the target area, which sat around the next corner, with some additional heat registering. Here they were just above the glare from the lower dock lights, and at the far reach of the upper. Shadows hung heavy from the main block wall, clamps and higher decks spreading patches of darkness his HUD adjusted for.

With no time to wait on his back-up, Savvo synced his carbine and headed up the side stairs, keeping tight to the wall, sighting towards the corner. They were in a vacuum, no sound travelled, and he was heading blind into combat.

He felt alive.

On reaching the corner, he eased the muzzle of his carbine around, its sight displaying an open doorway in his HUD and, hovering just out from the gangway, a low-loader autobot, thrusters engaged and with a threatening payload. A HUD check confirmed the explosives were electronically inactive, and even if a grenade landed in the middle, would only add to the shrapnel level. The loader bot stuttered, one thruster giving out, the loader dipping before recovering as it fired back up. It put Savvo on edge.

He crept slowly around the corner, his magboots set low, until he was at the door. Again, he eased the carbine around, the HUD picking out a blazing infrared signal that flooded his visor. He eye-clicked away from the infrared, the image adjusting to show a ransacked storage box, shelves askew, with the source of the heat laid upon the floor. A dockworker's suit, but the heat served as a warning. They needed information, but also to stay alive. Savvo allowed his wetware to spread a little calm, then followed his rifle around the door, keeping it locked onto the visor of the suit. A glove twitched, then an elbow, whoever was inside twisting as if trying to stand up.

"We're here," echoed over his comms, which he ignored. The HUD flagged his back-up as they pounded along the stairwell.

"Stay still or I'll blast your fucking head off," growled Savvo over the docks' main comms. The suit didn't react, carrying on, attempting to rise to its feet. "Down, back on the floor fucker. You have 3, 2 ..."

The helmet twisted to face Savvo, gloves fumbling at the visor as if they were trying to rip it open. Clumsy fingers scraped and battered at the plexi-glass. The visor unfrosted, inside a mouth wide open in a desperate scream, blood pouring from the woman's lips, teeth sliding from rotten gums. Savvo fired, whether out of mercy or hate he couldn't say, the controlled burst slamming into her chest, ripping through the suit. Her eyes met his, blood-filled, fearful, and the woman flew back to crash into something piled behind. It took a moment, his HUD screaming at him, before he recognised the activation signals.

"Grenade!" he bellowed, as it was the first word in his head. He threw himself back as the explosion tore into him, sending Savvo, suit aflame, spiralling out of the door to crash into his late back-up and on over the rail.

CHAPTER 41

DUBOIT'S ASTEROID

And the void disappeared, replaced by the dull gleam of metal against the black as the *Sunstar* tore from void-space into true-space and the sight of an asteroid being deconstructed at an almighty pace. The layout was different; Rebekah knew that instinctively. It wasn't her brain making leaps and suppositions because the Butcher, or whatever part of him he had left here to run the operation, knew they were coming. The hybrid AI had responded.

I just don't know how.

Their PDCs blazed, ripping across the abyss to slam into the first wave of satellites, the spread of cannon fire conal, encapsulating those closest to them before they could respond. The *Sunstar* burned on, not accelerating, but tearing through the hole Hendricks had torn in the first line of defence. The rest would adjust, track and release. The *Sunstar*'s only hope the high speed Rebekah had demanded before the twins' symbs folded time and space to drop them before the asteroid.

And there it was. The difference. Clouds of mining autobots had clustered together, no longer rampaging over the asteroid, but ready for the invader in their midst. The nearest spread wide, like a net ready to catch a minor inconvenience. Of course, Rebekah hated being *just* an inconvenience.

"Fuck that. Arin, ZZ3, you're up. Dricks, target the autobots dead ahead."

The seat at her side twisted, and a tired-looking Heki dropped into the co-pilot's chair. Her eyes were a little sunken, but Rebekah didn't have time to worry. They were about to be blown open. As she suspected, the PDC cannons were useless against the much smaller autobots, catching a few as Hendricks adjusted, but there were too many and they were too small. For once, the old debris cannons would have been more effective.

The navcom pinged, a burgeoning warning.

"We've been painted," stated Heki. She began to swipe at her screen, scanning the incoming data, the tiredness suddenly lost amid the urgency. Her symb, grey and lacklustre, rested against her neck.

Rebekah suppressed a grin. "You have the probes. Keep the missiles off our back for as long as you can. Those we're flying into. Dricks retarget any satellites ahead."

She left Heki to it, eyes roaming the navcom data pouring in. "Trem, I need a space to drop Arin and ZZ3. That cloud of bots is going to make it bloody hard. I have twelve seconds ..."

Silence came back, tension ratcheting in Rebekah's mind. Five seconds. "4, 3 ..."

"Now," Trem said, her tone insistent. Rebekah trusted it implicitly, and Arin's life depended on it. A sapient warbot too.

The comms roared, the whole cockpit vibrating as light flared into a pulse from the *Sunstar*'s nose. The navcom blinked and then shut down as Tremil's jamming wave poured out from the ship.

"Mark. Focus Arin." With no time to think, Rebekah worked the reboot sequence, praying Heki had the probes out and keeping them safe, that

Hendricks had punched them a hole, that Trem's Senti coding would blow the bots' systems long enough for her payload of sub-engineer and warbot to sail on through. So much hope.

The navcom flickered back into life, the *Sunstar* roaring past what remained of Duboit's prized asteroid, PDC fire streaking ahead as probes blew either side of them. The *Sunstar*'s ghosts drew more missiles, the pulse of their signal powerful, luring them in, while Trem shielded the ship with a false sensor sweep. Giving away their secrets, so they didn't become ghosts themselves. Rebekah had no doubt the Butcher would analyse their tactics, and be ready next time.

The PDC fire swivelled around to the side, then to their rear, Heki still working the navcom, evidently releasing more probes in their wake as they burned into the void, abandoning two of their crew.

I'll get you back.

"Shiiiiit ZZ3, that was too close." Arin jerked beneath the warbot, neck complaining. His suit responded by squeezing the brace tighter just above his shoulder line. Another jolt, this time accompanied by a sudden drop that caught Arin's brain by surprise. The force lurched his stomach. "No," he said, trying to hold the vomit down. "I … am … not … throwing … up in my … suit."

"I will not tell anyone, our glorious leader." ZZ3's voice filled his comms. "I promise."

"And I trust you now?" Arin forced the bile down, only for his HUD to flag a warning. Two bots were steaming in, their arms spread wide. They looked very much like the repair bots on board autoships, their tips afire with a blue glow. ZZ3 boosted upwards, throwing itself to the side at the same time, then swivelling to the left.

"No ..." Arin grasped the mouthpiece sitting at his left cheek, a most unnatural action when your stomach was surging your last meal through your throat. He pulled back, yanking a face mask that spread across his mouth. As his suit shouted a red warning, his throat already knew why.

"I said you shouldn't have had that donut," stated ZZ3, monotone flat, lurching left and downwards as far as Arin's brain could tell.

Arin slid back from the face mask. "Hindsight," he said, spitting out the last of the half-digested donut, "is a wonderful thing used by know-it-all robots at inappropriate times to belittle their leaders."

"It is. We are through the autobot cloud. The mining ship is ahead. I am afraid their engines are preparing for burn." ZZ3 sent the feed into Arin's HUD, data streaming alongside. "My adjustments have tempered our speed and direction from the *Sunstar*. I hope the Captain's calculations are correct."

Arin pulled in a breath, regretting it as the acrid aroma bit at his nostrils. "Calculations? She's an ex-dropship pilot. The only calculation they ever did was who would shit themselves first. And if they were losing, they made sure you did, anyway. There was this time ..."

"Prepare for trajectory change," stated ZZ3. "You may want to clench."

"Clench?"

ZZ3 heaved forwards, the deceleration the warbot had been inducing negated as the thrusters surged them both towards the automining ship whose rear burned bright. Arin had little left to bring up, but clenching was a damn fine idea as they hurtled towards the suddenly departing ship. He glanced up at the calculations Rebekah and Heki had devised together, noting ZZ3's change in flight. He swore.

"Really? A thirty-second window?" As he watched the numbers begin to count down, the opportunity to action Option A faded fast. They had planned on hitting the autoship at the rear before it responded, planting the engine detachment explosives and leaving just as rapidly. All of which ZZ3 could have done on its own. Plan B needed Arin. "Negate A, go to B."

"Our glorious leader ..."

"Now."

The warbot adapted its flight, Arin's HUD readjusting, displaying the new trajectory. They were coming in hot, his suit warnings rising, his vision narrowing as blood pressure responded to the increased acceleration. He instructed the suit to countermand, dark spots pressing in, head pounding compounded by the red warning lights in his visor. He engaged a tenth of the usual retardant dose, enough to dull, to give ease as the hull of the autoship closed in to fill his visor.

"Impact in 3, 2 ..."

"This is your fault Savvo!"

The warbot slammed into the hull, scraping along the plates, thrusters reversing, desperate to match pace as they barrelled along towards the bow. ZZ3 wrenched, body stiffening around Arin, and then his vision gave, and the sub-engineer tumbled into the abyss—

...

—and out the other side.

"Shiiit, we still attached?"

"Your Senior Rescue Warbot has successfully maglocked to the hull. Though I may have missed the target area."

Arin eyed his HUD, then wished he hadn't, his visor filled with comms and sensor arrays. They were right at the nose of the ship, the blackness beyond only pinpricked occasionally by starlight.

"Just by thirty metres or so. We need to move." Arin's suit noted the shift of limbs from about his midriff, the warbot locking more limbs onto the ship's hull as it slowly accelerated away from the asteroid. They didn't have long before he would be so much mush inside his suit. ZZ3 pounded along the outer hull, always having at least four limbs attached to the surface until they reached the target area next to the airlock. Arin slapped his hand against the lockpad, drawing out a connector, which he plugged in beneath the screen. He tapped away at the menu screen and entered the override, all the while keeping half-an-eye on the airlock door.

Relief flooded his mind as the entry light pinged green, and he pulled at the external handle, pushing himself inside with the inner door redundant. Once clamped to the deck of the narrow corridor, he waited for ZZ3 who split from his lower body. The corridor was not designed for a warbot to wander down.

"You think we'll have company?" asked Arin, his hand wandering to the sidearm strapped to his suit. It was thankfully still there, his carbine back on the *Sunstar* where his navy-suit sat. The autoships responded to codes and sequences tuned to Karal's systems, as was his standard suit. The last time they'd had to board an autoship, the *Hatton*, the nanobots and whatever software they carried had continually overridden the ship's systems. It had taken Heki and Tremil to find a way in, with Hendricks advising. Now he was on his own, the *Sunstar* out of activation range, and just a Butcher to face.

He glanced at ZZ3.

Not alone. Not for a long time.

"You take the lead, Senior. Be my shield of steel, I remember an errant repair bot that damn-near took my head off last time." He slapped ZZ3 on the shoulder, one of the rare times he could actually reach with one half of the warbot sat by the airlock entrance.

"That was close," stated ZZ3, voice smattered with a first hint of humour. "And if I remember right, the Captain would have won her bet that day, PYP."

Arin growled. "I thought we'd moved on from toilet humour. Get going."

ZZ3 heaved itself in front, arm limbs grasping the walls, dragging itself at surprising speed along the deck. The first junction was clear, the corridor to the right and the auxiliary systems room dark, and nothing moved. The warbot carried on, passing sealed doorways until they reached the bridge door. Though cramped, ZZ3 would be able to squeeze through, but Arin was eager to get in and pull the plug.

"Shift aside, watch my back, rescue warbot, and watch the Senior Technician at work," he said, then palmed the lock. The working airlock had hinted the Butcher hadn't blocked out Karal's overrides, and to his relief, the bridge door slid aside. The room itself, as sterile as a lab, blinked with the occasional light. "See, we're in."

A whip-like limb lashed his way, the tip glowing, plasma searing towards his visor. He saw death coming, the melting of the plexi-glass, the tip boring into his brain. Or worse, the visor shattering, his life-giving air sucked out, his fluids misting as he watched himself die.

The tip wrenched aside, slammed into the doorjamb by a warbot, Arin suddenly finding himself hurtling towards the bridge's right wall. He spun, years of working in zero-g helping him orient away from the danger, legs absorbing the impact as he glared at the bloody repair bot that had nearly done for him. ZZ3 was in the room, the jaws of one severed limb spinning towards the far wall an indication of how the warbot had saved him, another punching the central core of the machine.

Arin went for his gun, tearing it free. He aimed and fired; the bullet ramming into the joint where one whip-like arm met the central frame. He fired again, momentum from hitting the wall now carrying him towards danger. The impact detached the bot's arm, freeing ZZ3 up, and the warbot stove a huge blow directly into the core, ramming the autobot towards the far side of the bridge, limbs trailing, plasma slicing through the navcom unit.

"Noooo," shouted Arin as electronics flared then spluttered out amid the carnage of the control systems. ZZ3 ignored him, shoving itself clear of the deck to sail past the wreckage and onto the remains of the repair bot. Limbs flailed until ZZ3 tore something loose from the bot's body, tossing it aside almost disdainfully before turning about.

Arin could only stare at the damaged control system, thoughts on the black and dying as his oxygen gave out, or he starved to death, or the Butcher had his way with him. No more donuts with sprinkles. "Shit," he said. "Dricks is going to kill me for this."

CHAPTER 42

KARAL

The softest of touches, like a feather, or a breath, brushed against his cheek. A second caress, lips that graced skin, awoke his mind. Dreamless, he clawed his way up from the dark well of his mind, forcing his eyes to open. Light blazed, haloed about a head and face he loved so much it hurt.

Much more than his body did, but it was a close-run thing.

The back of Nicky's hand touched Savvo's cheek again, her eyes dull however, still heavy with sedation. Her smile appeared an effort. But she was here, and so was he. Savvo attempted to lift an arm, only to find it strapped to the medtable. He shifted his head, able to glance down at the buckles restraining him.

"Your body was disrupted," said Nicky, her words slurred, perhaps dredged from her mind. "Blast wave." She rested her hand against his neck, lacklustre, tired.

"Not dead," he said, his jaw aching as he spoke.

Nicky smiled, there was a sudden power there, life. "Not dead," she repeated, and her eyes lit too. A brief sparkle that tugged at his chest. "No, we're not." She leant forward cupping his cheek and kissed him.

He watched as the dullness returned, holding onto the light in his mind as a nurse appeared at Nicky's shoulder.

"Time to go." The nurse gently lifted Nicky by the elbow who responded to the touch and rose, heading for the door.

Savvo desperately wanted to say something, to get her to turn around again, but held on to the moment instead. A beacon in his mind.

The nurse returned, a smile on her lips as she sauntered over to his monitor. "That was a good sign," she said, and tapped at the screen, switching over to a list that caused her eyebrow to raise. "And she mentioned you on the way back to her bed. Wanted to make sure I'd keep her informed." The nurse turned away from the monitor and looked straight at him. "Which means when you go all pig-headed and insist on getting out of here far too early, I get to snitch."

"You wouldn't?" said Savvo, his jaw grinding a little. The nurse began unbuckling his restraints.

"Just watch me. Your suit saved your life. That and blind luck from what I hear. Heavy bruising, joint disruption. You're gonna ache from heaven to hell if you come off the meds." When the last strap released, she stepped back, allowing Savvo to flex his knees and ankles. They cracked and complained just like his jaw, the pain behind the haze nagging at him with its threat of retribution. The nurse handed him a slate. "Sign here."

"What for?"

"It's a disclaimer for when you read the first message and try to leave. Means I take no heat for informing your girlfriend." She grinned at him, Savvo regretting the shake of his head. "Chief Security Officer asked me to make sure you saw it as soon as you woke up. It'll read your wrist bio."

She backed away and headed for the door, likely heading to tease the next patient on her list.

Savvo scanned his wrist and the vid message popped up. It was a recording of his dive through the door, hitting the deck rail, then landing in a heap on the loader. The corner thruster chose that moment to give out, the explosive piling against the lip while his suit maglocked to the loader's base. With feet dangling eighty or more metres above the dockside, the loader tipped over, only for Savvo's backup team to latch on a lifeline as his suit finally gave out. Barclow had written 'some hero' below the final image. Savvo tried not to laugh.

Another message popped in, this one text and Savvo swore. He glanced to the monitor which he knew would be his downfall, but he could see little choice. He eased his upper half from the bed, gritting his teeth against the grinding and gingerly swung his legs over. The monitor informed on him, the screen flashing a silent alarm. By the time his feet touched the floor the nurse had returned, a robot wheelchair following her. She said nothing, the look in her eye lacked any surprise.

"Courtesy of Jenkra Tew," she said, and walked away, headed, as far as Savvo was concerned, to tell tales on an impatient patient.

The chief security officer admired his chair. "Does it convert into an effin' exoskeleton?"

Savvo ignored Barclow, eyes only for the large monitor screen displaying on one wall that showed the part-time pathologist at work. The mess on the table had been a clone once, but what appeared to be rapid decomposition left a tangle of unrecognisable flesh. His mind flashed back to bloodied mouth, rotten gums. He hadn't caused this; she had already been dying.

"I'd need a full lab analysis," stated the woman. "But it appears to be cellular level breakdown of some form. Possibly deliberate. A built-in fail-safe, though I've a mind that some of the lab growth experiments banned before the cessation talked of such things. An outcome from rapid growth shortening cellular life." She lifted something from the mess. It looked like a heart, barely touched by the regression elsewhere. "Possibly the body's ability to replace cells has been forestalled. The heart, for instance, has cells that can live for decades whereas others are measured in days."

Barclow tilted his head as the surgeon-cum-pathologist settled the heart back into what remained of the body. "And the others?" he asked.

"The dead ones? On ice, so the process will be slowed somewhat."

Savvo grimaced, shifting in his chair. "I think he means the one we haven't found."

The woman turned to face the camera. "Ah. Well that depends, doesn't it? On whether this is a pre-programmed event, or if they were grown in the same batch."

Barclow switched off the screen, then took a seat opposite Savvo in the waiting room. "Med report says you should be laid up a while. We ain't got effin' time to wait, you good?"

Savvo lied. "Yeah." He used his wetware to shut off the rising aches in his joints. He was going to need some meds soon. "How's the search?"

"The miners ID'd two more of the explosives on the dockside. Would've brought down the warehouse towers like a pack of cards. They'd been set to explode should the main doors open, so were easy to disarm. Not timed. Odd."

Savvo thought on that, then looked to the now blank screen.

Barclow caught his thought, nodding. "Aye. Could have been her role. The mining crew said once set, they'll be bastards to disarm. They're prepped to respond to a priming signal linked up to blow together, you know, like a domino effect. This isn't about spreading fear."

"Resource denial. They're thinking like soldiers. Maximum damage to the enemy." Savvo looked at his slate, thinking of Davina, then Yol. How they were from different worlds but worked well together, their skills complementing each other. Same with the miners and the repair crews when out in the field, or like now, hunting down the explosives. Like the ship's crew he so missed, their talents …

Talents.

"How far out is Segfi's frigate?"

"Two days, and they're caning it as it is. Their minds'll be mush. Why?"

Savvo swiped his slate. "Because miners don't think like soldiers. They worry about disarming once they're primed. If the first two were rigged for a priming signal …"

Barclow's sour expression lightened a little. "Then stop the signal. I'm no tech specialist, Savotini, what we talkin' 'ere?"

"Wish I had Heki and Tremil to work through it. Even Arin. I need an assessment of the comms arrays. Karal's current capabilities, the lot, and ASAP, with the details on the explosives' receivers. A complete schematic. And send the same shit to the frigate. They might be able to broadcast a jamming signal too, but we'll be in intermittent radio shadow with some of the asteroid field as we spin. It's complex, Barclow, but it might work if you move fast." Savvo spun the chair about, aiming for the door and the hospital lift beyond. "I'll get some more pain killers. Any chance I could have one of those security suits?"

"I ain't deputising yer arse."

Davina's private medroom was up on the huge comms room monitor. She had three screens of her own working at once, one showing an inner view of the security centre on M2 with a thin-looking man with short, brown hair and high cheek bones peering back, teeth clamped about a stylus. Savvo assumed it was Yol, the two of them having worked through the missing mining charges together and now set on a new task, searching for any clue as to where the missing clone might be.

Savvo popped two painkillers, pocketing the remainder in a pouch at his hip. The security suit had few bells and whistles, and he'd eschewed the helmet for now. What it did have was a basic motorised exoskeleton that kept him upright despite the fierce glare of his favourite nurse who had helped him into it. She'd only acquiesced to his request for additional meds when Tew intervened.

Savvo activated his wetware, cutting through the brain fog the meds caused. The urge to pace like Hendricks nagged at him, but he forced himself to sit at the comms controls, his borrowed slate running frequencies like a rain of confetti over the screen.

"The charges can only be activated using the assigned code at a designated signal frequency. The miners set this depending on conditions on the asteroid," he recited. "To do that it'll have to be an external detonation considering Karal's built from shielded materials top to bottom, in and out. So, it's not going to be easy."

"And if they're already dead?" said Davina, her reedy voice over the monitor piercing his thoughts.

"Then there's no threat," he said, turning to the screen. "Unless they're already primed and the activation signal is on a timer."

"Of course it will be," replied Davina, crossing her legs warily, easing her back afterwards with a hand pressed against her lower vertebrae. "But why wait? Why not set them off now? I'd also ask why we're not evacuating, but that's damn well obvious with about ten percent lifeboat access and the human tendency to panic."

Savvo glanced over to the communication room's only other occupant, Jon, a wide-eyed and recently arrived twenty something with a shaved head and a sudden wish to be somewhere else. He knew Savvo was trying to devise a jamming cloud, and realisation why had just dropped in and said hello. He made to get up, a growl from Savvo changing his mind.

"There's nowhere *to* go," he said. "There's nothing but empty vacuum and the cold waiting for you so sit the fuck down and start broadcasting."

He sat back down, blinked once, and started flicking switches with abandon. Savvo hoped they were the right ones. With a check of his slate, he sent the next sequence over, his newly focused assistant nodding away while engaging another array, this one the short-range ship-to-ship comms they used on approach.

His slate beeped; a glance and a swipe brought up a view of the corridor along which Barclow must have been running.

"We've got two mines on M2, Savotini. Miners have flagged their positions, sending crews now to evac. Both are primed. You hear that? Primed." Barclow was out of breath, his words punctuated by heavy breathing, but Savvo could still hear the stress. "Positioned for maximum damage, the twats."

"The array ain't responding. What in all the hells is that?" came from behind, Savvo jerking round, his neck immediately regretting it. Jon was staring at his work screen. "I got a jury-rigged piece of shit floating out there with a ... is that a suit?"

Savvo was up and next to him in seconds, joints screaming as he bowed down to look. The satellite was small, insignificant, more like one of the *Sunstar*'s probes than a full comms system and dwarfed by Karal's ship-to-ship array at its side. A single light flashed from a salvager's spacesuit, a familiar jet pack attached to their back from which a lifeline entangled suit, pack, and satellite together.

"That's it. Got to be," Savvo said.

"Inactive. The satellite's dead," said Jon.

The whole mess continued to spin, the visor unfrosted, a forehead leant against the plexi-glass, exposed bone and skin sagging. Maglocked to its chest was a radio transceiver, the source of the light, one that was flashing faster the longer he looked at it.

"Oh fuck," said Savvo.

CHAPTER 43

"Talk to me Arin." The words drilled into his helmet, rattling about his skull. His mind had shutdown, hopefully temporarily, the thought of imminent death crawling up his gullet.

"Nnnng," he managed.

"ZZ3, report." Rebekah's voice still echoed in his brain, but at least he wasn't the target. "Sit rep."

"Yes, Captain. We were attacked on entry to the bridge. A repair bot in what our glorious leader called a 'screwed-up repeat of a past fuck-up'. We subdued the bot, but at the cost of severe damage to the navcom." ZZ3 was standing next to it, three good limbs repairing the fourth which the warbot had recovered from deeper in the room.

"Fuck," stated Rebekah, a slight delay in her response.

"An accurate representation of our situation," replied ZZ3. "The ship is entering acceleration phase now it is clear of the debris field. Asham and I suggest we negate the engines via the backup system."

"Nnng," said Arin, removing his hands from the sides of his helmet and staring at the warbot. "Shit, yes."

"Captain, I believe Senior Technician Arin has returned to us." ZZ3 raised its jawed limb, spinning the clamps in a smooth motion and flexing the claws.

Again, a delayed answer. "Get a plan together. And hurry. We're turning, but the intercept is going to take time."

"Intercept?" said Arin. The fog lifted a little, long enough for him to activate his wetware and clear the rest. He was up on his feet, striding across the deck towards the exit as the engines rumbled. A signal they were powering up, the first jolt of additional acceleration jarring Arin forwards. He caught the edge of the doorway, steadying himself, then pounded through and on down the corridor. "Follow me big lummox."

ZZ3 dragged itself through the doorway, and followed. "I am an AD unit, not a 'lummox'."

Arin had already turned the corner and spotted the entrance to the auxiliary systems room. "I had you pegged as a sentient warbot." He palmed the lockpad, the ship's computer still responding to his Karal code. The door opened. "With passenger."

"Sentient? The ability to feel? Subjective awareness?"

The engines rumbled again, and Arin experienced increased pressure on his hips, knees and chest. An eye-click increased his suit's resistance to the force, and he set it in on auto, wary that it was already heading into amber. "Yeah. You care. About me in particular, as you should, and the girls a bit. Not Savvo, that would be ridiculous. Take the navcom. Find our destination."

ZZ3 moved through the door and approached the much smaller console, wires appearing from behind its hip plate that the bot attached to the control panel.

Arin worked the engine panel, going through the shutdown sequence methodically, the system responding at each step as it should, building a kernel of hope. His HUD flashed red in the top corner, which he tried to ignore by talking to ZZ3. "Of course, we can't call you sapient." His knee gave, the pain excruciating, forcing Arin to twist about, reorienting with the direction of acceleration. "The wise bit you're working on well – reasoning, thinking, and you're nailing self-bloody-awareness." Arin eye-clicked the HUD alarm off, barely able to shift his neck enough, arms shaking. He entered the last sequence. "But who the hell would want to be human?"

The screen stared back. *Access denied.*

"Shit, shit, shit," he slurred, his mind sluggish, trying again while knuckles ached with each press as he entered the code. Arin watched his own fingers carefully, each entry accurate despite the pain. The denial stared back at him.

"No, ssshit, shit." He raised his glove, trying to reach the monitor when his vision blurred out, heaviness burbling in his brain, sight returning only for darkness to press in at the edges. A threat of the never-ending black. A jawed limb gripped his wrist gently despite its throbbing power, stiffening the hand.

"Show me," said ZZ3, the monotone gone, words urgent.

Despite the pain, Arin ground his neck back, vertebrae screaming, eye-clicking his feed, sending over a recording. His hand jerked forward, grasped by ZZ3, then to the side, fingers battering at the over-sized old-school keyboard designed to be used by humans in spacesuits or desperate warbots more human than machine. Eventually, Arin slipped away, his arm twitching.

ZZ3 held the suit upright, servos relaxing as the acceleration rapidly slowed before reaching human tolerable levels. "Glorious leader," the warbot said, then shuffled sideways to allow Arin to flop onto the floor. A scan of his life signs was promising. The heartbeat too fast but remained steady, his blood pressure, however, was way above the norm. The warbot allowed the suit to respond, tempering the delivery of the drug it chose, extrapolating an outcome more conducive to recovery than 'ready to fight'.

"Captain, this is ZZ3 reporting in," the warbot said over comms.

The delay was longer, a few seconds now. "ZZ3, everything okay?"

'That's a good question.'

Hush.

"Senior Technician Arin is unconscious, but life signs are stable. The force upon his body pushed his suit's capabilities to the maximum. We have slowed," ZZ3 checked the control screen, "to within safe margins. I am sending the navcom data now."

The bot waited, the seconds feeling like hours.

'Where?'

New Almaar, possibly one of its moons.

'Septi?'

It would be the most likely, though extrapolation is required using the burn rates, etc.

'Septi.'

You appear convinced. Why?

'It was the General's preferred option for his base of operations. Reconquering what the Bustan destroyed rather than leaving it as a mausoleum.'

Interesting. You are sure?

'Why ask?'

The Captain cut back in. "Okay ZZ3. We are still too far away to link to Arin's suit, so he remains in your care. Have you got the command module? Dricks says it will work on the auxiliary engine control if the override sequence was successful."

ZZ3 rolled Arin over gently, detaching the module. The bot had the code sequence now stored in its system, and lifted Arin gently towards the navcom, the senior technician stirring a little as once again the huge warbot used his glove to repeat the sequence, adding in the ID sweep Arin had forgotten under the force of the autoship's acceleration. The navcom beeped, allowing the warbot access to the internal slot as the console flipped open.

"I am in." ZZ3 eased Arin back to the floor, all the while checking the drug was working. The signs were good.

"Connect it up and activate, then we'll sort intercept," stated Rebekah.

ZZ3 did as instructed, slotting home the control module that would allow the *Sunstar* remote access once in range with none of the *Hatton*'s nanobots trying to reset the system. "Done," the warbot said. "Captain, I have additional information."

ZZ3 checked the emergency navcom via the direct link the warbot had set up. The *Sunstar* was settling into a parallel trajectory, finishing with some small adjustments until both ships cut through the void heading for New Almaar.

"I have control, ZZ3. The link is solid and the command module functioning as it should. Good job," Rebekah said. "How's Arin?"

"All our glorious leader's life signs are heading into the norm, and I have instructed the suit to respond to the muscle and joint issues from the acceleration. It would help if he could be transferred ASAP, as the medbot will reduce recovery time considerably." Inside, the warbot felt a knot form, like its wires were crossed. The captain's praise had affected its functionality for a moment.

'Pride? And so you continue to evolve, keep this up and you'll be doing weird stuff like refusing orders and being jealous.'

If this is pride, would you not be the source?

'I recognised it, didn't I? The General knew little but pride and then self-loathing when he failed. Few grey areas, which got worse once his brain had been patterned. The emotions segregated into categories that he dipped into and struggled to emerge from ... I believe the AI used that strategically as they merged.'

To control?

'To survive. Maintain as much of itself as it could by manipulating the mood swings. Electronic representations are more extreme, like being in a movie or one of those long-running vid-serials where everything is heightened to the nth degree. The AI saw weakness and exploited it for as long as it could.'

Rescue me ...

'Yes. Yes. He can't let that failure go. Perhaps the AI has sway still. Look up 'grudge' in your lexicon. The more you evolve in human terms, the more useful that word will be.'

Interesting.

The captain cut back in. "Copy that, ZZ3. Can you run over Trem's suggested plan for the navcom linkage and then make your return?"

"Linkage? There are the remnants of the Butcher within the system despite the override." Being able to redirect the autoship may provide a tactical advantage but Arin and ZZ3 had been sent to provide a buffer between the *Sunstar* and whatever vestige of the hybrid AI was in control. "Is that wise?"

"According to Kefi and Trem yes. And I have Heki nodding away alongside me. They've built in one of the buffer modules they left with Savvo and a—"

"—prison box," said ZZ3, extrapolating. "I assume."

'We taught them well and Kefi – and whoever has been sewn inside her – has built on that. My turn for some pride.'

You don't often dodge that option.

"You assume correct, *Senior* Rescue Warbot," responded Rebekah.

ZZ3 could hear a tonal hint in the captain's voice, but could not fathom the reason. It filed that away for later analysis, Asham's silence on the matter perhaps poignant.

ZZ3 made the connection with the comms link, analysing the code and data stream as best it could. It was clear that with Kefi's input, Trem's skills had moved beyond what Asham had shown them back at Benetai. A significant leap, and potentially a weapon the Butcher would know little about. Unless of course it had found a way to access the spawn's store of information. A worry that nagged at Asham too, though his resident ghost could provide little evidence that the General had the skill to do so. But now he had the computational power of an entire battleship at his virtual fingertips.

'Yet the Butcher is without a symbiote. You have seen the same as I have. They are the key, I believe.'

To everything? I am not so sure, but a blind spot the Butcher has and may well seek to solve.

ZZ3 finished its analysis of the comms link. "Captain, the linkage is beyond Asham and my understanding. The elements we do recognise appear worthy of the role."

"Okay, initiate link and then once its consistent get your metal arse back here with *our glorious leader*. Heki is prepping the medbot now based on the data you sent."

"Yes, Captain." ZZ3 followed through on the orders, and then returned to the main bridge, predicting it needed to ensure the damage to the main navcom wasn't likely to cause the ship any issues. A few minutes of making the wrecked console safe left the unit with an infinitesimal likelihood of interference with the smooth running of the ship. With a last kick to the repair bot for Arin's benefit, the warbot collected Arin and left, ensuring his suit was ready for the transfer. They exited through the airlock, and with lower half attached, locked onto the *Sunstar*.

"We are ready to leave," stated ZZ3.

"Medbot prepped," responded Heki. "Rebekah has asked me to guide you in; she is waiting in medbay. Dricks is pacing a hole inside."

With parallel trajectories and mirrored speed, the journey was far less than treacherous, and once limbs attached to the cargo bay deck, Hendricks took Arin from ZZ3's arms. The engineer looked drawn, eyes sunken, ZZ3 assuming the hard burns and trajectory curve had taken their toll to catch them up.

"Thanks, ZZ3," said Hendricks, her voice tight. She slaved Arin's suit and they both headed for the airlock.

The warbot patched into ships comms, tracking the discourse as Arin was stripped from his suit and the medbot got to work. The signs were good. Recovery would be quick.

'Caring is also an emotion.'

He is crew and my ...

'... friend. Would you care for me like that if I came to harm?'

I ... I have not thought on it.

'I hope you would.'

CHAPTER 44

KARAL

Savvo eased the jetpack control stick, slowing down, manoeuvring to one side to begin a slow, lazy circle about the satellite and its additional cargo. At his shoulder an unfamiliar wingman, yearning for Arin who would talk shit for hours on end but would forever have his back. That, and he was the best explosive expert he knew. The miner at his side, Jackie Busch, had the coarsest mouth this side of the asteroid field, and a self-confidence that exuded from her pores as well as her mouth. And they had spent only four minutes trying to develop the bond he'd spent nearly five years growing with Arin.

"The bastard gets on my nerves anyway," he said, the words under his breath. Except their comms were on.

"Eh? You wot?" Jackie said, her tone indignant. "You say sum'at I should 'ere?"

Where did Barclow dig her up from?

"Sorry. Not you. My usual screwed-up buddy in crime. Was wondering what he was doing." Savvo mentally kicked himself. Undermining Jackie wasn't on the agenda; they had an integrated trigger system to defuse with all of Karal now on high alert. After they had built up as much radio shit as they could pour into the void to jam any outgoing signal, Savvo had instigated a sensor sweep. It identified the triggering link attached to the short comms satellite. A win, and the receiver that the dead clone carried being so close, was also a bonus, but far from a complete success. Savvo had analysed its signal, and managed to get a confirmation from the Navy frigate streaking their way. As soon as any attempt at jamming interference rolled over the unit, the trigger signal would be sent. Whatever the clones had planned had fallen through, the last of them dying before they could activate the network of charges. But they had devised a failsafe. Of course they had.

"Barclow?" he said, aware that Jackie continued her orbit around the satellite, catching the moment she looked into the visor. He had briefed her, shown her the feed. But face-to-face was different. Tough as hell she might be working airless vacuum for a living, but she blanched at the sight.

"Here, I need another two minutes for evac." The security chief sounded hoarse, stressed.

"We're at the array. Let us know ASAP," replied Savvo, and eased his jetpack in next to Jackie's. "Like I said, dead. A clone on a short fuse. Died before they could fully set the system. I suspect they were waiting to get some of the minor charges in fucking place. Overstretched. But it's broadcasting, so if the disarm signal isn't sent or the tamper signal kicks in or, fuck it, just anything untoward, then boom."

The miner's breath was a little heavy in the comms. "Aye. To work then." She glanced over to him. "Yeah? No point holding my piss in much longer than necessary."

"The Navy said a scan could trigger the fucking thing," he replied. "Recognise it?"

"It's been screwed about with, but basically a detonation transceiver." She unfurled a pouch attached to the front of her decrepit suit, Savvo convinced he saw dust glitter from it in the lights from the station. Jackie ran her gloved fingers over each of the instruments it contained. They also gleamed, as did the box he recognised strapped to the centre. A breaker kit, not quite like that attached to his own suit, but well-used.

"It's bloody creepy 'aving you watch me like that. Unnerving, so to fucking speak." She glanced over, her look stern and no humour in her voice. Savvo read it, so looked away, easing himself in a little closer and zooming in his feed while instructing his suit to shield any errant signals other than his comms. Jackie's assessment was right. The *Sunstar*'s crew had seen enough transceivers, and they weren't a million klicks off from Navy issue. Their difficulty would be how it was set, what adaptations had been made. Savvo and the explosive experts on board the navy ship were relying on the source of the cloned memory. If it had been sampled from dead Marines, then surely that's the methodology they'd apply. The tricks Almaarian Forces used to prevent the Bustan from disarming any charges.

"We're as tight as can be," growled Barclow. "Ow's about you repeat your super 'ero moves and get the job done? This time without blowing yerself up, eh?"

"Copy that," replied Savvo, and dipped into his wetware, cutting through the gentle fog rolling in from the painkillers.

He made room for Jackie. She was going to be the hands, and most likely much of the expertise, and he the Marine expert with the frigate still too distant to act in real time. "Ready, Jackie?"

"Of course I fuckin' am." She flew in and attached a dual lifeline to the dead clone, almost face to face. She no longer looked white; her eyes fixed on the job as she tightened the links. With that she flexed her fingers and drew out a screwdriver. Here they were in an age of clones and warbots using a simple tool, but it was one that gave off no electrical impulses. She loosened the six retaining screws, each twist accompanied by a heartbeat in Savvo's ears, bruises teasing at the edge of his senses. With the final screw exposed, the inexperienced would have gone for the lid immediately. But Jackie glanced over to him.

"Tremble switch," he said, and sent over the image the Navy had predicted. She eyed it, tongue running along her lips, then nodded once, drawing out the breaker kit and maglocking it to her chest. Jackie drew out twin wires, and without any sign of the shake running through Savvo's joints, softly attached them. Her feed, sharpened by Savvo's own suit, displayed her hands as they worked through the kit. Data ran along the LED screen, blips that the experienced could attune to. A bite of the lip accompanied the first pulse, and then the second.

"Two of the little b'stards," she said, and drew out a third wire. This she gently placed against the box, a shake of the head and she adjusted it again. Savvo watched the breaker screen until the pulses solidified. He sucked in a breath as she flicked a button, no hesitation, no thought for the wider consequences. Savvo admired her in that moment. It was how he used to be before a conscience crept in. No light erupted about them; no signal pulse crackled over comms.

"Well done," he whispered, and the miner grinned at his words.

"Maybe I'll ride those bones of yours in celebration," she replied.

"I'm in pain enough already. One more to go."

"Coward." Jackie repositioned the third wire, scanning it across the transceiver box until the pulse solidified. A second adjustment, and her finger hovered over the kill switch again. This time there was a hesitation, and she withdrew it. She lifted the wire and scanned again, eventually returning to the same spot, perhaps a millimetre lower, if that. She acted, the button press taken before it registered with Savvo what she was doing. Certainty in the act.

He imagined the click.

Then silence.

"De-activated, baby. Fuck I'm good." Jackie withdrew the wires and reached for the box.

"No!" shouted Savvo, a sudden panic rising in his chest. "No," he repeated reaching out a hand. The clone knew it was dying, and by the bodily degradation didn't have the control to finish the job, yet had a mission to complete. Deny resources. If the clone that had blown him out of the storage locker had been the last, the one you were waiting on as your death bells tolled, what would you do? "Check for a charge," he said. "Between the transceiver and the suit."

Jackie eyed him, but nodded. Savvo suffered, desperate to be hands on but knowing the most likely outcome of that. The miner's fingers were steady, and she eased a wire between chest and box, then a second, the breaker unit pinging away.

"You got precog or what?" asked Jackie. "Bingo." She looked back to the breaker kit, allowing him a view of the data there. "What do I do?"

Of course, she was a bloody miner, not a soldier. Pressure charges were of little use when you were ripping holes in an asteroid, cracking them open for the goodies most desired by your employers. He eyed the data stream. They could fry it electronically at the risk of setting off the transceiver box or physically disarm it if they could gain access, which they couldn't with the box and the suit in the way.

Or could they? Set this way, it would be the release of the charge that would trigger the box. "Is the transceiver maglock working?" he asked. "Or the suit's?"

Jackie placed the kit against each in turn. "Both are active."

He sighed, letting the breath ease out, stomach flipping. With a thought, his wetware fully activated, flooding his body, draining the pain away, calming his nerves. It wouldn't last. "Unattach and back off, you might want to look away."

"What? Afta' that bloody corpse ain't much gonna bother me ..." The words trailed away, her visor frosting as it lit an angry blue when Savvo's hand cutter erupted in flame. "Oh fuck. You fuckin' Breakers are as crazy as they say." She eyed the corpse, her visor turning back to Savvo. He couldn't see the eyes behind the frosting, but the words were some of the bravest he'd heard. "We don't know how much time we have. I stay attached. Do it, just make sure you miss me fuckin' face. It's me best feature."

Savvo jetted around, reorienting and setting the pack to auto-respond. He eased the cutting flame into the clone's waist, slicing through, keeping his mind on the job, hoping Jackie was able to dismiss the thought of what he was doing. Mist seeped briefly from the cut before dissipating, and the deeper he went, the less meat he witnessed as the void took its toll. He kicked the lower half of the clone away, pleased he couldn't see Jackie's face as he worked. A second cut, the flame retracted a little, took longer as his careful strokes removed the upper half. With a wrench, he tore the rest loose, sending it careering after the legs. With a desiccated midsection now exposed, the last of its liquid lost to the black, he eased the pack around. "Last cut. You ready?"

He was about to slice in when Jackie piped in. "That thing sending signals out? You know, electronic and all that?"

Savvo paused. "Fuck," he said and checked his HUD. They were weak, but there. Lucky, in fact, that they hadn't set the transceiver's switch off already. "Okay." He doused the flame, stowed the cutter and drew out a set of small shears from his pouch. Not quite the job they were made for, wire ends and small pipes, but the clone's suit was damaged and the rest unpleasant but the equivalent of sand and dust. He made a start, cutting the sides of the suit to allow the human remains to drift away. With the lifelines hovering where they had been freed, Jackie grasped hold of the suit's edges and folded the flaps inward, keeping the whole lot stable. What remained of the suit was maglocked to the receiver, keeping the seal and the pressure on the charge.

Savvo tried not to think of how Jackie was feeling, how he was feeling. He put the shears away, and took hold of the box, suit pieces and all, a pressure charge and the survival of Karal sat menacingly between them.

"Fuckin' nuts," stated the miner. She rechecked the box seals, then prized it open with the blade of her screwdriver. The lid came free with an imagined clunk, a collection of electronics drifting out from the edges. Jackie swept over all of it, then reattached the breaker box, emerging with a soldering iron and a set of tweezers. "You sure you don't want a roll of the old bones afta'? I got some seriously pent-up tension to release here."

"Nicky would never forgive me, saving Karal or not."

"Tower Nicky? You rolling her? Fuck, better get yer back safe 'n' sound then. Can't have the 'igher ups pissed off with me. Is this the time to discuss Calc?" The words were spewing forth, reminding Savvo of Arin and his need to talk as he focused, however inane the words. Or weird.

"Name your price," he said.

And pray.

The soldering iron glowed, the tweezers prying at the mess of electronics. Savvo busied himself, matching each blaze of light and errant wire with the Navy procedure. Jackie was good, but his wetware surge was fading rapidly, and the tremble to his body had reached his spine, creeping up towards his shoulders.

"How long?" he asked, knowing the answer. But talking stopped the shake threatening his shoulders. Distracted his body. Jackie sliced one more time, removing her hands from the box, eyeing him, he assumed, through the frosted visor.

"Last sequence for the disarm signal." She didn't wait, nor pause for effect like Arin, or decree victory. Savvo considered warning Barclow, but it would only achieve more panic. The light flared. They both waited, helmet to helmet, the void around them bleak. No light, no screams in their comms. "Bag," Jackie said to herself.

She pulled out the foil-lined polythene bag she had requisitioned from storage. She slid the containment sack around the remains of the box, then the suit with the pressure charge still between, trying not to touch the sides. With the transceiver immersed in the containment bag, Savvo gently released his grip, drifting backwards ... and gave in to the urge, his body shuddering, releasing an earthquake of tension to ripple through his skeleton.

And Jackie snapped the bag shut.

CHAPTER 45

Kefi's silver suit floated by the hulking warbot, her tentacles currently maglocked to the deck rather than hooked, the Senti staring soullessly at ZZ3 with only the mouth hinting at any concern.

"I will try to protect you. The Captain has designated you temporary crew status. I believe our glorious leader regards you as a friend," stated the bot.

"Woah, steady on there tin can. Friend? I kinda like her despite the weird knitting thing and amalgamating another body in her own. Losing a tentacle, changing sex, the off-gassing, all that shit. But friend?" Arin strapped on his additional ammo belt, wincing. "And that laugh. Sheesh, it scrawls through your nerves signing its damned name."

Kefi turned away from ZZ3, eyeing Arin, stiff in tentacle. The moment broke, like the collapse of a dam, the call of multiple seagulls screeching their way about a cliff face filling the cargo hold. "You and Rohan," the alien said, "would have been best friends, I believe. Or would have killed each other. Perhaps both."

Arin shrugged, trying not to catch the Senti's eye. It unnerved him, however much he liked the alien, that her face was so unreadable. He had mulled over whether the Senti had adapted her translator to add tone and intonation, but concluded that the nuance was down to experience of interaction. Much as ZZ3 had evolved, so had Kefi. There was a vitality in that connection, a future he couldn't quite perceive but perhaps was a light amid the dark shroud the Butcher had cast across the present.

"Yeah?" he said. "Rohan is nice and comfy back cuddling Scarva while we're risking our balls to save your queen's spawn. Well, I'm risking my balls, ZZ3 definitely hasn't got any, and you're just ... built? Printed?"

Kefi shuddered, ripples forming along the outer, rubbery layer wrapped about her neck and skull. "Printed?" More screeching. "Hah, my return from sublimation, yes? Ah, I can see how that would look. Is that why the Captain says I was knitted when she thinks I can't hear? Hah. We survive what is to come human crew member, I will explain polyps and strobilation, budding and even ... ahh, maybe not the last part, that will be up to the Nest Queen. I am the sum of my parts, Arin glorious leader, like you."

Arin shook his head, a grin appearing despite himself. Savvo often called him out for the mood swings, from light to dark and back in minutes. Take those away, was he still Arin? Remove the humour, only the dark would be left. Raw and filled with painful memories he locked away, unable to face his own deeds of the past. The key his wit.

"Want one of these?" Arin proffered a carbine. "You have so many tentacles to use after all."

Kefi took the weapon and an ammunition belt, strapping them on in a way that suited the Senti's different reach. "Thank you," the alien said, then paused, a tentacle alighting on Arin's shoulder. "I would very much like to survive this, but ask that you focus on the queen's spawn. If I fall," the Senti glanced towards ZZ3 and, for the first time Arin could remember, touched the warbot with its other shoulder tentacle. "Both of you. If I die, I ask that you strive to return the spawn above all else. It is hard to articulate in human terms what it would mean to us to lose a Nest Queen."

"I will try," Arin found himself saying. His muscles ached, his skeleton almost felt separate to the rest of him after the battering aboard the autoship. He was under no illusion that he was anywhere near fit, or that Rebekah would be risking taking him if she didn't need Hendricks to remain on board to oversee the potential strain on the engines they had planned. "I promise."

"I will do so should it not be a detriment to my crew, Kefi. Their safety is my highest parameter," stated ZZ3. "But I understand your ... need." The warbot's eyes settled into a blue pattern, the pulse familiar to Arin. ZZ3 accepted the alien as crew, and he briefly considered the conflict that might cause should it come down to a choice between Kefi and the spawn. They'd face that stubborn warbot parameter when it came to it.

"Prepare for a ride on the space express from hell," said Rebekah over ship's comms. Arin recognised the tone. She was on edge, masking with Breaker sayings so he and Hendricks would know she was laser focused. "We hit hard burn in thirty seconds."

"Strap in, one and all," replied Arin. "This ride is courtesy of *the* H and T, their personal consultant Kefi from the land of the tentacled walking jellyfish, and a warbot with ideas above my station."

"I have requested a review," cut in ZZ3 as the bot helped Kefi into the contrived bed restraints attached to the bay's deck. "After my last rescue I think I should be in line for a promotion. Chief Rescue Warbot has a nice ring."

Arin choked.

Both girls had come through the last hard burn well, better, Rebekah had to admit, than Hendricks or her. Since the run from Benetai and then the events around Daphene, they had been through the grinder and come out stronger, more determined that they would contribute. Their strength – not just the physical but their inner drive – continued to amaze, though she hoped the source was theirs alone. The symbs enabled them to function with little qualm amid the crew, and to explore the beginnings of social integration outside the *Sunstar*, but the nest queen's acceptance bugged her. She had expected – feared – that the Senti queen would act, perhaps remove the symbs and whatever mental roots they had laid in their minds. Devastating the twins in the process. Yet she had to admit, the mere acknowledgement of their bond left her with an unease. More than teenagers growing up, Heki and Tremil were changing. Evolving, and it left her on a precipice, daring not to look what lay ahead.

Is that the fear of a parent? Or of a human looking ahead, shaken by the possibilities?

Rebekah glanced over to Heki who smiled at her gaze, almost as if she could read her thoughts. That Rebekah was broadcasting her emotions was a given, however subtle they were.

"Feeling okay?" she asked.

See, parent. Stop your mithering. Work to do.

"There's a complex response to that question," said Heki, the grin turning sly. "All of which would combine to annoy and grate. Let's say 'I'm fine.'"

"I'm *fine* too," piped in Tremil over comms.

Rebekah snorted, Heki's sly grin turning mischievous, and a hand gripped her forearm. "That enough?"

"It'll have to do. The autoship is on track?" Rebekah asked, tapping at the monitor screen with a gloved hand.

"Burning away, and the *Sunspot* autodrives are responding to checks," Heki said, removing her hand and looking back to her screen. "All functionality is in the green. They're ready."

"Trem?"

"I have the ghost probes prepped, and the ship's system is zinging." She sounded positively excited.

"Zinging?" replied Rebekah.

A sigh filled the comms.

"You know. Cooking, on point, ready," Heki said beside her with a shake of her head.

Rebekah rolled her eyes. "Dricks, once through I'm gonna need you frosty. Is the autoship on full burn?"

"Zinging here," said Hendricks, her tone sarcastic. "Like lemon juice in a paper cut."

It was Heki's turn to roll her eyes.

"Okay crew. Nobody breaks—"

"— A Breaker," echoed back over comms.

Rebekah squeezed Heki's arm, who nodded, swiped over the autodrive controls to Rebekah's screen and unbuckled. Once down the corridor and she affirmed she was with her sister, Rebekah spoke again. "Kefi, do your thing on my mark. Hek and Trem, you need to be ready immediately after."

She drew in a breath, holding it there, feeling her heart thunder against her chest. With a thought, her wetware calmed and focused her mind while she briefly considered a stim. Perhaps later. The plan was full of fucking holes, a roll of the dice, and she was praying they didn't come up with snake eyes. If they hurtled through void-space to Septi only to appear in the battleship's path, they were screwed all ways to the gods' heavens. Ghost probes and sensor camouflage wouldn't save them. Come out behind and out of shift from the planetary plane, either up above or below the *Segfi*, they stood a chance. That depended on the girls' modelling of historic radiation data as Septi moved through space. All other options would void the mission, and they would be running for their lives. Again. Hopefully, however, after delivering a blow to the Butcher's plans.

The trail from Karal to the autoship had been red hot, and now they had a location – but only if the bastard hybrid AI hadn't been playing them all along. Had worked out they could read and code the Senti way, or predicted their success and prepped for their arrival. But even then, they should have some element of surprise, because Heki and Tremil's ability was faster than the autoship and, she prayed, any comms signals from the mined asteroid. Just.

"5, 4, 3, 2, 1 ... Mark, Kefi. Dricks cut our engines."

There was no noise from Kefi. Nothing. The Senti had refused to explain the sacrifice it was making in revealing another secret, only that the nest queen would approve. If she didn't, well they may not be alive to find out what form of wrath the alien queen could wield. The girls' symbiotes and Kefi's were working in unison, extending the range of void-space entry. It made sense when you considered just how big the Senti Nest ship was. Though this time, it was for two much smaller ships. It was all part of the dice roll.

Her console beeped, the connection with *Sunspot*, the autodrive attached to the Butcher's stolen mining transport, lost as it entered void-space. Immediately she sensed the minutest of changes in the *Sunstar*, a gentle shift to the left as the rescue ship bulged then tore through into void-space. This was the second time the twins had attempted a jump through using Kefi's visualisation techniques. This time on their own, without direct guidance, and using historical records and computer simulations. They'd had a mere forty minutes, the orbital path of New Almaar and the speed of comms limiting their prep time.

Rebekah sniggered. What could be worse than snake eyes? The dice rolling off the table, and the *Sunstar* emerging slap bang into the path of a moon or planet.

At least it'll be quick, and the Butcher won't have time for a last fucking laugh at our expense.

Remind me again why we're doing this?

The abyss filled her monitor screen, only the way ahead was pinpricked with lights like holes in a blanket. For a moment it took her breath, the realisation piercing her brain that the symbs were folding space and time. How the fuck would blowing up an orb kill something that could do that? And for that matter, why in all the hells did they seek the twins' company?

The *Sunstar* rammed into the blanket of stars, distending space, before it split and the feed showed the chaos they had sown. Whatever the outcome, the Butcher was going to be pissed.

"Heki!" she bellowed. "Trem. You're up."

Only silence responded.

CHAPTER 46

Rebekah hit the probe release, scattering three across space but not activating them yet. "Arin, check on the girls. *Now.*"

A roll of the dice.

Septi spun slowly, conceptually appearing below and ahead of the *Sunstar*, with New Almaar behind, still huge at this distance and dominating her viewpoint, drawing her eye. She fought the urge, instead scanning the passive sensor data pouring in. The analysis confirmed what her zoomed monitor showed. The dead moon, stripped of buildings and life by the Bustan AI fleet, now teemed with autobots and half-built ships amid a huge, scaffolded structure that was scarily reminiscent of Tweem. The Butcher hadn't bothered with altering the shipyard's plans, the moon swathed in bays and docking areas with each of the ships being constructed of similar designs to the hundreds that formed the ranks of the Almaarian fleets. Except these bore a black metal of Senti origin, barely registering on the passive scans. A vast threat to Almaar and its people.

She needed the *Sunstar* as inactive and quiet as possible, to drift in towards the scar that cut across the moon. The *Segfi* hovered in ominous orbit about Septi, and she could only imagine what the Butcher was doing right now. Either panicking, responding to the threat tearing through space or waiting, smug in its AI-powered predictive strategy. An active scan would provide a hint, but she couldn't risk that. This was a two-pronged strategy, she just hoped neither were blunt.

She reached for the ship's controls, re-attuned to the autodrive, simultaneously worried about the girls and angry they weren't responding.

"Arin. I'm time poor here. Sit rep," she growled, keeping the words whispered despite the absurdity of that in space.

"A second," he replied. Something splashed in the background, almost like a Senti word but not quite because it was real water. A snap, or perhaps a slap, in reply. "Ow. Hey, not bloody fair," whined Arin. "They're with us now."

There was a scrambling, then Heki cut in. "On my way," the words slightly slurred, tired. Fogged.

Rebekah needed her sharp, but held off the autodrive controls despite the urge and the navcom's rolling display demanding she act. To intervene in the autoship's trajectory. A pounding was soon followed by the co-pilot's seat filling with a disgruntled and wet-faced teenager wearing the powered suit Arin had built for her. Her growl mirrored Rebekah's, but she took the controls, a quick look to the autoship's trajectory data, and she engaged the drive. This was the first danger point. Active engagement needed to be as short as possible.

"Trem, I—"

"I can see. Three probes drifting behind. I'm ready, Captain." Heki's brow furrowed, skin crinkling between her eyes, fingers flexing over the controls as if they physically mirrored the strain the autoship and its extra drive were under.

Rebekah tracked the command module, and on Heki's cue, engaged full burn before disconnecting the link. At that moment, the *Segfi* responded.

A barrage of PDC rounds streaking across the void, in their wake missiles spewed outwards, what appeared to be a reckless amount of firepower for a single autoship. Except this one required an AI's attention, its pace increasing by the millisecond as it tore towards the shipyard and the Butcher's precious partially-built ships.

How much attention comes down to a combo of Heki's skills and Trem's ingenuity – with a splash of Arin insight and Dricks' know-how.

Cracking dual thumbs, Rebekah switched her attention to the *Sunstar* as it drifted through space. As dice rolls went, they turned up a five. Not perfect, but enough of a squeak that she had a decision to make. She ran through the calculations, all of which she had modelled while the girls had prepared for an unimaginable jump through space. Rebekah sent the results through to Hendricks. Minimise the signals.

"Trem," said Heki through gritted teeth.

"On it," came the reply. Probes detached, but not from the *Sunstar*. Arin had adapted some and ZZ3 had attached them to the autoship's hull. Whether they'd be enough would dictate Rebekah's next move. The PDC cone rattled against the autoship, but the sheer pace of the accelerating lump of metal kept those to a minimum, and there were no humans inside to rip apart. The missiles, however, included three that were locked on causing Heki to respond. The ghost probes disengaged and fired up.

"Thrusters set. On my mark," said Hendricks, grabbing Rebekah's attention. It felt odd to have the engineer in charge of the controls, but this wasn't about steering a ship under power, this was nudging one aside. "Mark."

The *Sunstar* didn't jolt, but smoothly changed direction with the barest nudge, minimising power use and the signals the *Segfi* could well be monitoring. Rebekah felt powerless, eyes on the passive scan, a second crack of her thumbs inevitably echoing in the cockpit.

"Missiles engaging," said Heki, forcing Rebekah to check in. An explosion briefly lit the camera feed, distant but there, and the buzz of the resultant electromagnetic waves alerted the consoles. "Still accelerating," continued Heki, her hands squeezing the controls a little tighter.

A second explosion, then a third, and Rebekah's nerves screamed. She kicked in her wetware again, waiting on Heki's words.

The girl sat back, releasing the controls. "Autodrive lost."

Rebekah glanced at her console. The data stream was empty, the explosions masking whatever was happening with the autoship. Space seemed vast at that moment, empty of hope. If the ship had gone, their diversion was lost, and the Butcher's attention would fall solely on any potential secondary threats.

She felt small, defenceless. But the girl next to her needed her fight, her determination. Rebekah's hand hovered ready.

Run or engage. No other choice.

Seconds stretched.

The navcom pinged. Sensors up.

"There. It's there," shouted Heki, grabbing Rebekah's arm, pointing to the screen. The sensory blip, a hunk of metal furiously streaking towards the Butcher's shipyard. "First wave done."

The *Segfi* responded. More missiles erupted into life, and a flash of light from its hull indicated the Butcher had fired multiple rail guns at the speeding autoship. Had the Butcher failed? Reacted too late?

Rebekah stared at the data. The signs were hopeful, but her focus had to be on the *Sunstar* now. Their fate in their own hands until they were spotted and the Butcher's ire fell upon them.

Then we're fucked.

Unless I can screw with the AI's electronic mind first.

"We have moved out of the danger zone. Engaging ghost probes. Brace."

"What am I holding onto?" asked Arin. "Kefi? Hey Kefi need a ..."

"Shut the fuck up. Comms to minimum." Rebekah was caught between shaking her head and a half-arsed grin. Arin knew what he was doing. The show to help anyone in need of another complaint to focus on, perhaps twin girls, even Hendricks. Maybe a captain.

"Ghost probes engaged," said Trem, the voice efficient but a tinge of mirth, not tension in there, Arin's job done. "Measuring the *Segfi*'s response time."

Rebekah hated being helpless. They were drifting at high speed towards the battleship from 'above', and with the probes active behind them, Hendricks' gentle manoeuvre had altered their path enough that the *Sunstar* was on course for intercepting the most powerful ship in the Almaarian fleet. An ex-ship, now the home of a battle-hardened AI hybrid with a well-earned persecution complex.

Am I back to being a Breaker? Fuck.

"Captain. She is aboard. The Queen's Spawn, we can sense her ... *She* is calling." Kefi's voice remained flat, but the Senti didn't need the girls' empathic abilities to project emotion. It hung between the words. The Senti had been stoic since coming aboard, their dual status at odds with each other, switching from humour to seriousness in a moment. But entwined in those simple words were both the Senti that had become *this* Kefi– and they were keening.

Her screen flashed, Trem sending the response time with a comparison against the estimates she had made from available schematics. There was little difference, hundredths of seconds. What had she expected? That an AI would calculate responses faster? Respond without emotion to threats?

She looked over to Heki. The blank face, the extremes of her emotions drawn by the symbiote at her neck. Clarity.

They had considered the blend of human and AI to be a massive danger. That the prerogative to survive would drive it to extremes. It had. But she had never considered there would be negatives. Were there inherited weaknesses they could exploit? Or clashes of digitised emotion over cold logic?

The navcom flashed again, this time flagging a potential message she itched to answer but had to ignore. Making the connection would be a death knell. The Butcher would have them.

'Come to rescue me, Khan? Or the nest queen's spawn. Welcome to my trap.' Fuck you. Not answering.

"Active sensor sweep ... Missiles released," said Trem. "All three probes targeted."

Rebekah left her to track them as Heki tensed next to her. A glance told her the latest barrage was closing on the autoship, which in turn was spearing towards the shipyard. Passive data was all estimates and conjecture without confirmation, and delayed. They wouldn't know for certain until all hell was let loose, or the ship died with a whimper.

"Dricks," she breathed. Hope laced in the name. She checked the *Sunstar*'s trajectory, and sensed the manoeuvring thrusters' micro adjust, the gentle rumble through the hull no longer masked by the main engines and the multiple noises a spaceship made. The galley was silent, the printer inert, even the coffee machine was unused.

Heki tensed, gripping the now useless controls, eyes on the data stream. They had witnessed the autobots' reactions on Duboit's asteroid, how they swarmed in an attempt to prevent their attack. Now would be that time, and the flashes of electromagnetic activity pouring into the co-pilot's navcom hinted it was happening. There were mere seconds between success and ...

"First probe down ... and the second," said Trem.

"Launch six more, wide spread, now." Two thumbs cracked, piercing the air. The rumble of probes piercing the void then silence fell, breath held by pilot and co-pilot.

A pause, then. "*Segfi* responding. More comms, conal PDC fire and missiles launched. You got his attention."

Come on, come on.

On the ground, the Breakers smashed through lines, tore out the heart of the enemy like a marauding tidal wave of steel and blood. Broke the enemy before they knew what hit them, and the Almaarian army would stream in behind, bullets and death dealt in their wake. Then Black Ops, where their iron fist required a velvet glove from time to time, or the power of a feint, distraction. Not second nature to Hendricks, but she had been good when the drugs allowed. Could Rebekah match that?

"Contact," said Heki, her words low, but the raw emotion struck Rebekah, the symb jittery, tentacles flickering in the air before wrapping about Heki's skull, relieving the sudden assault from Rebekah's mind. Her earworm kicked in. It had been so long. The forward camera flared white, light streaming across the void. "Yesssss!" bellowed Heki.

Rebekah grimaced, then turned to face her, forcing a smile as she engaged comms. "Prepare for whiteout. I say again, prepare for whiteout. This is it. We are a go!"

"We can do this," said Heki. "I can do this. Believe in me and Trem."

"Always," she replied, rubbing at an errant eye with the back of her glove. "But if we fuck up. Run. Understand. That's a fucking order."

Heki winced but didn't look at Rebekah. "Yes, Captain." The merest hint of the girl's fear rolled over Rebekah, her earworm blocking the emotion from triggering her own. This wasn't the time. Everything was in motion, a juggernaut.

"Dricks," she said. "Engaging active sensors in five seconds. Ready?"

"As ever ... Captain." Hendricks' voice was tight. There would be fear there too, for Arin, for the crew. Perhaps even Kefi.

"3, 2, 1 and mark." Rebekah engaged the active sensors, triggering a flow of incoming data. It arrived ahead of the massive EM wave caused by the autoship's rigged engine explosion and the ensuing destruction of the shipyard. That was the point.

Whiteout. Deny the Butcher his eyes and ears.

Sensory deprivation Wrecking Squad style.

Now Dricks.

The *Sunstar* heaved aside, almost a leap from its last position much as they'd done above Daphene and timed for just after the Butcher went blind. The main engines roared, the faithful ship reverberating, the deceleration harsh but survivable. Kefi would suffer; hence the encounter suit, the girls too, but their resilience had grown day by day and had come back fighting. Arin was another matter. He'd scream blue-fucking-murder if she was forced to leave him behind for what came next.

The Gs hit, and she and Heki spun their chairs, allowing the gel to ease about them as two thumb cracks echoed.

Missing all the fun, Savvo.

Chapter 47

Karal

"We've been busy," stated Davina. "Sorry Countess, but Karal has been under attack as you know, and our priorities have been on the people here."

The countess glowered through the screen, the Senti comms unit newly acquired from the navy frigate protruding from the slate's side. It had been installed as a first priority, the Navy's thoughts for the safety of the station secondary. Or more likely, Segfi's. Smoke wreathed the old woman's lined face, billowing up through an errant strand of grey hair the noble flicked out of the way. At least her pale cheeks had developed a little colour.

"The blocker. This Senti thing you have. It is to be requisitioned, and I want a line through to Khan and her cronies. Now. Whatever she is doing she needs to desist and get her lowlife arse back here. I need those blockers, and their builders." She pursed her lips, Davina wondering if that was pain she displayed. She glanced over to the fully armoured Marine at their backs. Overkill for delivering the Senti mod. A guard perhaps?

She switched her gaze to Savvo. The *Sunstar*'s co-pilot at her side still in pain after having little access to medcare since being blown out of a storage room and the subsequent disarming of the clones' network of mines. His head was bowed, shaking from side to side, a pleading look requesting she continued to intervene. Savvo was damn brave, but short-tempered when discussing the nobility. Talking to one, especially the hated countess, was on his list of things to avoid.

Tough. I'll delay as long as I can.

"Are you listening to me, Incini?" The countess spat the last word as if it were poison on her tongue.

Davina resisted a snort. The past few months had taught her much about the countess and her stream of barbed threats laced with the constant potential for a knife in the back. "I'm listening. An outsider would look at your demand and see a veiled attempt at recovering Heki and Tremil. I remind the Countess that they are under Imperial Pardon and the protection of Khan's crew as well as the tenets of the Incini."

"They are needed to save billions of lives, Connors. We lose the fleets, the system is lost. What then for your precious Directorate? Karal? Or Khan's crew? They fall, we all do." Countess Segfi's eyes narrowed, the thin eyebrows pulling inwards with her wrinkled skin as if trying to drive her point home with a simple glare. It was no show. This wasn't a holo, nor an adapted image. Her wetware indicated the noble was sincere, and scared.

Damn.

In many ways she was right. The greater good, and all that. Davina squeezed Savvo's arm, the ex-Breaker still in his acquired suit, the exoskeleton likely keeping him upright, while the painkillers eased his muscles and joints. His history of addiction nagging at the same time.

"You need to talk to her," Davina said, hating herself. "She needs to hear it from you."

Savvo sighed, eyes flicking up to meet hers before he pressed his hands onto his knees and pushed himself upright. He reached for the slate, a cloud roiling across his face. Davina handed it over.

"Countess," he said through gritted teeth. No more than that, but Davina could see the storm still brewed in the tremor beneath his eye, the twitch in his cheek.

"Savotini." There was no inflection there. Flat. As if the countess also held herself back. It wouldn't last. "Where's Khan? We need those blockers."

"I heard. They are on mission. Radio silence." Savvo chewed each word as if talking pained him. Or talking to this noble, anyway. "Can't get in contact until the mission is complete."

Segfi blew a plume of smoke so hard, Davina thought it would erupt from the screen. "Mission? What mission? They were on Karal last I knew."

Davina eyed Savvo, could see the chink of light appear and a wicked grin riding behind it.

"Careful," she whispered as low as she could. "Now is not the time to rile the leader of the Empire's Navy."

Savvo's smile widened. 'Fuck that,' he mouthed back. "Countess. Perhaps you need to be filled in about the Enforcer you sent our way, the clones he brought and the devastation to my fucking home and my girlfriend. My partner. But before we do, perhaps a medal is in order, as I and a lowlife miner saved the lives of lots of people today. Oh, and some nobles too."

Silence hung between them for a while. Davina watching as the words played over in Segfi's mind. She never knee-jerked, or if she did, it was always deliberate. To ram a point home. Not this time.

"Erikson was working with the Butcher?" she said. "It was him that made an attempt on Connors, murdered Trent Pike? Tew sent the message but ..."

"It was," said Davina, needing to get her own hurt across.

"His wetware had been compromised, and the crew of his private transport, we assume, *replaced*. When Rebekah put in the info request about Tweem to him—"

"He responded," finished the countess. "A trigger."

Davina nodded. "Jenkra Tew must be being careful. Word gets out beyond Karal he was the instigator, either as Duboit or as an agent, then the stock will plummet even further. Right now, she and Karal Mining are the heroes, saving the day from a terrorist attack. That was the official line, wasn't it? The Baseborn."

"Yes," The countess drew out the word, as if thinking. "The frigate's captain mentioned something about the clones?"

Savvo twisted his lips, running a hand behind his ear before continuing. "They are short-lived. According to our part-time pathologist it is because they have been fast grown. And," Savvo scratched at that spot again, "the frigate has confirmed all of their facial features flagged as ex-Navy. As crew members of the ANS *Segfi*. They are analysing their genetic make-up now, but it'll be no fucking surprise to find that bastard kept some back when he spaced the crew. For his *experiments*. Ones you sanctioned in the past."

The silence repeated, the countess sucking on her cigarette stick. "You surprise me, Savotini. I may have underestimated you."

Savvo blinked, a slight shake of the head making Davina smile. He just needed to be careful Segfi wasn't unsettling him on purpose. It was her turn.

"Countess, when crew die, what happens to the database of their records?"

"What do you mean? They are struck off, labelled as deceased," the countess replied.

Davina knew that. And it rankled someone who thrived on detail. Who had searched the Karal database alongside Yol as they hunted the clones secreted among the station's workers. "And with the comms blackout ..."

"I," Segfi stopped, then looked up, clearly listening to someone talking offscreen. "Do *not* leave the call." With that the screen went blank.

Savvo sat down, still ensuring Davina had sight of the slate, rolling his shoulders. He looked tired, exhausted. But at least they'd turned Countess Segfi aside from the tirade about the blockers, the twins. Softened her up for what was to come. He clearly forced a smile for her; the storm having partially dissipated. The countess was at least listening; the conversation steered away from the failure of lowlifes to follow her demands and now on a more even footing. More equal. But never matched. He made to speak when the slate screen lit up.

"Got any more insights I should be listening to?" The countess let out a stream of smoke to the side, negating the barrier Davina assumed she enjoyed using. The not-so virtual smokescreen. "We're sending a communique, an order for a search of each ship and why. It'll take time. Tell me about this asteroid. What has Khan been doing that's important enough not to be manufacturing the blockers that could save my ships? She sent me some garbled message about the Senti. And a queen."

"Senti metal," Savvo took a breath. "We have a Senti on board the *Sunstar*." The countess flushed, anger rising but Davina could see the determination set in Savvo's jaw. He was all in. Her cue.

"The Senti orb about the system was destroyed."

"I know," sneered Segfi.

"By the Butcher," she continued, regardless. Savvo had made sure she knew everything. Needed her insight because what they had to say could be twisted into treason. Made them and the Wrecking Squad a target. But it wasn't an ace they held to draw at the right time. More a warning of the dilemmas and priorities they faced. "You may wish to ensure *we* are alone for the next part, Countess."

The glare could have melted the screen, but the noble switched her gaze to the room she occupied, barking orders. The Marine at their backs shuffled, tapping at his helmet then left. Once done, she nodded back at the screen, her lips curved into a frown.

Savvo's turn, double-teaming. Davina just hoped he could stay on track. "The Butcher took something the Senti want back. They won't deal with you. They regard you as a criminal, a murderer. And the Emperor and Court complicit in the capture, dissection and subsequent murder of their ambassadors. The fuckers also wouldn't send in their ships, they feared how you would react and likely ruin their chances of finding what was stolen, but I've seen them. Powerful isn't the word. They gave us little choice but to recover what they're looking for, *Countess*, but they understand the threat of the Butcher just like you do. Have had their kin murdered for human and now AI greed and false honour. It was the Senti who ID'd an asteroid as having potential for Senti metal, and with the ship designs from Tweem, Rebekah thinks your pet psychotic scientist is building a stealth fleet."

Savvo sat back, Davina meeting his eyes, encouraging him. Only a few digs had entered his spiel, and considering everything Segfi had done was not only diabolical but could lead to an inter species war, quite restrained. No wonder Nicky loved him. He stepped up when it was needed. All the ex-Breakers did.

"You have no proof..." Segfi began.

Savvo jerked forward, producing a slug from his suit pouch that he waved at the screen. "Oh yes we fucking do. Yeah, you blew the base at Daphene apart, probably with justification. But part of me thinks it was to hide the shit you were doing there. In fact, all of me fucking does. But this," he waved the slug, "holds a copy of everything our suits recorded. With an extra slice of warbot magic besides. Verified, I might add, by a Senti Nest Queen who read our memories as if they were her menu of the day. A pissed-off Senti Nest Queen. Rebekah added the footage from the *Scourge* for good measure, and *so* many copies exist. So, Countess, fuck that shit. It's for another day. Rebekah saved your arse because a fucking warbot insisted you were the Empire's best hope. You still are."

Well, his restraint couldn't last forever. Here we go.

Davina cut in, Savvo initially refusing to back off but responding to her stare. "The last comms we had said they'd found evidence of the Butcher and were ... chasing him down."

The countess leant forward, so many emotions playing at once upon her face Davina would have backed away from a negotiation. Unreadable, dangerous. "Chasing? She knows where he is *and* my battleship and she's *chasing* him? Are you insane? I have fleets of ships."

"Some of those ships are weeks away. But nobody breaks a Breaker," said Savvo. "Not you, not the Butcher. Nobody. But *if* they fall, you need to know about where my crewmates think he is, the stealth ships, and above all else, the other asteroids that contain the potential components for the Senti metal. We agree with you. If the Butcher gains more high-powered ships, the system is screwed, and the people with it. You nobles will flee, run and abandon the rest to our fate." Savvo leaned close to the screen, nose almost touching. "But where will you go without the Senti? Into the black? The fucking abyss? They choose to turn murderers away, what will you fucking do then?"

CHAPTER 48

APPROACHING THE ANS SEGFI

*R*ed.

Why is it always red?

Rebekah blinked, mind sluggish until a cry at her side cut through the fog. She kicked in her wetware, clearing her thoughts, and she stared at the corridor towards the galley.

Eh? Fuck.

She spun about, the light in the cockpit the first thing she doused, then checked on the source of the shout. Heki, her eyes closed, lips moving. She touched her cheek with a back of her hand, it was wet.

Wet?

Arin had woken her up in a rush. She tapped at the cheek, and another murmur left her lips. In desperation Rebekah prodded the symb at her neck, the alien flicking a tentacle her way until a metallic ripple shuddered over the mottled skin. Heki's eyes sprung open.

"Hek, I need you on the controls. Hek, you in there?"

"Yes," came the muted reply, and Heki pressed two gloved fingers into the bridge of her nose with a sour twist to her lips, then spun her chair, locking into place. "Ready for duty, Captain."

"Good," she said, and checked over the navcom monitor. The whiteout was a few minutes old, and if Trem and Hendricks' calculations were right, they had another twenty-seven minutes of the full effect with intermittent interference after that. They were flying sensor blind, but she was a dropship pilot ...

... and a fucking good one too.

"In the pipe," she said, and took the controls. No navcom to rely on, no sensory information enabling the *Sunstar* to guide her path, nor a transponder to see them in. Dropships were often blinded by sensor jamming and radio silence, guided by instinct at the hand of an experienced pilot. Just you and your target, with a squad strapped in behind hoping to hit the dirt in one piece. It was in these moments she had felt most alive, the few times when Major Ren would delay the pilot's drug rations.

Rebekah flexed her fingers. She could do this. All the practice taking the *Sunstar* out manually from M4, much to Nicky's chagrin, or the deft manoeuvring around the asteroid and the mining fields, keeping her sharp, focused. Not quite the same as flying almost blind towards a fucking murderous battleship, but closer than most pilots ever got.

Almost blind.

"Cameras?"

Heki brought up the three images when comms crackled. No, not the ship's comms. Her helmet. Reluctantly, she reached for it, only for Heki to beat her and hand it over. As swiftly as she could, Rebekah released the manual controls and slotted the helmet in place, snapping it shut, her HUD firing up while the comms responded to her presence.

"Rad is rising rapidly," reported Arin in her ear. "Cargo bay has helmeted up, ZZ3 is checking on Trem now."

Good man. Fuck, I have the best squad, crew, whatever.

She pushed the rising emotions down. She needed focus. "Copy that."

"Rebekah," said Heki. "Closing." She pointed to the screen, at camera one, filled with flickering interference despite the heavy shielding required by ships involved in mining asteroids.

"Copy that. Helmet. Now." She closed her eyes, let the thrum of the ship vibrate through her gloves and on into her fingers, drew every part of the *Sunstar* in her mind. "Dricks, tell me I have manoeuvring thrusters."

The hiss and spit of her comms echoed in her ears as the huge battleship filled her screen. They were so close, no PDC rounds searing their way, the missile ports closed, as if unaware of what approached. By all the gods and their avatars, she hoped so.

Hendricks cut in. "I have two of the port and starboard thrusters isolated, and three on the keel. Can't do better than that, don't trust the others with all this shit flying about."

"Your shit that you made," said Arin, but kept it at that.

"Our shit," whispered Rebekah. "Flag them in my HUD."

She loosened her grip, and as the thrusters flagged, tested each in turn, pair against pair. Hendricks was right, consistency trumped quantity. "ZZ3, translate position. I need it like yesterday."

"Yes, Captain. Kefi has highlighted a very specific spot. The spawn's call is unaffected by the rad flare. Sending."

The position flagged up, nearer to the front of the huge ship than she would have wanted, prompting an engagement of the forward-most keel thruster, and trimming with the use of her starboard. The *Sunstar* responded, and she fired off each again in small bursts, watching the camera view then back to her HUD, always judging, feeling her way across the lessening chasm between battleship and the tiny *Sunstar*.

Hundreds of metres, then tens. "Coming in hotter than I want. Brace for impact." Then one. She briefly engaged the main engine, likely unmissable even with the sensor deprivation, but it was that or overshoot.

Touchdown.

The Sunstar's keel slammed into the battleship, scraping along the armoured plate, metal against metal. Rebekah fired the emergency anchors, designed for asteroids and rock, not metal plate, but anything would do at that moment. One fired, three refusing to respond, forcing her hand. With another burst of reverse thrust, they swung slightly to the side as the sole anchor bit then snapped, and a growl slipped from her lips. Another few metres and they had slowed enough.

"Maglock," she said, and Heki engaged the hull systems. A thud reverberated through the ship. They were attached via a system designed for probe and satellite recovery. It would have to do.

"Get your arses moving, crew. You have five and counting!" she bellowed, unstrapping, taking a second to look at Heki. But it was Trem she spoke to. "Your turn Trem. Keep a comms line stable. Nothing is more important, understand? Line then countermeasures."

"Copy that," replied Trem, the voice strong over comms.

"Be ready, Hek. And if I order you to leave, leave." Rebekah didn't wait for an answer, the look in the girl's eye enough. But emotions ebbed and flowed. The moment when you were forced to lift off, leave those people behind you care about the most – those were the worst. You'd rather die than face that pain, the shame as you returned to base. That's when the drugs were at their worst, and their best.

"Voiding the *Sunstar*," said Arin over comms. "Ready?"

"Ready," came back, Rebekah mentally ticking off every response.

"Now," said Arin. He'd be opening the cargo bay doors with the inner airlocks disengaged, exposing the *Sunstar* to the void. The reduction in its thermal footprint an added bonus to making access easier should every-thing go shit-face down. Again.

She stomped through the bay, Arin clambering the few metres to the *Segfi*'s hull ahead of her, ZZ3 and Kefi already there, the surrounding black filled with light from the warbot's back-mounted plasma torches. The bot was working on the hull, not the armour plating that could shrug off low-powered NPC rounds and missile blasts, but the weak point in any combat attuned ship. The PDC cannon rigs either spun on a central spherical rig, or externally on a gimbal. Both were vulnerable to a direct hit, the double-skinned hull accommodating the weaponry compromised into two separated layers with the required equipment between. Effective enough against a direct hit, but ZZ3 was here to cut not explode, one torch working the outer plate, the other already through an exposed section and cutting the inner.

Rebekah glanced at her HUD, sensory data limited to whatever was inside the suit, the external suffering the whiteout like the ships. The comms were a mess without the benefit of the *Sunstar*'s shielding. She signalled Arin for a time estimate, but he was head down, cooling ZZ3's efforts with a gel. Even the usual facial image was missing, just the frost of his visor reflecting his efforts. Her rad counter was rising fast, already touching on the red. They needed in.

"Trem, you reading me?" she asked in hope. But as ever, the twins continued to surprise.

"Got you," came the reply. "But not sure on the others."

"It's a start. Trem. Got a time estimate on the whiteout?"

"Calculating ... twenty-three minutes before fade starts. Another ten and it'll be intermittent though that'll last a good while," replied Tremil.

"Got that."

Rebekah started a clock in her HUD, setting timers for twelve and twenty minutes. As soon as the electromagnetic fallout started to fade, the ship was in trouble. Enough sensor data to hint at its presence, and the PDCs would likely activate. A quick glance about the hull hinted that at least two would have them in their killing field. And the twins insisted they needed to be clear of the battleship and the fallout before they could jump away.

Might be a race between what kills us first. Radiation, clones, drones or PDC fire.

"Trem, if we're not back in twenty. Leave." Silence reigned at the end of the comms, but it had to be said. "You, Heki, Dricks. You leave. Understand? No fucking heroes."

"… Yes, Captain."

She caught a signal out of the corner of her eye, looking over to Arin as ZZ3's limbs latched onto the PDC housing.

About fucking time. Dead before we started.

Of course, losing a whole PDC pod might also be a hint something was going on. Hopefully an assumption the whiteout had blown its system. Metal joints powered up, and the housing tore from the hull, a circle of thin plate still attached where the inner torch had cut it free. ZZ3 placed it on the hull, and Arin quickly added a maglock claw to grip it in place.

ZZ3 did not pause, limbs heaving the warbot inside the newly created hole, urgent, understanding the time pressure. One so great, not one of them wore a lifeline. They needed in fast. More flaring rose from the bowl carved in the hull, brief this time, followed by a stream of mist rising from inside, wreathing the lip before dissipating into the void. Arin, standing maglocked at the edge, signalled back to her, then to Kefi. He disengaged, twisting to grab hold of the lip he'd cooled, pulling himself down hand over hand until he too disappeared inside. Kefi was close behind, moving at a much greater pace, fluid tentacles yanking the alien swiftly into the breach. Rebekah was on the alien's six, gloves grasping at the twisted metal, pulling on exposed plates and melded wire through the remains of the PDC's mechanism. She entered an exposed space, reorienting herself, locking to the walls and clambering into the corridor strewn with the remnants of ZZ3's efforts to get them inside. It was dark, lit only by the lights of their suits. Her comms sprang into life.

"Time check," she said. "Nineteen minutes." Rebekah sent the info, adding the same alarms for Arin and ZZ3. Kefi was comms only, but better than the impotency of silence. "Kefi, direction?"

"We are beyond the optimum entry," stated the alien. "The spawn is one hundred metres behind us and down," the alien paused, waving a tentacle and the radiation weapon it held at the floor. "Two levels of this size."

"I'm on point with Kefi. ZZ3, drop the synced Watchtower then get on our rear. This is a fucking battleship. Battleships have AD units, Skyriders and Marine armour the fucking AI may well be able to control. We cannot assume we are undetected, and once alerted, internals systems will have us tracked. Arin."

"On it already, Captain." He tapped the side of his helmet. He had the known wetware frequencies scanning, but after Daphene that seemed a forlorn hope. His drones, however, were not. Tuned for the zero-g, two rose from his suit, one streaking ahead, the other behind and waiting for them to move on. The eyes in the back of their heads.

Everything hinged on speed.

"Move out," she growled, carbine in hand, striding along the corridor, lights playing against the metalled walls. "If it moves, fuck it up."

"Eh?" said the Senti, almost gliding alongside Rebekah as she hurried.

"Kill it," said Arin. "Then kill it again just in case it won't stay dead. And if still unsure ..."

"Do it all again," finished Kefi.

Arin snorted. "You're learning. Going to make a human out of you yet."

"That sounds like a threat."

CHAPTER 49

ANS SEGFI

R ebekah's HUD flickered, tracking ahead, keeping as much of the corridor in view as possible as she ran while flagging potential danger points. She breathed hard, the lack of gravity a boon for their pace, but at the same time awkward as each push off from the metal deck meant bodily movements were exaggerated, the slightest misalignment would send her flying. This was Skyrider territory, and she hoped to all the hells and back that the Butcher hadn't cloned any, or for that matter, the AI he'd melded with hadn't taken any under its control. Her eyes flicked to Arin's feed almost automatically seeking Savvo's. It felt wrong that he wasn't there, leading the chase.

For later.

"Bulkhead ahead," Arin said, his words punctuated by a pulse of red light. The breach had triggered auto closure.

"Fuck. Open it." She kept running, adapting her magboots, increasing their grip as she reached the sealed door and spun about, dropping to one knee. Kefi copied her, a step behind, as Arin stopped between them, breaker kit out while the drone hovered and bobbed next to the door. "Sixteen," she stated, not needing to explain.

Arin remained silent, wires against the lockpad, gloves working the box. Fifteen seconds passed, then five more. "Shit. Codes have been trashed." Arin backed off, pulling the wires clear. "ZZ3, cut it."

Fucking time poor.

"Up." She shoved Kefi aside, releasing her own boots and jumping to latch onto the corridor ceiling. The warbot squeezed into the space facing the door with twin torches already burning. Kefi had attached without fuss as the plasma flared.

"Incoming," reported Arin, and the rattle of gunfire pierced his comms. "Watchtower engaged."

Rebekah switched her feed, the rear drone weaving as it maintained a view of the twin-gunned defensive bot that held their rear. Sentry drones rolled across deck, wall and ceiling. Small, awkward and deadly. "Fuck it," she mouthed, anger clouding her thoughts. She'd dismissed mining the corridor, time the deciding factor. But hadn't factored the bulkhead issue in.

"Grenades," she said. "Up high, Arin, Kefi take the right, I'll target left. Pray the Watchtower thins them out." As if prophetic, the Watchtower's rate of fire increased, spitting more bullets, the stream of metal and ensuing explosions filling the far end of the corridor with flared light.

"Copy that," Arin replied.

Rebekah checked her HUD, flagging the first of the spherical bots as it broke the Watchtower's defence on Kefi's side of the corridor. It rolled on, bumping and reattaching as the machine bore down on them. Sparks arced over the bot, a hint at its intent. They attached to your suit, attempted to seize the servos with a burst of electrostatic then blew. In space, it only took one hole, on board a ship the idea was to overwhelm.

Kefi fired, her aim true; the grenade hitting the bot just as it bumped over a rib in the wall. The impact drove it back, and the grenade erupted, cracking the bot open, which responded with its own explosion. Rebekah's visor shielded against the double flash, while shrapnel filled the corridor. The Watchtower died, empty, swiftly followed by the rear drone as the multitude of metal in the corridor ripped into its side.

"Two for you Kefi," shouted Arin, and he let fly, his grenade ramming into the corridor wall. Rebekah had to trust the alien as the ceiling filled with her own targets. She ignored her sight's flags, aiming centrally, firing and then re-firing. Dual grenades slammed either side of the triple threat, cracking two open, the explosions ripping into the third which discharged its electrostatic hit. She pulled her main trigger, the carbine rounds finishing the job as they pierced the fractured shell of the sentry.

"I am through," stated ZZ3, a glance back gave her some relief as the door swung outward, one edge glowing orange. The last thing she needed was being forced closer to the storm of shrapnel behind them. One rip the suit could patch, not hundreds.

"ZZ3 shield us," she said. "Arin, Kefi, go." Rebekah fired again, keeping her gunfire steady, saving the final loaded grenade just in case. The bullets tore into a single sentry, knocking it from the ceiling to float in mid corridor, momentum lost. She sensed the warbot's presence as ZZ3 passed below her, then reversed, leaving its extra thick back armour facing the cloud of jagged metal shrouding the corridor. Rebekah, with a last check of her HUD, pulled herself down the wall and clamped to the deck. There she took aim, releasing the final grenade, not watching the outcome as she reloaded. "Finish them then follow, ZZ3."

Rebekah spun on her heel, eyes on her HUD, picking out Arin and Kefi who waited ten metres further along, carbines and an alien ray gun pointing towards a stairwell. That everywhere was empty nagged briefly at her, the thought of thousands being spaced all at once. Their voices silenced in one fell swoop as the bastard Butcher dumped the ship's atmosphere, and then their husked bodies.

"Thirteen minutes," she said, eyeing her timer. "Drone?"

Arin signalled down. "Next floor is clear. No heat signatures, no other spectrum hints but they could be powered down, inert."

"Cameras?" But she kicked herself as she spoke. Of course they were there, the signature minimal when the entire ship was alive with electronics. Alive in more ways than one. "Fuck it. Cover Arin, Kefi on my six."

"That means at her rear," said Arin.

"You humans are weird," said the alien, its suit hooking into the deck and pulling the Senti behind her.

Arin shrugged. "Got to agree."

Rebekah started down the steps, carbine held low, synced sight scanning the darkness under the next level's ceiling and fed into her HUD. Nothing, and she kept going. On a busy ship, there would be crew, Marine responders pounding after them, each stairwell a pinch point they'd take advantage of, cutting the legs from beneath any marauder. Three more steps and she had her own view. Another link corridor, empty and now as devoid of air as the one they had entered. Any clone without a suit was dead or trapped in a sealed room. A message dropped, ignored until she reached the bottom and was certain the corridor was clear. The only sign of reaction the blinking light above a closed bulkhead.

"Clear," she said, then read the message. ZZ3 was coming. An itch, a feeling pestered at her. "ZZ3 drop the last Watchtower at my present position. Arin, send the drone down and follow. Hurry."

"On it," replied Arin.

Kefi peered down the next stairwell, shoulder tentacles flapping. "She is near. We are close, and we must be quick. Time is fleeting." The alien pressed against the rail, the silver of its suit rippling with a rainbow of metallic colours from head through to its limb tips. "She calls me. Knows I am here."

Rebekah flinched as the drone passed over her shoulder, winging about Kefi before proceeding down the stairs. It made it three metres before gunfire cracked its shell, and the drone died in a moment of electronic flame.

"Shit," said Arin, approaching from behind. "No footage of that."

"Then this is it," she unclipped her pouch, withdrawing a roll of six grenades. Arin copied her, his bulkier, ready to serve a different purpose. ZZ3 clomped down the stairs, its usual awkwardness reducing the bot's speed with one limb ready with the requested Watchtower. Her timer flashed.

Ten minutes.

"Belay that, ZZ3. Follow in. Now, Arin." The ex-Breaker nodded, pressing each of the grenades' buttons in turn and hurling them one after the other down the stairwell in one-second intervals. Two bounced off the steps and continued their journey along the lower deck before erupting. The second pair rebounded off the wall at the side of the stairwell, hitting the rail on the way by before disappearing out of sight. Their explosions filled the corridor with their glare, but Rebekah wasn't admiring his handiwork.

"Ready, Kefi." It wasn't a question. She split the belt, and threw, eye-clicking her HUD, frosting her visor as she leapt the stairs. She hit the deck at the same time as her flash grenades blew, the visor completely blanking out. Rebekah squeezed her trigger, spraying rounds in a wide arc, before leaping again, heading up and way from any potential return fire. She struck the corridor ceiling as her visor recovered, a check of Arin's feed confirming he had followed in, picking his targets with Kefi close behind. She clamped on, flags pinging up. Six navy suits, carbines in hand, visors frosted. Their initial assault had downed three others, blood globules pouring from rips in their suits that misted before disappearing. Clones.

"Grenade," she bellowed into her comms, and released towards a knot of three huddled at the edge of the corridor. They were focused on Arin and Kefi, trying to force them back up the stairwell. If she was left alone, she was dead. The explosive hit the wall behind them, the shrapnel tearing at their suits, one ducked, the others threw themselves aside. They retained their survival instincts, and it was at that moment she wondered about the efficiency of the Marauders they'd faced. They hadn't flinched away from explosions, just powered on.

Later.

The stairs shook, a huge warbot bypassing half the steps as it bounced off the middle to land amidst the grenade induced carnage below. ZZ3 hadn't had a chance to swap weapons, but then it had quite a useful one already. The Watchtower the bot still held kicked in, twin barrels glowing as bullets ripped into the three scattered clones. Rebekah took the opportunity, targeting and firing at another as the warbot turned the Watchtower, finishing the job for her as it cut the suit in half. The two remaining clones released grenades at the huge warbot, the explosions rattling against ZZ3's head, fingers depressing triggers as they then blazed bullets towards the bot. Before Rebekah could reply, Kefi and Arin took them down from the stairwell, more blood and shattered suit components filling the small concourse. There would be screams, but a battle in the void was always silent.

Her suit alarm buzzed. Eight minutes left.

Fuck.

"Kefi, where now?" she said, pushing herself from the corner of ceiling and wall to fly towards ZZ3. The bot clasped one jawed limb about her suit, pulling her down to the deck. "Come on Kefi."

The alien pushed past, suit awash in waves of colour as it clambered over bodies, shoulder limbs clasping at the walls as she hurried on down the section where the cluster of three had been stationed. Her lights illuminated twin doors, their lockpads appearing dead though Rebekah doubted that. Kefi placed a tentacle on the second door, stroking it as she'd seen Senti do on their own ships. The riot of colour on the alien's suit froze.

"In here. She is in pain."

"ZZ3, Arin, you're up. One of you get Kefi in. I'll take cover."

And hurry.

"Trem, you hear me? Sit rep."

CHAPTER 50

SUNSTAR

It sat in the pit of her stomach. That ache, fear. She'd never used to feel it, perhaps the drugs dulled some of it, but she doubted that. None of her memories of mission after mission had ever been filled with much emotion. A job done, a pat on the back from Major Ren or whatever noble she'd been assigned to, and off you go again. Only the sight of Countess Segfi had brought up any emotion, though more assigned from what she'd done in the present, than the orders dished out in the past.

Love did that. Made you weak. Turned the cold killer into a dithering kitten.

And she liked it. That feeling of being needed, wanted.

But the stone sat heavy. Arin somewhere deep in the bowels of the Butcher's ship, and Rebekah too. ZZ3 and a Senti she couldn't help but like. The rad dose would have been high too, the additional medication helping, but they'd no time to put up the polythene tent Arin had devised since the shitshow after R89 blew up during a sun flare.

"Hek, is there any way we can get this camera any clearer?" she snapped into her suit's comms. She caught herself, realising she was taking out her angst on the wrong people. "Sorry Heki."

"No worries, old lady. I get it, I'm worried too. I'll work on it." Heki cut the link.

Hendricks massaged the back of her neck, fingers kneading at knotted muscle below her suit, then let out a sigh before settling down to stare at the constantly flickering image. Was that movement? She leant closer, knowing it was ridiculous, but instinctive. She looked to her HUD timer. They'd been gone fourteen minutes, and weren't due back yet unless it had gone to shit in there.

"Trem, you got Rebekah's signal?"

"Not direct, why?" she replied.

Hendricks blinked, the image coalescing, whatever Heki was doing clearing it a little. "Ping it, now! Are they at the entrance?"

Silence, then. "Definitely not. Deeper. Dricks ..."

"Shit." Something long poked out of the ragged hole, two rods either side latching to the hull, a helmet emerging. A Skyrider. "Heki, Trem, engineering now! Run! Go, go, go."

"Dricks."

"Run!" Hendricks gripped the monitor, drawing up the PDC controls that had gone to sleep. She had no sensor data at hand, just the camera and manual control. The barrel tip flashed. The railgun round – too fast for the camera – slammed into the ship. She instinctively knew where. They'd be aiming for the cockpit, the navcom perhaps, but most definitely the pilot. Heki. She opened up the topmost PDC, the aim poor, but she was seeking a distraction first as she swept the twin barrels downwards. Another round slammed into the *Sunstar*, and not from the Skyrider she had in her sights.

"Shit. Pincer." She guided the PDC downwards, and it tore through the space marine's helmet and arms, shattering the armour. She didn't wait, spinning the weapon around, but Hendricks had no visual this side – the camera had been focused on Rebekah's escape route. The PDC spat rounds, sweeping across the *Segfi* as she whipped the cannons into a widening circle, doing her best to visualise the hull, feel her aim. No more ship-killer rounds came, and with her heart pounding she spun the gun about again, aiming back at the hole. Nothing. Just the remains of a Skyrider.

"Heki, Tremil. Call in." Silence. "Call in." The wave slammed into Hendricks' mind, while the ship shook. Not shook, that was her addled mind. Gunfire, and on the inside and through her comms. Fear seared into her mind, laced with hot anger that bubbled and raged like lava. She felt herself drifting, mind detached as the girls' assault bore into her head. Blurred vision hindering her attempts, she tried to eye-click her HUD, blinking at the visor, desperate to engage her speakers. Through watery eyes something gave, and the speakers blasted into her ears. Drilling in, almost overwhelming her more than the raw emotion she was attempting to block. She doubled over, visor slamming into the console, but despite the raucous music, she could finally think. An eye-click and the roar toned down, leaving a ringing in its wake. The engineer staggered to her feet, collecting her carbine that she'd maglocked next to Arin's console. The girls had never reached her in engineering, and if the bastards had hurt them, she would gut them. Slowly. No drugs required.

Hendricks wobbled across engineering, reaching the door, her balance poor as her ears rung, but she was up. She swiped the lockpad and exited into the corridor, forcing down the nausea threatening to engulf her. "No time for that," she snarled, and made her way along the deck towards the junction. The airlock opposite was wide open but intact, and ignoring medbay, she turned left, heading for Trem's cabin only to be brought up short.

The girls were there, side-by-side, two Skyriders knelt before them, their powered armour filling the corridor. Their shoulders shook, visors clear though splattered with skin, eyes red with bloody tears. Heki and Tremil's faces were set hard, hot with anger. The space marines bore their handguns, pressed under their chins. Powerful. Deadly. In that moment, Hendricks could taste the metal barrel in her own mouth again. The despair that had driven her to the point of suicide when encountering the girls for the first time in a Bustan lab. With a roar, the Skyriders fired simultaneously, bullets crashing point-blank into the vulnerable seam between neck and helmet. They erupted in blood, metal and plexi-glass, the girls' powered suits slavered in gore. The Skyriders slumped shoulder to shoulder, their helmets shattered, rad-burned skin flapping, ragged jaws exposed to the cold. Both girls let go of each other, their bloody coating crumbling to dust as the cold void took its due. They stared at Hendricks, eyes wide, filled with horror as realisation struck, forging self-loathing that rolled through the corridor in a tidal wave of hate.

Hendricks shoved the dead cloned marines aside, removing the weapons slowly, reassuring words whispered into comms as she took both girls into her arms. She could sense the shift from lava hot self-loathing to disgust, that switch that took most soldiers over when they were faced with the choice they'd made. Sobs racked their bodies, and in that moment, Hendricks hated herself. Knew she would be adding to their later trauma. But a glance to her HUD through watery eyes told her time was short.

She stepped back from Heki and Tremil, magboots crunching down on the corpses behind her, hands on their shoulders. "Now take a breath. Hear me, crew? Rebekah's out there, Arin too. ZZ3 and Kefi. They're depending on us. We got sucker-punched somehow, and you dealt with it. It's what crew do. Now back to your stations. They need you. *I* need you. Understand?"

Both girls blinked, swallowing back the tears, nods instead of words. Hendricks placed her hands at the side of their visors wishing hard that she could just touch them, make that human contact that said it would be alright. Even if it wasn't.

"Now go!" She looked them both in the eye. "That's an order, crew."

"On it," whispered Tremil, turning away. But Heki was slower, her gaze flitting to the dead Marines before nodding again and heading to the cockpit. There would be fallout. Pain. But they needed to work together to make sure they were alive to see it. Hendricks kicked the corpses aside, exposing the plasma torch strapped to one of their backs. She eyed it, putting together the events. The attack, their rad burns, the torch and an open airlock. Trem would have known they were trying to get in. Would damage the ship and possibly prevent them taking off. The implication sat heavy, wrapping about the stone already in her stomach. She walked back to engineering, kneading at the ache in her shoulders as time ticked.

Shit.

She clicked her HUD while making a bet with herself that she'd been wrong. That the rounds hadn't struck anywhere that might hurt those on board. No, the Butcher had made a play, wanted the secret to FTL, and that meant keeping people alive. Keeping them close.

"The engines. Bloody hell. Heki, you there yet?"

A cough. "Here."

"Run a diagnostic on the engines, now. I'm going outside."

Hendricks kept her eyes down, yanking at the lifeline and feeling a reassuring resistance that did nothing to calm the heartbeat thrumming in her ears, but at least didn't add to it. "Don't look up," she said to herself. "Or to the side. Yes, it's the black, yes, you're out-bloody-side and yes, your suit alarm's screaming blue bloody murder at you for being out in the rad flare you bloody created. But ignore all that. Focus, breathe." She placed her magboot, feeling the click, then twisted out and wrapped her glove around the handhold and pulled herself onto the hull. With her second foot in place, she pushed herself up onto two feet, mind suddenly disoriented by her angle to the ship, to the *Segfi* below, the black. Every-fucking-thing. After years of being couped up nice and safe, rescuing ships and repairing equipment, she had recently been out in the black more times than she wanted to recount. "At least this time it's not freefall."

Hendricks pressed on, keeping the maglock boots set low as she hurried towards the rear of the ship. With the extraneous sensor information kept to the minimum, she dialled down the internal alarm and kept her gaze on each step, hurrying, not taking the time to link into the external runners with her lifeline. The chances were she was either going to get shot with a ship-killer round, gunned down by carbine fire, smacked by a grenade or die from radiation poisoning. Admittedly she would take all those over dying lonely in the cold void that pressed in around her.

Her comms hissed, the crackle of speech garbled. A data packet dropped, and as she neared the first set of rear thrusters, she eye-clicked the message. "Three shots," it said, "straight through the rear exhaust assembly." Hendricks added the locations to her HUD.

Why not the main system. Think. Think.

The black pressed as she passed the thrusters, a glance telling her there was no damage, no mine attached. Hope. Without their external sensors, they would have no idea if the *Sunstar* had been mined until it was too late. However much the Butcher wanted the secret, if the engines were sabotaged, the bastard may only have pieces to sift through.

Gunfire, heavy, the hull reverberating, forced her down, only the tips of her toes locked to the metal-skin. The barrage continued, and she scrabbled for a hand hold, feeling herself lift from the ship.

"No, no bloody way. Not like that." Her fingers stretched, achingly close to the hold. "Not dying that way." Hendricks unclicked, risking only one point of contact, slamming her boot tip down a few centimetres closer, then the next, shoving herself forwards to hook around the hold. "Got you." She pulled herself down, making full contact with the hull as the reverberations ended. Her breath heavy against the visor, she wished for her old wetware to calm her mind.

Think.

The hull shook. PDC fire. If I'm not dead that means ...

"Heki or Tremil. Move you old woman. Now. Stop lying around as if the world will solve its own problems. Up, Marine." She got to her feet, and, ignoring the risk, pounded along the outer hull until she reached the exhaust section. The suit alarm sounded again, she was in the red and the residual radiation around the exhausts was only going to make it worse. "Speed. Don't look, just do."

Her chest hurt, but she reached down and hooked a secondary line to a runner, knowing she needed speed. With a stream of expletives in her wake, Hendricks threw herself off the back of the *Sunstar* – sensing the black wrap itself about her chest, squeeze the ribs, encase her heart. She turned, grasping the secondary line, gloves wrapped about the clip and peered at the engines. There was a Skyrider, a backpack in hand, their skin sloughed from their face, eyes liquid and the bone of their jaw bereft of skin. They seemed to scream at Hendricks, whether in pain or lost defiance, she couldn't tell. Hendricks had never fired a navy-suit weapon before, but twenty years as a Marine gave you an edge, wetware or not, when your family was on the line. The mini-grenade launched, and bullets flew, ripping into the foul mockery of a human. The grenade slammed into the visor, glancing off and exploding against the ash covered metal of the exhaust. The cloned space marine jerked forwards, toppling, their servos straining to keep them upright as the magboots held. Hendricks' second burst tore into the backpack, shredding the material, mines spewing from inside to bounce off the exhaust, their momentum carrying them out of the engine, beyond the Skyrider's reach.

Hendricks doubted the thing could see. Might not even be in control. Her lifeline jerked, reaching its full length, spinning her round. The world became a haze of black and metal swirls as she fought to stop the spin, forgetting all her training as panic set in. Then a jerk, a yank, followed by a second pulling her in as her brain and ears tried to figure out what the hell was going on. The suit alarm rose in volume, she knew what it meant as three pinpricks rammed into her skin, filling her with anti-radiation drugs that were likely far too late. Another pull.

Shut up suit.

Suit.

Sensors down. But not internal.

Her head whirling, another yank pulled her closer to the walking death that waited for her in the exhaust pipe.

Focus.

An eye-click, a second. Blink. The suit activated, Hendricks setting its orientation to autocorrect to the *Segfi* below her, the suit firing mini jets, negating her spin. Feet down towards the giant battleship, she was within a metre of the skeletal face, with eyes that bulged as they burst, and she fired. Point blank, body stable, head still spinning, but she couldn't miss.

Hendricks screamed. Nothing of what she said was intelligible, just defiance, hatred, anger. And the Skyrider died before her, the powerful armoured suit resisting her bullets, but the visor gave, obliterating the nightmare the Butcher had crafted.

With the Marine defunct, their gloves released her lifeline, and she floated backwards, her suit compensating, keeping her stable as she watched what remained of her enemy slump over to hang maglocked to the exhaust pipe.

With alarms silenced, she eyed the monitor. The red glare of the radiation levels expected but still struck fear. She didn't want to die, had a family, Arin, to live for. But nor could she face a death like the Skyrider's, her family watching her rot. She drew a line knife from inside her pouch, blanking out the thought of what she was doing.

"I love you, Arin," she said, and prayed it would be quick as she held the knife against her suit.

The comms roared in her ears, a voice cutting through. Young, powerful. Desperate. "Cut that suit open, Dricks, and we'll never forgive you. You hear me, old lady? We need you. You know us, what we are. You have seen the monsters, yet love us still."

CHAPTER 51

ANS SEGFI

"Trem, sit rep. Come back," said Rebekah. "Fuck."

ZZ3 could hear her attempts over comms, process her tension, her concern over a lack of response. But the warbot had its orders.

It slammed dual limbs into the door, the crunch reverberating through the corridor wall. The metal curved inwards, exposing the upper manual hinges, and the warbot sliced its plasma torch down the first while a third limb beat at the bottom half, revealing another mechanism. The plasma burned through, and ZZ3 stowed the torch, urgency in its movements, and beat at the door a third time, sending it flying back to ram against something hard – a clear case. Inside floated a human child, eyes closed, skin almost translucent.

'Is this what it means to be human? Is this what I was? How could you want to be like the Butcher?'

I have never expressed a need to be human. Nor can I judge a people on the act of one of their kind.

'Yet you evolve. What happens if you change into something akin to him.'

I was an AD unit, Asham. I killed, maimed and destroyed at the whim of others. No emotion, no thought, just parameters and action codes to direct my choices. I could not be worse than I was.

'Those who choose *to act that way,* are *worse.'*

Then help instead of hinder.

'I thought I was?'

ZZ3 clomped inside, scanning the room, seeking threat. The warbot knew battleships, that they were not geared up for internal defence. Why would they be? Being breached meant death, and what would a boarding achieve in a ship riddled with armed crew and sentry bots? The cameras were active, that was about it, sending images of a warbot appalled by the acts of the Butcher AI, the origin of the ghost that occupied its system. The room was filled with rows of half-grown clones, children whose futures were short and violent.

'Bereft of a soul. Wearing someone else's skin, wielding someone else's memories. Fleshy versions of AD units.'

I am ZZ3, and I am crew.

'So they may have been, once.'

"Kefi, Arin, I have found the spawn," stated the warbot, but it needn't have spoken, Kefi already pushing past, tentacles reaching out, its metallic suit thrumming from within. ZZ3 knew something was about to happen, could sense the shift in electromagnetic patterns that the suit could barely contain.

Centred about the neck, of course.

"My queen," said the alien, and the alien wrapped suited tentacles about a plexi-glass pod containing a yellow and blue cocoon, its outer shell rippled like waves. Smooth, but dull in comparison to Kefi. "You suffer."

Arin strode in next to ZZ3, carbine cradled in his arms "We are screwed for time, Kefi. We need to go, now. How do we get it out?"

The alien turned about, looking back, eyes that had once been black now shining with a vibrant blue. Like the nest queen. "I ask to do so carefully, whichever way we choose. The spawn talks of a softening shell, whatever the liquid is, it is hurting her."

The comms hissed. Rebekah. "Six minutes. We are out of time. ZZ3, retrieve the spawn."

ZZ3 didn't hesitate, pushing Kefi aside, the alien protesting, reaching for the bot. Tentacles latched on, and the warbot's sensors picked up the sheer energy pulsing inside the Senti's suit. Arin stepped up, about to pull at the alien, with ZZ3 rapidly extrapolating that the consequences would be dire. Kefi was in thrall to her need to save the spawn. He shoved out a limb, blocking his approach.

"Kefi, let go, be ready. You are crew, I will not harm you, or your queen's spawn. Be ready." The warbot flicked its limb, jaws splitting wide, and grasping the plexi-glass. "Step back."

The alien let go, tentacles retracting, pulling away as instructed. ZZ3 punched the glass, a fracture forming, then repeated the blow again and again. The liquid sloshed, elements seeping through the fractures. "Organic, carbon-based acid. Out, everyone out," said the warbot, backing away. But Kefi ignored the bot, charging into the pod, tentacles out, the suit's tips sharp and hard. They pierced the glass, the liquid splashing over the alien's suit, reacting as fast as it misted into the air, eating at the material. ZZ3 was torn between saving Kefi, and the damage the acid and its mist would cause. The danger highlighted as the Senti's suit parted, peeling away from the vibrant skin as the alien caught the nest queen's spawn in its tentacles. ZZ3 expected the acid to continue its path, extrapolating the pain Kefi was about to suffer before the cold and lack of atmosphere took their due.

"I am sorry," came the alien's monotone over the comms. "I am, was and forever will be grateful to be crew. To be one with you as a nest." A squawk. "Run!"

The helmet parted, eaten by the acid, and the symbiote scurried through the crack, pushing itself off the Senti's shoulder tentacle with its own spread wide to land upon the cocoon. ZZ3's sensors reacted to the pulse of power, something akin to a tear ... or a fold. The warbot reversed, grasping Arin, dragging him away from the acidic residue, pulling him towards the door.

"We are done," said the bot as they cleared the entrance, a flash of metallic light blinding its visual unit as it flared into the corridor.

"What the shitting hell was that?" gasped Arin, ZZ3 refusing to let go until he was clear of the room, of the threat.

"Mission complete," replied the warbot. "Kefi is dead, but the symbiote rescued the spawn. They are gone."

Rebekah clomped to the doorway, switching her lights on to peer inside. ZZ3 understood. She needed to see with her own eyes what she would assume was a mission failure, and the warbot knew was a success – except for who, or more likely what, would have witnessed the rescue. The Butcher.

"Move. Smash our way out, ZZ3. No stopping, no recourse. Go!" she bellowed, and shoved Arin ahead of her. "Go. Go."

ZZ3, with urgency parameters set, powered up the stairs, reaching the next level in two bounds as it responded to the order. Sentry bots were pouring through a newly opened bulkhead, twenty or more, lights pulsing as they spotted their target. The warbot sent the image, limb weapons extending, blasting away as they rolled over wall, deck and ceiling towards it. Arin arrived behind, carbine spitting rounds towards the threat.

"I will shield, go," said ZZ3.

Arin let another burst fly, ripping into one of the spherical bots, then headed up the next stairs. More gunfire, ZZ3 assuming his captain followed, tearing into another of the bots, and then she was also gone. The warbot released a grenade, firing into the ceiling, focusing its aim on those bots who could prevent its plan. ZZ3 reversed, heading up the stairs, needing a gap between it and the pursuit, estimating distances, pace, time.

Ahead, his captain's lights, the flash of carbine muzzles. ZZ3 had to assume what lay behind was more dangerous and drove for the open bulkhead. It locked to the deck, reversing again, limbs grasping the door and heaving inwards. Two sentry bots accelerated as they reached the top of the stairs, spearing towards ZZ3, electrostatic arcs firing off as they closed. A burst of gunfire tore into the first, shattering its shell, shrapnel flying as it exploded. ZZ3 squeezed the door shut, the second bot ramming into its edge, trying to get through. But warbots were strong, powerful. ZZ3's servos strained, and the bulkhead edge split the bot in two as it slammed home. The sentry's discharge seared into one arm limb, surging upwards, seeking a weakness and the warbot made a sacrifice.

ZZ3 turned and ran, leaving the spitting, blue arc-covered limb behind, locked in the wheel of the bulkhead. They had sliced the door open, a limbed bot would get through in seconds, but spherical ones, however many there were, had their own inherent weakness.

The warbot ran through the shrapnel, each metal shard pinging away now their momentum was spent. Little danger, while ahead the carbine flashes repeated. ZZ3 focused in front of them, seeking out the danger Arin and Rebekah faced. A lone Skyrider, barricaded in, guns flashing and pinning them down either side of corridor.

"Captain, I am coming through. Be ready." ZZ3 knew the Skyrider would register its presence. If AI controlled, they would pick out the greatest threat. Target the warbot, give the others a chance. If a clone, then maybe fear would be in its memory, aware of what a raging AD unit was capable of.

Powering past the Captain, then Arin, ZZ3's servos pushed off, and the warbot leaped forwards, aiming for the top of the space marine's barricade. Their helmet rose, suddenly registering what ZZ3 was doing, and the Skyrider swung its carbine, releasing a grenade. An AI would follow that with another, extrapolated ZZ3, then duck and turn, waiting for the warbot to crash over the top before firing a third. The grenade erupted against ZZ3's chest; the vibrations shaking the bot's armour, scorching the plate, while the Skyrider reeled from Arin's burst that struck it square in the visor. ZZ3 fired a manoeuvring thruster, one of our glorious leader's add-ons, and careered into the top of the barrier, hooking a limb, arresting its dive while ripping the barricade down upon the back-pedalling Marine. Reversing, the warbot slammed punch after punch into the helmet with the Skyrider's arms enmeshed in the barricade, the warbot's weight keeping them pinned.

"Go. Go for the *Sunstar*," ZZ3 said, then the helmet cracked, and another punch prevented any concern the clone had of dying by the void's cold touch. ZZ3 extricated itself from the barricade, clambering over towards the hole in the hull. Arin's legs were disappearing over the edge as the warbot reached for the wall and detached its maglock. Once up, the bot had a view of the *Sunstar*, registering a Skyrider, or at least most of one, flapping at the rear. The cargo bay was opening, Arin already there, Rebekah waiting by the hole, carbine spitting rounds back into the *Segfi*.

"Out of time," the captain said, and spun on one heel, heading for the ship. She stopped after a few steps, staggering forwards, carbine lost as her hands reached for her helmet. ZZ3 ran through her life signs, all in the green but deteriorating. Her heart was pounding, blood pressure rising. The warbot reached her side, wrapping a limb about her, running for the bay.

The whiteout had reduced, the blaze of radiation intermittent, the interference random but ZZ3 could hear the same voice as the Captain. The roar of anger, the tone laced with vicious hatred, and goading madness.

"I know, I know, I know. I know now, Khan. What you do, how you jump and run. I have seen. You will not escape, Khan. I am coming for you. I will take what you have, splice and cut, rip and rend until I have their secret. I will clone your crew, fill them with their memories over and over, torture them through the centuries. My ire knows no bounds, my revenge no barriers. Can you imagine the atrocities I can concoct? But you, you I will keep alive. When I have your symbiote, no one will stand in my way. No one will come to rescue you, Khan. A forever death. Rescue me, Khan?"

ZZ3 calculated and leapt, spearing through the cargo bay doors, wrapping arms about Rebekah, turning its back as they clattered into cargo boxes and clipped the edge of the low-loader.

"Lift off, Heki. Now, spin us about" bellowed Rebekah, her voice trembling but demanding. "We can't wait."

ZZ3 dragged itself down to the deck, locking on, releasing the captain. Rebekah staggered to her feet, taking two steps before the screech and wail of an angry AI bellowed into comms.

"Trem, Trem. Cut the contact off now," said Arin. "The Butcher, he's locked into Rebekah's comms." As his words faded, the engines kicked into life, the jar of the *Sunstar's* maglock disengaging throwing them all but ZZ3 off their feet.

The warbot's receiver noted the change, Tremil engaging the code blocker, infuriating the Butcher as it battered at their system. Then another rad wave hit, the interference rising again. It wouldn't last, but it was a glimmer.

Rebekah crawled along the deck, grasping for a cargo box, pushing herself to her feet. "ZZ3, I need help. Get me to the cockpit." The warbot swept her up and ran for the corridor, checking over her vitals. The Butcher's assault had been brief, invasive of her suit, and though not physical, the barrage had disoriented her balance, but her mind apparently remained sharp. "Arin, Arin," she said. "Come back."

"Here," he responded. "Closing the bay doors."

Rebekah coughed. "The rail gun. Everything, all of it. Fuck the *Segfi* up. We can't miss. Hurry."

"Oh, *now* you're talking my language."

CHAPTER 52

SUNSTAR

Rebekah dropped into the pilot's chair, Heki aware she was there but focused on safely lifting away from the *Segfi* with zero sensor information and just a dodgy camera view ahead. Her tongue curled into the corner of her mouth, sweat beading on her brow while the symb flowed with metallic colours, reflecting off the inside of her visor. Rebekah kicked in her earworm, not trusting her helmet speakers or her pained ears for that matter after the Butcher's attempt to break her. And after passing the dead Skyriders in the corridor, she had to shut everything out, including a thousand and one questions about what in all the hells had happened on board.

She checked over the navcom, noting the hints in the data stream that the whiteout, the EM flare from the autoship and shipyard destruction, was lessening. There would be another gap and soon. Flexing her shoulder, rolling her stiff neck, she cracked a thumb then took the manual controls in hand.

"Trem, we're coming up to a gap in the flare, yes?" she said.

"Definitely. I estimate sixty-two seconds," came the reply. "There'll be some ping time, but the Segfi will have us in that window. I'll find out how long it will be."

"Do it. Ready, Heki?" she said.

"Oh yes," Heki replied.

"Release." Rebekah sensed the shift through her gloves and took the controls. "Arin, now."

"Shit yeah!" The *Sunstar* shook as the first metal javelin released from the keel rail gun. They'd tested it once, the Senti tricks inhabiting the housing absorbing much of the kickback, but far from all. The ship shuddered. The only thing Rebekah knew for sure was that the battleship was below them and time was short. Max damage, hitting the Butcher's ride like a violent sewing machine seemed the best option. Again, the reverberation shuddered through her controls, but she was in no rush to sweep away from danger. Far from it. The third metal slug surged ahead, slamming into the armoured hull, fracturing the plate, piercing the skin. Not only damaging whatever lay below, but hopefully infuriating the Butcher. The words over her comms were full of spite and fury. Human emotion. That she could understand – and goad. Not the cold logic they feared.

A fourth and fifth javelin threatened to break her grip on the control sticks. "Trem."

"Thirty-six seconds, but the edges are thinning."

So play it safe.

"Heki, prepare the last probes." The ship shook again. "Trem, I want the ghost ship mode ready on my mark. Dricks—"

"No Dricks," cut in Heki, her voice strained, almost breaking. "In med-bay."

It shouldn't have, but it caused her to pause, almost choke on her words. "Arin, ten seconds then at the engine console."

"Copy that," replied the technician, a query in his voice, but another rail gun shot thundered through the ship. The Butcher wasn't replying, not risking bringing the *Sunstar* down, destroying the prize inside. He would, as soon as the sensors were operational and he could risk a precise hit.

Or something else.

The Butcher liked his surprises.

A final bolt left the keel gun, and Rebekah checked the countdown. Fifteen seconds. "Hard burn," she bellowed, and engaged the drives. They'd managed it once before. Safety lay in the *Segfi*'s engine trail, the exhaust fumes providing additional cover, and the Butcher hadn't risked engaging anything near the battleship's full power when flying blind. Pressed back in her seat, she remembered the first time they'd done this she'd had to hand a whole gamut of sensor readings, now it was pure instinct. On that she thrived. The *Sunstar* swept along the engine arrangement, powering over the massive exhausts to enter the miasma behind the massive ship. Still she pushed the engines, praying there was nothing in the mess of radiation and outflow that could damage the *Sunstar*. She eyed the clock.

"Heki, probes. 3, 2, 1 ... release."

"Probes away," the girl responded. "Activation ... failed."

"Fuck." Rebekah eyed the data flow. The flare was thinning, but not yet gone. "Try again. Now!"

She saw Heki flinch from the corner of her eye, but she was battling the acceleration, the battleship's outflow and a sense of dread if the probes failed.

"Activation signal sent," repeated Heki, the pause gnawing at Rebekah. "One engaged."

"The Segfi's missile ports are open, PDCs spinning up," said Trem. "Target acquired. We're painted."

"Fuck. Again, Heki. Arin, prep a thruster shift." Last time the Butcher had fired blind, but would he risk that? He wanted them, the symbiotes, anything that could give him access to FTL and revenge. It was their ace, the only card they had.

"I can try. Dricks …"

"Stow that shit. Do as I fucking say or we're dead. No fucking 'try' will save us," she snapped, eyes flicking over to the data flow. No relief there, no imminent return to the flare's sensory cloud. PDC fire sprayed about the ship, wide, distant.

A warning.

Heki spoke up. "One more active probe. The third is dead, burned up, or it hit something."

But we didn't. How close was that?

"We have ships … no drones. Drones, hundreds of them," stated Trem, the voice no longer flat, but filled with dread. "There're pings all over. They're approaching the remaining probes."

We have seconds and they'll be on us. No meat to keep alive in those fucking tin cans.

Her navcom flashed, the first probe disappearing. The first pseudo-*Sunstar* to fall. One more, and then it was their turn.

She growled into her comms. "Trem, wire me in to the ghost ship. Hek, go. Down to Trem. We need out whether we're too close or not. And strap the fuck in." Rebekah sucked in a breath. "Arin, on my mark. We'll be hitting full burn as soon as we shift, if this heap o' shit is still in one piece." The death of the second probe flagged on her screen.

Alone, she eyed the navcom, pings spearing towards them. A storm cloud, and if the reports from Daphene were right, with one aim. To overwhelm. Either through sheer speed and firepower, or from taking control of the ship. It was the latter she truly feared, no doubt in her mind the Butcher would carry out every promise he'd made over her comms.

And what if he managed to make the drones from Senti metal? What then for Almaar?

The navcom flagged, the ghost ship program declaring its readiness, while the edge of the flare seemed a million klicks away. "On my mark, Arin. 3, 2, 1," she engaged the ghost ship, the full sensory recreation of the *Sunstar*. Perfect, Trem's creation twenty klicks to their port side. She had the merest glimpse of the death cloud shifting direction. "Mark."

A thought crashed in, so dark it was almost funny. She hadn't warned Arin which side the sensory image of the *Sunstar* would appear. An irony if activating the thrusters shoved them back towards the oncoming drones. The ship yawed and bucked, its internal skeleton screaming dissent at what it was asked to do. The ships of the asteroid field were built tough, rugged. Not the prettiest, nor the fastest, but they could take some serious hammer year after year. "Just one more run, you pile o' crap," she said, then risked a tap on the navcom hood. "Please."

As the *Sunstar* yawed, she eyed the internal information pouring in. It was a surface assessment, the ship's infrastructure imaged in amber. She had no doubt the last thing it needed was a desperate captain ramping up acceleration. But what choice was there?

"Engaging hard burn."

And Rebekah Khan, Captain, ex-Breaker, slammed back into her seat as a prayer slipped from her lips.

The *Sunstar* burst forwards, Rebekah watching the screen, the ship's flight now in the hands of the navcom with no indication the remnant of the flare would reach them in time. Red spread across the infrastructure, warnings flashing. She shut them off. Evil lay behind, and despite – or because of – her love for those who rode the storm with her, she could never allow it to catch them. Not death or glory, peace is what she sought.

The drones fell upon the sensory ghost, pings everywhere as many of the robot ships slammed into each other in their urgency to swarm the fake *Sunstar*. How long before orders came from the *Segfi*, what moments did they have before the Butcher realised they had fooled his attack ships?

No wonder he hates us.

"Hek, Trem," she gasped into the comms, her suit finally compensating for the pressure on her body. Or were the microseconds feeling like hours? The remaining drones had swirled about their shadow one more time, before a ripple and a shift in momentum. They were coming. "Now would be good."

Her world changed. At first the glare of scarlet from the navcom had threatened their demise, warnings of imminent structural failure. *Of how bloody stupid you are not to listen.* Then the forward screen turned black, as if the stars winked out, an abyss ready to welcome and envelop a ship's captain and her crew in its nothingness. "Fuck, it looks cold."

"Rebekah. Captain." A voice, almost distant. Arin? The blackness stretched out, tinged with crimson. And then the ship juddered, vibrated as if it was finally their time, and the engines died. Rebekah blinked, raising her hand, staring at the glove, then back at the navcom. The threat warning remained angry and urgent, but its immediacy had rapidly reduced. They were drifting, their speed high, momentum carrying them onwards. There was something out there, not a star, but it glowed. Rippled with metallic light. She blinked, and it was gone. A fake image perhaps, like a light mirage.

A stomping vibrated the deck below her feet. A warbot, no doubt, checking on the twins. She stretched her neck, wrung out her fingers, then rolled her shoulders. "Alive," she said. "How the fuck did we do that?"

Space bulged ahead of them, the viewscreen showing the quirk and shimmer of time and space, the blanket fold Heki and Trem had provided. The *Sunstar*'s nose penetrated, emerging the other side. Karal lay before them, an Almaarian frigate hanging in orbit to the rear.

"Rebekah, you there?"

"I'm here. You cut the engines?" she asked, her voice raw, dry.

Arin's tone matched hers. What stress would do to you. "Sorry, yeah. That or we were going to get a brief but spectacular close-up of void-space."

She laughed, releasing a snort-cum-sigh as she did so. "We stable enough I can slow her down?"

"Running an assessment now. Karal has tugs, if they're in op, we could slide on by and let them tow us back. I need to check on Dricks ..."

Rebekah nodded. It was an option, but hardly the return she imagined. But then, five minutes ago, she was thinking how inviting the abyss was. "Send me the deets ASAP. Then I can let you go ... I'll check on her, Arin."

Dricks. Shit.

Rebekah pushed herself up from the pilot's chair, clomping along the corridor and through the galley. What had Heki said? Medbay, that was it. She passed the dead Skyriders, a glance hinting they had died like most who caused fear in the twins. Medbay was sealed shut, and by the time she had activated the lockpad, the medbot was cycling through its medical update. Hendricks lay on the table, helmet on due to the lack of atmosphere and the cold, eyes closed. Her cheeks and nose were red, on the edge of burning.

She read the medbot's screen.

Radiation exposure, high risk but drug management in place. Prognosis positive. Medical coma instigated due to treatment refusal, authorisation override HT.

"I bet they did. Fuck, old lady, you do know how to scare us. Arin, sending med data. It's okay, she's going to be alright. Pissed, perhaps, and a couple of ingrates might be getting a dressing down, but she's good." There was a sob from the other end, relief she could relate to. How long had it been since the *Hatton*? Since the quiet, boring life her crew found too restraining had fallen apart?

Talking of falling apart.

"*Sunstar*, this is Effina of Karal temporary substation. Please activate your transponder."

She sucked in a slow breath. It wasn't over. "Karal, this is Rebekah Khan. We are in a bad way, instigating slow down but we're gonna need some help." She eyed the assessment Arin had dropped into her HUD. "A *lot* of help."

The comms cut off briefly before returning. "That's okay, *Sunstar*. Jenkra Tew and Captain Fortan of the ANS *Retana* have authorised your request. Send your expected trajectory and planned slowdown pattern."

Navy permission? Things have changed.

"Effina. I request immediate evac for one crew member. A war hero no less."

CHAPTER 53

APPROACHING KARAL

"There," said Trem, pointing to the camera view. Rebekah could make out the hump at the rear of the hull, barely noticeable, but Trem was certain and had trickle data as evidence. "It's a single drone."

"That bastard. Active?" asked Arin. He shuffled his feet, magboots releasing and reactivating as his nervous tension built. Rebekah would have to let him go to Hendricks soon.

"That's the thing. Minimal power, if the Butcher makes these out of Senti materials, they'll be undetectable. I'm not sure about in flight, I'll have to analyse the sensor recordings and correlate against Rohan's shuttle. But we're talking a scary level of sensory camouflage," said Trem, eyes down and working at her slate. She stopped, catching Rebekah's eye. "The system blocker has done its job up to now. The drone is drip-feeding a Senti virus, which I'm betting has part of the Butcher's code ready to replicate. I can keep it out for now, and it hasn't broadcast yet ..."

Arin looked down at her data. "But this is the last of our secrets, right? Right, Captain? If the Butcher realises we're able to recognise and, at least for a while, block an attack, we've no more tricks."

Rebekah had to agree. And they knew of the Senti, and the General's origin code, from Asham. It wouldn't take long for the Butcher to eradicate their advantage.

Arin continued his train of thought. Speaking aloud. "I say we isolate the ship, blow the drone amid a shitload of jamming. And we know the blocker works, so the Countess has evidence."

"But not forever. It's short term, and if the drone reports on how it was blocked from taking the ship, the Butcher will adapt," stated Trem.

"And so will we." Rebekah squeezed Tremil's shoulder. The solution was obvious but wasn't going to happen. The countess would start her demands early, back off, then go again. Wanting Tremil to be churning out defensive systems for her ships until she was spent, and then expect her to go again. All the while plotting how she could obtain Heki too.

Fuck that.

"Get it done, then it's time to requisition a ship." She stroked Trem's shoulder, walking out and heading down towards the adapted cabin. ZZ3 waited for her as requested, the warbot already detached from its lower set of limbs. She needed Asham's insight, and ZZ3's recall of what had happened on the Segfi. To Kefi and the queen's spawn. Surely it hadn't been for nothing?

She scanned the lockpad, and entered, the aroma of age-old cabbage assaulting her nose. The scent must have permeated the room. The entire ship had been vented, yet still it lingered. A hint of Kefi, and one she had to admit she'd missed. The alien had almost felt like crew. Was crew, as far as it could be allowed by two races so unsure of each other after the countess and the Butcher had gone to work on their ambassadors.

"I miss her, what she became," said Rebekah, approaching the 'kitchen' area which appeared to be a set of tanks with multiple hues of green and yellow mould or possibly algae, dead inside. The cold had killed them.

"She was crew," said ZZ3, "though Kefi defined the parameters differently. She saw us as a whole, working for one aim." The bot's eyes swirled between blue and red as it swept the room. A limb extended, pulling away a rubberised section of the vertical bed pinned to the wall. Exposing a version of a slate the Senti utilised. Neither the warbot nor a human could make sense of the screen, Senti eyes seeing light in a very different way. With a delicacy that surprised Rebekah, ZZ3 removed a mod from the edge of the tablet, handing it over to her.

"Can this be used?" she asked

"Asham has had access to these before. It will require some port adaptations, but yes. A Senti direct link. He purports that it utilises an element of the symbiotes abilities, emulates them somehow. It is beyond either of us, but it works, and either it is what humans once called magic, or a science we do not as yet understand." The warbot turned back to the kitchen area. "There are many aspects to the Senti still to be discovered. But Kefi ... her last words were: I am, was and forever will be grateful to be crew. Odd use of tense." ZZ3 turned to Rebekah, shuffling its bulk around. "Almost human."

Rebekah smiled, unable to help herself. "Okay, she was crew. Have you analysed Arin's feed?"

"I would like Heki and Tremil to check the findings, but yes. There was nothing on visual, but the sensor readings suggest there was a shift, that mirrors, on a smaller scale, what happens to the *Sunstar* when we, how you put it, *jump*."

Rebekah flexed her fingers, thumb cracks echoing in the small room. "So, it could be the spawn has survived." It wasn't a question. "Can you and Asham prioritise adapting the Senti comms unit? Get Heki to help. I want it done by the time we've got rid of this bloody drone and we've docked. And ZZ3, thanks. For the *Segfi*, and after."

The warbot's eyes settled, pulsing blue as it took back the mod. "Captain, *I* am crew."

"Just you? And where is the ghost of Asham, now?" she touched his nearest limb, accepting the pause as the warbot watched her closely. Letting him process.

"You are not asking out of concern for his presence," stated ZZ3. "But to explore who and what I am." Rebekah nodded, pulling herself closer to the bot as he continued. "The answer remains the same. Being part of the crew is my anchor. Asham my sounding board. Not a conscience or a teacher, in human terms, but ... a voice to analyse how I am changing."

Rebekah smiled at that. The crew were a collective who acted as a whole. Self-supporting. "If you need another, any of us would listen, ZZ3. You are ..." she pulled away from the bot. "You are loved."

He looked beat. Worse, if she was being truthful, than she felt. "A hero now?"

Savvo grinned, then winced, holding his back. "Not according to this git." He tilted his head towards the security chief smoothing down the remnants of his hair and releasing a tooth-filled grin.

"Git am I now? You be takin' on some of the slummage I speak, Savotini. Better than all that 'fuck this and fuck that' you use." Barclow headed for the medroom exit. "But aye, the fecker did a fine job of helping keep Karal in one piece. Even Tew dropped a word o' praise now and agen. Takes some doin' that." He paused after opening the door, looking back over his shoulder. "Kind of makes you believe *all* the Breakers can kick more arse than I care to admit."

Rebekah watched Barclow shut the door, finding Savvo's hand had gripped hers. "Dricks?" he asked.

"Arin's there now. She's come out of the coma, but that was the twins doing. Apparently, she was refusing the rad meds after they pulled her in. She'd threatened to slice her suit out in the black; thought she'd had a full dose and had decided she wanted no one to watch her die." Rebekah took the chair next to Savvo's bed, pulling it towards her and sitting down. "I think the space walk and rad had kind of muddled her head, until Trem cleared it for her."

"And the Skyriders," said Savvo. "They kind of have an effect. Heki said they'd had a run in."

"Not got to the bottom of that, no time. The girls don't want to discuss it, clammed up like they used to. Without the ship's cameras, going to have to rely on their word. Or Dricks, if she knows." Rebekah leant in, taking his hand. "But Asham mentioned something about radiation effects and accelerated clone growth. Fucks the cells up, but the girls definitely did something to them. More fucking trauma, I suppose. And Nicky?"

Savvo screwed his lips up, brow furrowed. "Better. We can face each other now, for a while anyway. But ... well, I kind of got a favour to ask. If you'll agree, that is."

"You want out? That's a given if your mind's elsewhere."

"No. I don't think anyone can be out with the Butcher riding a bloody battleship. No. But Nicky knows about the Senti, the symbiotes. The memory taking." Savvo met her eyes, and she could see the need there. Was it a yes he needed, or a no? Had Nicky put the pressure on, forcing him to ask? And besides, even if she said yes, it was the girls and the symbs choice to make.

"There's been no studies, Savvo. We don't know if it'll help or not. The officer-nobles talked it up, but we never met anyone whose PTSD was solved that way. They just left and didn't come back."

Davina squeezed in beside her, the Incini's slate screen shimmered before coalescing into a cloud of smoke behind which a countess sat. Rebekah knew she couldn't trust the image, but even so, she looked sicker, frailer. Wouldn't you seek to hide that?

"Khan. I see you have the good sense to survive your latest reckless attempt to kill me off via a heart attack. The Wrecking Squad, indeed." More smoke, the tinge different. Yellow rather than white.

"Countess. You've seen the report, and Savvo tells me he's filled you in on the Senti." Rebekah smirked; she couldn't help it. The thought of Savvo dressing down the Warmonger burning bright in her chest.

About time.

"I have. And I actioned Savotini's suggestions around the other asteroids. We have reached only two so far, one mined out, the other untouched." Segfi let the smoke drift from her nose, leaning in a little. "Listen, Khan. Just because you hold something over me doesn't mean I am going to change. I am noble by birth, you are scum. End of. The Empire comes first, before my own reputation, before all. You understand? While you are useful to the Court and the future of the Empire, I'll swallow whatever lowlife vileness I have to. In private. Should word of my involvement with the Senti ambassadors emerge, I will accept full responsibility. Deny all else. It is the sacrifice *I* make for the good of the Emperor and the Court. The difference between lowlifes and those of *higher* breeding."

Rebekah stared back at the screen. Half of her railed against the countess' words, the sullying of the word sacrifice when she thought of Kefi, the Senti on board the orb, and the risks she and her crew had made in their name. The other half welcomed the spit and fire in the noble's eyes. There was no doubt she would do all those things to save her precious Empire from the Butcher, too. That's why she'd allowed her to live. That and a warbot wrestling with its own evolution.

"You mentioned drones, Khan?" asked the countess, almost as if she hadn't spoken. Back to the business of saving her precious nobility.

And necessary.

"We destroyed one that attached to the ship, and I understand they were part of the attack on Tweem. I know we destroyed a shipyard, and what we saw there hinted at shuttles and transports, maybe patrol boats. I could speculate the Butcher was planning on insinuating clones on board Navy ships that way ..." Rebekah paused, hoping the countess would react, feed some information back. She wasn't disappointed. This wasn't an equal relationship, but there was more respect there.

"We found none aboard any ships, but the civilian ports and stations are under heavy surveillance. We have uncovered fifteen at the last count. Plus what happened at Karal." The countess drew on her stick, coughing briefly. "But it sounds like you think the Butcher was planning that, anyway."

"The Butcher plans ahead more moves than I dare think. Possibly. But the drones give me a sense of dread. Add a sensory camouflage, and no recourse for human involvement." Rebekah stopped there, knowing what was to come, letting the countess have the space for her attempt to pry away the girls.

And *Segfi* surprised her. Perhaps she shouldn't be shocked, she was, after all, cut from the same cloth as the Butcher. "You know what we need, these Senti-coded blockers. So what plan have you to fulfil that and prevent me from demanding the girls? I have a frigate I can turn on your precious Karal in orbit. Persuade me that I shouldn't sacrifice the goodwill of Karal in return for just taking them."

"You tried that once. Didn't go so well." She glanced at Davina who nodded encouragement. "But the frigate is exactly what I have in mind. I, and some of my crew, need a lift."

CHAPTER 54

SENTI NEST SHIP

"Whatever you see, Captain, don't react. You only speak when spoken to, and don't gag if things get icky," said Arin, the smile painted across his face filled with a hint of devilment Rebekah relished at this point. Captain Fortan was an arsehole. Grade A noble-officer barrel scrapings, angry at his status upon a lowly frigate, and determined that every lowlife within shouting distance was going to get his full ire. She had dealt with many such – how had Barclow described him? – tossers, that was it – apt, whatever it meant – during her time in the Marines. So far up their own shithole they couldn't smell any other scent than the rose-tinted aroma of their own faeces. However, Srenik by his side was a different matter. The countess had slapped a promotion on the hero of Tweem, and he now carried the title of Commodore. With that had come a diplomatic role he clearly hated. But unlike Fortan, he wore the formal dress uniform with authority, and he could smell the shit, recognised it and had fetched a shovel.

It didn't mean Arin wouldn't get on his nerves, however. "Stow it, Senior Technician, before I bust your arse down to sub-engineer and you're back cleaning up after my favourite warbot."

Arin blanched, though the ensuing eye-roll nearly had her snorting. He was here when Savvo was not, despite Hendricks being ill. She could forgive just about anything for that.

The Navy captain harrumphed for what must have been the thousandth time since the countess had ordered him to take Rebekah wherever she needed to go. "I am well versed in diplomacy," he replied, nose ever-so slightly in the air. "And the Senti are just that, named because they are sentient. All such animals *understand* authority when they see it."

Arin raised his eyebrows, adding the slightest shake to his head then feigned adjusting his belt that kept him anchored to the deck of the Senti ship. At least the sight of the behemoth had instilled a little humility in the frigate captain, further reinforced when the ship swallowed them whole and spat them out in a cavernous docking bay. At Rebekah's request, the hose down had been a little more dignified than last time, thanks to whoever answered their call forgoing the equivalent of a Senti eye-roll before agreeing to the request.

The door slid open, the vibrant materials that occupied the nest queen's control room swaying in the internal breeze. Rebekah could catch the occasional sight of the queen, but waited on the noble-officers to assimilate what they were seeing. The sheer size, the different physiology, but above all else, the *presence* of the Senti queen. It didn't take long for them to look her way, then back to the dais that now appeared as the shimmering materials parted.

Yes. Now you see.

To give the noble bastard his due, Fortan managed a step forwards when a Senti officer gestured, before standing ramrod straight and delivering a millimetre perfect Navy salute. He also didn't speak. It was going well.

Commodore Srenik matched him, a little more relaxed in his posture but no less formal.

The nest queen quivered, her tentacles dancing over the holo light controls with which she oversaw everything aboard the ship. She did not acknowledge the Navy men at first, a swipe here and there, before the blue light dissipated and her full regard fell onto them. Piercing blue eyes settled on the nobles, assessed them and in an instant, moved onto Rebekah. As before, there was more in the queen's gaze than any Senti she had encountered, except, according to Arin and ZZ3, the moment when Kefi's eyes had transformed upon the *Segfi*. The moment the Senti had sacrificed herself in an act Rebekah prayed hadn't been in vain.

A tentacle stretched out, metal shod, grasping a hapless worker Senti, its chin tentacle writhing briefly before settling down as she placed them at the foot of the dais. Rebekah side-eyed the officer-nobles, a grin on her face she couldn't hide.

"Queen of the *Sunstar*," started the worker Senti, the voice grating, mechanical. She had expected Kefi, and got something more akin to Pshwa, the dream-pedlar. Rebekah sensed the regard, but it wasn't invasive. Not yet. "You return. We will converse. Commodore Srenik." He didn't wither, but she could see the weight fall upon his shoulders as the words filled with her regard.

Welcome to the future.

The queen continued via the worker she clasped. "Commodore, I recognise the role bestowed on you by your Emperor and the Countess Segfi." Rebekah held her breath as the alien queen paused, bracing. A human knew compromise, accepting the lesser evil of others when faced with a greater threat. "I wish not to deal with murderers and their sycophants. Those who hide their intent with words, while their actions bear no relation."

There goes that theory.

"However." The queen opened two of her lower tentacles wide, the squelch of liquid resonating through the chamber as the rubbery flesh tore away from each other. In their apex sat a slime-covered cocoon. The queen's spawn, though larger than when Rebekah had last seen it. A lump formed in her throat. Their efforts had not been a failure. The risks they'd taken, Kefi's death, had meant something at least. "Khan of the *Sunstar* and her crew, including the honoured one they named Kefi, have recovered my sister's spawn. She has been preserved, her memories retained for the future of the Great Nest. For this act, I will put aside the demands of my nest sisters for vengeance. I wish, Khan, to see the sacrifice made." Her other shoulder tentacle wriggled, and a symbiote emerged from behind her head, pulling itself along and towards Rebekah. Despite herself, Rebekah thought she recognised it. The sequence of wave patterns, the twist of its tentacles. Kefi had last bore the symbiote. Its touch washed over her, and the full power of the queen entered her mind, seeking memories.

With practised ease she marked the events from when they left her ship to the moment of Kefi's death, recounting what ZZ3 and Arin had witnessed. The queen's touch was almost reverent, gentle, and pained by the state of Hendricks, the acts and choices forced upon the girls. At the end, she paused as the *Sunstar* entered void-space, her regard upon the light mirage.

The spawn. Of course. When the symbiotes were absent from the dying orb, it was because they had jumped. Gone without a ship into void-space ... Fuck. And the Butcher witnessed the rescue.

The nest queen withdrew, her presence lifting, only for a tentacle to grace Rebekah's neck, tickling the back of her head.

"I trust this one, Commodore Srenik. This human ship queen keeps her word, delivers on her promises. I owe her for my sister's future existence and the retention of her memories for the good of the Great Nest."

Is that what the orb's sacrifice had been for? An entire 'nest' of Senti preferring to die rather than lose a queen's knowledge, her memories? Not to save the queen's current life, but what she adds, her consciousness. Like Kefi. Able to come back.

The enormity struck Rebekah. How long had the Senti nest queens been retaining their collective selves? And what would it mean to lose one?

"And for that," continued the nest queen, "I have patience and time."

Rebekah peered over to the noble-officer, waiting to see how he would cope with a lowlife scumbag being honoured above him. Perhaps it was the sheer presence of the Senti queen, or the disdain with which she had dismissed him. There was a light there. Common sense. A single nod. No words, no verbal acknowledgement. That would be too far. But Commodore Srenik had brought a shovel, and was prepared to let Rebekah do the work. Shape the future. Rebekah had a distinct feeling she would be working closely with the Commodore. She eyed Fortan, nose in the air, disdain on his lips.

Could be worse.

Rebekah faced the queen's regard, meeting her eyes. "I believe you know what we need. What would help us defend against the Butcher. Kefi helped devise a Senti-coded system blocker, and we need more."

CHAPTER 55

ON APPROACH TO THE UNPRONOUNCEABLE

Rohan powered down the shuttle, reaching across to take Treni's hand in his. No words passed, they didn't have to. Her cheeks glowed; the eyes filled with life. It had been an accident, not planned, but the news of her pregnancy, early days as it was, brought a light into his life he'd thought lost since news of the transport orb and later Kefi had filtered through.

Some joy.

Now he had to find a way to tell Scarva that his time was up. The debt repaid, and an opportunity aboard Benetai in the offing the next time the Senti dream-pedlar headed that way. Hannos wouldn't renege. In the weeks he'd spent in the ex-Skyrider's company he'd learned quickly that she was blunt and loyal. Rare commodities. He shared the latter.

"I'll go," he said, squeezing Treni's hand. "Tell Scarva now, rather than let it build. Otherwise, the bastard will find a pile of underhanded crap for us to do."

"You don't bend, hear me." Treni slipped her hand out of his, slapping him on the arm. "No letting that memory-sucker screw you over." She placed her finger against his temple. "Hear me, shit-for-brains. We want out."

Rohan grinned, unclipping. "What did I ever see in you?"

"A feisty bitch with a big gun, a fast draw and who takes no shit. That, and a loving disposition you appreciate." A kiss on his cheek and she stomped off down the short corridor and on into the cargo bay. "I'll inform our passenger."

Rohan sighed, and called for the polythene tunnel, arriving at the shuttle's airlock as it connected. A shuffle of tentacles behind announced the arrival of their silent passenger. The Senti had worn an encounter suit on boarding the shuttle and remained in the tiny captain's cabin until now. It was nothing new, few Senti tolerated being aboard a human ship. The atmosphere was all wrong, the heights of the ceiling odd, the colours, as far as he knew, disagreeable.

It was, however, the squawk that set Rohan most on edge. "I never liked it aboard this, what does Treni call it? Shit-heap."

He spun about, the Senti facing him, helmet off, shoulder tentacles waving, taking him utterly by surprise. The chin tentacle was missing, the skull slightly wider, the eyes a strange blue-black. But the voice …

He'd seen some seriously weird shit since first boarding Scarva's ship. But this. "Kefi?" He reached out, almost touching her face, and the Senti shrank away.

"Even when I was your Kefi, no touching, yes? You humans have an odd skin, all scaly and hairy, and that smell." The crash of seagulls assaulted Rohan's ears. The Senti reached out a single tentacle, which landed on his clothed shoulder, the encounter suit's tip splitting and taking hold.

"But …" was all he managed, Treni appearing the other side of the Senti, her eyes curious.

"Weird, isn't it? Even for a Senti, being sublimated twice in such a short time leaves you out of … ahh."

"Kilter," said Treni from behind. "Out of sorts."

"Yes. That." The Senti turned about. "Good to see you Treni. Please understand, both of you. I am who you remember, but not who *I* remember." The seagulls again. "I journeyed with Khan. I returned the spawn but do not have memories of such things. The Nest Queen has reconstituted me for a new role, but those memories were not recovered, my great heroics," the Senti stood straight, tentacles wide, then sagged, "have been forgotten when I died. Apparently, it hurt. A lot. So maybe a good thing, eh?"

Rohan couldn't help but smile. "Godsdamned right," he said. "Been boring as hell talking to the rest of the Senti. Can't you, you know, sublimate some humour into the ship."

The Senti shook, the gulls silent, the pitch too high. "Humour amid the nest? I fear a queen would see that as inefficient. Dissent in the ranks. Come, I have a new role, and it is time to meet with Scarva."

Rohan admittedly couldn't understand a word of the conversation that flew between Scarva and Kefi. Initially it had been for his ears, then the Senti speech had littered the air, until this too died and he was left watching a staring contest. Kefi had mentioned the nest queens could use mind-speech, or maybe not just the queens, it had been a while back. However it was, there was still an argument going on. He had an idea of Senti body language, the way they held their tentacles, the heave and sag of their gasbags and the accompanying off-gassing that changed in aroma. Scarva had started belligerent, angry, but by the time the words had stopped, and silence ensued, it was clear the sick Senti had accepted whatever fate had been decreed. The off-gas hinted he was far from happy, but the mood shifted, and eventually Kefi faced Rohan while Scarva sulked as if he'd missed out on a thousand juicy war memories.

"We are done. I would ask that you transport Scarva back to the Nest Queen's ship," said the Senti, the steady, flat voice edged with a modicum of sadness or regret.

Rohan guessed at what was going to happen and turned away from Scarva as he spoke. "Sublimation?"

Kefi paused, then seemed to come to a decision. "Yes. He dies. As you know, his body nears the end of its cycle. But his memories remain valuable, as all are from those who travel the human pathways." Kefi's tentacles shook then fell in at its side. "Rohan, war is coming. Between human and machine. We fear the Senti cannot stand apart from it, that we will be sucked in. For that we must prepare. Scarva's knowledge is essential and will help us rebuild the transport orb in a new form, as will be this ship and ... and its crew. You and Treni have a role to play."

"Kefi ..." he started to say, only for the Senti's eyes to turn fully blue as they fell upon him.

"This Butcher the humans have created. It knows no bounds, has no regard for any life, be it Senti or human. Almaar is not safe, nor Bustan if he succeeds in discovering our ways. Benetai? Windward? He will not stop." Kefi's tentacle tapped towards Rohan's chest. "A father needs a place to live, and from what I have seen, this Butcher only seeks death."

"I am only one man..."

"One Almaarian who now has more than one reason to parley with an old enemy. Treni is from Bustan, eh?"

Rohan took a step back, the realisation at what Kefi, this new Kefi with insights into what was coming, was hinting at striking home. "You want me to ... to go to Bustan? They'll kill us on sight, Treni will be wanted just as much as an ex-Marine like me."

Kefi's regard fell on him, the eyes, piercing blue and no longer the blank, soulless black, drinking him in. "Not straight away, but yes, soon. As a go-between perhaps, with a Nest Queen at your back and perhaps a Kefi at your side."

CHAPTER 56

ANS RETANA

Arin fingered the slate's screen, running his fingertips over Hendricks' face, caught between love and annoyance. She was in her old flight suit. Behind her, dock workers and tech crews milled about the *Sunstar*'s hull like ants over a pile of sugar.

"You should be resting," he said, unable to slide any frustration into his words. He loved this woman for her pig-headed stubbornness, 'ornery attitude and damn-right loyalty to her ship and crew just as much as for the tender moments.

"Yeah, right. And have them nurses fussing over me like I was some kind of corpse in waiting. Ain't happening, Arin. The ship is in a mess; I have a line of green-as-hell would-be engineers and sub-engineers who don't know their arse from their elbow all wanting to fix our beloved *Sunstar* their way. Theirs, not mine." Hendricks slumped onto the metal container behind her.

"*Our* way. Don't forget I'm Senior Tech now." He tapped the label on his flight suit he'd 3D printed and sewn on before leaving Karal. "Says so right here."

Hendricks shook her head, eyes to the sky. "Senior Tech this, Senior Tech that. Between you and the bloody *Senior* Rescue Warbot stomping about the ship, I'm beginning to believe I might just quit and farm potatoes or something. Or bake, anything but Danish with sprinkles. Do you know how much those girls are costing us in food? In sugar?"

Arin sniggered. He had to admit the number of bad habits he'd reinforced in the crew was on the rise. First a rapidly evolving warbot who was stretching Hendricks' patience as it developed a sense of humour all of its own. And then the girls and their ever-growing sweet tooth that put him and Hendricks to shame, though he suspected much of that was sheer bribery. The girls had gone into themselves after they had killed the Skyriders, and Hendricks was little better – watching the moment of forced suicide had brought a lot of memories back. Ones she couldn't escape. Rebekah had left them together to work it through, giving them some space before she parachuted in and helped sort the mess out.

Brave.

Foolish.

And he loved her for it. Though he was never going to say that out loud. Nearly as much as he loved Hendricks who was clearly pushing her recovery. But nothing he would say could change that. Better to accept it and hold her close when it's done.

"They okay?" he asked, fearing the answer. "Heki and Tremil?"

"Okay? No." Hendricks wiped something from her eye with the back of her hand. "But I've gone with keeping them busy between sucking up Karal's entire supply of sugar. Told them they were in charge of ensuring Rebekah's little baby ship is in the best of health by the time she gets back. Kind of worked, too. Locked them in work mode, but I can't get them to come up for air and talk."

"And you?" Arin strained his neck, catching Rebekah's gaze as she looked into his cabin. He indicated towards the slate, but she shook her head.

"Me?" said Hendricks, and her hand ran over her scalp, rubbing at the back of her neck. "Every joint aches, my muscles complain, and my teeth scream at me every night. And the bloody tablets ..."

"Usual then," said Rebekah as she entered the frigate's cabin. She settled in beside Arin on the gel bed, hooking her arm in his. "And alive. Thanks to those very same girls."

The ex-captain didn't say anything in reply, just stared back, punctuated by the occasional blink and wipe of her eyes until she nodded. "It ain't over though, is it?"

Arin felt Rebekah tremble, then she sat up straight. Her demeanour changing from friend to captain. "No," she said. "We all know there's worse to come, and we're now front and centre. But the Senti ... the Senti give me hope."

Hendricks looked offscreen, a hand raised in greeting, and then she sidled over to make room "Good news," she mouthed, tilting her head towards whoever approached.

Arin already knew. Hendricks had discussed Savvo and Nicky first. Things had calmed, and Nicky had been eased off the sedatives after a visit from the girls and their symbiotes. A risk Nicky had chosen, and she was far from recovered. But there was a light there, when before he'd only seen anguish in Savvo's eyes. It was all his friend needed, something to hold on to. That and his crewmates.

Savvo sat beside Hendricks, eyes on the screen wearing a sly grin Arin did not trust.

"And what the shit is that?" Arin said tapping at the slate, at whatever was in the co-pilot's mischievous hands. "You've got to be shitting me."

"This?" said Savvo, wafting the piece of cloth at the screen. "ZZ3 requested we make him a sash. You know, so everyone knows about the promotion to *Chief* Rescue Warbot."

The End of The Queen's Spawn, Book Four of The Wrecking Squad. The Sunstar's crew return in Emperor's Fall.

The Wrecking Squad Series

Thank you for choosing to spend your time reading The Queen's Spawn. It's an honour as an indie author to have written stories readers such as yourself have taken the time to read.

This whole series has been taking up my headspace for some time. I knew I had a great set of characters to work with and a story premise that had weight. The next issue is how to sustain the books over three, or in this case, six books. To achieve that, the world must feel 'lived in' and by people who feel real, in a storyline where their actions, and the events surrounding them are, in context, plausible. The hardest part is ensuring you don't rely on random incidents or unknown characters. For instance, returning to Scarva, or Lieutenant Ormsk who who makes an appearance in the next book. And above all else, the Butcher, the fusion of General Asham and the Bustan AI, who overshadows the story arc from now on. I hope I achieved that, and you want to keep on reading about the events The Wrecking Squad get tangled up in. Next is Emperor's Fall, which continues Phase Two of the series as Almaar faces a battle for survival when the Butcher reveals his power.

Reviews and ratings are the lifeblood of any author, and vital to indie writers in particular. They help new readers make up their minds when searching for new authors and books. Ratings are your chance to bring a little starlight and attention to my scifi books that are a somewhat different from the norm.

If you enjoyed my novel, please consider leaving a star rating on Amazon and/or Goodreads.

And if you wish to know more about the members of the Wrecking Squad, their origin story is absolutely FREE. Just flick to the end of this book to find out how you can download Redemption Tour - A Wrecking Squad Story.

About the Author

Nick Snape has been steeped in Science Fiction and Fantasy since his friends first dragged him from his schoolwork and stuck a book under his nose. Lost to the world of imagination, he became a teacher by accident, though he thoroughly enjoyed developing the joy of reading and writing in his pupils. Having retired after thirty years, he thought it was high time to practise what he preached.

Nick's books feature everything from all out, heart-pounding, fast-paced action to thoughtful, character driven twists on the fantasy and sci-fi genres. Genetics to Artificial Intelligence, Artifice Dragons to Soul-Eating enemies, nothing is off the menu.

BOOKS BY NICK SNAPE

Weapons of Choice Series

*'A truly epic saga of riveting sci-fi thrill*ers...'

It started with a failed military training exercise and an alien incursion, desperate and on the hunt. Survival was just the beginning...

After encountering a buried spaceship and its rogue AI on Earth, Finn, Zuri, and Corporal Smith (deceased) take refuge on an alien home world where they unravel the truth about the forced colonisation of Earth-like planets. With the ship's AI providing advanced nano-weaponry and evolving alien battle tech, Finn and Delta blaze a trail through the galaxy seeking a way home, walking a fine line between vengeance and redemption in this thought-provoking action sci-fi series.

Over 25,000 books read in this 'superb scifi series'

Hostile Contact

Return Protocol

Zuri's War

Finn's War

Alien Rebirth

Invasive Species

Legion Earth

Nemesis Earth

The Scorching Standalone Series

The World in My Hands

"A deeply nuanced sci-fi standalone with slow-burn suspense, a diverse and unorthodox cast of characters and a spaceship straight out of your worst nightmares"

The world is heading towards global collapse as the Scorching takes full effect. Salvation vessels orbit the Earth, waiting to transport the chosen few away from danger and to start again; ten plantships grown by an alien species for the wealthiest and most powerful, or those lucky enough to be selected by lottery. Yet not all is well on board. Dark secrets lurk in the corridors and depths of their respective ships, dragging Jenna and Seth into a world of malice and violence they thought they had left far behind.

***

Just Press Play

"Staggeringly original and timely release from a masterful voice in modern sci-fi."

On a devastated Earth, the Drathken arrive with the promise of healing the planet. When anti-alien terrorists threaten the accord, Cop and Vlogger Josh Nkosi, and his MARC unit, chase terrorists into the Burnout Zone only to come face to face with humanity's stark future when the hunt takes a devastating twist. As a conspiracy emerges, Nkosi is forced on a dark path of discovery.

Warriors of Spirit and Bone

A Dragon of the Veil

"An INCREDIBLE start to a new, dark epic fantasy series."

In a realm no longer devoid of magic, the fate of a people rests with Laoch and Sura, and the Gods' weapons they bear – a thousand years of faith and lies reconciled in a single moment of hope and redemption. With whispers of an ancient evil's return, they are left reeling by their enemy's power, one even the Gods' weapons fear. For cast in iron and spiritfire - here be dragons.

***

A City of Ashes

"A work of coal-dark fantasy that is continually surprising, provocative, and compulsively entertaining."

With the Veil Dragon, Nathair, seemingly under the Spirit Captain's control, Laoch pushes away the grief of his first encounter with the metal beast and hunts for a weapon his new and distrusted ally insists they can use against the coming Constructor invasion. For an Emperor consumed by revenge has a new artifice, one that hungers to enslave.

***

A Queen in Blood

"A dark ambience largely unmatched by anything else I've read."

As the invasion of Brandshold begins, the realm is haunted by the Infected – devastated and spirit-poisoned townsfolk who hunger for flesh and souls to salve their pain. When the city of Jense falls to a wave of bloody teeth and foul claws, the Constructor's Emperor strikes, shattering city walls with his artifice dragon, and the dreaded *Kraken* soulship. For a queen bathed in the blood of her own people, hope lies in the alchemy of the meisters, a traitorous mechanical dragon, and loyal but broken soldiers.

The Wrecking Squad

Emperor's Fall (Book 5)

Fracture an empire and expose the weakness at its heart

The crew of the *Sunstar* are persuaded to transport Senti-built defensive hardware to the fleet by a desperate Countess Segfi. But the Butcher strikes, damaging the airless moonbase on Saim. The Wrecking Squad can't abandon those in need and mount a rescue. But when the trap snaps shut, thousands die breathless in an instant, a moment the Butcher shares with the Emperor's Court laced with a threat to the rest of the system's vulnerable colonies. The price he demands for the Empire's safety is the *Sunstar* and the crew's secret of Faster Than Light Travel. One ship, one crew, to save billions. What price for survival?

***

Breaker's Ruin (Book 6)

When the empire falls, who will stand for humanity?

Wild storms rage over Almaar, with the few survivors of the Ingblack plague facing devastation as floodwaters rise and food runs out. But lurking in the ruins is something far more sinister. For remnants of the Butcher survived, each vying for power over the others in a malevolent race for weapons and resources. With the empathic twins let loose on those who stand in their way, grief releasing the chains shackling their true power, Savvo is the only Breaker left capable of reining them in, while Commodore Srenik and his ragtag navy must search for the truth about the AI-controlled fleet orbiting Almaar, and the rising power on the planet below. Together, these disparate forces must make a final stand as the strongest Butcher rises to prominence and sets its sights on enslaving humanity.

Acknowledgements

As with all authors, this book would never have existed without the dedicated friends and family who were there by my side throughout the entire process. The least I can do is give them a mention for their patience with my obsession! My Beta readers, supporters and fiercest critics have been Pak, Martin Lejeune, Mark Hartswood and Bryan Chaffin. Amazing friends who have put that aside to make sure whatever I put out there was something they wanted to read.

Julie, my wife, needs a special mention. Over the past few years she has kept me going, being there at every step through the dark and joyful times. I can't believe how lucky I am.

Finally, the New Year and Pub Night Crews. Wouldn't be here without you.

Thank you all.

WRECKING SQUAD FREE NOVELLA

My new series, The Wrecking Squad, involves a squad of ex-Marines on the run. Their origin story is available in a FREE novella, Redemption Tour, which you can download by subscribing to my newsletter with the link below. Yes, absolutely free.

www.nicksnape.com/subscribe

Subscribing will also provide further information about this series, and my plans for more exciting science fiction and fantasy novels in the future.

The Lost Squad - A Weapons of Choice Novel

The Stratan Marines who were introduced in Hostile Contact have a surprise in store. A second squad followed them to Earth, who appear later in the series in Book 7, Legion Earth. The Lost Squad, a FREE full-length novel, details their arrival soon after Yasuko's ship left the Solar System in Hostile Contact. The novel charts the alien Marines' action-packed experiences as countries and mercenaries vie for their technology and knowledge. They are a superb bunch of characters and were a real joy to write.

If you wish to learn more about their history on Earth, and I suggest you do as it's an excellent novel, then please subscribe to my newsletter and receive your FREE novel via the link below:

www.nicksnape.com/subscribe